'There are echoes in here of Gene Wolfe's *Book of the New Sun* and Walter M. Miller's *A Canticle for Leibowitz* but to these greats Adam Roberts has added a twist of high-concept originality.' *SFX*

'The oddly helter-skelter elegance of *On* marks the novel as one of the notable SF books of the year – the sort of experiment in form and perspective that the genre sees too rarely . . . Adam Roberts is a purveyor of illusions that underscore the real, a beguiling dispenser of cruel instruction. Heed him. Harsh medicine is not often so entertainingly administered.' Nick Gevers, *Sfsite.com*

'A fantastic story.' *Scotland on Sunday*

'*On*'s main attraction is not hard SF worldbuilding, but its skilful subversions of the well-worn story of the picaresque adventures of a magic kid; Roberts's inverted world is crueller and far less friction-free than most in SF.' Paul McAuley, *Interzone*

'The central mystery is a joy to puzzle over, and Roberts's imagery and style are striking.' *Starburst*

'Roberts's first novel, *Salt*, was nominated for the Arthur C. Clarke Award and was widely praised. *On* looks to be a worthy follow-up and confirms Roberts as a writer to watch.' *Sfrevu.com*

Also by Adam Roberts in Gollancz:

SALT
STONE

ON

Adam Roberts

The right of Adam Roberts to be identified as the author of this
work has been asserted by him in accordance with the
Copyright, Designs and Patents Act 1988.

This edition published in 2002 by

Gollancz
An imprint of the Orion Publishing Group
Orion House, 5 Upper St Martin's Lane, London WC2H 9EA

A CIP catalogue record for this book is available
from the British Library

ISBN 0 575 07299 7

Printed in Great Britain by
Clays Ltd, St Ives plc

Contents

How fearful
And dizzy 'tis to cast one's eyes so low!
The crows and choughs that wing the midway air
Show scarce so gross as beetles; half-way down
Hangs one who gathers samphire, dreadful trade!
Methinks he seems no bigger than his head.
The fishermen that walk upon the beach
Appear like mice, and yond tall anchoring bark
Diminish'd to her cock, her cock a buoy
Almost too small for sight. The murmuring surge,
That on the unnumbered idle pebbles chafes,
Cannot be heard so high.

King Lear, 4:6

The soul, like fire, abhors what it consumes.

Derek Walcott, *Another Life*

1
Prince

1

On Tighe's eighth birthday one of the family goats fell off the world. This was a serious matter.

The news of this loss, of losing so valuable a thing as a goat, went all round the village. Of course, it completely eclipsed Tighe's birthday. Tighe's pas were struck down by the news, his pahe reacting in what was a typical manner for him, sitting gloomily in the shadows of the house; and his pashe reacting typically for *her*, shouting her anger. Tighe was only glad, as his pashe raged, kicking chunks out of the house-wall in her fury, that he was not yet old enough to be given the task of tending the goats, or he could have been responsible and then he would have been on the receiving end of the rage. It was a girl called Carashe, who had been paid to tend the winter flock for the moment, until he was old enough to take on the job. A couple of months earlier Tighe had gone up (to see how it was done because a Prince's son ought to know about these things) and watched Carashe tending the animals as they grazed the higher ledges. There was no doubt that goats were the stupidest things ever put on the wall. It was a puzzle why God had created them. They looked sideways at you with their lunatic eyes, grinding their mouths never-endingly; and then you'd try to come over to them to tug their hair or pet them or something – and they'd leap to the side, or scatter away like midges evading a swatting hand. They'd leap with no thought to where the edge might be. It was as if their pearl-small brains had not registered that God had put them on the worldwall in the first place.

'It's because they're animals,' Wittershe had told him. 'They have *no* brains.'

But that didn't make sense because there were lots of animals on the wall that never lurched about with such a suicidally myopic sense of where they were. The monkeys never did that, for instance.

Tighe preferred the monkeys, in fact. He knew (if only because he had been told so) that goats had a higher status than monkeys; that it was appropriate for the Prince's family to own goats and that everybody in the village looked down on an old monkeymonger like Wittershe's pahe. But monkeys looked nicer, nearly human. And they acted smart and Tighe liked that.

'I guess I've always wondered why goats are better than monkeys,' he had said a few weeks before his birthday. It had been a bad moment. Pashe was sitting in her chair, reading through her tattered edition of the Sayings. 'Pashe, why is it that goats are better than monkeys?' His question sent her flying into a rage. Sometimes it took the slightest thing to send her exploding with her anger. Even as a little boy Tighe could sense that she was a woman stuffed so full of anger that the merest rip in her outward skein of mood would cause it to come bursting out. She didn't get up this time (which was good, he knew, because it meant she wouldn't actually smack him), but she sat there screaming. 'This boy will drive us all over the ledge, will he *never* stop with his questions? Will he smash my head *apart* with all his questions? On and on and on . . .'

Tighe's pahe, who had been mending the dawn-door with some mud-patched grass-weave, heard the raised voice and came through. Tighe, sitting in his alcove frozen with sudden fear, saw him come in. Recognised the delicate, graceful pad of his walk; the way he lowered his head and hunched up his shoulders, placatory. It was a delicate dance, but one that Tighe had seen so often he thought it ordinary. Surely everybody's family was like this. Pahe would try and calm pashe, would say things in a smooth low voice, would start to stroke her sides. If her anger settled a little, he would stroke her head and maybe kiss her. If it didn't, then she might well start hitting him, or pulling at his hair, and then Tighe would watch his pahe bend double, bring his elbows up to defend his head, and his own heart would shrink within him. But on this occasion it didn't take much to calm pashe down.

'It's that boy,' she said loudly. 'He will drive me to madness. He will drive me over the edge.'

'I think', said pahe, sucking at his words and letting them out slowly, 'that maybe the boy had better come and help me mend the dawn-door.'

Pahe had taken him by the hand and led him out of his alcove and out into the vestibule. But, of course, pahe had no need of his help mending the dawn-door. So, instead, Tighe sat and watched his father work, plaiting the grass-stems together and smoothing plastermud over the mat with a spatula. His pahe was a handsome man; he was certain of it. His skin was smooth, as richly brown as the mud he worked with, his features regular. His eyes were pale, the irises violet like a flame in daylight. His straight black hair was neat. Tighe admired his pahe.

'What had you said', pahe was asking, 'to get your pashe so riled?'

The question burned in his head now. He wished he'd never asked it. He wished he'd never thought it. He hated the way he couldn't sit still, couldn't

4

think still, the way his pashe did. She could sit and be absolutely motionless for hour after hour. But he fidgeted and wriggled, and kept thinking of questions. But his pahe had asked, and so he said, 'I was only wondering why goats are better than monkeys.'

And, of course, his pahe was not angry. It was, he said in his quiet, slow way, a good question. It was a thoughtful question.

'It's only', Tighe went on, 'that monkeys look so much more like human beings, don't they? They *look* like human beings. And Grandhe always says that we are humans, and that we are closer to God. He says that God looks like us.'

'I think', said pahe, pausing between every word to stroke mud on to the wattle, 'that he said *we* look like *God*.'

Tighe stopped. Wasn't that what he had just said?

'Goats are better than monkeys', said pahe after a pause, 'because we get more from goats. We get milk, for one thing, which we don't get from monkeys. And the meat is better eating. And monkey hair is bad for weaving, it's too short and it frays. And monkeys are difficult to keep. Tether them and they pine and grow thin, but let them run free and they scramble all over the wall and you lose half of them.' He was fitting the panel over the broken panel in the dawn-door, fastening it with palm-nails which he pushed sharply into the fabric of the door with smooth movements of his forearm. 'Goats like to stick together,' he said. 'They like to stick with the herd.'

Tighe scratched at his scalp. There was a long scar on his scalp, from an old injury; he had cut his head when he was too young to remember and sometimes now the line of the scar itched a bit.

Tighe thought of his pahe's words later, on his eighth birthday. One of their six goats had evidently decided he didn't want to stick with the herd. He had danced, skittering and trilling his legs, right over the grass tufts of an upper ledge and over into nothingness.

Months before, Carashe, the goatherd they had hired, had been sitting with him on a tuft and together they had chewed stalkgrass and looked out at the sky. His days were idle because he was the son of the Prince; so he was mostly bored and loitered around. But because he was the son of the Prince of the Village, the villagers gave him their time, talked to him, humoured him. Carashe did the same.

'You need to keep an eye on the goats,' she had told him. But she didn't act out the caution her words suggested. In fact she had a thoroughly blasé attitude to her charges. She would sometimes look round to see where the goats had got to, but they were quietly munching and seemed at peace. 'Keep an eye, and make sure that none of them go over the edge.'

Carashe was nine and no longer a girl. She had been a woman for the best part of a year now. Tighe could remember when her front had been flat as a board; now she was as ledged and creviced as the wall itself, her breasts standing out from her ribs, her belly folding out over her lap as she sat on the tuft. Tighe found his wick stiffening as he watched the way the fabric of her tunic creased and smiled with her shifting about. Carashe had a man friend down at the middle of the village and everybody knew that. Tighe had no illusions. He knew she looked at him and saw only a boy, for all that he was a Princeling. But he liked spending time with her, being with her; he liked sitting on the higher ledge, nobody else around but the goats with their straining bulging eyes, listening to her talk about how to tend the animals.

'Why not just tether them together?' he asked.

She shook her head and sucked a little more on a piece of grass. 'They need to roam about, to find the sweetest grass. They won't get fat unless they get at the succulent tips. Besides, six is too many goats to tether. They get cross with one another and fight and butt. They'll end up tearing up the tether post, or chewing through the leather straps.'

Tighe nodded and watched the goats again. One was cropping vigorously, stepping towards the edge of the world. It seemed blithely unconcerned. Tighe felt his stomach tighten in sympathy. He hated going to the rim of a ledge; he hated the raw yank of the endless drop, the way the downward distance somehow pulled and distorted the inside of his head. There was something truly terrible about that looking down. It sucked at his heart, some magnetic yaw towards destruction. Looking up, and seeing the wall stretch upwards and upwards over you into the haze was also disconcerting, but it wasn't as heart-tickling as down.

Down was a terrible thing.

Yet the goat was unconcerned. It leaned its tool-shaped head right over the lip of the ledge and yanked up some of the spikegrass growing over the void. Then it shifted round and started grazing back towards the wall.

When their time was up, Carashe had pushed with her legs and hopped off the tuft. Then she had looped each of the goats in turn, draping the O of their tethers easily around their necks. They barely noticed even this, but carried on munching the grass. As Carashe led them towards the slope down to the lower ledges of the village, Tighe stood up too. He watched as her now adult body rolled easily from foot to foot. Tighe fell in behind, hypnotised by the pull of cloth across her seat. He expected nothing. He was only a boy and barely even that (his pashe still called him boy-boy from time to time). Carashe was a woman, with a man interested in her from the middle of the village. But the whisper was that the man was nobody special, only a technical sort of man, a machine-mending man. Tighe knew himself to be better than that; because he was a Princeling, because his father was

6

the Prince. It had dawned on him recently that being a Prince didn't mean a great deal, not compared to the splendour of his Grandhe's house (but then his Grandhe was a Priest); or the Doge's house (but then the Doge looked after all the trade, so you would expect her to be wealthy). But Tighe's pahe was still the Prince, and the Prince was notionally the boss of the whole village – of the whole Princedom. Besides Tighe's family wasn't poor. After all, they owned many goats – not the largest herd in the village, admittedly, but six whole goats and the carcasses of three more salted and hanging in the storeroom dug out at the back of the house. So he watched the beautiful roll and pull of Carashe's body with a certain hopefulness. Surely there would be more of a chance next year, if only his manhood would come on (and eight was about the right age for that to happen), if only he could grow some hair from his face like the monkeys and bulk up his wick a little so that it took on a man's thickness. And it only took that for his imagination to start pressing his own body close against Carashe, to imagine what it would be to put his hands underneath the fabric of her clothes.

But then, on the day of his eighth birthday, things changed. The goat went over the edge; a sixth of the family's wealth. His pahe might be the Prince of the village, but a Prince without money would starve as quickly as the meanest beggar. Tighe didn't quite understand it, but it seemed that his pas were involved in a network of promises and exchanges, of debts and double-debts with other people in the village, and that the whole thing depended upon goatgoods. On milk, on promises of flax and meat. Losing a sixth of the family wealth tipped this delicate web towards collapse. Pahe tried to explain it to him in his alcove, whilst the sounds of pashe's sobbing shuddered louder, softer and louder again in the main space.

'We promised a salted haunch and fourteen months milk to old Hammerhe at the Dogeal end of the village for the work he did sealing off the cold store.' Tighe shook his head. His pahe had dug out the cold store with his own hands. He had watched him do it, had even helped him carry away the dirt in grass-weave buckets down the ledges to the allotments on the lower reach of the village.

'But yo-you d-dug it yourself,' he stuttered. His own eyes were sore. He had been crying. Not, he thought, for the goat, because what did he care for a stupid goat? But because his pashe was crying so hard; and because Carashe was in disgrace now and he wouldn't see her again for a very long time. And because . . . well, just because.

'I dug it out,' said his pahe in his soft, slow voice, 'but we needed to get it sealed. That meant plastics and that meant old Hammerhe. And plastics don't come cheap, so that was a whole haunch. And we promised the hide to your Grandhe Jaffiahe, which is why he's been so good to us recently. If you ask me . . .' and pahe's soft voice became softer again, soft as a flow of water, and Tighe sucked back his sobbing so as to be able to hear his father's deep, melodious voice, '. . . if you ask me, we should simply call the debt to Jaffiahe *off* – in the name of family. But your pashe won't hear of that. You know she and your Grandhe don't get on. You know how they fight. It's been that way since she was a girl. But that puts us in difficulties because if she would *only* go and speak to him then a lot of this difficulty would go away.' He was whispering very low, now, bending his head towards his son so that the words didn't go astray. 'Don't tell your pashe I said so, though.'

That night Tighe lay in his alcove. He could hear his pas talking in a low, burbling stream of words. He couldn't hear the words themselves, just the mellow burr they made in the air. Like music. Every now and again his pashe's voice would warble and rise, would transmute into a reedy wail; then it would be shepherded by pahe's soothing grumble until it was calmed and dropped away again. It took Tighe a long time to get to sleep. He kept twisting and wriggling in his alcove. Outside the dusk gale roared. He fell asleep, but woke up again in the dark. Everything was still; no sounds from his pas' bed through the wall; no nightwind, which must have meant it was deep in the night. Tighe put both his hands between his thighs and pressed his legs close together, for the comfort of the gesture. Eventually he fell asleep again and this time he dreamed. The goat was in the dream, but it was as bald as a baby, pink hide catching the sun with its occasional stubbly white hairs. It danced and danced and Tighe pressed his arms around its neck. There was some sense of familiarity about it all, as if the intense particularity of the pressure of skin against skin reminded him of something. But the goat was right on the edge of the world now, and with a horrible lurch in his stomach Tighe knew it was going over the edge. And he knew that he could not let go of the goat, and that he

– was over the edge of the world. The whole worldwall arced, and tilted, and slewed round and then he could see nothing but sky. His limbs convulsed, and he was suddenly alone, no goat, with the rushing of clouds past his head

and he woke with a sweaty start. The morning gale was blowing, loud as thunder outside the house. Tighe's hands were digging into the grass-weave mat of his bed. His face was cold with old sweat. His heart was thundering.

He tumbled out of the alcove and staggered to the family sink. He drank deeply and then (looking around, because his pashe got furious if she saw him doing this) ducked his head into the water. His pas were still asleep. The house was gloomy with dawn and absolutely still with a kind of unnatural vacancy. Only the battering of the gale against the dawn-door disturbed the lifelessness.

There was nowhere to go whilst the morning gale blustered outside, so Tighe went back to his alcove and lay down. For a while he dozed and then his pashe was at the door of the alcove.

He couldn't help himself; he jerked on his bed, jittery with the jolt of sudden fear. But she didn't yell, she didn't strike him, she only said, 'My sweet boy-boy,' and came in to hug him.

There was a swift unloosening of feelings inside him. His eyes even prickled with moisture. 'Pashe!' he said, returning the hug.

'You know I love you very much indeed, my little boy-boy,' she was saying, her voice woven through with tenderness. And she was crying a little bit and hugging him so hard it pressed his breath out of his chest.

'I'm not a boy-boy any more, you know, pashe,' he said, his voice warm and breaking. 'I'm a proper boy now.'

'Oh I know,' she said, holding him back at arm's length to have a good look at him, her eyes dawn-red with crying. 'In another year you'll not even be a boy, you'll be a man. But you'll always be my little boy-boy in my heart.'

And – as miraculously as the sun appearing from nowhere on a cold day – everything was all right. After the broken, bruising mood in the house the day before, this morning was golden. He was eight now, grown up, and that was what was important about his birthday, more even than the gift-giving. His pas and he took their breakfast milk; and when the morning gale had died away they all three went out on to the ledge and started downways towards the village.

2

But that was his pashe. Everything balanced, teeter-totter. Some days she would be wonderful; some days she would scream at you and flail out, trying to hit you with a stick, or whatever came to hand. It was as if his pahe lived in the deeps of the house, solid as the groined roof and the flattened, mat-covered earthen floor of the cold store; but his pashe lived forever on the very lip of the ledge, precariously balanced, forever poised to fall.

But then, his pashe had visions. He knew this was the case although it was rarely mentioned; and perhaps it explained the precariousness of her mood. She would wake in the night screaming – really screaming. This would happen once a month, as regular as regular, through all twenty months of the year. Each time the yelling from his pas' room would startle Tighe from his sleep. He would sit straight up so hard it made his spine ache, and there was the noise – *ach! ach!* – shouting, or sobbing, crumpled and muffled by the walls between him and them. And his pahe, the Prince, cooing and soothing her.

Life continued with its usual rhythms after Tighe's eighth birthday, despite the loss of the goat. The remaining animals still had to be pastured, of course, even if Carashe could no longer be trusted with the task. They were still hungry. Their wild-orb eyes held no knowledge that their fellow had fallen to his death. They cared nothing for that. Their minds were as rooted as the grass they ate; food, food, and then (in season) mating. There was a solidity in that, too, Tighe supposed.

'We can't have Carashe any more,' his pahe said to him, on the ledge outside. It was the day after his birthday. 'Best not even mention her name again, in front of your pashe, you know.' They both looked at pashe, forty arms away. She was leading the five goats out of the village pen, where all the animals spent the night. She was still smiling her tearful smile, still luminous with her joy at being alive in the morning.

'But anyway,' said pahe, cupping his hand on Tighe's shoulder, 'you're a boy now – eight! – near enough a man. You can herd the goats yourself, with your pahe to help you the first few times.'

10

Tighe's breast swelled with joy. 'I'll look after them,' he said.

But in the end Tighe didn't herd the goats. His pashe, her mood wobbling a little, said no. It was obvious that she didn't want to risk losing any more of the animals and it was obvious, though unspoken, that she did not trust Tighe to take care of the goats. It wasn't what she said: she said that it was below the dignity of a Princeling and the grandson of the Priest, but Tighe realised that that wasn't the true reason. He was, he knew, almost wholly inexperienced with tending goats; but the rejection hurt him none the less. Of course, it was not to be argued with. Pashe waited with the goats by the mouth of the pen until another goatmonger came to collect her animals. Then they chatted for a few minutes, pashe striking some bargain whereby their animals would join the larger herd for a day or two until a new herder could be arranged.

After that, his pas went down to the village to start the elaborate negotiations that followed on from losing a goat, and Tighe had nothing to do. He was the Princeling of the village, he never had anything to do. He could have sought out his friends, but he wasn't in the mood. So he loitered outside the pen, watching people come and go. He offered to help the stallmen set up their food booth, in the hope of some free food in payment, but they shooed him away. Then he thought about going down to the village and seeking out Carashe, telling her that he personally had no hard feelings about the lost goat. But that was a stupid idea, a non-starter. And so, instead, he went off to be by himself in the sunshine.

He made his way along the main-street shelf where most of the market traders set up pitches, jostling through the growing crowd; then, with a duck into the church and out the back, squeezing through the narrow cupboardways and along a dim alley, before scrabbling up a bamboo ladder set into the wall (a public ladder, of course – he had no money to pay for private passage), and out again into the sunshine. The ledges up here were shorter and narrower, more thoroughly overhung, and the houses correspondingly more primitive. Two grassy ledges slanted up zigzag from one another, and then he was into the newest part of the village – mostly people from Meat, a village several thousand yards above and to the Right. Tighe had never been to Meat, but he knew from report that it was a large place, founded on a great broad platform that jutted out from the worldwall. He knew it was a place rich with all sorts of meat. Some of the poorer people from there had migrated downwall to Cragcouthie in the hope of a better living, but as Tighe walked along the muddy stretches outside their houses he wondered if their life was any better downwall than it had been higher up. The shelf seemed so miserable. A switchback and then a few grassy crags, barely more than crevices. Then another row of new houses, dug out of the wall barely a year before. Many still had raw dirt walls in their vestibules and some of them didn't even seem to have dawn-doors; which made Tighe wonder how they managed when the dawn winds got up every morning.

Then he was past the last houses and up on to the higher crags. Nobody lived here and even the goatherds didn't bother to bring their charges this far. These crags were too small, and their grass too meagre, to provide grazing; so Tighe was able to settle himself with his back against the wall and be alone. The wall stretched above him for a thousand leagues, and below him for a thousand leagues, for all that he knew. And yet he was inches away from the edge of the world.

He stared out into the sky. Birds swooped and curled in the air. Several popped down on to the ledge in front of him to see if he had any food, but they lost interest and waddled off the world again, falling into space and swinging up on their magical wings.

An insect landed on his cheek and tickled; he slapped it with the flat of his palm.

He pulled up fistfuls of stalkgrass and started chewing on it. Stalkgrass never filled you up, but it was better than nothing. You could always tell people who had nothing but stalkgrass to eat because they got thin in a particular way. Their faces became sucked out, dented with starvation. You could last for a long time eating nothing but stalkgrass, but eventually you'd waste away and die. It was a mystery how the goats managed because they grew fat on nothing but the grass. And, following from that, Tighe found himself wondering again about the lost goat from the day before. Scampering near the edge and, then, suddenly – gone. He crawled on his knees the four or five yards to the lip of the crag, covering the last yard on his belly. Finally, inching himself, he put his head over the edge of the world.

There was still that horrible griping in his stomach and the prickles all over his scalp. But there was something beautiful, too. He was lying on his belly looking down, back down the way he had come. The crags were layered narrowly on to one another so he saw the pathways of the newest parts of the village directly beneath him. Their ledge-lips, pressed close together by perspective, gave a vivid sense of depth. Below him somebody, a woman, came out of one of the houses and stood for a moment, lighting up a thorn-pipe. She hunched to get the flame to take and then stood up. Her head, from above, was as round as a pebble, furred with the bristles of her cropped hair. Then she walked off and Tighe lost sight of her.

Wisps of smoke, from cooking fires and curing benches, spiralled out and curled into nothingness from lower down. Sucking in his breath and trying not to concentrate on the thundering of his heart, Tighe pulled himself a little further out over the ledge. The perspective shifted a little and the outside edge of the main-street shelf came into view. Below that was nothing for a hundred yards, just flat wall, too steep to build on. Tighe knew the layout of the village so closely he did not have to think about it; the shelves leading away right and down from market shelf, the warren of smaller ledges spread in an arc, the dugouts leading back into the wall. The sun was rising, well past the lower limit of sight, and as Tighe angled his head higher he had to shade his eyes. Where did the sun come from every morning? How did it climb its way upwards, from the base of the wall to the top?

The day was getting warmer and the morning scatters of cloud were dispersing.

Tighe pulled himself back in and lay on his back. The wall stretched above him, impossibly high, enormously tall, vanishing into blue haze. How high was it? Toweringly high.

Insignificant crags puttered out into nothing above, into the smooth face of the wall, on which nothing grew but a few hardy strands of grass. Directly above Cragcouthie there was nothing; just one of those stretches of almost perfectly flat wall. Meat was somewhere up there, but away several thousand yards to the left. There was passage between the two villages, of course; crags that wound and connected zigzag, linked sometimes by stairways dug through the wall itself. And right and down was Heartshelf (not a shelf, in fact, but a motley collection of ledges, barely even enough to keep goats on). Heartshelf made its living mostly as an intermediary because it was on the only direct pathway between Smelt away downwall and Cragcouthie, Meat and the rest. At Smelt they dug ore out of the wall and fixed it up as metal. There were smelters in Cragcouthie too, of course, but ore was harder to come by up here. So metal was traded downwall and it went through Heartshelf, which took a percentage.

Up beyond Meat were some other villages, and it was said that the wall became more wrinkled in that direction, more prolific with crags and ledges, easier to find a living on. But Tighe thought the stretch directly above him now was the best; the flatness of it, the *purity* of it. The wall blued away into the distance, where it got hazy and vanished in a blur. If only his eyes were good enough and the day uncloudy, Tighe thought, maybe I could see all the way to the top of the wall. *All the way to the top of the wall.* The words gave him exquisite little chills on his scalp and neck. But there was a haze in the mid-morning air that muddled vision after a few thousand yards. Away to the Left big bustling clouds were nudging up against the wall, like great animals nosing some huge breast. Perhaps that was what happened to the far-off walltop, Tighe thought to himself, barely voicing the words. Perhaps it was transformed into clouds. *Clouds. Transformed.* Words could distil such intensity. Words were as high as the wall.

There was a noise at his feet and Tighe looked to see a monkey. He launched a kick at the brute, but it danced out of his way with a screech. Scrambling to his feet, Tighe chased the thing, but it swung upwards on handfuls of stiffgrass and was gone where there was no crag for Tighe to follow.

Laughing, Tighe settled down with his back against the wall again. He munched on some more stalkgrass and stared out at the sky. The colours changed the further up the sky he looked, from the flusher tongue-colours of the lower sky, where the sun was, to the darker, more plastic-blue tints of the upper, but Tighe could not mark the place where the one set of colour shifted into the other. What gave the sky colour? Was it just the sun? But the air was invisible (he flapped his hand in front of his face) so there couldn't *be* any colour.

The sun must be shining on something to make the colour.

With a jolt, as if the idea were so charged it sparked jerkily in his mind, Tighe wondered if what he was seeing was *another* wall – one so distant that he could see no details on it at all, and yet one so huge that it filled the sky from horizon to horizon, from Right to Left. The thought possessed him with wonder.

Another wall?

Inside Tighe's head there was a peculiar sensation of dislocation. Senses swimming. It felt as if there was simultaneous shrinkage, a freezing down, and a sudden expansion, an outrushing of something from the point at the centre of his skull. Another wall. The idea grabbed hold of his mind.

And perhaps people living on it. People like him? Or maybe quite unlike him. He shut his eyes, and tried to imagine what *his* wall would look like from that impossible vantage point. What colour would it be? Blonds and greens from the grasses; browns and blacks from the exposed dirt. Maybe stretches of grey from the exposed rock and concrete. He tried to push his brain out, to swoop outwards on impossible wings, to see the worldwall from even further away. What would the mash of colours end up as? But he could only imagine it dirty and stained-looking, an ugly patchwork of blobs and dabs. That wasn't how the sky looked. He opened his eyes again and tried to map precisely the grain of what he was looking at.

Maybe it was a completely different sort of wall; maybe it wasn't made of rock and dirt and vegetation, as his wall was. Instead it could have been built by God wholly out of grey plastic, say (why not? God could do anything). Or even metal. The thought of it! A wall as big as the worldwall itself, but a wall smooth and pure and perfect, every surface glittering metal that sent back the sunlight touched with blue. And metal people living on it; people as glossy and smooth as chrome, who melted together in lovemaking. Smooth shiny skin on skin; blurring together in sex.

Tighe's wick stirred, but he was too sleepy to do much about it. Instead he dozed.

He woke with a horrible start, with the certainty in his belly that he was falling. He hated that sensation. It was happening more frequently than before. The world would tilt and he would have the certainty in his clenching stomach that he had been rolled off the world and was falling. It always woke him and he always woke up desperately clutching at the ground beneath him. It took him a long time to calm himself down.

He sat up straighter, pressed his back against the comforting bulk of the wall. Looking out at the sky again, the balance of colour had shifted. If it were another wall, then was there another wall behind it? And another behind that? Wall after wall, like the pages of a book, with just enough space in between to allow the sun to thread its way through, lighting one side then the other.

It was an unwieldy vision, but there was something about it that Tighe liked.

Like the pages in a book. His pahe had two books. Some people in the village had more than a dozen. They called it wealth, but Tighe's pashe was always contemptuous of that. She would say, 'Can you eat books?'

Tighe scratched prickles away from the back of his head. Everything was touched by the aftertaste of his daydream now, that dreadful sensation of tumbling into nothingness. It was frightening to consider that he had lived through eight full years, all through his childhood and into his adolescence, and for every minute of that time he had never been further than a few yards from the edge of the world.

It was all so precarious. That was it, yes. Some bitter truth at the core of living, precariousness. Maybe even the goat, even something as dim as the goat, was granted a glimmering epiphany as it stumbled over the edge of things – an understanding of the delicate balance of things. Life is a balancing act and death a sort of falling. He thought of the goat, falling. He thought of his pashe, living on the emotional edge of things, always tipping. He thought of the ancient hierarchy of the Princedom, of the villages together: Prince and Priest and Doge in balance, ruling the law and the religion and the trade, and all the people in their place underneath the ruling order as his pahe had explained it to him. Life involved so many things fitting together: take any one of them away and the structure started to topple.

Was there a brick (he thought) somewhere at the very base of the wall itself that could be picked out, a single brick that could lead to the collapse of the whole worldwall itself? The whole thousand-league structure tumbling down? The thought brought an edge of panic to his mind and he tried to block it out. Concentrate on something else.

Look at the birds flying rings in the air.

Look at the sheen of the clouds running striations up the cool blue of the sky behind.

Look at the dismal brightness of the sun, hot and yellow.

3

From Tighe's house the village was largely a series of stepped ledges, each one a little further west and further downwall from the one before, that led away from the main-street shelf.

Boy-boys would play in the smaller crags at the edge of the village. Games came and went. When Tighe had been a boy-boy, the craze had been to weave kite-planes out of stalkgrass and throw them over the edge. Sometimes these constructions would merely dip away and be lost, but from time to time the breeze would catch them and spin them through the clear air, and the boy-boys would whoop and halloo. But Tighe was a boy now, a Princeling, with a boy's sensitivity not to be mistaken for a boy-boy, so he no longer loitered about this playground. On the day after his birthday he wandered down there, bored, and saw four boy-boys playing a new game, which involved running up and down the crag squealing and trying to catch one another. He couldn't stay. He couldn't bear it; it was so blind to the appalling reality of the drop. How could they be so blithe? If they were to stumble, to fall the wrong way, they could vanish over the edge of the world and fall *for ever*.

He made his way down to Old Witterhe's house; a dingy narrow dugout down a rickety private ladder from the market shelf. Wittershe had once told Tighe that her pahe couldn't widen the house; its space was hemmed by rock on the one hand and manrock on the other. Outside was a tumbly stretch of broken wall too near vertical to make a useful space for humans. Old Witterhe kept monkeys here.

Wittershe's pashe had been young when she married Witterhe and had died giving birth to their one daughter. The thought of it gave Tighe a clench in his gut – to have your pashe *die*! – but Wittershe was blasé about it. She had no memories, she felt no loss. In a way, her situation was more grounded, less precarious, than Tighe's. She had no pashe to lose.

And Wittershe had a pretty face, with lips as broad as fingers and shiny eyes. Her skin was a little paler than was conventionally considered handsome, a sort of timber-coloured light brown; but it was at least smooth, without the pocks that marked some other girls' complexions.

Tighe knew his pashe disapproved of his playing with Wittershe, but he didn't know why. He knew also that his Grandhe particularly disapproved of Old Witterhe, who held some strange opinions concerning God and the wall. Heresies, really, to give them their proper name. But the old man's daughter, Wittershe, was the person in the village nearest to Tighe's age; she was seven years and fourteen months old. Nor was she a girl any more, not really. She didn't have the bulging body of Carashe, but her figure defined several slow arcs, a line Tighe would trace with his eye from neck to small of back, from chest over belly to leg.

Old Witterhe was smoking a thorn-pipe and squatting in the door of his house. His monkeys were placidly picking insects from the tuft grass; a few of them were chewing the grass itself. The sun was making Witterhe hide his eyes in wrinkles.

'Who's that?' he asked, holding his hand like a ledge-flat over his eyes. 'Boy Tighe? Sorry to hear about your goat, boy. Sorry to hear about that. 'Course,' he dropped his hand, 'I lost a monkey yesterday, but nobody considers that much of a tragedy.'

'Sorry to hear about your monkey,' said Tighe automatically, in a monotone. 'Is Wittershe about?'

Old Witterhe poked into the bulb of his pipe with his little finger; like all pipe-smokers, he grew his fingernails long for this purpose. 'They're bringing down some wood from Press, I hear. She's up on main-street shelf to see what manner of price they'll want for it. I could do with building a ledge-flat outside my door.' He pointed with the spire of his pipe. 'There's been some crumbling away at the crag edge there. It's not a good crag, in all. A bit of wood to strengthen it, and maybe build a little overhang, would make my life.'

Tighe thought, *If the traders from Press really have some wood then they won't be trading it for a few monkey carcasses.* But he didn't say anything so rude. Instead, he stepped back a little away from the edge, feeling the comforting press of the wall at his back. Crumbling crag-lips made him nervous.

'I'll climb back up and see if I can find her then,' he said.

'Reckon I should start charging a toll on that ladder of mine,' said Old Witterhe. 'You seem to use it enough. Still, it's good to see you getting some air. You spend too much time in your pas' house, burrowed away in there like a mole. You're not a mole, you know, little Princeling. You're a boy.'

But Tighe was already scrambling back up the ladder.

Up on main-street shelf a crowd was gathered around the traders from Press. The Doge was there, with her retinue. In the middle of the knot of people Tighe could just make out the tall figure of one of the wood traders, his precious package strapped close to his back. Wittershe was there too, but she was making no serious attempt to engage the wood traders in any dialogue. There were too many wealthier villagers with more to offer. Tighe approached her.

'Hello,' he called. 'Wittershe.'

She noted him with a sly smile, utterly distinctive to her. 'Well well, is it the little Princeling?'

'I spoke to your pahe,' he told her, coming up close.

She tossed her head, the short black hair flipping. 'My pahe sent me up here to trade monkey for wood,' she said, 'but there's no trading here for such poor exchange.'

'Are you free then?' Tighe asked.

'Why?' Wittershe giggled. 'You want us to go play? Like boy-boy and girl-girl?' Tighe flushed and Wittershe giggled again. 'I can't do that now, little Princeling. But why don't you come down our ladder this evening? I have chores until the end of the day, but when the sun goes over the top of the wall we might do things.'

'Yes,' said Tighe, too eagerly. 'Yes, I'll come.'

She leant towards him to kiss him on the bridge of his nose, and he got the fleetingest scent of her, the odour of her skin, of maringrass and cheap chandler's soap, and then she was moving away from him.

Tighe felt a ridiculous joy in his heart, but almost at once the sweet emotion fell away. His Grandhe grabbed him by his shoulders, scaring him, and shouted into his ear. 'Young Tighe!' he bellowed. 'My grandchild!'

'Grandhe,' squealed Tighe, squirming round to evade his Grandhe's grip. There was the old man, leaning close to him, his ancient face as wrinkled and ledgy as the face of the worldwall itself.

'What are you scheming at here, boy-boy?' shouted Grandhe. A few of the people who had gathered on the main-street shelf to join in the trading haggle turned to see why the chief Priest of the whole Princedom was shouting. Tighe dropped his shoulders and slunk about in front of his Grandhe.

'Nothing, Grandhe.'

'Nothing? Nothing! It doesn't dignify the office of Prince', he bellowed, 'for the heir – and the grandchild of the Priest as well – to spend all day skulking about doing nothing.'

'I'll be off and find something to occupy myself then, Grandhe.'

'You should be working!'

'Yes, Grandhe, I'll just be away and find some work now.'

But his Grandhe's hand bolted out and caught Tighe's hair, yanking it painfully. Tighe stumbled and almost fell. The old man was speaking in a much lower tone now. 'And I like it *very little*', he was saying, 'that you converse with that girl, Old Witterhe's sluttish girl. Hear me?'

'Yes Grandhe!' The tender hairs near the base of his hairline felt as if they were being torn out.

'*Hear* me?'

'Yes Grandhe!'

'You'll do *better*', he said, with an emphatic tug of the hair, 'to shun the company of that girl.' And he let go of the hair, and stalked away. Tighe took hurried steps backward, and saw the old Priest fold into a company of his deputies, and the whole crowd of them moving away over main-street shelf.

4

His Grandhe's words made a deep impression upon Tighe, but come the end of the day and the disappearance of the sun over the top of the wall, he could only think of Wittershe: the pretty constellation of her features; her smell; the lines of her figure. He slunk down the ladder to Old Witterhe's house with a guilty look up and down the main-street shelf.

She met him outside her pahe's house, and brought him in. Old Witterhe was there, smoking his thorn-pipe vigorously, and offering grass-bread and a monkey bone to chew on, pulling out bits of marrow. They passed the bone round and Witterhe talked. His daughter sat at his feet. 'You're a boy who likes to ask questions,' the old man said.

'I am that,' said Tighe.

'You want to know how the worldwall is, I think.'

Tighe kept stealing glances at young Wittershe. Her hair. Her mouth when it smiled. It was murky and very close inside this part of Old Witterhe's house; a single grass-torch gave off smouldering light that threw swollen shadows on the wall.

The smoke from the thorn-pipe was sparking tears in Tighe's eyes. He kept grinding the heel of his hand into his eye-sockets, but that only made them redder and more sore. Old Witterhe kept stroking the top of Wittershe's head, smoothing her hair.

'Now your Grandhe,' the old man said, raspingly, 'your Grandhe.' He stopped, a look of concentration came over his eyes and he coughed suddenly, loudly. That seemed to clear his voice. 'Now your Grandhe,' he went on, more fluently, 'he says that God built the wall, but if you ask him *why* he just says that *whys* are for God and not for man.'

Tighe tried to clear his throat, but the smoke was going right into his lungs. Wittershe didn't seem to mind it; but she was used to it, he supposed. He nodded.

'Now I don't see why we can't look at questions like *why*, you understand,' said Witterhe. 'Why did God build the wall?'

'The other day I thought', said Tighe, 'that maybe there was another wall.

21

A perfectly blank wall, away in the distance. I thought maybe that was why the sky was blue.'

But Witterhe wasn't listening. 'Now when *I* build a wall, it is for a particular reason. I build a wall to keep something out, or to keep something in. That is what a wall is *for*, do you see? So we have to ask the same question. What does God want to keep in? Or out?'

He glared at Tighe, as if expecting an answer. But apart from the *frisson* of knowing that he was listening to heresy, that his Grandhe would fly into one of his cold rages if he heard these words, he had little interest in what Witterhe was saying.

'God lives on top of the wall,' said Tighe. 'He has the best view up there. Maybe that's why he built it, to give himself the view. Maybe he built the wall to sit on.'

Witterhe coughed, then cackled. 'No, no, that's not it. Let me ask you about the sun.'

'The sun.'

'The sun goes up. That goes direct against the law of gravity. So how does it happen?'

Tighe pondered. 'I never thought of it,' he said.

'You did *not*, no indeed,' said Witterhe. 'Nobody thinks of these things because they seem so plain and straightforward. But we still need to explain ourselves. You know what the sun is?'

Tighe wasn't sure what the question meant.

'The sun is a hot-hot ball of stone. It's rock, like the wall, but it's heated up. That's why we feel its heat and its light. So I ask you again: how does this enormous flaming ball of stone rise *upwards* against the pull of gravity?'

'You're teasing him, pahe,' said Wittershe and smiled at Tighe.

'Oh no, oh no,' said her pahe. 'He's a bright boy, our little Princeling, I'm trying to bring out the thinking in him. It needs to be practised, thinking, or it withers away. When he gets to be Prince himself, he'll need wisdom like this. So how does the hot, *heavy* stone rise up against gravity?'

'I don't know,' said Tighe.

'If *you* wanted a stone to go up,' said Witterhe, 'what would you do? You'd *throw* it up. What else?'

'I'd throw it up,' conceded Tighe.

'And why do you think God is different? Now don't tell your Grandhe, or he'll have the village band together and denounce me as a heretic. But isn't it plain, isn't it *logic* that this is what happens? Every night God heats a giant ball of stone, one of the pebbles from God's beach. He heats it up till it shines with heat, and then come morning he *hurls* it upwards. That's what we see, rising through the day, God's missile. And every day we watch it, without thinking about it; it goes up and over the top of the wall. So that must be where God is throwing it. He is tossing flaming missiles over the wall.'

Puff on the pipe, and another. More thick brown smoke clouded the lamp.

'There's a war, that's what there is,' Witterhe announced grandly. 'We cling to this wall we live on like monkeys and the war is fought right over our heads. *That's* why God built the wall. He built it to keep something, some things, away from Him. Something evil lives on the other side of the wall and God has declared war upon it. Every day he bombards it and he will continue doing so until he has destroyed it.'

And, dozy with smoke, Tighe's imagination flared. He could see the dark abyss on the far side of the wall and sense some nameless evil seething at the base. And then, every night when he lay in his alcove asleep, when he thought the universe was peaceful and at rest, on the other side of the wall divine catastrophe was raining down. Every night another blazing fireball would come screaming down, spitting sparks a thousand yards wide. The smoke wound around Old Witterhe and around Wittershe's clever, narrow face, with its baffling smile. Some dark, smoky abyss on the other side of the wall. Creatures sliding, plotting their evil. And then, every night, the howling apocalypse of divine wrath.

'What sort of creatures, though?' Tighe asked, his voice changed more to awe. 'Why is God so angry with them?'

'Well,' said Witterhe, stretching a little, 'that's a little difficult to say, isn't it. Now, I know somebody, here in the village. He's a good man, works with artefacts and old machines. Maybe I'll introduce you to him. Now, he has a theory.'

Witterhe stopped, gauging the effect of his storytelling.

'This is what he reckons,' he went on. 'He thinks that there is Good and Evil in the universe. That, in some worlds, this Good and this Evil get mixed up. It happens with us on the wall, we can't deny it. Good, yes. Evil, yes. In the same person, often. On our level, which is a small enough level, that's the way. But in the world which God inhabits, maybe it is different. Maybe God built the wall precisely to separate out Good and Evil. Ever think of that?'

Witterhe sucked his pipe again. The air was fragrant and clotted with smoke. Tighe was starting to see blobs of light, deep blue and purple patches that flickered at the edges of vision. His chest heaved, but no matter how hard he breathed he didn't seem to be able to draw enough air into his chest.

'But we are God's favoured because we live on the face of the wall that looks out over Good. We see the sun rise. But what of the people who live on the crags on the *other* side of the wall, eh? What drear and miserable lives do they lead? Living in the stench of evil, living in the dark and then running into their burrows to hide their heads as the wrath of God flames roaring down the sky.'

'Think I need some fresh air,' mumbled Tighe. He stood up, but his feet seemed unsteady. The narrow walls of Witterhe's house seemed to be drawing together. The lamp swung slowly about and Wittershe's face came into view. 'It's the smoke,' Tighe heard her say, 'he's not used to it.'

'Take him out,' came Witterhe's voice, somehow removed from things. 'Fill his lungs with fresh air.'

The nameless evil. Tongue of smoke. Something down there, something roiling around, but he couldn't see his feet. Through the door, leaning on somebody and stumbling – and then, like cold water, the wash of night air. The smoke coalesced into blackness and only the pricks of light in the huge blackness.

Tighe tried to focus on the stars. His head resonated with a swift headache pain that passed away as soon as it struck. Then he knew where he was: sitting on the turf outside Witterhe's house, Wittershe sitting beside him with her arm hanging about his neck like a stole. To his right, the muttering of the apes in the darkness. An occasional shriek of appalling-sounding outrage. Tighe rested his head on his knees, looking down at the grass before his feet. A dozen or so pale mushrooms seemed to be growing on the grass in front of him; but he looked again and saw that they were the bodies of sleeping doves, roosting on the crag. Their heads curled down, their bodies had a weirdly insubstantial appearance. Balloon bodies. Foam bodies. Bulging patches of a ghostly paleness.

'Doves,' he said.

'I know,' said Wittershe, in a whisper. 'Don't speak loud or they'll vanish. Pahe likes to snare them, but they don't often roost on our crag. You stay here and keep an eye on them and I'll slip back through and tell him. He has a net.'

And the pressure was lifted from his neck. Tighe looked around, but Wittershe was gone. The air was soft, falling only gently. Why did the air seem to blow around so much at dusk, but only draw gently downwards at night? Why was dawn always accompanied by a fearful gale? God firing his blazing cannonball, making war on evil. Tighe felt the rightness of Witterhe's cosmology. God setting the great rock alight at dawn and that was the growing of the light way down at the base of the wall; and then God hurled it, from His muscled arm, and the air boiled and howled. That was the morning gale. If it could cause such fierce storms on launching, then what must it be like crashing down on the dark side of the wall?

As if in sympathy, Tighe felt his own insides lurching. Nameless evil. A wall netted with smoke, hideous shapes moving. Tighe's throat clenched and he toppled forward vomiting noisily, a spattering stream. And the doves, cooing as if to reassure him, broke into the night sky in a flutter of starlit wings, pale and ghostly as grey smoke, feathering the stars themselves.

Old Witterhe was furious when he came out to find the doves gone. 'There's good eating on one of those birds,' he said. 'They're valuable. My girl said there were six.'

'I'm sorry,' Tighe groaned. 'I couldn't help it.'

'And you've thrown your puke all over the lip of our ledge,' raged Witterhe. 'My girl'll have to clean that tomorrow. That's disgusting, that is foul. Did you puke and scare the birds away?'

Tighe tried to say something, but the words clogged in the burnt dryness of his throat.

'You puked and scared the doves away,' yelled Witterhe, really angry now. 'Is that the most stupid thing ever? I think it is!'

Tighe felt too awful to argue. He begged some water, in a croaky voice, but Witterhe stumped back into his house shutting the dawn-door behind him. Tighe's throat felt scraped and raw, his stomach teetered on the edge of convulsing again – although he was certain that there was nothing more inside his belly to vomit out. And he was ashamed to have Wittershe see him like this. He tried to gather himself, but she came over and took his hands. Slowly, he climbed the ladder with Wittershe's help and stumbled along the main-street shelf, with the deep blackness of the night apparently swaying and shifting towards him. The journey was patchy. One moment he was trying to say something to Wittershe, to express something, but the words were crumbling in his croaky throat. The next thing, without a sense of continuity of time, he was at the dawn-door of his pas' house fumbling through the webbing to get the latch pulled over. Then, he was at the family sink, slurping messily. His head felt funny. Mostly he was tired; but later, in his alcove, lying on his back, he couldn't sleep. He turned on his side, and turned to his other side, but did not seem able to push himself away into the bliss of unconsciousness. Left side, right side, squirming back to his left side.

Visions arrowed through his head. Old Witterhe's creased face. The doves, sitting motionless on the ledge. The drawing-out massive blackness of the night, open to everything, ready to swallow anything that fell off the world. A mouth that refused no morsel. It was as if Tighe was drunk with the enormity of the universe. The game of God, tossing the sun over the wall of the world. In his twitching half-sleep, Tighe's memories blurred, his atomised vomit scattering over the edge of the world and the filigree tips of the doves' wings folding and unfolding, the two things blending together.

Doves. Even at their moment of most intense effort, with the wings jerking and flitting, their bodies struggling into the air with the epiphany of panic – even at that moment, the expression on the faces of the doves was calm. Nothing could touch the seraphic blankness of those birds. Coasting in flight, settling on the ledge, roosting, bursting spectacularly into the air again; everything was the same to the dark eyes of the birds. The beak-smile of their narrow face.

Tighe turned again. Something was itching deep inside his mind. He turned again. Neither side was comfortable to sleep on. He wished for a third side. Turned again.

He had to sleep. It was stupid. In a few hours the dawn gale would begin sounding, and after that he would have to get up. It was Old Witterhe's stupid pipe-smoke; it had irritated his mind, had rubbed it raw. Now it wouldn't settle.

He wondered if, outside, the doves were still flying; or if they had found themselves another roost. Old Witterhe would still be angry with him in the morning, but it was better that the birds fly in the starlight than that they get their necks corkscrewed and their bodies hung up dead in his smoky old den.

Then Tighe was on his back and thinking of the stars. The nailpoint precision of the stars. Were the stars windows lit in the night-time of that other colossal wall? Was that where the gods lived? Free from the acid tang and muscular ache of bodies; pure spirits; pure as the placid flight of doves.

Then, with sleep in his eyes, and light filling the room outside his alcove, his pashe was shaking him awake, and it was morning.

5

He expected to feel awful, but after washing himself and taking his morning
goatmilk, Tighe actually felt purged. 'You look tired,' his pashe told him,
but he didn't feel it. There was, behind the tenderness of the ache that still
haunted his throat (he *hated* being sick, it was the worst of feelings) – there
was, behind that, still the enormous feeling of pure light, of having been
initiated into mysteries known only to the few. It cradled in his chest; he
wanted to tell his pashe, but she would not have understood. In that
respect, and even at his early age, Tighe recognised her as Grandhe's
daughter.

Then Tighe thought of Grandhe Jaffiahe. Of how outraged he would be if
he knew what Tighe had learned. Of how heretical this truth was, the
knowledge of this cosmic war.

And then – a coincidence that seemed to chime with Tighe's new sense of
insight into the universe – Grandhe Jaffiahe came to the door. But Grandhe
never visited! There was a quarrel between Grandhe and pashe. There was
always one quarrel or another between the two of them. Tighe had realised
that the particular disagreement was not important, but was only the form
taken by some more fundamental clash. Pahe would sometimes make faces
at Tighe, as if trying to look at his own eyebrows, and the whole thing was a
joke. Except that it could never exactly be a joke when Grandhe was so
important in the village. So Tighe was scrubbing the inside of his goatskin
with stalkgrass, getting the last of the milk out (so it wouldn't go bad and
stink the place out) and eating the soaked grass, when Grandhe shouted
outside the door. It was as if he had been thinking about Grandhe and had
summoned him. But the figure at the door was no wraith.

'Daughter!' Grandhe called. 'I am coming to your house. Daughter!'

Pahe always shrunk in on himself a little when Grandhe Jaffiahe was
around; and Pashe, opposite in everything, always bristled outward a little.
But they invited Grandhe in and he sat at the bar with them, and even took
a little milk. Tighe couldn't help staring at the old man, snatching looks.
His face was so weirdly deformed. This is what happened if you lived into
old age; the cheeks became cluttered with wrinkles, the nose spread and

became pitted with tiny dots, the hair blotched white and started coming away from the head in patches at the top and back. Yet the very fact that so few people survived to any great age gave Grandhe a distinctiveness that fed into his habitual gravity. He slurped his milk noisily and then lowered the skin, a white line painted on his dark upper lip. He was looking straight at Tighe.

'You are my only grandchild, boy,' he said, sonorously.

Tighe nodded, unsure. Grandhe had a way of making even the simplest statement sound charged with terrible significance. Was this just an observation, or was it leading into something profound?

'My enemies,' said Grandhe and stopped. The three of them, Pashe, pahe and Tighe waited. Grandhe often began sentences with the words 'my enemies'. He looked, slowly and seemingly with an effort at penetration, into the faces of Tighe and pashe in turn. 'My enemies say that my grandchild frequents the house of the known heretic, of the dangerous man. This is damaging to me.'

Tighe's heart bucked. His thoughts went back to the night before. He had been to Witterhe's house a few times, but last night was the first time anything that might be styled *heresy* had been spoken to him. And surely news about last night had not gone round the village already?

'You', said Grandhe again, lowering his gaze on Tighe once more, 'are my only grandchild.'

Tighe nodded again, but he could feel his face flushing. His heart was moving rapidly. But Grandhe said nothing more and a silence settled in the room. Grandhe Jaffiahe slurped up the rest of the milk, and wiped the eyebrow-thin line of white from his lip. Then he cleared his throat.

'Daughter,' he said, without looking at pashe, 'you have lost a goat.'

'I have, pahe,' she replied in a soft voice.

'I am sorry for your loss.'

There was a quiet period. Tighe could see that his pahe could barely control an expression of astonishment from possessing his face. Pashe was unreadable.

'Daughter,' said Grandhe, 'some of that goat was mine.'

'That is true, pahe.'

'At a time like this,' said Grandhe, making a swoopy gesture with his right hand, 'there is no need to press such debts.'

Even pashe was surprised by this; her face showed it. But she struggled. 'Why thank you, pahe,' she said.

Grandhe sniffed, dropped the hand to his side. Tighe stole another look. There was a rheum in his eyes that looked very like tears. His cheek quivered once, like the twitch that will sometimes pass over the face of a goat when bothered by flies. The motion dislodged some of the moisture from his eye and a bead of water slid downwards over his seamed cheek. Tighe had never seen Grandhe like this.

'When God built the wall . . .' he declaimed, suddenly loud as if beginning one of his sermons; but he broke off. There was a moment of silence.

'Konstakhe is dead,' he said, more softly. 'He died in the night. God took him in the night.'

Nobody said anything for a while. Then pahe offered, 'What terrible news,' in a tentative voice.

'Death comes to us all,' boomed Grandhe suddenly. 'That is God's way. That is why he has placed us on the wall, to remind us at all times of the precariousness of life, of the immediacy of death.' But his preacher's passion faded from the words as he spoke them and the sentence ended in little more than a whisper. Another tear trembled on the ledge of his underlid and then tumbled down his cheek. 'He was a friend,' he said.

'I know,' said pashe and reached out with her hand. But the touch seemed to spur Grandhe back into his manner. He stood up, abruptly, and spoke noisily. 'We'll be burning him today, of course, and it would be good for the whole village to watch the ceremony. He was a great man. He was a *good* man. We must burn him and send his soul up the wall with the smoke. God is waiting for his soul. God sits atop the wall and sees everything.'

And he was gone, sweeping enormously out of the room.

For a while Tighe simply sat, watching the looks his pahe and pashe were exchanging. Then pashe shook her head and got up from the bar.

As he helped pahe give the house its brief morning tidy, Tighe said, 'Grandhe was very close to Konstakhe, wasn't he?'

Pahe gave him a quick look, but then said, 'Well, yes, very close friends, they were that. Known one another for many years. More years than you've been alive.'

But Tighe found himself thinking: at what moment in the night did Old Konstakhe actually die? Had it been when Tighe had been with Old Witterhe? Or afterwards? The rush of doves' wings in the starlight; Tighe vomiting up his stomach, like the cold glitter of a soul leaving a body. The whole thing made his head feel strange.

Afterwards Tighe walked through the village. Down on main-street shelf a couple of Grandhe's junior preachers were building the pyre, roughly weaving together plates of the high bamboo that grew on the most poorly watered crags and was therefore brittle and flammable. Tighe stood and watched them for a while. People passed and re-passed, and a few stopped to watch the process. The priests bent the flimsy boards of bamboo to

29

shapes, and boxed a funereal shape. More grass and bamboo were laid around the edge. Onlookers watched for a while and then moved on.

Tighe went up a public ladder and along the series of shorter ledges to the up-and-to-the-right of the village. Here there were a number of mechanical shops; a friend from boy-boyhood, Akathe, was working in the clockmongers. Though no older than Tighe, his family was not as elevated and Akathe spent most of his days in the outside alcove beside the shop entrance, working with various clockwork devices in the daylight.

'Did you hear?' Tighe said, sauntering up to him. 'Konstakhe died in the night.'

'Everybody has heard that,' said Akathe. He didn't detach his attention from the little clock he was working on. It was a plastic device, cogwheels worn and grooved with use. Akathe prodded it with a needle-thin spatula, working clockworker's mud into the workings. He had a little plate of the stuff at his elbow.

Tighe sat himself on the grass before Akathe. 'Shall you go to the ceremony?'

'If I get this finished.' He looked up, but kept one eye shut in the clockworker's squint. 'Yesterday somebody traded power-book parts with my pashe. We got a regular pile of the parts now.'

'Which parts?' Tighe asked, although these sort of clockwork details meant nothing to him.

'Well, there's a sort of membrane that pashe thinks was the screen. We also have the teeth of the thing, pulled teeth each marked with a symbol. Even I could recognise some of them – an R, an A, something that is either a C or an S.'

'That's good,' said Tighe, but without enthusiasm. 'So will you go?'

Akathe sniffed, and looked again at the clock. 'Don't know. Maybe, maybe not. This is an odd plastic, this one. The mud won't seem to set and when it does it comes away in lumps. Something about this plastic that resists the glue of it.'

'You don't go much to religious ceremonies,' said Tighe.

'Don't have all that much time, really.' He was prodding at the clock's innards again.

'I was thinking, you know,' said Tighe, snapping off a blade of grass and twirling it in the sunshine. A striking purple-and-red beetle was twitching its way through the stalks at his feet, climbing some until they bent and tipped him over, weaving through others. 'Thinking about God, you know.'

'God,' said Akathe, without inflection.

'You know how we're taught he sits on top of the wall,' said Tighe. 'Sees the universe.'

30

'You should really ask your Grandhe this kind of stuff,' said Akathe.

'But you know about that.'

'Sure.'

'Does it sound, uh, *right*, to you?'

'Don't really think much about it.'

'It's just that I heard some other stories, and they made me think. What if God doesn't sit on top of the world? What if God lives at the *bottom* of the wall – what if he built the wall to keep somebody out? To keep something out?'

Akathe stopped and gave Tighe a serious look. 'Well,' he said, 'I had heard that you were chasing after the girl, the Wittershe girl. And everybody knows that her pahe is a mad old boy-boy.'

'Well,' said Tighe, staring intently at the strand of grass in his hand, 'I was just wondering.'

'You'd be careful, that would be best,' said Akathe. 'Old Witterhe is a dangerous sort to be around. I say if *my* Grandhe were the Priest I'd be specially careful who I spoke to. And I'd be specially careful who I let know about strange cosmic notions.' He shook his head, and sniffed again. 'You think that Wittershe girl is worth anything at all? You're a Princeling, after all. She's beneath you. Your pas own half a dozen goats, you know.'

'We lost a goat,' said Tighe.

'Well, I heard that, but that's not the point. You still come from an important family. You can do better than a monkeymonger's daughter. You'll be Prince of the village one day, and you can do better. She's beneath you. That's what my pashe reckons, at any rate, and I suppose she knows.'

'Wittershe is all right,' said Tighe.

'Sure, but there are better, that's all. And be wary of listening to heresy, Tighe. Just because your Grandhe is the preacher won't protect you, I think. You know the way he is, better than any.'

'Grandhe came by the house today.'

Akathe didn't say anything.

'He came by and he was actually crying. He is upset by the death of his friend, by the death of Konstakhe, he really is.'

Akathe was working at the watch again. 'My pashe has some things to say about that too,' he muttered, darkly.

'What?' said Tighe, genuinely surprised.

But Akathe wouldn't say any more.

Tighe wandered back through the village. The sun was hot today and he took off his shirt. Life in the village went on. Death made no dent in it. Tighe thought of the tear trembling on the underside of his Grandhe's eye. He had never seen the old man cry before. One person's death could put

31

such a wound in a single mind, and yet the village carried on without there being a visible gap in the weave of life.

He climbed down to Old Witterhe's ledge and found Wittershe cutting pelt from the monkeys. She held one captive creature firmly with her thighs and scraped his hair off with a razor. The beast screeched and muttered, but Wittershe kept a tight grip. The shaved hair was going into a cloth sac, to be used as stuffing. When Tighe said hello she scowled at him.

'I had to clean your vomit off the ledge this morning, you foulness,' she said, sourly.

'I couldn't help myself,' said Tighe. 'It was the thickness of your pahe's smoke. What is that, anyway, that smoke? What does he put in his pipe?'

'Something too strong for a boy-boy like you,' she said.

'Don't say that,' said Tighe, a little stung. 'I'm sorry about the vomit, but, you know. I was thinking about all the stuff your pahe said last night.'

'So?'

'You've heard it?'

'I know what the truth is,' she said, scraping her razor down the leg of the squirming monkey. He looked comical, piebald, with one side pink and naked and the other still furred black. 'And I know that your Grandhe would like to push my pahe off the wall for heresy.'

'It's not my fault that he's my Grandhe,' said Tighe, defensive. 'I don't think it sounded like heresy. I think it sounded right.'

Wittershe stopped what she was doing and looked at him. 'I'd be careful of saying that too much about the village,' she said. 'Your old Grandhe wouldn't hold back at throwing *you* off if he smelt heresy.' But there was a smile flexing her lips.

'Nobody gets thrown off the world for heresy, not really,' said Tighe, feeling the mood relax. 'That's just grand talk.'

'There was a man my pahe knew in Meat,' said Wittershe, starting to scrape again. 'He spoke some heresy and he got thrown off. Or he was chased off. Before I was born.'

Before I was born was an impossibly enormous length of time to Tighe. He came over to where Wittershe was sitting and reached out. Her neck was stretched over the ape she was dealing with. There was a little nobble of bone at the exact point of the nape. Tighe let his hand rest gently on that place. His heart sped up with the proximity, with the touch of her flesh.

'Now,' said Wittershe, 'you'd best stop that. I have work to do.'

Tighe danced back, skittering. His heart was full of light. The softness of her skin on his fingers' ends. 'You hear about Old Konstakhe dying in the night?'

Wittershe looked up sharply. 'What's that? Old Konstakhe dead?'

'There's the ceremony today, the burning. To send his soul up to God, they say. My Grandhe came round today crying because of the death.'

'Well,' said Wittershe. 'That's something. A burning today.'

'I never saw my Grandhe cry before,' said Tighe. He pushed himself against the wall and rolled slowly, pressing front and then back and then front against the warmth of the soil. Particles of dirt stuck to his skin.

'Well,' said Wittershe, with a sly look. 'You know what they said about your Grandhe and that man.'

'No,' said Tighe. 'What was that?'

'So you never heard?'

Tighe was genuinely puzzled. 'No.'

'What an innocent you are!' Wittershe laughed briefly, and then turned back to the monkey. 'Can it really be that you never heard?'

'Heard what?' Tighe brushed the dirt from his chest. His shirt was tied like a fat belt about his hips. There was more of a breeze now, falling from above and coaxing goosebumps from his arms. He unravelled his shirt and wriggled back into it.

'Oh, nothing,' said Wittershe, with a strange smile on her face. 'You'll be at the ceremony?'

'Sure,' said Tighe. He had nothing to do, so of course he would go. 'Will you go?'

'Well, I'm supposed to shave all these monkeys, but I guess I could spare a little while.'

'Seriously, Wittershe,' said Tighe, coming over to her again. 'What is it that I never heard about my Grandhe? What won't you say to me?'

'I'll tell you at the burning,' she said with the same minx-smile on her face.

'But what is it?'

'I'll tell you at the burning,' she repeated. 'Only, your Grandhe and Konstakhe were more than friends. That's all.'

'What do you mean?'

But Wittershe wasn't to be drawn, and eventually Tighe climbed back up the ladder and roamed around the village again. The pyre was ready now, on the market shelf; one of the junior preachers stood solidly beside it. Tighe loitered a little more.

Soon, though, the sun was up to the level of the village and the shadows shrank right to the back of the wall. It was time for some lunch. Tighe made his way back Left through the village to his pas' house. As he arrived back at the door the air was very still and the sun's heat was undisturbed. He was sweating a little as he fingered the latch of the dawn-door aside and stepped into the cool of the hallway.

His pashe was home, lying in the dark of the bedroom. When she heard

33

Tighe moving around in the main space she stirred and came out of her room. For a while she was silent, only watching whilst Tighe cut up some sprouted grass-bread and smeared it with watery cheese. Her silent audience began to make Tighe nervous. She was usually in a weird mood after any encounter with Grandhe, but if she were going to explode at him she would probably have done so by now. He wiped the spatula and put it away and then came over and gave his pashe a kiss. She turned her cheek as he walked over with a strange something in her expression, but she accepted the kiss.

A little unsettled, Tighe took up the bread and cheese and ate it in large mouthfuls. He wanted to say something, to draw pashe out of her motionless silent watching, but he didn't know what to say. He looked around, hoping his pahe was somewhere in the house, but he clearly wasn't.

'I went by market shelf,' he said, at last, his words sounding clumsy and loud after the quiet. 'They've built the pyre.' Silence. He finished the bread and wiped his hands on his shirt. 'It looks handsomely done.'

A fluttery smile had come to her lips. His heart lurched. What did that mean?

'You're a good boy-boy,' she said, in a distant voice. The smile was a full smile now and she held out one hand towards him. Feeling more than a little sheepish. Tighe went towards her and was received into a desultory one-armed hug. Then he broke away and slouched about the room as he spoke.

'It was strange to see Grandhe so upset,' he said. 'I don't recall ever having seen him so upset by anything.'

Pashe was leaning against the wall by the doorway into her bedroom. 'You know your Grandhe,' she said. There was a floaty, disconcerting edge to her voice. Tighe found himself getting wound up inside, like one of Akathe's clockwork devices.

'I guess. I remember another ceremony of burning, I must have been three, not yet three. I remember that, though, and Grandhe seemed almost pleased to be able to do it. I remember all his preaching.' He stopped speaking and stopped his slouching. Pashe was following him with her eyes without turning her head.

'I don't recall ever having seen Grandhe so upset by anything,' Tighe said again. 'I guess he and Konstakhe had been pretty close friends, had they?'

The merest contraction of her eyelids, but pashe didn't say anything.

'It must be terrible to lose somebody you're really close to.' Tighe's own voice sounded strange in his head. It was the silence. But he couldn't stop talking. 'I heard in the village that there was some story about Grandhe and Konstakhe, but I never heard that before.' As soon as he had said it, he knew it was the wrong thing to say. He stopped, his heart faster, wondering

34

if he had spoken the spell that would summon up the angry pashe. Poised. But she hadn't moved, her expression hadn't changed, except perhaps for the faintest tightening around her nostrils. Tighe was breathing shallowly.

'Anyway, I guess I'll go along to the ceremony and hear Grandhe preaching,' he said, hurriedly. 'Will you go there? Will pahe be there?'

Pashe's hand went up to her mouth, her fingers' ends touching her upper lip. 'Will I go?' she said. She was standing straight now. 'Will I go to the ceremony? Will your pahe? Do you know where your pahe is? Do you *know* where he is?'

Heat was building in her words. Tighe felt sickness in his own belly. He had got her angry after all and now there was nothing he could do except stand there and watch whilst her rage built itself and built itself until it exploded. His eyes and mouth were equally open, frozen, a horrified look. 'Do you know where your pahe is? Shall I tell you? Whilst you *maunder* around the village like a goat lost on a crag, your pahe has been *working* on the higher ledges. Have you *forgotten* already that we lost a goat days ago – a whole goat? Is that how *selfish* you have become? Don't you know what that means, in terms of the extra work your pahe and I have to do now?' Her voice was loud now, her hand clenching to a fist before her face with each emphasis. But Tighe could only stand there and watch. 'Do you assume everybody is as idle and worthless as you are? Is *that* what you assume? People have work to do – not you, not you of course, but real people. People like your pahe and *me*.' She was trembling now, shivering with the rage as it built up inside her. Her other hand came up and clutched sharply at the fist. 'I wonder how I could have raised a boy-boy as *selfish* as you. It's mockery, it is mockery, mocking your Grandhe when he came here with *tears in his eyes*,' and with that she lurched forward and swung out with both her linked fists. Tighe knew better than to dodge. The blow caught him at the side of his head and he dropped himself down. It was better to go down. He curled up, wrapping his head in his arms and bringing his knees to his shoulders. It wasn't that it hurt him physically – he was too large for that now – but there was something horribly penetrating about her anger, emotionally penetrating, and that made it gruelling. He didn't understand it and yet he did understand it. Deep down it made sense and the sense it made had a kind of perfection because deep down he was bad and his pashe could see that.

She had taken up one of the wall paddles, a yard-long slightly curved and polished piece of wood that pahe used to work patterns into the drying mud of the wall. It was wood and therefore valuable, but pashe was using it feverishly, slapping and smacking his whole body. In some distant part of his brain, Tighe wondered whether she would break it and what they would do then. He didn't want the paddle to break because it was expensive. But also, some logical part of his mind deep inside his head decided, because if it broke then he would have to explain to his pahe how it had broken. And that would mean including pahe in this ritual of pain. Which was not something Tighe wanted. Impact burned on his hip, chest, head, stomach-side. And then, suddenly, it was over.

When he looked up, tentatively, his pashe was sitting, panting a little, with her back to the wall of the open space and her legs out straight in front of her. Sheepishly, as if complicit in some unmentionable game, she caught his eye. He unwound himself and got unsteadily to his feet, and during the whole time of this manoeuvre they never broke eye contact. It was a kind of bond between them, a horrible intimacy. But he knew he brought it on himself. So he bowed his head, and shuffled out through the door and out on to the ledge again.

6

After he had wandered about the village for a bit in the sunshine the beating receded into the distance. It became a memory, and memory (he told himself) made little distinction between yesterday and ten years since. Thinking about it like that helped. As if it had not happened, not quite. Or, perhaps, as if it had happened to someone else.

There was the sun, there were the faces of the people passing, that was enough. He sat and stared out at the sky for a while: his whole theory of there being another wall, a pure, clean blue-grey wall in the hazy distance – was that a kind of heresy too? He wondered what his Grandhe would say if he broached it to him. He squeezed his eyelids together, trying to bring the distant artefact into some more detailed resolution, trying to trick optics with the pressure on his eyeballs.

He touched his bruises slightly, with his fingers' ends, through his clothes. One more feature on the landscape of his body.

He drew in three long, slow breaths. He actually felt better.

After a while he made his way back along. On market shelf the crowd was starting to gather. It was about to happen. Both the junior preachers were standing by the pyre now, something stiffer in their posture. Tighe watched shop alcoves in the side of the wall shut up, their owners scurrying in knots of two and three and accumulating on the broad shelf. People were coming up the main stair at the far end of the street one by one, each head growing into a body with legs and feet, and each person emerging to be followed by a new head. The sun was cooled by a strong breeze from below; an afternoon breeze rising as the day warmed. The sun was above them now, throwing shadows and spreading darkness into doorways and cubbyholes.

Tighe pushed through the crowd looking for Wittershe. For some reason he couldn't quite pinpoint, the thought of her *neck* was very strong in his imagination. It was so beautiful: the brown tone of her skin; the tiny black filaments of hair that were just about visible on it, the arc of the bone under skin. A wave of intense yearning passed through Tighe and he wanted to touch Wittershe. But he couldn't find her in the crowd.

The crowd had now reached a certain size, and was gelling as a mass of people. Tighe, always nervous in groups when too near the edge, elbowed his way through and pressed his flank against the wall itself. He had an oblique view of the pyre as the two junior preachers moved off and made their way into the chapel behind. Tighe had been friendly with one of the juniors when they had both been boy-boys; but now he took his apprenticeship to preaching seriously. Tighe hadn't spoken to him from summer to summer, a whole half-year.

A hum started in the midst of the crowd and Tighe raised himself. They were bringing out the body; wrapped in a grass-weave shroud, slung between the two juniors. And there was Grandhe, hands folded together as he paced the ground out to the pyre. The crowd was excited now, with mutters rippling back and across. The juniors were sliding the body into the inside of the pyre.

There was a touch at his shoulder: Wittershe.

'My pahe don't know I'm here,' she said into his ear, breathy from just having climbed up. 'I mayn't be able to stay for the whole ceremony.'

'You're just in time,' said Tighe, his chest burning with excitement. He tried to turn round, but she pushed his shoulder. The crowd was close around them and there wasn't much space. Tighe had to content himself with reaching behind himself and letting his knuckles trace the side of Wittershe's hip.

'There's your Grandhe,' she said, putting her mouth close to his ear. When she leaned forward to talk, her body pressed against Tighe's left shoulderblade, her warm breath tickled the side of his head. His wick was hard as stone with just that fleeting contact. 'There's your Grandhe,' she said, 'weeping over his woman.'

It took a moment for Tighe to realise what she was saying. 'What do you mean?'

But Grandhe's voice came bellowing out and the crowd hushed. Wittershe's hand found Tighe's and her fingers curled into his.

'God sits on top of the wall,' he called forth, in clear tones. 'God sees everything from there. What God wants, God gets. He wanted the soul of our dear friend Konstakhe.' And he broke off. There was no expression readable on his face. The crowd was becoming more excited, jostling back and forth, motion passing through the gathered bodies like wind through the grass. Grandhe's expression was unreadable.

'God placed us on the wall as witnesses,' he said. A few people in the crowd moaned or murmured. Somebody put his hand into the air and then others did the same. 'Konstakhe was a good man. He was a good man,' Grandhe was saying, but his voice was becoming submerged in the increasing hum of the crowd.

'He'll be flying up,' shouted Grandhe, his voice loud suddenly. The congregation hummed like the wind, and somebody towards the back took up the shout. 'Upward! Upward!' Tighe felt his heart jerk, twist inside him. Everything shifted, seemed to pull closer. Bodies, red faces. Everyone calling out, faces stretching to open the mouth wide. Up! Up! He was joining in the shouting without even realising it. Up he had to go; he had been a good man. Grandhe was shouting, his words barely audible over the storm of shouting.

'Upwards! Upwards!'

Grandhe kept talking, and with a sort of impalpable eddy the jostling crowd stilled. The shouting died and the Funeral Speech became more audible.

'. . . of the Divine, his spirit. With the flames that struggle upwards, with the smoke that tumbles into the sky, with the hot air rising, his spirit. His body shall relinquish it and only the downward dust shall remain. And dust shall feed the earth and the earth will bring forth flowers in the dirt. Flowers, my friends,' said Grandhe, lifting his arms in a theatrical gesture, and smiling. 'Flowers know their nature is from the Divine! They struggle upwards, struggle like green flames, though tethered to the ledge. They struggle in the direction that he has gone!' A murmur spread quickly through the mourners; Grandhe beaming, casting his glance amongst these people. For the briefest moment his eyes lighted on Tighe.

Tighe's heart leapt up again, but for a different reason. The unholy thought had occurred to him just how ugly Grandhe's face was. Broad brown nose like a piece of goat-dung; semi-coloured face, blotched with a disfiguring paleness in a spilt pattern, like milk unwiped away. He joined in, heartily, to cover his own evil thinking.

'Upwards! Upwards!'

Grandhe ducked down and Tighe couldn't see him past the crush of people. But moments later boulders of smoke hurtled upwards and a shower of flames stretched after them. How did they get bodies to burn so quickly and with such ferocity? Tighe didn't know.

Wittershe was at his back, pressing herself against him. 'I could hardly hear,' she said, leaning close to his ear. 'Did he say anything shocking? Did he admit to anything with Konstakhe?'

Tighe breathed sharply, sucking in a laugh. It was the tart delight of being close to Wittershe, of her saying the unsayable. He half turned and leaned a little forward, so as to bring his mouth close to the side of her head. 'How do they get flesh to burn so fierce?' he hissed in her ear.

She snorted with laughter, stretched up so that her lips were close to his ear. 'They douse the body. They dig a pit and douse it with this stuff, leave it all night. But only if the dead is a virtuous dead. My pahe told me.'

'Your pahe doesn't know anything past monkeys,' said Tighe, drunk with the delight of speaking the unspeakable. But the cheering had got louder and Wittershe probably didn't hear. Which was doubtless for the best since Wittershe was close to her pahe.

'Stand there,' said Wittershe. 'I want to climb up on your back and have a look at the body burning.' He turned to face the front again and her tiny body was scrambling up his back, pulling herself up with her hands over his shoulders. She reached as high as she could go, her belly pressing into the back of his head. She was holding his shoulder to steady herself. His bruises ached a little where she put pressure on them, but he didn't mind that, not really. He reached up with his own right hand out, pressing the small of her back to steady her. The goat-hair cloth she was wearing scratched his neck, but his head, neck, back could feel the sliding of her naked belly. It was so close, pressed so close against him. His heart swam, his wick strengthening and standing. With his free hand he jostled it, so that it wouldn't bulge his pants. 'Can you see it?' he called. 'Can you see it?'

It wasn't comfortable and it obstructed his own view of the scene, poor though that had been. He could just about make out the shimmy of the flame-tops over the people ahead of him. Everybody had shuffled forward as the burning began and closed together, almost as if they wanted to soak up the warmth. He tried to look up, to see if the old man's spirit was visible as it bounced up free through the air, looking like – he didn't know what. Dancing on the flame-tops, perhaps, or climbing each strand of yellow flame like a spirit creeper. But he couldn't see anything other than the backs of people's heads and at the top of his vision only a mess of broken smoke. Wittershe was leaning forward, her head and her hair stopping him seeing properly upwards. Tighe got a sudden perspective of a folded chin, of nostrils and sight up the nostrils. It was weird. But the press of her flesh against him, the sagging curve of goat-hair cloth that was only a thin veil hiding her small breasts, was more present in him. His wick was straining now, so stiff it even hurt a little.

Then she was climbing down and the crowd was breaking up. The cheering had died and was now only a muttering as people filed down the ledge, or else climbed the footholds to the ledge above. 'Did you see?' Tighe asked her. 'Did you see him burning?'

She nodded. 'I couldn't see his face, though. I wanted to see his face, but all there was was a kind of black shape all covered in fire. It was a man-shape, but it didn't have anything, you know, *personal* about it.' She sounded disappointed. 'Let's go and look at the ashes.' She pressed forward.

He followed her through the crowd, almost breathless. The excitement of it was all concentrated in his wick. All that death and holiness, all the yelling and cheering at Grandhe's speaking; the intense anticipation that he might see old Konstakhe's rising spirit was one with the anticipation that he would be able to take hold of Wittershe and press himself upon her. That he would be able to push her down to the turf and put himself on top of her. It was all packed into his wick, all crammed into that funny little tube of flesh. Tighe had watched goats and the way their wicks hung flaccid most of their lives, except when the mating fever was on them when they became hard as rock. And then afterwards they would be placid, their thoughts far from sex.

Sometimes Tighe felt as if he were living in a continual mating fever.

He pushed himself through the crowd and tumbled against Wittershe again, pressing himself against her a little more forcefully than he needed. The rasp of cloth, the distant, slippery sense of flesh underneath it. Wittershe didn't seem to mind; didn't seem to notice. She was peering down at the still-hot ashes, gleaming with dots of red.

'That used to be Konstakhe,' she said, as if to herself. 'Old Konstakhe. That used to be him.'

'That used to be my Grandhe's closest friend,' said Tighe, and Wittershe sniggered, hiding her mouth with her hand. Tighe grinned to return her grin, but in fact the thought unsettled him. A human being was now only a pattern of ashes on the ground. The glow paled from red to black. Somebody was standing next to the remains of the pyre with a bucket, ready for the ashes to cool to take them to one of the gardens. Grandhe had vanished. Tighe looked around; the crowd was dispersing. So little distance between these walking, breathing people and this little pile of black sand.

'You should piss on it,' said Wittershe, putting her hand on Tighe's arm.

'*You* should,' countered Tighe.

'I can't, I'm a girl. But you could quickly piss on it. Put the fire down.' She sniggered again and suddenly she was darting over the shelf. Tighe lurched, took a step after her, but stopped. She was gone.

7

Things changed. It was hard to pin it down. For Tighe it was all somehow clouded with his infatuation with Wittershe, which took up more and more of his thoughts. But it seemed difficult to deny that some sort of change began with the loss of the goat on his eighth birthday. For weeks pahe was not around, and pashe was in an even more precarious mood than normal. Pahe was working all the hours, trying to make good some of the debts that the loss of the goat had brought upon them. He told Tighe that he couldn't spend time doing the work around the house that needed doing and then he paused. 'I could do that,' said Tighe, prompted by the sad expression on his pahe's face. 'I'll do the work around the house.'

His pahe almost smiled. 'You are my son,' he said. 'You are Princeling and one day you'll make a fine Prince.'

He spent an hour showing Tighe the basic repairs that the dawn gale made necessary on the outside, patching the dawn-door and so on. It seemed clear enough, but left to himself Tighe found it hard to get right. He couldn't seem to concentrate. His pahe was gone and in the main space his pashe was lying on the floor and sobbing noisily, intrusively. It was hard to concentrate. Normally Tighe would have gone out and roamed the ledges and the crags; but his pahe had left him in charge of the house and another layer of mud needed to be applied to the outside of the dawn-door – it needed to be done in the morning so it could dry in the midday sunshine. So Tighe bit his teeth together and smeared the mud over the front of the dawn-door, making quite a mess of it. But always there was the *ah-ah-ah* of his pashe crying in the main space.

He sat back on his haunches and listened to the noise. Difficult to know what to do. Then the sobbing changed to a single rising wail, *ullahhh*, and the noise slid like a needle into his head. He made a few more swipes with the spatula, but the noise was too much. Tentatively he made his way back to the main space, putting his head round the door. 'Pashe?'

Only her huddled shape on the floor, bulging and shaking with the effort of crying. She was sobbing again now.

He stood in the door, scratching his head. Then he tiptoed over towards her, and crouched down beside her. 'Pashe, what is it? What is the matter?'

The sobbing stopped and Tighe's heart jumped, not knowing whether violence was about to spring up from the floor. Pashe lurched and sat up and Tighe couldn't prevent the reflex that jerked him backwards. But his pashe's face was so blurred with crying, her eyes so red and desolate-looking, that he paused. 'Oh my boy-boy,' she moaned and grabbed his neck in an awkward embrace. 'You're the only man in my life. You are my life! You are why we do all this, all this struggle, when it would be so easy to give up, to give over, to fall away.'

And she sobbed and cried on to his shoulder and Tighe did not know what to do, so he just held her and tried to make a comforting hum with his mouth. And, as the moment stretched out, there was an almost warm feeling in his belly. That he and his pashe could enjoy this intimacy; that she could depend upon him. Or maybe it was only that the terror of his pashe was reduced to this bundle, this series of hot desperate breaths against his neck. It was a sort of power; but at the same time he felt awkward because of its incongruity. The moment swelled and then passed, faded. Pashe gently pulled herself back, away from him, wiping her face on the sleeve of her shirt. Tighe sat looking at the floor. The intimacy had evaporated and now there was only the awkwardness.

He went back to the dawn-door and made some desultory passes over the front of it with the spatula. Then he threw the equipment down and lurched outside and along the ledge. The sky was brass coloured, scratched like old plastic with some streaky clouds running vertically. A fresh breeze, the last remnants of the dawn gale, was pushing up and rustling Tighe's hair. He made his way along the ledges and down the public ladder to the main-street shelf. There were a few loiterers hanging about the shelf, hoping for work; thin men and women in raggedy clothes. That was a sign that things were changing; even Tighe knew as much. There would usually be three or four people squatting with their backs to the wall hoping for any sort of chore or job that would earn them their food. But here were more than a dozen people, some faces that Tighe recognised, some completely new to him.

He went up to Akathe's booth to talk to him about it. 'All the traders are talking about it,' the clockmaker told him, with an eyepiece clenched between eyebrow and bulging cheek. 'Bad times coming. If you know how to sense it you can feel it, like the stirring of the air before the dawn gale.'

'I saw more than a *dozen* people waiting on market shelf hoping for work – think of it! There were several new faces there.'

'They came along this ledge late yesterday,' said Akathe, 'trying to beg work directly from the traders – as if that was the way it works! They really don't understand the way it works.' He shook his head sagely.

'Who are they?'

Akathe shrugged. 'From Smelt, I think. They've made their way upwall to Heartshelf and then to us.'

'Why come to us?'

'Who knows. I suppose work is thin in Smelt, and in Heartshelf as well. So they come here because this is where the Doge lives. And the Priest and the Prince too,' he grinned and made a little mock-obeisance with his head in Tighe's direction, 'but it's mostly the thought of the Doge living here that brings them. But there's no work here. Mostly we have animal tending and this is too valuable to trust itinerants with. The rest of us serve the goatmongers. They'll get no work with us.'

'So what will they do?'

'Hang about the ledges getting thin,' said Akathe. 'How do I know? They can go jump into the sky for all I care.' He fiddled with something and then plucked the eyepiece from his face. It made a faint popping noise. 'Now that they know there's no work here I guess they're just trying to raise enough money to pay for the toll ladder up to Meat. That's the biggest town in this part of the wall, so they're more likely to find something up there.'

'But if they can't get work they won't be able to buy food, let alone pay for the toll ladder.'

Akathe shrugged again. 'I dare say, if they get too close to actual starvation, the Doge will let them pass and climb her ladder, if only to stop them messing up the market shelf with their dying. Or maybe she'll let them die so we can burn them and put their ashes to fertilise our gardens.' He grinned as he said this, but Tighe shuddered, wondering if he were half-serious.

Tighe wandered back down to the shelf and watched the newcomers for a bit. A bone-worker passed and recruited one of the loiterers; presumably she had some stripping and rendering she needed doing, hard smelly work that an itinerant could manage. But the bone-worker (a short, hunch-shouldered woman called Dalshe) of course hired one of the village's known tramps. It went without saying that she was going to give the work to somebody she knew. The faces of the newcomers rose as she approached; they forced smiles, stood a little straighter. But as she left their faces tumbled again and they slouched or sat gracelessly back on the ground.

Bored, Tighe climbed down to Old Witterhe's, but the dawn-door was shut and nobody answered his calls. He climbed back up and made his way back to Akathe's booth.

'You again? You're not here to buy anything, are you, you wastrel

Princeling. You're just here to loiter, like the spoilt boy-boy you are.'
Akathe grinned. 'If your grace don't mind me saying, you're worse than an
itinerant.'

'It's sad,' said Tighe, 'watching those newcomers. They're going to be
hungry tonight.'

'I wouldn't waste your energies on worrying about them,' said Akathe.
'I'd worry about your own kind first. There are people from the village who
will be hungry tonight, and I worry about that. Your own Princedom, think
of it that way. Because that could be me in a few weeks.' He sighed, and
clambered out of the booth to stretch his legs on the ledge. 'People don't
buy clocks or clockwork when times get hard. My pahe is worried.'

'You'll be all right,' said Tighe unconvincingly.

'As if you know anything about it! *You'*ll be all right. People always need
goats.'

'But we lost that goat,' said Tighe, eager not to be outstripped in the
misery game. 'Don't forget that.'

'No,' said Akathe, sucking his lower lip. 'I suppose that's true. I heard
your pahe was working on old Musshe's house up on top ledge. He may be
Prince, but he has to work like anybody else. Labouring up there on top
ledge.' Nobody knew why it was called top ledge; it was not the highest
ledge in the village. But old Musshe had the ledge to herself, so perhaps it
reflected her status in the village. 'He owed her some goathair from the
beast you lost, I heard, and some candles indirectly. So now he's single-
handedly digging her a new room. Must be back-breaking. It's itinerant
work, too, so I don't suppose it's paying off the whole of the debt.'

Tighe had not heard that his pahe was involved in anything so
demeaning. It was a shock. Part of him wanted to hear more detail, but
the stronger impulse was to deny that his pahe was in any trouble at all. He
decided to change the subject.

'What's happened in the village, then?' he asked. 'Why has it come down
like this? It was fine only weeks ago.'

Akathe didn't answer this straight away. He was staring out at the sky,
tracing the paths of birds circling on the last of the warm upwinds. Black
dots like pieces of the night sky torn off and blown about in the fresh
sunlight. Eventually he said, 'Who knows how it works? A village is like a
large clockwork machine. A hundred parts need to work all together for it
to function. Who knows why it goes wrong? Everything seems to be like last
year, only there are more people begging work on the market shelf, only
there are fewer people buying the traders' goods. Suddenly everybody is
hungry and nobody can afford anything.' He spat.

After a while Akathe said, 'My pahe says the world is running down.
Maybe this is just the front of it. Maybe things will only get worse indeed.'

Tighe felt his stomach shrinking; there was a sensation in his sinuses, almost as if he were smelling something burning, some sharp potent odour. But he knew he wasn't smelling anything. It was a sort of intensity, focused in the middle of his head. Everything was running down. The end was coming.

'Let me tell you,' said Akathe. 'I work with clocks. Clocks divide the day into ten hours. But sometimes I have seen old clockfaces, and they divide the day into twelve sections. Do you know why?'

Tighe said, 'No.'

'The world is changing. I think so. I think the day once had enough space for twelve hours; I think it was a golden age. Now there is space only for ten. Days were longer in the great old days. There used to be twelve tithes in a year too, not the ten we have these days.' He spat again, shook his left leg, then his right.

'They used to have twelve of everything,' said Tighe, remembering his schooling. 'Twelve months, twelve fingers, twelve toes. Twelve tribes, twelve degrees of separation.'

'So?'

'We have twenty months. That's longer, though.'

'They came from a different world,' said Akathe. 'They were a different people.'

'Maybe they did come from a different world before they found the wall,' agreed Tighe. 'But we have followed on from them.'

But Akathe was bored with this conversation. 'Anyway,' he said, 'back to work.'

Tighe left him feeling weirdly elated. The world was running down, like an antique clockwork. He started marching smartly along the traders' ledge until, he didn't know why, he was running, sprinting all the way along. Then clambering down the dog-leg and dashing over the main-street shelf. His heart was filled with a desperate sort of joy. He was running as hard as he could, really pounding the ledge with his feet and digging his elbows into the air, past the astonished looks of the people on the shelf, running as if he could burn himself up with the speed. And then, abruptly he was at the end of the shelf and he pulled himself up in a few jarring strides. There was no space to run any further.

Back home Grandhe was paying a second house call: unheard of previously. He was sitting in the chair in the main space, with pashe standing near. Tighe came in with a fresh expression, a little sweaty from his dash, but grinning. One look at the two faces of pashe and Grandhe took his mood away, though.

'Hello, Grandhe,' he said. 'Hello, pashe.'

46

'My boy-boy,' said Grandhe, sonorously. Tighe remembered the tear that had gathered on the underlip of the old man's eye; the swell of the beady water, the way it had paused on the very edge, and then the way it had abandoned itself and fallen streaking down his wrinkled cheek.

'Grandhe,' said Tighe.

'Listen to your Grandhe,' said pashe sharply.

'What I have to say will not take long,' said Grandhe, climbing to his feet. 'I saw you at the ceremony, boy.'

'Yes Grandhe.'

'I saw you were with that girl-girl. The girl-girl of Old Witterhe. He is a dangerous man and a heretic. I do not want you to associate with him or his daughter. My enemies will make much of it.'

'Do you *understand*?' said pashe, shrilly. There was something alarming in her face. Tighe shrank back.

'Yes,' he said. 'Ye-yes. I understand.'

There was a heartbeat's silence.

'You are a Princeling of this Princedom,' said Grandhe. 'You have a place in the order of things and this girl is beneath you.' Grandhe paused and looked so intently at Tighe that he felt as if he were being stared through. Then he said, 'Well, well enough.' He stalked awkwardly to the door, his knees creaky with age. 'That is well enough.'

'Show your Grandhe *out*,' hissed pashe, and Tighe, as if slapped, lurched away and shepherded the old Priest through the dawn-door. Then he stood in the hall and tried to summon the courage to go back into the main space. His pashe was waiting for him, he knew. He felt the desperate desire to duck out the door, just to run; but there was nowhere to go. It made more sense to get this out of the way now. He turned and shuffled back into the house.

'So,' said his pashe. 'Do you understand what has happened there?'

She was holding something behind her back. Tighe wanted to see what it was. He said, 'No,' in a sulky voice.

'You know, *don't* you, that we owe a debt to your Grandhe? You know that the loss of our goat has put us in a very difficult position. He comes round now to make me *feel* my humiliation. He knows I have to agree with him because he has the *debt*.'

She paused, as if expecting Tighe to say something, but he didn't know what to say. He stared at his feet.

Pashe took a step towards him. Her fury was very real now, very sharp; it possessed her features. 'You associate yourself with that girl-girl and you give him more power to humiliate *me*. Do you *understand*? Do you –' but she broke off and swung round with her right arm. Tighe flinched back. He didn't mean to, he knew it was better to take the first blow and simply go

47

down, but he couldn't help himself. Something whistled past his nose and his pashe's face was frozen for an instant in a curl of pure rage.

Then her momentum spun her round a little and she grunted, trying to regain her footing. Tighe could see that she held a stone in her hand, one of the large flat pebbles from the ledge outside. His brain, working with an odd exactness, wondered if she had gone outside to fetch it whilst Grandhe waited in the main space for him to come home; or if she had chosen it on a previous occasion, had prepared it for the next time anger took grip of her. But she had taken a step to brace herself and was swinging her arm back. Tighe's thinking stopped, jarred, frozen. This time pashe's motion was accompanied by a scratchy cry, pashe's mouth open, and Tighe had just enough wit to hold himself still until something solid clobbered the side of his temple with the sharp compression of impact and he flipped to the side and down.

On the floor. He lay static, like a doll, aware only vaguely of his pashe standing over him panting. Some sort of pummelling should, by rights, have followed, but instead pashe simply stood there. Eventually she moved away. Tighe lay still, even calm, with his eyes open and looking at the join of wall and floor. There was nothing, then the hurting started. Like a distant grumbling that grew louder in seconds, a headache caught and swelled at the place where he had been hit. He put up a hand; wetness.

Trying to get to his feet proved more difficult than usual. He tripped and sprawled, struggled up again and then skittered left and right instead of straight on. Like a newborn goat trying out its legs for the first time. Somehow he managed to make it to his alcove and to collapse on the matting in there.

But his head started thumping with pain as soon as he lowered it, so he struggled up and sat with his back against the partition. He could hear his pashe moving around in the space outside. He wanted a drink, but was not about to leave his alcove whilst she was there.

Something tickled the side of his head. He put his fingers up to his temple and felt the wetness dribbling. He felt dissociated from the wound, from the heat and the sharp fall of blood. Except for the thumping of his pain, which was very real.

He did not exactly sleep, but his consciousness went woozy and everything shrank away except for the pain. It went dark. Only a small patch of matting was visible to him. He tried to put up his hand, but the nerves refused to convey instructions down his arm. He started sliding over, toppling, and was unable to stop himself falling all the way over. When his head slapped the matting he felt a surge of pain.

For a time he lay like that, a great dark upon him, and in his head, behind the pain, the strange sensation of falling. Then somebody was helping him up, words were trying to pierce the pain, and his pahe was mopping at the side of his head with something. Tighe could barely even focus on the familiar features. The well-scored lines that ran from nostrils' outside edge to the corners of his mouth. The little crag of his chin. Hundreds of dots of black hair, shaved that morning, speckling the cheeks and around the mouth.

His pahe wrapped his head in something and gave him some water, together with some willowgrass stalks to chew. With those the pain receded a little and Tighe was able to lie down and sleep. He awoke with a very dry mouth and was able – however unsteadily – to make his way to the family sink and douse his head. That made him feel a little better.

His pahe was at his back, putting a scuffed hand on his shoulder. 'You doing better?' he asked, in his soft voice.

'Better,' agreed Tighe.

His pahe looked into his eyes carefully, like a doctor might. Then he smiled, or pressed his lips as close to a smile as they went. 'You'll be fine.'

He did not ask, *How did you hurt your head?* There was no need. For one moment, fleetingly, Tighe felt the bond between pahe and boy solidly, the unspoken affiliation. He said, 'Maybe I'll take some fresh air.'

'Good idea,' said his pahe.

So Tighe wobbled to the front and through the dawn-door and just sat himself down outside. It was late in the day now. He had been in his alcove for most of the day. Sunlight came straight down, split by high clouds into luminous shafts and spears that stood vividly against the darkening brown-mauve of the sky behind. Birds wheeled and flopped, swooping near the wall and pulling away from it into the enormous air. Looking for roosts, finding places away from the dangerous habitations of man. Tighe let his eyes go slack watching the patterns they made.

With a rush in the air and a sudden whirr of wings, a pigeon landed on the turf a few yards from Tighe. He reached out towards it, but it leapt into the air, kicked out with its extraordinary wings and was away.

8

Matters worsened in the village. Akathe and his pahe packed up the clockwork booth. Akathe's pahe said he knew somebody in Meat, thought he could find a little work there. They paid the Doge the toll for her ladder. Tighe saw the two of them off. 'When will you be back?' he asked.

'If it goes well, who knows?' said Akathe, shouldering his pack. 'If it goes badly, we may be back inside the week, begging off all our friends for food to stop us starving.' He laughed at this and Tighe laughed too, but there was a desperation behind the fun and behind the too-hard hugs they gave one another.

The market shelf was now always busy with people loitering and hoping for work. Some of their faces were starting to look very drawn indeed. These were people who had eaten nothing but stalkgrass for weeks. When Tighe would wander up to his usual crags, up to where the goats were pastured, he was never alone any more. There was always a group of people, with sucked-in faces and rips in their clothes, pulling up stalkgrass and munching at it with a frightening desperation. Sometimes they would call to him for work; or for money, food. But he avoided these encounters, turned and scurried back down the dog-leg to make his way down.

For about a week he avoided going to Witterhe's. Then he met the old monkeymonger on the market shelf. 'Well, my boy,' he called over to him. 'Haven't seen you in quite a while, quite a while. My girl, she's been asking about you.'

And despite himself Tighe was drawn in. 'She has?'

'Sure she has.'

Tighe grinned. 'Well, I was thinking of going down this afternoon. I've got to buy a candle now, but I could come by this afternoon.'

'Evening's better,' said Old Witterhe. He spat, the saliva coming out dark with whatever it was he was chewing. 'She's off in the Rightward crags gathering some vegetation for now, some apefeed. Come in the evening. What you do to your head, boy?'

'Knocked it on the door,' Tighe said, automatically. The thought of seeing Wittershe again had filled his stomach with light and excitement. It was an uneasy feeling, too; a knowing transgression. His pashe would be furious if she knew, his Grandhe also. But his Grandhe need never know. His pashe need never know.

Most of the traders on traders' ledge were closed, but his pashe had told him to get a candle, so Tighe went to the chandler. Even hungry people needed light at night and the chandler – a woman called Anshe – had had a long relationship with Tighe's family. Candles were made mostly out of wax secretions scraped from the leaves of a number of plants, but a degree of goat fat was an important ingredient in the mix to stiffen the finished product. Pashe had told him that Anshe would hand over a candle, part of some complicated arrangement of debt and counter-debt, and Tighe had agreed eagerly to collect it. Anshe was leaning over the bar of her dawn-door, smoking, when he arrived.

'Well met and hello,' said Tighe, a little shy. 'I have come for a candle. My pashe says you and she have an arrangement?'

'I'll fetch the one I made,' she said. 'I made it for your pashe a few days ago. I've been expecting you.'

She went inside and returned with the candle all wrapped up in grass-weave, handing it over with a smile. Tighe smiled back.

He loitered on the way home, and found a crevice in a not too busy ledge to sit in and stare out at the paling midday sky and the bone-coloured clouds. He toyed with the candle. It was so heavy; like stone. Yet he could press his thumbnail into its pliancy. How could it have the weight of stone and not the hardness of stone? That was an interesting question. Wax must be made out of different stuff from stone. Two different sorts of matter. He pondered for a while, trying to reckon up how many different sorts of matter there must be. Air and water, for example; then brittle and solid and pliant. But it was too tiring. The sun was warm against his face. He slowly cleaned out one of his nostrils with his little finger.

A monkey skittered along the ledge, running with legs and draping forearms. It was gone before Tighe could notice if it was collared, or to whom it might belong.

There were ants in the grass, following a line through the blades. Tighe tried to think himself down to their level; imagine the grass stalks as enormous pillars, imagine the specks of dirt as boulders. How did they see the Universe? As a flat plane created by some man-sized Ant God; planted with great trunks of grass to test them? He got on his knees and peered closely. The ants were black and red, the colours striped down their plastic-looking carapaces. Each of them waved filament arms from their head. Tongues? Eyes on stalks?

Grandhe had once said that Tighe wondered about the wrong things. Spent too long asking questions that had no answer instead of learning about God and being silent. Tighe sighed. Time to go home. He picked the candle up and brushed ants from the parcel.

He trotted along paths worn to dust by many feet, paths that were worn into his mind too. They were so familiar he felt he could shut his eyes and make his way along them blind. But he didn't shut his eyes. There was still the threat of the edge, the yaw and tumble promised to everybody. It still made his stomach ache and fist inside him. He still chose the path that went closest to the comforting bulk of the wall itself.

Down the dog-leg, along main-street shelf. He was so familiar a wanderer through the village that several of the itinerants waved to him. But he hurried on, to the end of the shelf, up the public ladder, zigzagging up the briefer ledges and out along the ledge where his house was.

The walk had made him hot and the cool of the hall was pleasant. Out of the sun his eyes were murked briefly, but adjusted to the dimness. He called out, 'Pashe, I have the candle,' and went through to the main space.

There was nobody there.

That was odd; pashe rarely left the house these days. Tighe went through to the storeroom at the back, empty except for the salted remains of a few goat-joints stacked against the wall. Then he came back and helped himself to some food from the store. The candle, still packaged, was sitting on the bar shelf. On a whim, Tighe unpacked it. Anshe had streaked it with a spiral pattern of red dye. That was a nice touch; she could just have given them a plain candle to settle the debt, but she had put the extra effort into patterning it.

Tighe wondered where his pashe was. Something about her absence bothered him. He tried to picture where she might be, but no image came. That bothered him. He shut his eyes and tried to call up an image of his pashe at all. It was the oddest thing. He tried to build up the picture, eyes, nose, mouth, but the image kept slipping out of his mind. Wittershe. Other women from around the village. Anyone but his pashe. The effort made his head throb at the scraped temple and suddenly there came a striking visual image of his pashe straining with the effort to bring her fist round. Her face was darkened with rage; the lips pulled back, the face in the rictus of anger.

Tighe banished the picture hurriedly.

He had to find his pashe. Where could she be? It was only a small village; it shouldn't be too hard to find her. He felt a sudden burning urgency.

Where *was* his pashe?

He finished the grass-bread and took a swig of water from the sink. Then he went out through the door and made his way back along the ledge. He assumed his pahe was still working on the house on top ledge.

The route up there was complicated and involved switching back on several levels. It took him past some of the wealthiest houses in the village,

52

large doorways opening on to spacious ledges, almost all of whom made their fortune with goats – with herds of tens, twenties of goats. Many of these houses even employed a doorkeeper, a raggedy man or woman who squatted in front of the dawn-doors and shooed passers-by away. Tighe watched several beggars approach one particularly splendid door like persistent flies, be waved away by the shouting doorkeeper (who had armed himself with a stick) and scatter to several places near the lip of the ledge; but then gather themselves and approach again. Tighe, passing, marvelled at their persistence. How could they think that there was any chance at begging from somebody's doorway? Desperation indeed.

The turf at top ledge was patterned, scythed regularly by a specially employed gardener and then pressed by boards into diamond patterns. It felt sacrilegious somehow even to walk upon it. Certainly the doorman at Old Musshe's doorway was giving him a very hostile look.

'Get away,' he barked. 'This is not a ledge for boy-boys to play on.'

'I'm no boy-boy, I'm a boy, near enough a man,' returned Tighe, bridling. He was the Princeling for the whole Princedom and better than any doorman. 'I've come looking for my pahe and he's the Prince, you know, and you'd do best if you let me in to have a word with him.'

'Your pahe,' said the doorman. Tighe had sometimes seen the man on market shelf, but didn't know his name.

'He's working on Old Musshe's house, I know.'

'I know him, I know Old Tighe,' said the doorman. 'He's been working here for a week or so.'

'Well, he's working right now. I'm thinking he came today with my pashe, maybe she's helping him.'

The doorman laughed briefly, then coughed, then spat. 'Your pashe is not here,' he said firmly, 'and neither is your pahe. My mistress is pretty angry with him. She's doing him a favour, you know. She's been kind and he repays her by not turning up for work.'

'What do you mean?'

The doorman scratched at a gum with one fingernail. 'You're not smart for a Princeling,' he sneered.

'My pahe didn't turn up for work today?'

'Deaf, are you? That's what I said. You want that I should shout?'

Tighe scurried away.

He was getting anxious now. It made no sense that pahe would miss work. That was not how pahe was. Tighe worked his way round the tight dog-legs of ledges and down the ladder to the main-street shelf. A woman he knew, Becshe, was carrying a pallet of new-baked grass-bread and some morsels of insect meat around the restive crowd of itinerants. Few had money and what little they did have they were saving for the toll of the

Doge's ladder to get up to Meat and find some proper work. Grim, drawn faces shook left and right; *No thank you*, a few closed their eyes and turned themselves right around to face the wall, as if to deny the very existence of the food. But every now and again one of the itinerants would be unable to contain him- or herself, would give in to their hunger and give away their precious money for the passing satisfaction; a full belly for an hour, the taste on the tongue.

Tighe touched Becshe's arm. 'Well well, Becshe,' he said. 'Have you been here all through the day?'

'Since the air settled after dawn.'

'You have seen my pahe pass through here? With my pashe on his arm, perhaps?'

Becshe gave him a strange look. 'Lovely food,' she said in a loud voice. 'Work better on a full belly, you know it, gentlemen, gentlewomen.' Then in a quieter tone she added, 'I'll tell you boy-boy, I've not seen your pashe out of the house for months. Not since you lost that goat over the edge.'

'But you saw my pahe passing this morning? He would have been on the way to work?'

'I see him most days,' said Becshe, 'but he didn't come through this day. And the very thought of your pashe coming down along the main-street shelf is improbable, I think.'

'You could have missed him.'

Becshe hawked and spat. 'More than my business is worth to miss the passage of people,' she said. 'He didn't come through.'

Tighe was off, running. He was not sure where he was running to. If pahe had not come through the main-street shelf, he must still be somewhere on the Leftward ledges; but that was a small enough ground, and there was no reason for him to stay there. Up the Leftward ladder and along to the goat pen. A man with one hand missing, Rothroche, was tending the pen. He hurried out of the cave mouth when he saw Tighe.

'You think your family can just *leave* the goats for me to look after?' he shouted.

'Have you seen my pahe today?' squealed Tighe, dancing out of the way of Rothroche's stretching arm. 'Have you seen my pashe?'

'Deleshe came by this morning,' snarled Rothroche. Deleshe was tending the goats now, after the disgrace of Carashe. 'It was the usual arrangement; she came and we both waited for your pahe to come by. But he didn't. I couldn't hand the goats over to that girl without your pahe being there – what if something had happened? So she had to go off and try to find him, but she said the house was empty. So the goats have stayed here all day and I'm sick of them. This is a goat pen, not a pasture. They've nothing to eat in here and they are messing the pen. They keep bleating. I'm not supposed to have to wait around all day – I have other work to go to.' This last was probably a lie; Rothroche was lucky to have this one job, given his deformity – he probably spent his days sleeping in the sun. Tighe felt anxiety inside him, sharp and tart. He suddenly felt young and small, not the eight-year-old near man. Something was very wrong. Pahe always came by to check the goats of a morning and to pass them over to the herder for the day. The family's wealth depended on the goats. It was inconceivable that they would be ignored.

'Where is my pahe?' Tighe blurted.

'Never mind that,' shouted Rothroche, waving his good arm. 'What about these goats? They can't stay in here all day. You take them – take them up to pasture and feed them for the day.'

But Tighe was away. There was one more place in the village where his pahe might be. It would be surprising, but it was the only place. And he was panting now, not with the exertion. He was walking quite slowly, not running any more. He was panting with fear. And that was why he was not running because a part of him did not want to discover that his pas were not there. Because if they were not there then they were not in the village – and if they had left the village, then the unmentionable, the wordless void swelled up and over the lip of the ledge like a great blank tongue and licked them away into nothingness. And Tighe could not think about that. He could not think about that.

Grandhe's house was at the far end of main-street shelf, not far from the Doge's house. Tighe had rarely visited it and never in the last year. It would have been alarming enough to be scraping at the door for any reason.

Grandhe's voice came from inside. Since the death of Konstakhe and the ceremony, he was rarely seen about the village. But his voice sounded strong. 'If you are going to knock, knock, don't scratch like a monkey.'

'Grandhe,' called Tighe, 'is pahe with you? Is pashe in there? I have come to speak to them.'

'What are you saying?' called back Grandhe. 'Your pas never come here. God forbid they should ever pay *me* their respects. What are you saying?'

'Grandhe,' called Tighe again. He was surprised that his voice wobbled so; and surprised to realise that he was crying. 'Grandhe?'

Silence. Then, 'Come in, boy,' and Tighe pushed the latch up and tumbled into the smoky darkness of Grandhe's house.

9

Tighe's life changed. His first thoughts were that if he had not loitered on the ledge watching the ants, if he had come straight back with the candle, then maybe he could have caught his parents before they disappeared. He had visions of them, packing bags with things in the silence of the house. But this was not right because they had taken nothing with them. Nothing had been removed. Everything in the house was as it had been. But still Tighe clung to the possibility that they were still alive. There was some pressing reason why his pas has needed to go. They had sent him off to fetch the candle and then swiftly, quietly, they had simply gone.

'Where would they go?' he asked his Grandhe, in the first few days after the disappearance. In the early days he had shown his grief to Grandhe. It had taken a time before he learned to hide it from him. 'Would they go to Meat, do you think?'

Grandhe had a staff. It was real wood and Tighe had often seen him carry it. Without thinking much about it, he had assumed it had some religious purpose. Now he discovered it had a new function. Grandhe would whip it around his head and catch some part of Tighe's torso or head with the end of it. The end was blunt, but the blow jarred with a fierce pain. He did so now.

'Your pas would never abandon their village,' he declared, as Tighe whimpered on the floor. Then he marched out.

In a strange way, the disappearance had given the old man a new surge of life. After a month of hiding in his house all day long, Grandhe had suddenly emerged. First, he had claimed the goats – legally the goats were probably Tighe's. Boys could inherit, if the village thought them mature enough and Tighe was only months away from legal manhood now. But Grandhe had simply swept the goats up: marched up to the goat pen with one of his deputies in tow and announced to old Rothroche that the goats were his. He dismissed the herds-girl pahe had been employing and set one of his deputies to tend the animals.

The next thing he did was to gather many of the possessions that were in the empty house and sell them. With the village as depressed as it was there were few buyers and much of the stuff ended up stacked in Grandhe's own, smaller house. Tighe heard, from tight-lipped people uncomfortable about gossiping over a preacher, that Grandhe had tried to sell the empty house too; he had been up to top ledge to try and exchange the house for some more goats, to build up the herd. But houses were not in demand. People were moving away from the village, going up the wall to Meat and Press to try and make a living. The population was thinning visibly and several houses stood empty. Only the itinerants, coming up the wall from Smelt and Heartshelf, swelled the numbers and not one of them had the money to buy a house – or they would never have left their original villages.

To begin with, Tighe was simply too stunned to pay much notice to what his Grandhe was doing. He might, he thought, have contested it. Maybe gone to the Doge and asked for a ruling of law. But the Doge and his Grandhe were friends, neighbours, and that would likely lead nowhere. But he didn't really think about that. Instead he found himself replaying over and over the possible scenarios of his pas. He imagined them slipping away. Yet nobody had seen them go, nobody had seen them pass through market shelf, and the Doge was certain she had received no toll for her ladder up to the path to Meat that morning. So perhaps they had disguised themselves, slipped through the crowds on market shelf and made their way down the crags to Heartshelf; although why would anybody want to go down to a village where, according to the itinerants, people were now dying of too meagre a diet, stalkgrass only? Maybe, Tighe pondered, they were on their way further down. The wall became more sheer further downways, and general wisdom was that eventually all paths, all crags, petered into blank nothing when you went far enough downwall. But there were also traveller's tales, mutated through repeated retellings, of difficult pathways, of golden chances for the adventurer, far away to the down. Maybe his pas (how unlike them! But maybe . . .) had been seduced by these stories. Yes, Tighe thought to himself, the loss of the goat had thrown their finances into disarray. The poverty that infected the village had made it impossible to recover their status. Maybe they had gone off questing for a new wealth to the down. Maybe they would return with sacks of salt, metals, plastics, wealth of all kinds. Maybe they would return next week, leading a train of servants all carrying baggage stuffed with treasure, to rejuvenate the village, for his pahe to take his position as Prince with a new magnificence. And Tighe would be crying by this stage of the fantasy because as he built it up higher and higher he knew in his heart how impossible it was. And he was crying, too, for the absence in the heart of his imaginings, the thing he could not permit himself to think. He was crying for the nothing in the middle of his dream, the unspeakable void that cleaved to an image of his pas, like the goat, simply stepping over the edge of the world and into death.

Nobody said anything about that. His Grandhe never mentioned it. It was the truth, but it was unsayable.

There was a meeting, maybe half the entire village of Cragcouthie gathering on main-street shelf. Grandhe Jaffiahe herded him out for that, but left him between his two deputies. 'Now you'll be quiet when I address the village, boy,' he had said to Tighe before coming out. He did this thing, ordering Tighe to stick his tongue out of his mouth and then grabbing it agonizingly between his thumb and finger to compel attention. 'You'll be quiet?' Tighe had mumbled his assent, unable to speak or even nod with his tongue pinched that way. So when they had come out on to the shelf he stood between his Grandhe's two deputies, who often kicked him about the lower leg, or pinched his bare arms, just to keep him silent.

Grandhe spoke to the crowd. 'The Princedom needs a Prince,' he said, 'few would deny. Yet are we certain that our Prince has departed for ever? These are hard times, people, hard times.' People were nodding and fragments of Grandhe's speech went about the group in various mouths. *Hard times, true. Princedom needs. Are we certain?* 'I say', orated Grandhe, raising both his arms, 'that our Princedom needs a Prince. The boy, my grandchild, will be of adult age by the year's end and then he can take up the burden of the office – if our Prince has not returned. If he does not return, then let us crown the boy Prince at the year's end.' This would be ten months past his coming into adulthood, but Tighe didn't say anything. The crowd was murmuring approvingly.

'And until that time', said Grandhe, dropping his voice and his arms at the same time, 'I – your Priest, your intermediary between God and the people – will care for the boy. He shall live in my house, my own grandchild.'

Somebody cheered and there was a polite smattering of applause. But a drizzle was starting up, droplets swarming through the air, and people started dispersing and making for shelter. Grandhe's deputies grabbed Tighe painfully by the tender parts of his arms, up near the armpits, making sure (it seemed to Tighe) to dig their nails in, and practically carried him back to his Grandhe's house.

His pas' house was emptied now and shuttered. Tighe slept in the main space of his Grandhe's house, curled on the uncomfortable floor. By day he would mope inside, whilst his Grandhe went about the village ordering his affairs as a man of renewed wealth. There was a certain amount of restrained debate in the village about whether debts should be inherited. The people who felt they had a right to parts of the goats, or to the whole carcasses, would sometimes petition Grandhe. But Grandhe called the

Doge and the Doge said that the law permitted no such thing. Besides, people were more than a little frightened of Grandhe.

In fact, the law was hazy. If Tighe's pas were really dead then their debts died with them. But, claimed the creditors, there was no hard proof they *were* dead. Grandhe had not inherited the wealth, he was merely tending it until they returned, and therefore he was tending the debts as well as the animals. The Doge ruled on law, but that didn't stop a few people hammering on Grandhe's door and demanding payment. People were intimidated by Grandhe, but a few of them still braved it. Times were hard and people desperate. These bangings on the door were some of the hardest moments for Tighe.

'Come along,' somebody outside would yell. 'Your girl is still alive, somewhere, and so her debts are still alive!' But hearing somebody say this shadowed the opposite in Tighe's imagination, made it hard to blot out the thought of his pas dead.

Dead. Fallen to God at the bottom of the world.

For Grandhe, Tighe thought to himself, it ought to have been harder. If his girl and his girl's husband had truly fallen off the world, then their souls were forfeit; the village could not burn the bodies and release their spirits in the smoke to ascend to heaven. But Grandhe seemed unbothered. He went about the village and went about his business. He was accumulating wealth, he said, for the glory of God.

People were intimidated by Grandhe and Tighe knew why. Tighe flinched whenever Grandhe so much as looked at him. He would wield his wooden staff like a young man and catch Tighe expertly about the body or face with the end of it. One time he beat Tighe so hard he was certain his cheekbone was broken: it throbbed and ached for hours, although eventually the pain dispersed.

Tighe tried to keep out of his way, not to bring himself to Grandhe's attention at all. But he missed his pas, and sometimes that feeling overcame him. Once he said, 'Maybe my pas slipped up the Doge's ladder.'

Grandhe glared at him, smoking his grassweed pipe. 'Eh?'

'Maybe they disguised themselves and went up to Meat. Or maybe the Doge had an arrangement with them . . .'

Grandhe had to lean forward to reach his staff. 'Have my enemies been talking with you? The Doge is a friend of mine, longstanding,' he said, getting creakily to his feet. 'You say that the Doge would lie to me?' And he brought the staff cracking on to Tighe's left shoulder.

If Grandhe stayed home during the day, as he sometimes did, then Tighe slipped out and roamed the village in his old fashion. In the early days he would go from crag to crag, ledge to ledge, combing the village thoroughly as if hoping to chance upon his pas laughing together, coming out of somebody's house, or sitting arm in arm in the sun. He would work from the lower ledges up to the higher, or work downwall the other way.

From time to time he would go back to his old house. The dawn-door was broken, presumably by itinerants, and it was clear that somebody had gone through the whole house looking for food or valuables to sell. But Grandhe had removed all the valuables and there was no food. The first time Tighe went back to the house he thought, at some level, that it might be more comforting than the hostility in the air at Grandhe's. He had curled up in his alcove, the same space he had slept in since he was a boy-boy, and tried to lose consciousness. And he had drifted away, only to have a series of gut-lurching nightmares. Falling. His pashe's face, stretched in an agony of rage, furious with him. Dismembered parts of their bodies scattered from ledge to crag.

'You wander about the village like an itinerant,' his Grandhe barked at him one night. There was less food, and it was less tasty, at his Grandhe's than had been the case at home. Tighe still got his goatmilk, and Grandhe baked a form of grass-bread, although without the seeds and with fewer tasty insects embedded in it than his pashe had done. Tighe was sitting legs folded on the floor chewing on an underbaked piece of this bread as his Grandhe said this.

'Do you hear?' Grandhe had repeated, louder. 'You wander about the village exactly like an itinerant.'

'Yes, Grandhe.'

'It must stop. We'll find work for you. You're old enough to work. You've lived a sheltered life. Well, soon you'll have to stop being a boy and start to be a man, work for your living.'

Tighe almost asked if that would mean that, as a man, he would inherit his pas' Princedom, even his pas' wealth; but he stopped himself. Grandhe would have raged. The staff would have come down hard on Tighe's back for such a comment. And it was not even as if he particularly cared. He didn't care much about being Prince. What good was it? He didn't even care that Grandhe had stolen his family goats. He really didn't know what to do with goats, how to tend them or how to trade them.

'You don't ever go down to that heretic's monkey palace?' Grandhe asked in a menacing tone.

'No, Grandhe.'

'Good. I would *not* want to hear from people that you'd been down there. That would be fuel to my enemies indeed. You are my charge now, boy-boy, and I intend to look after you properly. Your pashe was too mincing about it, too soft.'

'Yes Grandhe.'

'I'll not be soft if I hear you've been about that poisonous heretic.'

And, truly, he hadn't visited Old Witterhe. It was gone a fortnight since his pas had disappeared and he had not so much as thought about going down the ladder. Instead, he filled his thoughts with a dream Wittershe, as he curled on the floor in his Grandhe's house. He pressed his thighs close together with his hand between them, curled under the grass-weave rug and stretched his muscles very gently. The pressure on the end of his wick brought it stiff and hard as plastic; and he would close his eyes and imagine Wittershe, the thought of her skin, of her nakedness under the rough weave of her skirt, of her smile. And usually on the smile his wick would surrender up its load, and the sunlight would blare in his soul, and he'd shudder to a stop with a sticky mess starting to glue the hairs on his stomach.

One evening he was curled in the corner, overhearing a conversation his Grandhe was having with his two deputies. They were planning to slaughter a goat and have a feast. Tighe was astonished, repulsed. If the richest family in the village were celebrating an important wedding, they might – conceivably – slaughter an animal just for the eating. But for a man such as Grandhe, at a time such as the present (his daughter and his marriage-son probably dead, their souls lost over the edge of the world) it was incomprehensible. From what Tighe could hear most of the conversation was about finding a way of avoiding the opprobrium of the village. The Doge was mentioned several times.

Eventually, a little stupefied by the smoke from three pipes, Tighe drifted off to sleep. And in the morning he found he could not get up. It all seemed so pointless. His pas were dead. Gone for ever. Why should he bother? The inside of his head felt stricken, consumed with drought. He turned over and lay in a painful motionlessness.

Grandhe discovered him in this state at lunchtime and roused him with several sharp blows of his staff. Whimpering like a monkey, Tighe struggled up and ran zigzag, dodging the blows, out of the door. Grandhe's voice followed him. 'We'll find some work for you soon.'

Tighe blinked in the sunlight, and wandered across main-street shelf. The crowd of itinerants was greater than ever, dull dead faces staring out at nothing, squatting on the ground or sitting with their backs to the wall. Tighe fought the urge to yell at them. *My pashe has gone. She is gone for ever.* There was an itch in the centre of his skull. His mouth was dry. His path wobbled and at one stage brought him towards the lip of the shelf. The thought was even in his head, *If I fall, I fall.* This was closely followed by *I hope I fall, I hope I die.* Maybe he would fall all the way to the God Grandhe denied lived at the base of the wall. But the actual proximity of the edge of the world was a different matter: his gut lurched and without conscious control his feet steered him back away from the great fall.

He was hungry. Lying on the floor all morning had meant skipping breakfast. His stomach felt like a clenched fist. But he had no money and he was not about to go back to Grandhe's house to try and find some food. His back was still smarting from the blows. He maundered up and down the shelf, without the desire to go anywhere in particular. Then he sat himself down on the Leftward side of main-street shelf and shielded his eyes from the sun with his palm. Birds flocked, patterns of dots that zipped themselves together and then pulled apart.

A hand on his shoulder.

'Well, boy, once again.' It was Old Witterhe.

'Hello,' said Tighe, squinting.

Witterhe was carrying a small sack salt. 'Apes need it as much as we do, salt, you know,' he said. 'There was a trader come up today with a backpack of the stuff. Prices are depressed, they are.'

'I'm hungry,' said Tighe.

'Come down,' said Witterhe. 'There'll be something to eat. My girl, she's been asking after you.'

In a daze, and yet acutely aware of the transgression, Tighe followed Witterhe down the slant and then down the ladder to his ledge. Tighe stood at the bottom, sheepish. 'I'll get my girl out here,' said Witterhe. He turned, stopped, turned back. 'I was sorry to hear about your pas,' he added, awkwardly.

Wittershe was out in moments, smiling to see him. She smiled at him. Tighe felt tears at the back of his eyes, but struggled to keep them back. 'Hello,' she said. 'I've got to take this salt to the monkeys. Come with me?'

Tighe followed her.

They made their way along a narrow pathway, Tighe looking wallward to avoid the drop. Then they were amongst the crumbling rack of grassy crags that housed Witterhe's monkeys. A few decaying pegs were driven into the wall, but no monkeys were actually attached to them. Witterhe had been keeping monkeys so long they were almost habituated to the place. The hairy, child-sized bodies clustered round Wittershe as she broke off pieces of salt and passed them out. Black, clutching fingers. Chattering and shrieking, with occasional sideswipes and bared teeth.

'Sorry news about your pas,' said Wittershe, raising her voice above the clamour.

Tighe didn't say anything. He found a crag wider than the rest and pressed his back against the wall. When Wittershe had finished feeding the apes she came over and sat next to him.

'Difficult time for you,' she said.

'I suppose.'

Her fingers touched his shoulder and even through the depression of his spirits, even with the deadness in his heart, his wick responded, straightening a little in his pants.

'There's talk in the village,' Wittershe said. 'They say you should be the Prince now, with your pas' wealth, that your Grandhe has no right.'

Tighe looked at her. There was an eager expression in her eyes. Through the fog of his mood, Tighe recognised the look. If he were Prince, then he would be an adult, a single man with five goats and his own house. That would be some catch for a monkeymonger's daughter.

'I suppose,' he said.

Wittershe sat back, so that her eyes glittered in the sunlight. 'I know your Grandhe is close with the Doge, but there ought to be a way. If you pushed it there might be a way. Claim the goats. Claim them – why not? Think, Tighe, six goats!'

'Five,' he said, in a small voice.

Then she was leaning on him, her breath on his neck. 'It's yours, you know. You need to *be* the Prince, to act as the Prince would. You need to *take* it.'

'I suppose so,' he said again. He felt an enormous weariness in his body, a terrible sense that there was nobody for him, nobody on any place of the wall. He was not a person, he was only the legal channel for an inheritance. And yet, despite this profound sadness, his wick was hard and upstanding. It was betraying his mood.

'I've always liked you, you know,' Wittershe was saying. Her voice sounded distant, despite the fact that the words were spoken directly into Tighe's ear. He was staring straight ahead. The blue sky. Was there really another wall, a pure smooth wall, in the far blue distance? Was that what made the air blue?

'You do know that, don't you?' she said.

Tighe turned his head a little and Wittershe pushed a kiss against his lips. Then she giggled. All around them monkeys were settling back into their crags, muttering to themselves, fumbling at one another's pelts for fleas, plucking stems of grass, slapping the tops of their heads with the palms of their long, narrow hands. Tighe felt his heart pummelling inside his chest.

'Better not let my pahe see me doing that,' Wittershe said. She glanced at him, almost coy.

On an impulse, Tighe jerked his head forward and snatched a kiss from her. His wick was so stiff now it actually hurt. He reached up with his hand and grasped her shoulder, then let the hand slide down the clay-like softness of her right breast. She was still smiling, but she briskly removed Tighe's hand. He tried to dart forward and kiss her again, but she pulled her head back.

'Wait,' she said.

She reached forward and pushed Tighe back, her two hands flat against his two shoulders, until his back touched the wall again. 'Some of the boys like this trick,' she said, in a low voice, and laughed again. Even as she was reaching for his belly, Tighe felt the words scrape awkwardly in his mind. Some boys? Which boys? A chasm of the possibilities of jealousy opened up. Which boys did Wittershe mean? Who did she spend her time with? Which boys did she practise this on?

But sensation drowned out contemplation. Wittershe had, with a slight edge of unpractised awkwardness, placed both hands on his stomach and then slid them under the band of his trousers. His wick was straining up towards them. She had to lean a little forward to get purchase, bringing her profile directly in front of Tighe's face. There was a distracted smile on her lips. With her left hand she ringed the base of his wick, and with her right hand she grasped the head of it. Tighe shuddered. Then she began roughly rubbing it up and down. The suddenness of the gesture, and the friction of dry skin on skin, made him cry out. She stopped, looked at him, her smile cupping down a little.

'What?'

'Hurts,' he said.

She paused, withdrew her hand, spat into the palm, and replaced it. Then she started rubbing again, a little more smoothly with the lubrication. The pressure was instantly there, just below his bladder; similar to the pressure felt when he needed to piss, but also different. It grew, building swiftly towards something hard and definite. Tighe dropped his gaze. The motion of the arm, back and forward in a small arc as her hand moved up and down, imparted a little jiggle to her torso. Underneath the rough weave of her shirt Tighe could see the wobble of her breasts. With a breathtaking jolt he came, his wick hurling up a glob of himself, then a second smaller one, and then nothing. Wittershe had stopped. There was a broad smile on her face.

'There,' she said, 'what do you think?'

Tighe was staring at her, open-eyed.

'Lost for words?' she teased, extracting her hands and wiping them on the grass by her side. Monkeys chattered all around.

He started to say something, stopped as if blocked. Then with a heave, as if the words were leaving him by a similar mechanism to the way his seed had just exited, he said, 'I love you.'

Wittershe's smile shrank and then broadened. Tighe felt immediately stupid, as if he had over-extended himself.

'I'd better get back inside,' she said, 'or my pahe is going to get angry with me.' She leapt to her feet with monkeyish rapidity and scattered along the crag, jumping to make the ledge outside their house and ducking inside the door.

For a moment Tighe was in a kind of daze. He put his hand on his belly, felt the snotty stickiness of his own stuff where Wittershe had massaged it out. He brought out a glob between finger and thumb and examined it. It was the colour of nothing. The colour of sky.

Then the sunlight swelled; clouds parted and the glory of light squeezed Tighe's eyes shut. His heart was beating. The image of his pashe came into his head. Why did he think of that? She always seemed angry when he remembered her; the skin of her face darkened with the anger. He seemed only able to think of his pashe angry. Then, suddenly, blocks of hollow misery burst up inside of him. His pas were dead. His pashe was dead. It was his fault, somehow; somehow he was to blame. His pashe had fallen off the earth. How had it happened? He saw a picture of her, features contorted with the rage that rendered her so close to fear. Fear and anger the same. Then the image was replaced with another and this was somehow much more terrible; his pashe simply stepping over the lip of things with a blank expression on her face, a nothingness. Going over as empty-minded as the goat they had lost. Anger and emptiness the same. A hollowness seeking out the enormous void of the air; to fall for ever, to fall into the fiery lap of God.

Away to the left, some monkey bickered shriekingly with another; and then, as swiftly as it started, the commotion died away.

Tighe was crying now and still he didn't really understand what he was crying for. He balled his fists into his eye sockets, but the grief wouldn't be contained. He could sense sobs trembling in his ribcage. Some distant apprehension of shame told him that he didn't want Old Witterhe, or worse Wittershe herself, to see him in this state. His eyes bleary and his breathing shallow he struggled up and lumbered over to the Witterhe ladder. There was motion behind him; monkeys. Or Witterhe coming out of the house. Panicked, Tighe scrambled up the steps of the ladder.

He was making odd little *whoo*ing sounds by the time he got up to main-street shelf, a combination of distress and being out of breath. Careless of who saw him, he stumbled and wove over to the wall with tears tumbling from his eyes. Amongst the itinerants he collapsed, tucked his knees up and wept into his own lap, doubled over himself.

10

Tears eventually fall away and the eyes are left dry. Tighe reached a less hysterical state, a wider ledge of calm. For a while he simply sat, the comfort of the wall at his back, and stared out at the sky. The sun had climbed and shadows were concentrated on the ground. People came and went on the shelf. He saw his Grandhe come out of his house and scurry over the ground, punting himself onwards with his staff.

Tighe sat. He looked around at the itinerants. They were sitting, knees up, elbows perched on top of the bony kneecaps, simply staring into space. Many of them were now so thin that it looked as though their bones were struggling to burst through their skin, just as their bodies had burst through the sun-wearied rags of their clothes. Everything about them, Tighe saw, was slow. The man squatting next to him would turn his head like a figure in a dream, the face turning with the inexorable slowness of the sun rising through the sky. His eyes were milky with hunger, his skin was speckled with mauve dots. Even his breathing came with enormous effort, as if the air were scaling the ridged wall of his ribcage with difficulty. He would stare at Tighe as if he were as perfectly remote and as perfectly featureless as the sky itself, and then he would turn his head slowly back to face front again.

'You're dying,' said Tighe. Saying the words added detachment to his perception of the man.

He breathed out; a sigh in answer.

'How long since you last ate?'

He breathed in again. 'Months,' he said. His voice sounded strong, for all the stretched feebleness of his body. 'I been eating grass,' he said, the words coming slowly but distinctly, 'but it don't support your strength.'

'So you're waiting for work.'

Another exhalation, more like a laugh. 'Nobody going to employ me now. Am too weak.' Tighe looked at his arm; the elbow was like a seedpod in a slender black stem. 'Once every few days somebody calls up,' he said, and paused to get his breath. 'Calls up one of the stronger ones. From the group over there.' The slightest inclination of his head. 'They get a bit of food and join the group again.'

'Why do you just wait around here to die?' said Tighe, suddenly. 'Why not just walk over the edge of the world and end it quickly? If I was like you I'd just walk over the edge of the world. That's what I'd do. Why don't you?'

The man rotated his head a second time, patiently. When he was meeting Tighe's intense gaze, he said, 'Sin.'

'What?'

He turned his head back and said nothing.

'What does it matter if it is a sin?' said Tighe. 'You'll be dead either way in a few days.' Saying that gave him heart. It was cruel, but the world was cruel.

After a long pause the man said, 'I get to watch the world go by.' Then after a pause, 'I get to watch you.'

'Do you know who I am?' said Tighe. Then, more urgently, the idea occurring to him for the first time, 'Do you know my pas? Did you ever see my pas?'

But the man was breathing out. 'Don't know you. Seen you. You live with that old man.' Tighe followed his gaze to see his Grandhe storming back over the main-street shelf. He looked angry.

'I'd say', said the man, 'he's looking for you. He's been back and forth.'

'But why,' said Tighe, his impotence and his rage focusing in a moment of sharp, painful intensity, 'why do you *give up* like this? How can you just sit here and give up?'

The man didn't turn his head; didn't say anything. There were tears in Tighe's eyes again. It was all so pointless. It all fell into death in the end. People clung to the precarious wall of life, but eventually their grips loosened with exhaustion and they fell away into nothingness.

A shadow fell over Tighe. 'What are you doing *here*?' demanded Grandhe in a high-pitched voice that threatened greater rage later on, in a less public place. 'Sitting with the *itinerants*?'

Tighe's face was wet now. Crying. He couldn't help it. He looked up to his Grandhe standing over him, the old man's face darkened with the shadow, the sun firing his halo of hair with light.

'My pas are both *dead*,' he said.

'Have my enemies been talking to you?' demanded Grandhe. Tighe realised he was still thinking of the inheritance.

'I'll never see them again,' said Tighe in a loud voice; or that was the sentence on his lips, but on the second word Grandhe's staff struck sharply under his chin. His mouth clacked shut and there was a sharp pain right on the end of Tighe's tongue.

'You want to sit with the *itinerants* do you?' Grandhe said in a voice of stifled fury. 'You want to beg low work to fill your belly? We'll see – we'll see how you like *real* work, you thankless wastrel.'

Tighe, startled into silence, tasted blood in his mouth. His tongue was stinging unpleasantly. Grandhe leant forward and dragged him up by the collar of his shirt. 'I've wasted the morning looking for you,' he barked. 'You will come with me.'

Tighe was led back to Grandhe's house, where the dawn-door closed to unleash a torrent of furious denunciation, accompanied with whacks from Grandhe's stick. Tighe felt himself – actually felt himself – retreat from humanness. The words the old man spoke mussed into incoherence in his head, a stream of sharply inflected noises without specific sense. Grandhe's face lost definition in the shadow of the main space. Nothing but a conglomeration of shadow spouting the music of anger. Tighe's jaw hung slack. Only the blows reached him, punctuating his blankness with spikes of pain, making him yelp like a monkey and try to draw away.

After a while Grandhe seemed to grow tired and Tighe crawled away to a corner, where he could lie curled in a ball. He was crying again, although there was no sense, no content in the bawling. It was all a nothing.

He stopped because he was hungry. Feeling sheepish, as if he were betraying his role, he scrabbled a loaf's end of grass-bread and went back to his corner to gnaw it.

He ran his fingers over his head, feeling the scalp between his hairs. The old strips and bumps were there, the scar tissue. They stretched a fair way over the curve of his head; it must have been a serious sort of wound when he was younger. He didn't remember the wound, but his pahe had told him about it. Hit his head and broke open the skin. Now there was just the corrugation of the old scar tissue. Either his head was very hot or his fingers were very cold. His heart felt chilled, as if clutched by the hand. The lines where Grandhe's stick had touched his torso blurred sensation with heat. Moving his shoulder hurt him.

When Grandhe came through again, Tighe was not able to meet his gaze, and so he stared at the matting on the floor. There was a gruffness in the old man's manner, which came as close to apology as he ever did. 'Now', he said, 'I can only hope that you have learned your lesson. It is for your good. God punishes with greater fury than a weakling such as I can muster. You should learn that lesson early before you have to face the wrath of God Himself.'

'God lives at the bottom of the wall,' said Tighe. He had no idea why he spoke.

Grandhe stopped, swallowed, decided to ignore the words. 'Now, I have spoken to Tohomhe. He is a good friend of the village, a good friend of mine. You will work for him.'

'Yes, Grandhe.'

For some reason, these two sullenly uttered words pricked Grandhe's anger more than the heresy of the preceding sentence. His voice rose. 'You should thank me – you've no more wit than a *goat*. If I hadn't taken you in you would have starved on that ledge like those God-abandoned itinerants you have been so friendly to.'

'Yes, Grandhe.'

'How you were bred from my line I do *not* know. You've no more wit than a boy-boy though you're nearly a man. You'll never have the savvy to be the Prince. You're some changeling, I think me.' He stormed out.

Later that night, after Grandhe and Tighe had eaten a small, silent evening meal, the old man seemed to be in a more conversational mood.

'Times are hard in the village now,' he said, picking the shells off beetles and chewing them. His two deputies sat with him, each with their own bag of snacks. Tighe watched them hungrily.

'Times are hard now', said Grandhe Jaffiahe, 'and people leave the village. But times will not be hard for ever. The human world is mutable, like the changes of day and night, like the eddies of a wind. They fail, they recover. And when times get better, then we will be in a better position. We will be above circumstance, and we can rule the Princedom better, just better.' It was as if he was talking to Tighe, but in fact Tighe could see that he was not. His words were promising nothing to him. Grandhe was talking to himself.

The two deputy preachers said nothing. Grandhe's deputies rarely spoke.

11

The next morning Tighe made his way to Tohomhe's place soon after the dawn winds had died down. In a village where the majority of people were perfectly competent at weaving their own grass matting and rough clothes, a grass-weaver could only make a living by specialising. Tohomhe made fancy-wear, treating the stems in various ways to make them soft and dyeing them to create multi-coloured cloths. These had been bought mostly by the richer inhabitants of the village. He was unambiguous when Tighe scratched at his door.

'I have no work for you, though,' he said, almost straight away. 'I said I'd take you on as a favour to your Grandhe. He thinks you should learn a trade and you're plenty old enough. But people don't buy fancy cloth at a time like this, so I've no call for another pair of hands to help me weave. I don't need you and I certainly won't feed you.'

Tighe had nodded, looking at the floor. But Tohomhe was a jovial man, even if his face had been sucked in a little by hunger. He laughed.

'Don't look so mournful, boy-boy!' he shouted. 'It's not as if the world ends because I've no work for you. When I am weaving, I'll call you up and you can watch, which is as good as learning. Why, it's as if your heart was set on this weaving and I've crushed it!'

He came over and put his arm around Tighe's shoulder.

'But of course,' he said, 'it's not the working. You have lost your pas. That's a terrible thing. I lost my pas.'

Tighe looked up into the saggy face of the taller man. 'How?'

'Years ago, now. My pashe died trying to birth a sister to me, such that the baby and the woman died together. My pahe never really recovered. He slipped off one of the upper ledges gathering weed for weaving. There was a party of people and they saw him. They say he was plucking the longer stems from the edge of the crag – that's where the longer stems tend to grow, you'll need to know such things if you're to be a weaver – and slipped. Simple as that. Just went over.'

Tighe was silent, absorbing this information.

'It's never talked of,' Tighe said in a soft voice, 'yet it sometimes seems to me that people fall off the world all the time.'

'Well,' said Tohomhe, taking his arm away and going over to sit on a tied-up bale of woven cloth in the corner of the room, 'life is precarious. God has made it that way for us, it's not our business to query Him, now is it?' He fished a clay pipe from a baggy pocket at the side of his trousers and lit it with a flint box. 'But I think you're right, my boy. People don't like to talk of it, it reminds them of their closeness to the edge of everything.'

Tighe squatted down on the floor, his thighs resting on his calves and his back against the wall of Tohomhe's main space. 'My family lost a goat over the edge.'

'I heard. People talk more about that. It's a loss, in money terms, of course it is. But a goat is, well, a goat.'

He puffed in silence.

'I was sorry to hear of your pas,' he said, ruminatively.

'Do you think they fell off the world?' Tighe asked.

Tohomhe shrugged. 'They're not around. Nobody saw them leave the village. And why would they leave the village anyway?'

'Times are hard now.'

'Not for a goatmonger. Times can never get that hard for a goatmonger.' He puffed some more. 'And your pahe was Prince of the whole village, of the whole Princedom. A Prince shouldn't leave his people. No, I'm sorry to say it, but I think they went over the edge.'

A lump materialised in some place in Tighe's chest. He could feel tears trying to come to life in his eyes, but he said, 'But why? Why would they go over the edge?'

'Like I said,' Tohomhe sighed. 'People do fall.'

'But both together?'

'Well,' conceded the older man. 'That's true. Did they go out in the dawn gale? Believe me, I've been out at that time, caught in the night somewhere in my travelling days when I was young. Those winds get pretty fierce. They can pull a person clean off the broadest shelf.'

'They were still in the house when I left to fetch the candle,' said Tighe. 'That wasn't it.'

'You went to get a candle?'

'Late morning and my pashe sent me to collect a candle. And when I came back they were gone.' Tighe was crying again, little tears squirming from the corners of his eyes.

'Well,' said Tohomhe, flushing a little, 'I'm sorry to say this boy, but they wouldn't be the first people simply to step off the world because things were hard. They had lost a goat, after all.'

71

That thought had occurred to Tighe too; but just having it spoken aloud was enough to set him off crying properly. He wailed. Tohomhe was flustered. He put his pipe out, humming, and then came over and embraced Tighe as if he were only a tiny child. Tighe cried; the words from the old man, 'There there, now now,' washed over his head.

When the sobs had dried up enough to speak, Tighe said, 'I know it's true, but it's hard. It's hard.'

'It is that,' said Tohomhe, disentangling himself. He seemed extremely flushed.

'It's a sin, though, is it not? Just stepping off the world like that. Everybody knows that it is a sin.'

'Yes,' said Tohomhe. 'Well.'

Tighe took several deep breaths. 'I'm sorry, Master Tohomhe, to come in here bawling like a boy-boy barely weaned.'

'Not at all,' said Tohomhe looking away. 'No, no.'

'And I'm sorry I can be of no use with your work. You have been kind to me and I would have liked to be of use to you.' The words sounded pompous in his own ears, but for some reason his crying had been followed by an acute sense of his own dignity. Maybe it was because Tohomhe had taken his grief seriously. He was a Princeling, after all.

'Well well,' said Tohomhe, dismissively.

'I'm also afraid that my Grandhe will beat me if I go back saying there is no work for me here.'

'Is that it?' said Tohomhe hurriedly. 'Well, well. Your Grandhe is a powerful man; a forceful man. There's no call to tell him that you can't come. You can come, if you like, and we can talk. Maybe you could bring a little food and we could share it?'

'Food,' said Tighe shyly.

'If your Grandhe could spare it. I have some stuff stored, but I don't like to eat it too quickly, so I go hungry many days.'

But Tighe had already completed the unconscious transaction in his mind. He would steal Grandhe's food and give it to this man. It would be a kind of trade. He would transfer from anger to tenderness, from rage to this softness. It made a perfect sense.

'I'll do that,' he said.

The rest of the day passed pleasantly. Tohomhe showed Tighe round his store, unbinding and holding up some of his finest cloths; and Tighe was suitably impressed by the softness and flexibility of the weave. Then Tohomhe led him through to the room he had dug out at the back of the house where a weaving harp was propped against the wall. Its shuttles were plastic and several of its cords were genuine old-cord too, although most of the original cords had broken and had been replaced with gut. Later, hungry, Tighe crept back to Grandhe's house and grabbed some bread and one of Grandhe's special apples, wrinkled and dried since the summer. The feeling of creeping away from the empty house with food hidden under his clothes was intensely exciting. Tighe fairly ran over the market shelf and up to Tohomhe's place.

That afternoon Tohomhe and Tighe ate and Tohomhe hugged the boy again. Tighe felt a sweet feeling in his belly. Tighe left after the meal and spent the rest of the day roaming the upper pastures, watching the goat-boys and goat-girls with their little herds. He came back late, with the sun already vanishing over the top of the wall. The itinerants on market shelf were starting to huddle together. They spent the night that way, for warmth; and then again for protection against the fierce winds that accompanied dawn. One of their number had died, starved entirely away, and a small pyre had been prepared. Two of the village's farmers, a fruiterer and a pulse-grower, were arguing over who had the rights to the ashes. It was nearing spring and the rich dirt could bring out an early crop – very valuable indeed in times of hardship.

Tighe passed by, barely noticing. In his head he was starting to plan how he might petition the Doge to have Tohomhe adopt him as legal heir. Maybe Grandhe would be happy to surrender him if he agreed to give away all the goats and the house.

Through the dawn-door there was a candle burning in Grandhe's main space; a surprising luxury. The old man was sitting in his chair, the staff between his legs. Tighe knew, as he came through the dawn-door, that the night was going to be troubling. The smell of freshly baked bread gave the interior an incongruously homely feel.

'How was your day of work, my child?' Grandhe demanded.

'Gu-good,' said Tighe, slinking a little towards the wall. 'It wh-was good.'

'Don't *stammer*,' snapped Grandhe, twirling his staff. 'Now, I will speak of how my enemies have persecuted me.'

There was a pause, so Tighe filled it with a tentative 'Yes, Grandhe?'

'Theft is an *abomination* before God on the Top of the Wall,' Grandhe declared in clear tones. 'Do you understand?'

Tighe nodded, waiting for the blow.

'Today one of your *friends* – one of those itinerants you have such compassion for – stole into my house, into *my* house, and robbed me of food. They took winter apples and the rest of the loaf.'

Tighe said nothing, but he thought to himself, *It was only one apple you lying old man.* But he said, 'Yes,' in a dull tone.

'They are nothing. My enemies put one of them up to it. The Doge and I have agreed. Tomorrow they will be sent away from the village. We have tolerated them too long. They are a sickness in the village. My deputies will attend me tonight and we shall prepare for the morning. They are sick, but they have numbers. You are a strong boy and you will also help.'

'Yes, Grandhe,' said Tighe.

The deputies slept that night in Grandhe's main space and come morning they huddled round the old man. Tighe loitered, but Grandhe shooed him away. 'You have work to go to now, don't mope around.'

As he passed the itinerants on market shelf, he stopped, as if there were some way he could warn them. But there was nothing he could do. He tried to pick out the itinerant he had spoken to the other day, but the bony faces all looked much the same.

He made his way up to Tohomhe's, but the weaver didn't seem to be in. So he wandered a little, along the higher ledges. The sun was higher and the air was luminous with light.

He slumped down on a ledge, back against the wall, staring straight out at the sky.

Sky, air, light. Birds cooing and falling through the air. A stray piglet, branded with the mark of Lipshe, from one of the richer families higher up the wall, snuffled along the ledge, rifling through the short grass with its snout looking for edibles. The piglet ambled over to him, sniffed at his crossed legs, snuffled at his left foot and then moved on. The thought, as random as a dice throw, came into Tighe's head to kick the beast off the crag. Let it fall off the world as his pas' goat had done – as (and this thought brought a choking sensation back into his throat) his own pas had done. Why should Lipshe keep her pig when his own pas had fallen to nothingness? But by the time he had got to his feet the piglet was a dozen arms' lengths away and the impulse had passed.

There was some commotion from below. A crowd gathered on main-street shelf. Tighe started along the crag and down the slant to the public ladder. By the time he got to main-street shelf it was mostly over.

The crowd was jeering as the beggars were sent away. The more able-bodied of the itinerants were being shoved and spat at as they shuffled their way to the Doge's stairway. The Doge herself was standing there, waving them on. Clearly she had decided to waive the usual fee, happy to be ridding the village of all strangers. The crowd was unusually animated: gestures and words. Tighe dodged and hid at the back, but stole glances through the shaking shoulders and raised fists at his Grandhe, standing next to the Doge and looking holy and impassive. Two of his deputies were standing half an arm behind him, flanking him.

The itinerants shuffled slowly, exhausted and ashamed, their heads down. But the villagers were finding their own release in abuse.

'I had to pay to go up that stairway only last month,' yelled one, 'and now you go up it for free, you bastard!'

'Bastard!'

'We should throw you off the wall, that's my counsel!' yelled another.

A third voice, a woman's, shrieked, 'You've brought ill luck on our village! You've brought ill luck on our village!' This was taken up as a chant. 'Ill luck! Ill luck!' A few people plucked out pebbles from the trodden mud of main-street shelf and threw them, without particular conviction, at the retreating line of men and women. Tighe saw a pebble strike one of the itinerants on the back of the head, but the victim barely even flinched.

It did not last long. Soon the crowd lost its focus and milled about. Some people went off, talking animatedly, a few others clustered excitedly about Grandhe and the Doge. Only then did Tighe realise that three of the itinerants had not gone up the ladder with the rest of the group. They were in their old positions, backs to the wall, bone-narrow faces staring out in utter exhaustion.

Grandhe strode over to these three, his deputies a pace behind him. With a gesture, he ordered his men to take the body nearest to the stair. 'You'll pollute our village no longer,' he said to the man in a ringing voice. A few of the remaining villagers standing about cheered.

The itinerant was clearly too exhausted to stand. The deputies lifted him and shoved him towards the Doge's stair, but he fell straight back to the floor, face down. They picked him up again and tried to force him on, but he sagged like cloth between their hands. It was clear that, unless they carried him physically up every step of the stairway, he wasn't going anywhere. The two remaining itinerants stared with unearthly, passionless gazes at this action.

With an exasperated expression, Grandhe barked at his deputies, and the two men carried the unresisting stranger back to his place at the wall. They dumped him like a bundle of bamboo sticks in at the coign of wall and shelf. He lay exactly where he fell.

'Perhaps', Grandhe declared in a loud voice, standing over him, 'God will judge you. Perhaps the dawn gale, or the evening winds, will pluck you from the world and rid our Village of your curse.'

He turned and strode away. The last of the villagers went their ways. Tighe stayed in the inset where the public ladder began and watched for a while.

The scene became still as stone. None of the three remaining itinerants moved. Two were sat, backs to the wall, staring ahead. The third lay where he had been dumped.

12

Tighe himself didn't sleep well that night. Grandhe kept moving through his house, coming and going. To begin with it woke Tighe up, but Grandhe hissed at him to lie still and return to sleep or he'd feel the sharp force of his staff, so he said nothing. For a while he lay completely still. Grandhe walked through the room and a little while later came back. Tighe drifted off to sleep, and woke again to the hushed sounds of conversation. Grandhe was in the other room with both of his deputies. Tighe thought about getting up and creeping over to try and overhear more clearly what they were saying, but thought better of it. If his Grandhe discovered him it would mean a beating. So instead he tried to listen in from where he was lying. That was hopeless, though: the words warbled and burred, mere music without sense. The men were deliberately talking in low tones. There was the occasional clink of baked clay beakers and Tighe wondered if Grandhe had opened one of his precious bottles of grass gin. Perhaps the men were celebrating something.

Tighe drifted to sleep again and woke with a jolt. He had been dreaming of his pashe, but it was a strange, jumbled dream. It had been his pashe that Grandhe's deputies had been lugging across the shelf, although she was as thin and scrawny as a vagrant. And, somehow, at the same time, it had been inside his pas' house, and Grandhe was his own pahe. Then he had looked again at his pashe's face and, horror, it had been a bird's face, with a great white beak.

Awake, Tighe shook his head and rubbed at his eyes with both hands. Everything in Grandhe's house was quiet now. It was perfectly dark.

Tighe was awake for a long time, trying to rid his mind of the savour of the nightmare. He would force himself to think of happier memories, concentrate on good thoughts. It was like trying to rinse away the taste of a poisonous insect from your mouth with water; each rinse and the foul taste would recede, but when you stopped it would reassert itself.

Eventually he slept again and then woke again. Then he woke at the noise of the sunrise gale rattling the dawn-door outside. It was starting to get lighter. He lay for a while listening to the music of wind and rattle, and then fell asleep again. When he woke properly it was because Grandhe was kicking him, none too gently. 'Still asleep, slugabed? God loves no sluggard. Up! Up!'

He breakfasted and then cleaned the house, as was his routine now. Some of Grandhe's deputies arrived at the house shortly after and Tighe was sent to sit in the corner of the main space. He felt, for some reason he could not put a finger on, immensely sad. Sadness filled him.

By contrast, Grandhe Jaffiahe seemed unusually cheerful. He even laughed, briefly and startlingly, at something one of his deputies said. Tighe skulked out of Grandhe's way for a little under an hour before he was noticed. 'Will you loiter here all the bright day?' Grandhe demanded, gesticulating with his stick. 'Away, my grandchild, and to your work. Go to the weaver's, and learn a trade that will benefit you.'

Tighe slunk out of the house.

Outside it was a glorious day. The sunshine was bright and sharp, and all the colours of grass and clothing shone brightly. Flints embedded in the worldwall shone like carbuncles, looking as valuable as perspex. The shadow thrown up by the breadth of main-street shelf ended crisply a quarter-way up the Doge's house, up the two largest monger-shops in the village. People moved back and forth, busy, their top halves in sunshine and their hair gleaming, their bottom halves still in morning shadow. Carashe, looking thin but happy enough and whistling as she moved, was driving a single goat-he with a crumpled horn towards the Doge's house. Tighe hadn't seen her in ages. A cluster of villagers was standing outside the Doge's main door and the Doge was there herself, smoking her clay pipe and nodding at something being said. Tighe put his head back and could see some of the higher ledges, set back in the wall over the main street. A pig's face peered down over a crag's edge forty arms up.

Tighe's mood sank. So much happiness, so much energy, and he felt exhausted and depressed. He knew why, deep down, but did not think about it. He did not want to think about it.

He crossed to the wall and bent, to try and slip past everybody without being noticed. He had no place here. It was impossible for him to go up to Tohomhe's house. There wouldn't be any work for him anyway, but the thought of the weaver's simple jollity was more than he could bear. He wanted to find a dark place and lie down. He wanted to sink into shadow.

He made his way along the wall with small steps towards the public ladder, thinking to go up to the higher crags and ledges and find a peaceful place to be alone. But here was Wittershe, her pretty face smiling its unique smile, a bundled package of fodder grass for her father's monkeys under her left arm.

'Hello, my Princeling,' she said, reaching out and touching his face with her right hand. 'I should say, my Prince.'

'Wittershe,' he said. He felt tears prick through the blankness of his misery. She was so pretty.

'You haven't been down our ladder in a while, my Prince,' she said, in a sultry tone. 'Did you not have pleasure when you were down before? Are you not anxious for more?'

Tighe tried to speak, but words didn't come out. How could he explain it to her? His blankness of mood, his hopelessness. She moved closer to him and he could smell her particular smell again. It reached past his misery into the core of his body, started the twinkling sensations of desire bubbling in his belly. 'Wittershe,' he said again.

There was something he wanted to tell her, but he didn't like to think about it. He did not want to think about it. Couldn't she see?

'My sweet Tighe,' she was saying, her breath touching his cheek. 'I think about you and miss you. Why not come down the ladder? Why not do so now?'

'The itinerants,' said Tighe, with a gasp.

'You say?'

'The strangers. They were starving.'

'The Doge sent them all up the stairway yesterday,' said Wittershe, leaning a little away. 'Everybody has talked about it. Good riddance – they were a curse upon our village, everybody says.'

'Three were too weak to go,' said Tighe, his voice deep with misery.

Wittershe looked quizzically at him. 'You say?'

'They were too starved even to stand up – but they are not here this morning.'

'I suppose they have gone as well,' said Wittershe, offhand. 'I have to take this fodder down to my pahe, but then I'm free for a little while. Why not spend the time with me, for an hour?'

There was a spurt of something in Tighe's breast, breaking the ice a little. 'No! Wittershe – *can* you not see it? Where did the last of the itinerants go?'

'They went up the stairway. My pahe was cross that they were given free passage when he and every other villager has to pay a debt to step up the Doge's stair, but even he thinks it good riddance. They were a curse.'

'Some of them went up the stair,' said Tighe, grabbing her arm, eager to make her understand, 'but there were three too weak to go up the ladder.'

'Tighe,' said Wittershe, dropping her bundle to the floor to prise his grip from her arm.

'Where have those three gone?'

'Gone away,' said Wittershe. 'How does it matter anyway? Up the stairway.'

'No.' He pulled her towards him. 'Don't you see? Don't you see what my Grandhe has done?'

'Tighe –'

And then, with a voice like thunder, or the strongest of dawn gales, Tighe heard his Grandhe. 'Grandchild!'

He looked around. Grandhe was standing on the main-street shelf looking straight at him – pointing at him, holding his wooden staff up to point in his direction. His two deputies were behind him, as always. Everybody on the main-street shelf had stopped their labour and all were staring at him.

'Grandchild! Leave that heretic's slut to *herself.*'

Wittershe looked mortified. She wriggled free from Tighe and stepped back. But Tighe's blood was running through his head now, making pulsing noises in his ears. He felt a curious raising of spirits, a feeling of lightness in his torso as if he might float away and up, all the way up to God sitting in majesty on top of the wall. He turned to face his Grandhe.

'You killed them!' he screeched. He didn't intend for his voice to come out so high-pitched, but his emotion was too strong for easy control.

'Grandchild!' bellowed Grandhe.

'You killed them – you came in the night and *threw them from the world.* Killer! Murderer!' He was crying now and his outstretched arm was trembling. Everybody was silent. Tighe could sense even Wittershe absolutely motionless behind him. Only his Grandhe's face moved, the rage and astonishment warping the features.

He opened his mouth to speak, but only a strangled, furious sound emerged. Then he sucked in a deep breath, and shouted 'Be careful, my daughter's son,' he bellowed. 'I say –'

'You killed them and you killed my pas!' screamed Tighe. 'You did it! You threw them off the world to die.'

'You *may be* my daughter's child,' yelled Grandhe, his face distorted strangely by his wrath, 'but you'll be punished like a criminal for saying such things.'

'Everybody knows, but nobody says,' screamed Tighe, the tears coming fluently now. 'Everybody knows you killed my pahe, killed the Prince. You killed my pashe, your *own daughter.*'

Grandhe howled, really howled. Then with a gesture of both arms he sent his deputies forward. The two young men started lumbering towards Tighe, crossing the main-street shelf in large strides. And Tighe could barely see them through his tear-bleared eyes. The sound of Grandhe's voice came upon his ears again. 'How dare you say such *wicked* things,' but Tighe was already turning on his heels, already lurching away down the main-street shelf. It was less than conscious. Some animal part of his being refused to be snatched by his Grandhe's men, refused to be beaten again. He had no idea what the villagers were doing or saying. He was blind to everything except the blurry sense of his own feet pounding the pressed mud and patchy grass of the shelf.

He ran clumsily, trying to clear his eyes by rubbing the back of his hand over them. He could hear his own sobs and the thump of his pursuers behind him. He felt as if he had spoken the unspeakable and had got no relief.

He reached the far end of main-street shelf quickly, and doubled back to clamber up to the ledges that led away and up to the Left. His pas' house was on one of these ledges. Somebody – Tighe didn't recognise who – stood stupefied as he rushed past and the Priest's deputies hurried after him.

The deputies were older than Tighe, with fuller strides. They closed the distance between them rapidly. Fingers clutched at Tighe's clothes. They almost had him. The sensation of near capture brought a sharp, sudden nausea into Tighe's stomach. He shimmied to avoid their grasp and kicked out to accelerate up the sloping ledge.

And, with a nauseous flurry in his torso, his foot went over the edge. The ledge swung up, and Tighe braced himself for the impact of his face against the hard mud. But no impact came and then the ledge was withdrawing from him. Wind leapt at his ears, smacked into his face and body.

His stomach clenched and bucked within him. But it was appallingly true. He was falling.

Falling and turning.

There was the fleetingest glimpse of ledges whipping past him, and then he was head over toes and nothing but sky, and the distant clouds. The wind was screaming now, its voice huge in his ears. He was screaming too, probably. Probably, but he couldn't tell because the enormous rush of air took everything from his mouth and whisked it away. It cloaked him in soundproof stuff; it chilled him and robbed his body of heat.

Everything.

A strong taste of metal in his mouth. His mouth was dry.

He tumbled again and the wall panned past him. He realised then that his arms and legs were thrashing, kicking and clawing at nothing, at air. With another great visceral lurch he felt himself propelled awaywall, so violently that his head slumped back and his limbs trailed behind him. Then he toppled, twisted, and was pushed hard again. The wind was a giant hand, pawing him, flicking him outwards. His stomach contracted violently and his breakfast came gobbling up at his throat. A streak of pale vomit spread away from him and he flailed and cried.

Then, miraculously, he was tossed upwards. His pulsing stomach registered the shift in direction, not *down* but *up*, as if a spectral cord was attached to his back and was now yanking him upwards. He was facing the wall, too, so the shift in motion made itself plain to his eyes too. The landscape of the wall slowed, stopped, began rewinding. A broad ledge heavily overhung, very distant, uninhabited, probably a singleton, moved judderingly down his vision, and he knew he was travelling up. The thought that the Divine had intervened occurred to him; that the Divine was going to lift him back up to his village. Or maybe this was what it felt like to be dead – maybe he had died of falling. Died of fright. And now his body was tumbling still, falling to wherever it was that people fell to, but his spirit had been pulled out and was going to fly upwards upwards to heaven. To see his pas. To see pashe, *I'm sorry pashe . . .*

Or, he was dreaming.

But no dream could be this solidly present in his stomach. And his guts registered it again, and the visceral tumbling, lurching, started once again, built rapidly from nothing like a seed growing in his deep insides. He was dropping again, falling down and gaining speed. Had it been a freak gust of wind carrying him up?

And the horrible sense of starting to fall, of moving down again faster and faster. Another violent push wallwards, then a turbulent juggling, wallwards, awaywalls, wallwards, awaywalls. His eyeballs hurt. His throat was hoarse. His skin shivered with the extreme cold in great jerky convulsions.

The wind was playing with him throwing him around like a fallen blade of grass. He barely had time to register this realisation.

It was the cold. That was the worst. He realised the immediate terror of the fall was shrinking, but the cold was getting worse. His fingers and feet were painful-sore with the chill of it, and the wind was pushing through the webbing of the weave of his shirt and trousers to give his body genuine aches. He was falling – no, moving sideways, hurtling back towards the wall – no, falling again, diving down again. But the surprise was going and now the cold was the worst of it.

Falling to wherever fallers went. Wherever the starving itinerants had fallen to. Wherever his pas had gone. To the very bottom of the wall, maybe.

But maybe there was no bottom; maybe those who fell did so on and on for ever. But they still died – a part of him was amazed that he could be so rational, that he could think it through like this – he supposed. Died of the cold, most like. Or of hunger. Or thirst, maybe. He looked up. Much closer to the wall now. Maybe that was how fallers died. Maybe they just smashed into the wall as they went down and were broken to a million pieces.

Then he thought, with his whole body stabbed with pain from the cold of it, that maybe he could steer away from the wall. If he stretched out, and tried to dive down, maybe the direction of fall would be awaywalls. If he got far enough out he could avoid the –

Instant blackness, and

And breath was punched away. A profound jarring, like a slap from a giant's hand. His spine howled with pain, his face was numb but dribbling a spout of warmth from his nose, as he lurched away and sharp fingers snagged him in a spiky embrace. That was the last thing: being grasped by unyielding spars of something.

Only a period of shady perceptions and most of those perceptions of a wall of pain that stretched right through him. It hurt, in crescendo pulses, as he breathed. His left foot hurt terribly. A pain pulsed through his sinuses.

2
Kite-boy

1

He began emerging from the darkness. It was sometime.

It was difficult to tell the time, and

His whole body ached. He kept his eyes pressed shut and tried to think the pain away. It was no good. His left foot hurt swingeingly. He tried not to think about it, but the pain kept intruding itself in his thoughts. He couldn't think a way round it. It was no good.

His eyeballs stung with the light. Grey light, sharp. He looked around, and it took a time to piece together the

Fell asleep again! He kept falling asleep in the middle of things. He had the sense of people moving about him, sometimes of soup being dribbled along a stick into his mouth. When he had been younger he had fallen ill with fever and his pahe had nursed him in this way; pouring a little sticky broth from a cup so that it ran down a fat stick and trickled into his mouth. But his pahe was dead, and his pashe too, and with that memory Tighe started crying.

People hushed him, and words flowed through the air. But the words meant nothing to him.

He tried sitting up one morning, but the effort was too much and it made his feet hurt badly and his back. He cried out. 'Ach! Ach!' Somebody, wearing face paint and a bizarre headdress, moved from the shadows and leant over him. More of the words, but they made no sense to Tighe.

Without sense, the words were like music, and the music acted like a lullaby. He slept again.

It seemed to him that he was never able to sleep for very long, because the pain woke him up. He tried explaining this to the person with the painted face and the headdress, but there was no sign of comprehension on the other person's face. Sometimes it was as if there was another person, with the same paint on his face and the same strange headgear, but different features. It was hard because the pale paint on the face made the features somehow difficult to see.

'How long have I been here?' he asked. But they just ignored his question.

By now he was able to sit up, although it rasped his feet pulling them over the mattress. But it meant a great deal to him to be able to bring his head up, to look around. When they came to feed him again he took the spatula and the bowl himself and spooned the soup in like an adult. He felt all right in the head, not hot about the temples or sweating from the eyes. His back was not as sore. Only leg joints hurt, and his feet in particular. The left one was broken. He couldn't see it because, for some reason, it was covered in a fat cake of mud.

When Tighe examined this mud – a strange pale mud, but dried mud none the less – he scratched away with his fingernails and started pulling fragments away from it. One of the attendants hurried over and stopped him, gently but firmly moving his hand away from the thing.

He understood. Once a boy-boy had fallen from an upper ledge, and had been lucky enough to land on the main-street shelf rather than falling all the way off the wall. But he had put his arm out of the shoulder and broken the bone. His pas had strapped thick bamboo to the arm and smeared it all with mud too to hold it steady whilst it healed. Only that mud had flaked off in hours and they had had to replace it every morning and evening. This pale, dried mud seemed to stay intact the whole time.

He ate, slept, drank. The soup was called *poltete*. One of the attendants pointed to it and repeated the word, until Tighe copied it. Tighe tried the other way about, 'My name is Tighe, Tighe,' but the other didn't seem interested.

He woke early every morning and hauled himself upright into a sitting position. He was in a low, wide space; only recently excavated from the wall to judge by the roughness of the walls. There was a line of a dozen mattresses, each woven from fat reeds unfamiliar to Tighe, spaced equally between one wall and the other. Tighe occupied one of the mattresses near the middle. In his early days in this place there was another body on the mattress three along from his, an impressively large body that lay on its back rasping as it breathed. By the time Tighe was able to sit up the body had gone, dead or recovered, he never found out.

He was struck, as soon as he could clear the dried, snotted blood from his nostrils, by how antiseptic the air smelled. It was remarkable, as if the walls had just been scrubbed with soap.

As Tighe's health improved, he moved on from eating only the poltete. Sometimes grubs were mixed into the soup and once he was brought a piece of something so delicious it had to be meat, although not a meat he had ever tasted before. He started each day with grass-bread so warm it was evidently just baked.

When he needed to piss he rolled to the edge of the mattress and pissed on the floor, in the way he was used to doing, the way he had always done it at home. He even tried scooping dirt over the puddle, as he would have done at home, although the gesture of stretching hurt his legs. But one of the attendants came over speaking their gibberish, obviously horrified at what Tighe had just done. An elaborate mime made it clear that Tighe was expected to piss into the bowl on the other side of the mattress. The bowl was filled with platán leaves, and Tighe slowly came to understand that he was expected to take the leaves out of the bowl and keep them to shit into; that the bowl was to be used for his piss. After he had taken on board this alien concept he did as he was told and used the unfamiliar devices as instructed. Attendants sometimes carried the bowl outside and each time he filled a platán leaf with his waste it was carefully gathered up and removed. Maybe they used it for their gardens outside, or maybe cast it over the edge of the world. Tighe couldn't know.

Another patient was brought in, bleeding from his nose and ears and whimpering like a piglet. He was the centre of attention for half an hour; all four medical attendants hurrying around him, leaning over him, mopping him and applying something to his lips. But he stopped his noise after a while and lay still, and half an hour after that a strange smell started from that part of the room. The attendants carried out his nerveless body and Tighe was alone again.

He realised early on that these people were not wearing face paint as he had thought. No, their skin was that colour naturally; an ash whiteness that looked like a religious mask. Tighe had been startled and a little scared when the chief medical attendant had been leaning over him one morning checking his legs and Tighe had realised that the peculiar ashen colour was not painted over but went right down to his pores, to the scalp between his hairs, to his hands and feet.

The headdress was not a headdress either, but an enormous mass of tangled hair. Their hair was different from normal, strange; thicker, somehow, each strand frizzed out so that the whole made limbs of moss-like excrescence rather than the normal threads. This hair covered their

89

heads and sprouted up and over, falling in ropy strands over their shoulders. They all wore the same clothes, too: deep blue tunics that went down to their knees and black leggings to their bare white feet.

These people were strange enough to seem barely human, and Tighe – with nothing else to do but weave fancies out of his brain – sometimes wondered if he had indeed fallen all the way to the foot of the wall and discovered it populated by devils. Or animals. Or some other alien beings. Perhaps, he thought, he was dead: but he banished that idea because he was so clearly still alive, with living hungers and thirsts, living pains in his legs. He could be on the bottom of the wall, but he felt sure he should have been killed by the fall.

The fall. It had a weird, dream-like quality for him now. It had clearly never happened. Or he had fallen fifty arms, maybe, and hurt his feet on landing, that was all – except there were no villages fifty arms downwall of Cragcouthie, he knew that. There were no villages a thousand arms downwall, or ten thousand. Directly below the village was a long stretch of flat worldwall that nobody could traverse.

But he was clearly in some village. How to make sense of it?

One of the medical attendants had a higher ranking than the other three. That was obvious from watching them together. The ranking medic was a little shorter, but the two men and one woman deferred to him. From watching and listening carefully to their babbling, Tighe heard them use the word *Vievre*. He never used it himself. It was presumably a name, or a rank.

The next time the man came over to check on him, Tighe spoke the word, 'Vievre.' The man's strange, ashen face broke in a broad smile.

'Aouee,' he replied. 'Vievre.' And then he gabbled a stream of distorted words and strange sounds that lost Tighe.

One time when he had still been a boy-boy a traveller had come up from Press carrying perspex jewellery and pipes to trade in the village. He had done well and had stayed several days, and Tighe – bored as usual, wandering about as usual – had had several conversations with him. He had, Tighe remembered, spoken with a peculiar intonation. 'You speak funnily,' the young Tighe had told him and he had laughed and explained that he had learned correct speech only late in his life, and before that had spoken some completely different speech. This had been a revelation to the young Tighe.

That there were more languages than one! The intimacy with which his words had related to the things he talked about seemed diminished by the news. 'Say something in your other speech,' Tighe had asked. 'Say what?' asked the trader. 'I don't care what.' And the man had rattled into a stream of nonsense. For weeks after that Tighe had experimented with his own nonsense words, telling his pahe that he was inventing a new language. But the gibberish he had come up with had sounded oddly unsatisfying to his own ears and he had given up his game soon enough.

Now the game was his whole world. As the pain slowly withdrew from his foot, he was able to concentrate more closely on the things being said between the orderlies. But names – or maybe they were ranks – were all he could deduce.

One day a whole parade of people came into the low space, and all to see Tighe. There must have been more than a dozen, all cramming into the space, some so tall they had to stoop. All were as ashen faced as the medical attendants, and all had similar black (or brown) hair in great tangled clumps – indeed, some of them had jewellery, plastic and other precious things woven into their hair. They were wearing similar dark blue uniforms, although some of their uniforms were more splendid than others, with yellow thread woven through the cloth of the sleeves.

They crowded about his mattress and stared down at him, gabbling loudly in their barbarous tongue, pointing and (it seemed) laughing. Tighe, bewildered by the sudden commotion, quickly became scared.

He flinched back as one of them bent over and started prodding him. They laughed at this. Great booming laughs from bone-coloured faces and tangled masses of hair trembling in time to the shaking of their heads.

Then, as swiftly as they had arrived, the delegation departed, pausing by the door to converse a little with 'Vievre'. Then all was quiet and Vievre was by Tighe's side examining him again.

There were bruises all down Tighe's left side, yellowing now, and his leg was blotched all over with bruising. He prodded the bruised skin. There were some scars too, but they seemed to be healing up.

The language spoken by these strange pale people percolated into Tighe's consciousness somehow. He found words stepping up from the general babble. Poltete meant soup (or perhaps it meant liquid?). Homb meant person, or maybe man. Vievre was a name, the chief medical attendant. He was a large man, tall and broad, with a face of alarming whiteness and a great mass of tangled hair that made him seem even taller. Tighe repeated the foreign words with which he began the morning conversations back at him for several days – to delighted smiles – before he realised what the words themselves must mean. *Nee* for new, and *or* for day.

'Good new day, patient,' Vievre would say. 'Are you feeling well?'

'Yes,' said Tighe. 'Yes.'

The big breakthrough came with learning the form of questions. How do you say? What is that? Tell me . . .

'How do you say?' Tighe would begin, and then touch his foot.

'Ah, the *foot*,' Vievre would say in his strange tongue.

'How do you say?' and touching the leg.

'Leg, yes. You anaprehal trop good, yes.' *Trop* meant *very*, Tighe thought. He thought so, at any rate.

How do you say *stomach, arm, hand, face, head, hair?*

'Hair,' said Vievre, chuckling. 'Your hair is very malpuea, meshalamme dela troppa.'

How do you say – and Tighe made gestures with his hands to indicate size, pulling his hands in different directions, puffing up his cheeks.

'What? What?' Vievre asked. 'You mean – empheu? No, no, you mean *granda*.' That was *big*; the word was almost like Tighe's familiar 'grand', so it was easier to remember.

'Big hair,' said Tighe, pointing at Vievre's enormous coiffure. 'Big hair!'

Vievre laughed now, pulled at his own locks, leaning down and pulling Tighe's much thinner hair.

Tighe tried starting conversations with the other medical attendants, but they uniformly ignored him. They would not so much as meet his eye. Tighe didn't understand this. Were they angry with him? Or were they too menial to think about holding a conversation with somebody like him?

Some days Vievre was not in the mood for the language-learning game. He would stomp about, shouting at his subordinates. With nothing else to occupy him, Tighe was bored almost all the time, and he waited with exaggerated anticipation for Vievre to come through, to give him something else to talk about, something new to learn. But he learnt rapidly not to bother Vievre if he was in the wrong sort of mood.

Vievre explained to him that the people who had crowded around Tighe had been part of an army. A great army! After the visitation by this group of military personnel, various individuals would sometimes put their head through the door of the ward and say something to Vievre or some of the nurses about Tighe. From time to time Tighe would catch these words: 'Is that him then? The sebstynapul boy?' Sometimes the words would be so rapid or unfamiliar, or the individual's accent so strange, that Tighe would catch nothing at all.

Vievre's attitude to these occasional visitors was strange. Sometimes he would shoo them away, even running from the far side of the ward to the door yelling. Other times, though, he would beam and smile and invite the individual in. 'This is Bellievra,' he would say. 'This is Prier-Vallio. Masters, say good-new-day to Master Tig-he.' Tighe had tried correcting Vievre's pronunciation of his name many times, but he always put too much and the wrong kind of emphasis on the 'h'.

'Master Tig-he,' the stranger would say, nodding.

'Good new day,' Tighe would say, politely. The stranger would grin, pat his head, look him up and down, ask some questions of Vievre.

'And so it seems I am a *celebrity*,' Tighe said to Vievre one day after such a visit, using the word from his own language. But it proved too difficult to explain the concept with only his halting command of the new language.

He learnt the words for *hungry, in pain, bored, heart, lung, breath, up, down, difficult, broken, mattress, piss, shit.* He learnt the different shapes of a word in motion: he learnt *to fall, I fall, you fall, I fell, they fell.*

'You fell!' chuckled Vievre, but there was a look of something close to awe in his eyes. 'Certainly. You fell.'

One morning, with a strange hopeful sensation in his belly, Tighe laboured through halting explanations and questions until he arrived at the word for *pas.* 'My parents,' he said. 'They fell, my parents.'

Vievre nodded at this news, uncertainly.

'They fell, I fell,' said Tighe. 'Here? Are they here?'

'Your parents?' Vievre looked unsettled. 'Here?'

'Yes. Like me, skin,' pulling at his own skin to underline the point, 'skin like me. They fell – here, perhaps. I fell here, *they* fell here perhaps. Are they here?'

'Skin like you – there are people with shuart skin, like you, in our glorious Empire. Our Holy Popes regnielle over many people.'

'My parents,' said Tighe, again, his heart fluttering now. If he fell off the wall and survived – in this strange, new place – then perhaps his pas had done the same. Perhaps his pahe and pashe were still alive, perhaps they were still alive in this place. 'Are they here?'

'Your parents are not here, Tig-he the boy. I'm sorry.'

Tighe paused, let this sentence sink in. 'Not here.'

'Not here. I'm sorry.'

'They fell. I fell. I fell to here – they fell to here?'

'They are not here, your parents, Tig-he. I'm sorry.'

He wasn't surprised. It was clear that his survival had been something extraordinary. He learnt the words for *lucky,* for *blessing* and *God* (which was the same as *Sky Father* – a strange concept for Tighe to digest). He began to understand why so many individuals crept into the ward to look at him.

He had fallen into the midst of an army preparing for war. Soldiers –

dozens, so many that Tighe forgot who had been to see him and who had not, too many new faces to remember – visited a boy fallen from the sky. A boy fallen from upwall and survived! He was a byword for luck.

Soldiers are always interested in luck.

One day Vievre decided that it was time for Tighe to try standing up. He and one of his assistants took the weight under Tighe's armpits and pulled him vertical. His senses swam as the blood drained from his head. 'Now,' suggested Vievre.

Tighe put weight gingerly on his good foot. It tingled unpleasantly, unused to the load, but it seemed all right. Then he tried shifting a little weight on to his other leg, and the joints sang with pain. 'Oh, oh,' he cried. 'Oh, oh.'

Vievre and the other hauled him around in a little circle about the mattress, with each assisted step causing twangs of pain from Tighe's knee joint. After no more than a minute Tighe was slicked with sweat, and the two medics lowered him gingerly back on to the mattress.

2

The food was excellent, though. Varied and tasty. Vievre brought him a bowl of broth in which Tighe was certain – once again! – that there was some meat. He ate hungrily. He was healthier, fatter, now than he had ever been.

Tighe noticed that there was something yellow in Vievre's tangled hair. It was the length of a little finger, but much narrower. Tighe noticed it early on in his stay, but at the beginning had too little of the language, and then was too shy, to ask about it. One morning he summoned up the courage.

Sarre. 'That,' he said, pointing. Saico. 'What?'

'You mean this, this little ossionetta, lai dela mam. It is', said Vievre, fingering the object, twirling it deeper into his hair, 'the dela of the Empire, of the army. Do you understand it? This sayno speaks of my dela.'

'Dela?' asked Tighe. He was running his finger around the clay bowl as he spoke, scraping up the last of the gravy of his meal.

'Sayno speaks of dela, it is a thing that – I don't know. Culoe, narre deliparta mash puentilio. Every man and woman in the army, do you understand it? Every jentolle man and woman in the army is *in* the army, in a place. Yes? Yes? From so high, to so un-high, from the Holy Father down to bottom, to sevarre boys and camp girls. Yes? All have their dela.'

'Rank,' said Tighe.

'In your language, yes. It is a strange and ugly sound, your language. But that is right. So, the sayno speaks of rank.' Vievre smiled. 'This, my sayno, says that I am under-prelette, but that is a luche rank, not fighting.'

'Luche?' asked Tighe.

Vievre sighed noisily, waving his hands in an exaggerated gesture. 'It is ballio to jentolle speaking, your questions don't end. I do not have the tempievre, do you understand it?' He turned to go and then turned back with another sigh. 'Luche is making bodies well at war, not killing or outanutelle. Do you understand it?'

Tighe nodded and said nothing. He had deduced that Vievre was in the army from his uniform, and he had clearly been spending his time returning Tighe to health, so if he had thought about it he could probably have worked out what *luche* meant by himself.

The language was coming a little more easily each day. Some days Vievre was full of laughter and good spirits, and Tighe felt emboldened to ask after the meanings of more of his words. Some of these stayed in his memory, occasionally he forgot some, but in general it seemed to him that he forgot fewer than he might have expected. Other days Vievre was in a worse mood, swearing and slapping with the palm of his hand. *Jentolle* meant 'fucking', as Vievre once vividly mimed in response to a question from Tighe.

The word ossionetta for the thing in Vievre's hair came from a word that meant bone. At first Tighe thought it meant 'finger' because that was what Vievre used to demonstrate the word. Tighe even used the word in conversation with that meaning and Vievre did not object. But later on Vievre was explaining how the ossionetta in Tighe's knee had been cracked but not broken (which Vievre demonstrated by cracking and then breaking apart a piece of bread) and he realised the true meaning of the word.

Each member of the army had a bone to indicate rank, it seemed; the bigger the bone the higher the rank. It was often tied into the hair to make sure of not losing it, but some officers, it seemed, had them woven on to their uniforms, or even pierced through their cheeks. Their cheeks? Tighe asked, horrified, patting his own cheek to make sure he had the right part of the body with the word. Yes, said Vievre, nodding seriously. Through there.

This rank-bone was, despite its name, not actually a bone. It was in fact made of some hard substance. In the light Tighe could see that it was the colour of urine, and when he touched it it felt warm, heavy, like some very high-quality polished plastic. He could even see the tiny scratches where the polishing had taken place.

'Not plastic, said Vievre. 'It's metal. Prise it is called. We have stores of it in Vale Ounlempre, where I was given this.' He tapped the rank-bone with his fingernail. 'It was lou-paral a Cardinelle herself who gave me this, at a military cue doffo ourelle. When I was raised up from ordinary medical-soldier to under-prelette.' He smiled. 'There was a large crowd. Many hundreds. All sal-darra and happy to watch the army of the Empire come up the world to fight the enemy.'

Vale Ounlempre, as Tighe understood it, meant simply 'City of the Empire'. It seemed to be, from Vievre's reports, a city of enormous proportions – scores of shelves, hundreds of ledges 'broad enough to walk ten abreast', many thousands of crags and smaller eyries. *Thousands* of people living there: thousands. It seemed incredible to Tighe, but when he expressed polite amazement Vievre was adamant. Imperial City was the greatest city in the world, he insisted. The centre of the Empire, home to the Three Popes, the most *valepul* city on the world.

Valepul was a word presumably related to vale, city, but Tighe couldn't figure out exactly what it meant. 'The most cityish city' didn't make much sense to him.

The Imperial City, it seemed, was some distance downwall. It was clear, also, because so much of Vievre's conversation related to this fact, that the Three Popes had sent an enormous army – thousands, said Vievre, flashing the numbers with his fingers to build up to the enormity of the number – thousands on top of thousands of soldiers – upwall to defeat a mighty enemy.

Tighe found *thousands* a very hard concept to accept. Could there be that many people on the whole of the world?

Thousands, Vievre insisted. A mighty army. That was why Vievre himself was here, with his three luchombes, his three nurses (homb meant man, but one of the medical assistants was a woman), and his medical equipment. He was to be ready for after the battle, when many injured would come in. But before the battle there were few soldiers who needed any medicine or care. Vievre was bored, that was the truth. And then you fell!

'Yes,' said Tighe, his stomach tightening. 'I fell.'

Why hadn't Tighe died as a result of his fall? Tighe thought of the ways of phrasing this question for Vievre.

Died was not a linguistic problem. One day two soldiers carried in a third so bloody his uniform looked black and wet instead of the usual blue. He had fallen, too, from the sky, it seemed. He was flatar.

Vievre worked busily, wiping away the blood from this boy's pale face; but it flowed back out as soon as he wiped it away. The boy's breathing was extraordinarily loud, it filled the low-ceilinged ward. Pink bubbles like spiders' eggs congregated in a mass at the boy's half-open mouth. His breathing had a liquid, gurgling quality that sounded to Tighe like farting. Tighe was horrified by his injuries, but then there was that noise and he felt himself giggling. It was so comical a noise. He tried to stop laughing and even prised his lips together between his thumb and finger to lock the noise in, but he could barely contain himself. *Prrprr-ahh. Prrprrphrprl-ahh.* It was appalling and hilarious at the same time.

Then the breathing stopped.

Vievre and his helpers stood around the corpse for a few minutes; then they wrapped it in a blanket and two of the assistants carried it out of the ward. Vievre himself mopped up some of the spilt blood, a menial job he would usually have delegated.

There was a gloomy mood in the ward for an hour or so after that; but it didn't last for ever. A military medic cannot afford to let himself be too moved by death.

'Who was that?' Tighe asked, when Vievre came to check on him later on.

'Some boy.'

'Some boy,' repeated Tighe.

Vievre made a gesture with his right hand. 'He merden.' *Died*, there it was. Tighe knew what the world meant without having to ask any further questions.

'How?' he asked.

'He was flatar,' said Vievre. 'Soldier in the sky. They practise in the sky and he fell. It is sorry. A sorry thing.'

'Flatar?' asked Tighe.

Vievre wrinkled his face. He clearly wasn't in much of a mood to explain words today. 'Flatar,' he said. 'Flatar.' He made a swooping gesture with his hand flat.

'Like a bird?' Tighe pressed.

'And what is *buhhd*?' Vievre asked, without much energy.

'A thing in the sky,' said Tighe. He put both palms together at the thumbs and flapped them like wings.

'No, no, that is owso, owso,' Tighe would have asked him more, but Vievre was walking away now, walking through the door and out into the light.

The next day Tighe didn't see Vievre at all. The assistants served him food in their silent way, and then sat together by the door looking out and chatting amongst themselves in low voices.

Tighe was full of fidgets these days. He could barely keep still. His knee still hurt if he pressed it or put weight on it, as he did from time to time, walking around the ward supported by the medics. But his foot in its mud casket had long since stopped hurting; now it mostly itched and Tighe wriggled in an ecstasy of discomfort when that happened. Or he just wriggled around anyway. He was so bored. He sat up and strained to see through the open doorway.

'What is flatar?' he asked one of the assistants, but she ignored him as she usually did.

Vievre came back the following day. 'Good new day to you, my little bird,' he said, laughing and flapping his hands together in wing-shapes. 'My little bird! The boy who fell! How are you?'

'My foot itches,' said Tighe. 'It very itches.'

'You should say *it itches badly*,' said Vievre. 'But no language teaching today! Today I have a conversation with the Sky Cardinelle of the whole army! He is very interested in you, my little bird. Escoutiens have gone up the wall, up the wall, and there are no people for ten miles or more. Think of it! Some paucie ledges, some solitarris, but no people, no villages, no cities. Ten miles.' A *mile*, Tighe had learnt, was some two thousand arms' lengths; nearly two leagues.

'If there are no ledges,' said Tighe, 'then how did your people go up there?'

Vievre laughed at this. 'They went up in the air,' he said, 'of course. Derienne, they travelled up for many miles and there is nothing there.'

'Nothing at all?' asked Tighe.

'Think how far you must have fallen, my little bird,' said a delighted Vievre. 'To fall so far and still to live! It is a mark of God's especial gressa. So Master Elanne will have a conversation with you, he tells me.'

'Master Elanne?'

'Master Elanne is the Sky Cardinelle of the whole army – think of it! Assistant-at-war to the War Pope himself. A very great man. A *very* streesha man.'

'He will speak with me?'

'You are a good fowlel – a good thing for the future, a good sign. You know?'

'Omen,' said Tighe. 'We say.'

'Fowlel – *ommen* – yes. To fall so far and not to die. All the men and women in the army think so, a good omen for the future. To fall so far and not to die.'

'Vievre,' said Tighe, 'how *did* I fall so far and not die?'

Vievre laughed aloud at this. 'Admiraculla!' he declared. 'It has never been known before. The army was gathering itself, setting its camp – yes? – in this place. We go to war with the enemy. We bring thousands of men and women in the army to know this part of the wall. Master Elanne was readying the flatars and the calabashen, those parts of the sky army.'

'What are they?' asked Tighe. 'What is flatar?'

'Part of the army. A flatar is', he paused, 'a thing. Each with a boy or a girl.' Vievre made the swooping gesture with his flat palm. 'You will go walking outside, on the ledge outside, soon; then I will show you. And a calabash is a bag, yes? Full of air, the hot air. It is a big thing.' Vievre mimed a great sphere in the air in front of him. 'A big thing that goes up in the air. The army has a dozen. Two dozen.'

Tighe tried to picture this strange thing, but had no imaginative purchase.

'Well,' said Vievre, a little downcast that his explanation had brought no flicker of recognition from his charge, 'you do not know the calabash in your land?'

'No,' said Tighe.

'Well,' said Vievre, 'you doubesse your life to the calabash. When you came it happened that one was being exhalpenen, made big with hot air. It was half full, beginning to rise. Then you fell on to it! One boy saw you far up, then everybody saw you, shouted, pointed. You fell from high and landed – pouff!' (Vievre blew all the air out of his lungs through his mouth to make the noise) '– on to the calabash. Pushing the air out of it, nan alderienne all covered up in it like a blanket at the end. So! The fabric of a calabash is thick – yes? But your left foot entrelatte, pushed through it. This is why your foot was all souped'– there was the word for soup, poltete, used as a verb. 'All mashed' – another food word. Vievre made a face. 'But otherwise, you were alive! Many bruises, cuts. Much blood. You slept – yes? De conaissep. But alive!'

'Alive,' whispered Tighe.

'So Cardinelle Elanne will speak with you tomorrow or the tomorrow after that.' Vievre was clearly delighted with this development. A genuine military celebrity to visit his ward!

3

For much of the rest of that day Vievre fussed about Tighe: preparing him, he realised, for the visit of the high-ranking officer. With one of his assistants he walked Tighe round and round the ward, calling off 'One, two, one two,' in time to the steps.

Over the course of his stay Tighe had learnt to count up to twelve in his new language. And, of course, he knew the word for *thousands.*

They rested for a meal, and after that Vievre called for some equipment – Tighe's ear was not skilled enough to overhear exactly what kind – and he folded his legs under himself to sit at the foot of Tighe's mattress.

'I shall remove the cast, now, my little bird,' he announced. His face was beaming and he was actually cooing in his happiness.

'Vievre,' said Tighe. Then, to be more respectful, 'Master Vievre.' Vievre looked up at him. 'I have a question.'

'You have?'

'What is your family?'

Vievre's head tilted a little. 'How do you mean?'

'You have family?' Tighe rephrased.

'Father and mother,' said Vievre. 'Brother and sister.' He might have been answering, or he might have been clarifying for Tighe what the word *family* meant.

'You are father,' said Tighe, blushing a little. 'Pahe and pashe, we say in my land. To me, you play at father.' He didn't want to use the word meaning *play*, but he couldn't think of a word that meant 'act' in the more serious sense. But having said it, it didn't sound right. He tried again, 'You work at father to me,' but that sounded wrong as well.

Vievre was looking at him in a slightly puzzled way. With a flurry, wondering if he had somehow offended the medic, Tighe coughed, and tried again. 'You must have a son,' he said, 'I think. You are good, I think.'

'I have no son,' said Vievre in a distant tone.

Tighe looked up, but Vievre's face had taken on a frightening, stony aspect.

There was a silence. One of the medical assistants came through carrying a leather satchel. Tighe wanted to say, *I hope I have not offended you – it was not my intention to offend you*, but he did not have the language for it.

In silence Vievre took the satchel and the orderly withdrew, leaving them alone together again. He opened the bag and brought out a serrated spatula.

'Vievre,' said Tighe, again. He felt – for some reason – close to tears. 'I say: thank you.'

'For what?' replied Vievre, without looking at him.

'You are good, I think. You are father, I think. To me. My pashe, my mother, she good, but she break me sometime.' Tighe slapped the mattress with the flat of his right hand to illustrate what he was trying to say. 'She go ill every month, she' – he slapped again – 'every month.' The tears were coming out now more freely. He wasn't even sure why he was saying this. 'You are good to me,' he said, finally and then sucked in his lips to stop sobs from emerging.

Vievre still wasn't looking at him. 'Don't cry. You have wounds on your head and body, I donerete – I saw them, when you were first here. Under your hair particularly. Deep old scar on the back of the head. Some said you were a soldier and they were soldier's wounds.'

'I had that as child,' said Tighe. 'I not remember when.'

Vievre looked up suddenly. His own eyes were bright. 'It happens sometimes. Your mother, I think. I am sorry to hear of your mother breaking you, to hear of your family. But she loved you, I think.'

'She loved me,' said Tighe, trying to breathe more calmly.

'Family is like army, family is like war sometimes. Sometimes people get hurt in the war. You know this?'

'She was', said Tighe, but didn't know the word for *unstable*, the word for *precarious*, and he couldn't think of a roundabout way of expressing it, so he said, 'she fell off the world.'

'So you told me,' said Vievre, more briskly. 'Anyway, good, I shall cut off the cast with this coutno here. It looks sharp, but it will not cut your skin.' He smiled. 'So?'

Tighe nodded.

Vievre sawed at the outer part of the dried mud-cake, and then pulled fraying chunks of the stuff off with his fingers. Then he cut more carefully closer to the foot itself. Tighe was aware of a lessening of pressure, a vague sensation difficult to assign specifically to his foot, but happening somewhere down his leg. Finally Vievre put the spatula down and pulled the cast apart in different directions. It came away in a miniature puff of mud-dust and there was his foot, wrapped in a flimsy show of dirty fabric. 'There!' said Vievre.

'Good,' said Tighe.

Vievre cut easily through the cloth and together they peered at the foot. It looked a little misshapen, the toes all warped in the same direction, the top of the foot hunched and bulbous. There was a prominent lump on the side that wasn't supposed to be there – Tighe put his other foot alongside for comparison. But otherwise it was his foot, as he remembered it.

'I will wash it now,' said Vievre. He packed up the spatula and went over to the ward sink, filling a bowl with water.

He came over and settled himself down again, starting to stroke the foot with a cloth soaked and wrung through. Tighe felt the chill of the water and the strangely sensual action of the cloth over his tingling skin.

'Having a person to wash your feet!' Vievre exclaimed, still not meeting Tighe's eyes. 'Only the Popes themselves have such pleasure, such luxesse.'

Anxious now for conversation that would lead him away from the painfully personal subject on which they had just touched, Tighe asked, 'Master Vievre, you say *Pope*. What is Pope? Is it a Prince?'

'What do you mean by *preense*?'

Tighe thought for a little about the best way to answer this question with his limited language. Finally he said, 'If society is a body, then, the Prince is the head. Prince and Priest and Doge are the three heads.' He thought of adding that his pahe – his *father* – had been Prince of his village, but for some reason he decided it was wiser to keep that information to himself.

Vievre shook his head gently, wringing the cloth again over the bowl of water. 'Your words are ugly words in your language, I think. But Pope is moncher, true. They are head of the body, of the Empire. You have three, we have three.'

'The Prince is head,' said Tighe. 'Priest is head for God. Doge is for', but he did not know the word for trade so he trailed off.

Vievre seemed to grow larger as he spoke, to breathe in more deeply and hold his shoulders back. He said, 'The Empire is in the hands of the mighty Three Popes. A Law Pope, a Pope Espitpul and a War Pope. But the Empire is a large land, it stretches many many miles up and down the worldwall, many many miles east and west. Where we are most at war, that is where the War Pope is mostly – and now he is here, he is Law, Espivre and War in one person.'

'Espivre,' asked Tighe. 'That word. It means God?'

'It is here,' said Vievre, tapping his head with his free hand. 'In here.' He gestured towards his chest. 'That is Espivre.'

'Soul,' said Tighe.

Vievre shrugged with his eyebrows, and went back to washing Tighe's foot. 'The Soul Pope is in the Imperial City now,' he said. 'There she is at the heart. The Law Pope, he is many miles downwall. That is land we eparven last year and the last year before.'

'Eparven?'

Vievre stood now, carrying the bowl back to the sink and emptying it. 'We took in war. It is Empire now. It has a large need of law and the Law Pope is there.' He turned. 'And now your foot is clean and you are ready to meet Cardinelle Elanne.'

Tighe was starting to intuit some sense of the structure and hierarchy of the Imperial Army. Under the Pope, it seemed that the Cardinelles had the most power. Beneath that were Caponelles and Prelettes, and other junior officers. So many ranks, so many levels of command, spoke of an army more enormous than Tighe could easily imagine. Thousands, Vievre said. Thousands.

4

Cardinelle Elanne came early in the next day. He was a small man, much smaller than Tighe expected, but there was a fat *prise* bone tied around his neck with a leather strap. His hair was woven together into thick strands like crude cloth and tied at the back. His skin was wrinkled and he was clearly old, but he wore no beard. Looking at him, Tighe realised that he had seen no beards at all since waking in this ward.

'I am pleased to meet you, Sayonar Tig-he,' said the Cardinelle. He was attended by two blue-uniformed soldiers, who waited several steps behind. One of these was carrying a small case; at a signal from the Cardinelle she opened the thing, pulling legs from the underside to create a small stool. It seemed to be made of wood, except that Tighe could hardly believe a material so valuable would be used in the construction of something as menial as a stool.

The Cardinelle positioned the stool and sat down. 'You fell from the sky,' he said slowly, speaking each word carefully. 'It is a miracle that you are alive at all.'

'I know this,' said Tighe.

'We sent scouts up in a calabash. There is no settlement directly up the wall for many miles. How long did you fall for?'

'I don't know,' said Tighe.

The Cardinelle seemed to think that Tighe had failed to understand his words. 'What I mean by that question', he said, more slowly, 'is what period of time? How long did your fall last you?'

'I understand your question, Master Cardinelle,' said Tighe, meekly. 'But I do not know the time. I do not remember.'

The Cardinelle was staring at him with an unsettling, unblinking stare. 'It must have been a long time, I think.'

'A long time.'

'Were you ventien at all? East? West?'

Tighe blushed. 'I do not know these words.'

'*East*,' said Vievre, 'leftward – west, rightward. Were you *ventien* left-ward or rightward as you fell?'

'I do not know this word, Master Cardinelle,' said Tighe, in a small voice.

'Ventien,' repeated Elanne briskly. He blew through pursed lips, then blew on his hand and mimed it being pushed back by the current of air.

'Ventien,' said Tighe, understanding. *Blown.*

'Yes. Were you blown at all by the wind as you fell? Perhaps you derit-nabur from some land far to the east or west above us. We do not know.'

'I do not know. The wind blown me up a little, sometimes the falling felt less – less falling,' said Tighe.

Cardinelle Elanne puffed noisily. 'The wind *blew*,' he corrected. 'But anyway. Are you from a large land? Your people – they have an army?'

'A village,' said Tighe.

'What word is this?'

'A small land,' said Tighe.

'And your army?'

'We have no army.'

This was so astonishing to the Cardinelle that he made Tighe repeat it twice. 'But what happens when you are at war?' he pressed.

Tighe thought how to phrase himself. 'Once, when I am boy,' he started, 'there were', but he couldn't think of the word for *bandits*, 'bad men, women, they come to take goats and things. Then two, three villages gather men and women together, and they fight the bad men, women. Then they dead, thrown away off world, and men, women are able to go to work again.'

Elanne became increasingly impatient during the course of Tighe's halting explanation, and started waving his hand as if he would wave away the whole narrative. He said something very rapidly, out of which Tighe only caught the words 'small' and 'story-telling', then he paused and said, 'Your doctor. He says you are better.'

'Much better.' In fact Tighe had started the morning with another half-supported walk about the ward, his first with his cast off. It hurt in a jagged sort of way when he put too much pressure on his left foot, but otherwise it was not bad.

'Good. Abliou, get up. Get up now and show me how you walk with your mended foot.'

Vievre, who had been hovering in the background throughout the interview, started forward to help Tighe up off the mattress, but the Cardinelle held out his arm and Vievre stopped in his paces. It was clear that Elanne expected Tighe to get up himself.

Tighe sat up and pulled his left foot underneath him. Pushing with his hands against the floor and straining with his right leg, he lurched up a little way, collapsed back on to the mattress, and tried again. On his third attempt he wobbled unsteadily to his feet, lurched forward and had to hop several times to avoid falling over. The Cardinelle did not move from his stool, only moving his head to follow Tighe's progress with an unblinking gaze.

Once Tighe got going it wasn't so hard. He was able to hobble, brushing his left foot against the floor and then falling back on to the right with each lopsided step. He made a painstaking circuit and came back to the mattress.

The Cardinelle nodded, once, as Tighe stood resting his poor foot on top of the good one. 'You can walk.'

'Not good,' said Tighe.

'Good enough. Flatar hardly need their legs anyway. You are talked about all through the army, little boy. It is a good omen that you fell on us as we embrolal here and it is a very good omen for the sky army. Everyone agrees, so you will become flatar. You will train quickly, I'm afraid to say, but that is dioparad manifolle of things. But your flatar platon will treasure you as a good omen.'

He stood up briskly. One of the Cardinelle's soldiers collected the stool on which he had been sitting and folded it back up. The Cardinelle made a single jerking gesture with his head, bending it forward and back again. He turned and made the same gesture to Vievre, who virtually fell forward upon the floor to bow low in return.

He marched to the door. 'Prelette Vievre,' he announced. 'You have worked well at bringing health to this omen-boy. He will bring luck in the campaign. Say your goodbyes to him tonight.'

Much later that day, with what amounted almost to tenderness, Vievre took Tighe through his last language lesson, and explained as much as he could about the army. 'It will be different tomorrow,' he said. 'They will train you in your platon.'

'What is platon?'

'A part of the army. Larger than the smallest part. You will have brothers, sisters there.'

'But no father!' Tighe declared. He found that he was crying. It was stupid to cry, but there you are.

Vievre's own eyes were bulging with moisture. 'Your platon chief will be father,' he said. 'You will fly again – they choose you for the flatar because you are small, thin. Flatar need to be small because the flat cannot carry much weight. But they choose you also because you have flown – flown here like a little bird. Fallen here.'

'No father!' repeated Tighe. 'None like you!'

Vievre gave himself over at this point and started crying as well. 'My purepul little bird,' he said, putting his arms around Tighe's neck. 'To lose you!'

'I will come here', said Tighe, 'many times to say good new day to you, Vievre.'

'Only if you are ill, I think,' said Vievre. 'Only that would be allowed. But never mind! Never mind! You will have a new family. You will have training. You will fly.'

He sat in silence for a long while.

The two of them ate together, sharing an evening meal. As the day moved to its close the light through the open door bulked, darkened. The patch of light cast by the sun through the doorway shrank away faster than a snail could crawl, as if it wanted to leave the ward, until eventually it was gone altogether. Vievre stood up in the dusk and lit one of the wall candles before pulling a door shut. For a while they sat in silence as the dusk winds grew and thrummed on the far side. Eventually Vievre spoke.

'I will tell you this, my little bird,' he said. 'I had a son and a daughter.'

'You had a son and a daughter,' repeated Tighe.

'When my daughter was navien, my son became – you will not know the word. We have a word to describe it, othalpul. Angry, unhappy with the girl. That the girl was there. He had been the only one, now he was the second – oldest, yes, but my daughter was more balienette. This made him angry. Do you follow?'

'I think so,' said Tighe, although in truth he didn't really understand what it was Vievre was telling him.

'He was a boy, only a boy. Then one day he pushed his sister off the world. He was only a boy, you see, and I think in his head', and Vievre tapped his own head to force the point, 'he only thought: she will be gone and I will be first again in the family. I think he had no thought to kill her, you see. He was only a boy.'

Tighe said nothing. Vievre sighed.

'She was small and he was small too; but he was big enough to do this wrong. He pushed her away and she fell. In that part of the Imperial City where we lived was the ward, near the army house and the trulano. That's a place where the City is layered on a slope, so that each ledge from below sticks out further. It is like that for ten or twelve ledges, so my daughter only fell a little way. But she was small and boudun and she broke many bones. She lived a week and then she died. But I think he had no thought to kill her and after he was very sad. There was real pain, I think, in his head,' and again Vievre made the gesture, tapping his head, 'not headache but his feelings, you know? We say: confla.'

'Conscience,' said Tighe.

Vievre was silent.

'What did you do?' asked Tighe.

Vievre shrugged with his shoulders and made his way over to the door to fit the windbreak. The howl of the evening winds was starting to become audible. As he wedged the panel in place he said nothing, then he returned to Tighe's mattress and sat himself, cross-legged, on the floor.

'In the Empire there is only one treatment' – he used the medical word – 'for such a thing. For cramla, for killing another, in your family or in the city. Even if it is a child who cramla deriginal, it is the same. If an adult kills, the adult is cast off the world. That is the law. If a child kills, it is the same. My son was crying, saying again and again how he had killed.' Vievre was looking at the floor; without raising his head he made the shrugging gesture with his shoulders. 'My son was thrown off the world for what he did. So now I have no daughter and no son.'

A silence settled between them again. Tighe wanted to say something, felt uncomfortable in the speechlessness of the moment, but wasn't sure what to say. Eventually he asked, in a tiny voice, 'You have a wife still?'

'I have two wives, as is right for a man of my position. But they were very unhappy with what happened. Very saddened. Now they live together in the Imperial City and I am with the army. The air between me and my wives', he made a nonspecific gesture with his right hand, 'it is not good. Sick, now. They and I cannot be together long without shouting and swearing.' He looked up and Tighe was a little shocked to see that he was smiling. 'But I go to war soon, and maybe there I will find another wife. With another wife, maybe more children. War makes many things possible.'

The candle threw shuddering patches of light on the floor and walls and roof of the ward. For a while Tighe watched the pattern.

After a long silence, Vievre got slowly to his feet. His joints creaked and sang as he rose. 'Anyway, my little bird,' he said, in a soft voice, 'I think it is that, well, with you I dreamt of my boy *flying* – do you see? You fell and you are alive. Perhaps he fell, past the Downwall Lands of the empire, past the empty stretch below – fell many miles, perhaps. But maybe he is still alive somewhere, far far downwall. Maybe he lived, somehow, and now has a new life. You are a good omen, they say. Perhaps you bring luck to us all.'

And he squashed the candle flame between finger and thumb like killing a butterfly, lay down on a mattress by the wall and fell asleep.

5

In the morning Tighe practised some more walking, making several circuits leaning on Vievre's shoulder, and several more hobbling along by himself. 'It will get easier with use,' said Vievre.

He seemed subdued and Tighe could think of nothing to say to cheer him up.

At some point in the morning a young girl came in with a bundle: it was a rolled-up blue tunic that stretched down almost to Tighe's knees. She also had some leggings, but they proved much too baggy and she went away again to fetch a smaller size. 'You will need the clothing,' said Vievre mournfully. 'Flatar feel the cold, out in the air. You should wear as much clothing as you can get.'

Tighe nodded at this. When the girl returned with the smaller leggings she was accompanied by a uniformed boy. He was taller than Tighe, but skinny and angular. His skin was also less sick-looking, although not as dark as a normal complexion. He marched through the door and struck a particular stance, planting his feet an arm apart and putting both hands on his hips. 'I am flatar,' he said, putting his head on one side. 'My name is Ati. I have been told to come fetch the bird-boy. He is to be trained as a flatar and fight in the war against the enemy.'

'Here he is,' said Vievre, 'as you can see with your own eyes if you weren't acting so mensona. What did you say your name was?'

'Ati,' said the boy, a little taken aback. He shifted his stance so that it was angled towards Vievre. 'I have orders.'

'Ati,' said Vievre. 'Is that a Downwall name? You have a Downwall look about you.'

'My family', said the newcomer, with a little spurt of pride, 'are from downwall, it is true.'

'All Downwallers are the same,' Vievre said loudly. 'You are all bad. I never met anybody from that far downwall who is good. My little bird,' he turned to Tighe, 'believe me. God puts culpaiden further down the wall, further away from Him. I was born upwall from the Imperial City and so I know.'

110

'My family is a good family,' said Ati, outraged.

'You are shit, as all Downwallers are,' said Vievre, his temper rising. 'Your family is shit as well. Shit falls downwall, as the proverb has it, and you are proof of that. Do you contradict me?'

'Have you ever travelled downwall?' demanded the boy.

'Ati – my rank is Prelette. Are you calling a superior a liar?' Vievre was speaking very loudly now. 'I will report you – I have met the Air Cardinelle of the whole army. I *will* report you for pride and un-army behaviour.'

'Sir,' said Ati, in a quavery voice, 'I meant nothing, only . . .'

'Shut up! This boy is as a son to me,' said Vievre, gesturing with both his hands. 'You will watch him, estarre him, treat him well. If not, you will be thrown off the wall! Shut up!'

There was a frozen moment. Then Ati saluted – Tighe was later to learn that this gesture, a touching of the forehead with the hand, was an Imperial army tradition, from a junior to a superior. 'Sir,' said Ati in a dull voice, 'I have orders to bring the sky-boy to the flatar house. He will be trained and will become an assievre to the flatar platon.'

'I know he will,' growled Vievre. But when he turned to embrace Tighe, there were tears in his eyes. 'Goodbye, my little bird,' he said. 'Go with this boy, even if he is downwall shit. And you,' he said, turning again on Ati, 'take care of this boy.'

With that Vievre dashed out of the ward, with Tighe and Ati staring after him in varying degrees of astonishment. For a moment there was silence and then Ati turned to Tighe.

'You,' he said. 'Sky-boy. Will you please to come with me?'

They stepped through the door and on to the ledge outside. It was a bright morning, the sun was below their feet and shining straight up into their eyes. Briefly Tighe couldn't see anything other than the great wash of white light, the heart of silence and a clear morning. There was the hush in his ears of morning air settling after the dawn flurries. Then he blinked and his eyes adjusted. The boy Ati was standing next to him, looking at him strangely.

'Your doctor has gone I think,' he said.

Tighe scowled at him. 'My foot hurts very,' he said.

Ati snorted. 'My foot hurts very!' he mimicked. 'My foot hurts *badly*, you ignorant barbarian. Your hair is stupid. How do you keep your head warm with that stupid hair? It looks like grass, it is so feeble.'

Tighe felt a wave of weariness go through him. His foot was throbbing uncomfortably. He leaned against the jamb of the ward door and breathed out. 'Is it far to walk?'

Ati picked something out of a pouch from around his neck, slotted it into his mouth and started chewing. 'Far?' he said. 'Not far. You smell funny. I don't *like* your smell. I'll tell you something, you *azhnazd* barbarian.' Tighe felt certain that word wasn't part of the Imperial language. It didn't sound right. Ati spat a little globule of black spittle from his mouth. 'I'll tell you something. When you get to the platon, you won't have any high-rank doctor to look after you like a mummy-mummy. You'll have Waldea and he's a hard father. And you'll have *us*, you little barbarian, with your golzg hair and funny smell.' He was suddenly in motion, striding away along the narrow ledge and Tighe hurriedly bundled himself into a halting limp behind, trying to keep up.

'Hold!' he called. 'So fast! Wait!'

The ledge sloped down, rimmed with wild mushrooms growing on the far edge. They turned a dog-leg and rounded a spur of the worldwall, and suddenly – breathtakingly – the whole base was laid out before them. Tighe forgot his discomfort for the moment in the splendour of it.

He had never seen anything like it.

The landscape was a series of ripples across the face of the worldwall; perhaps it had been a village once, although now it was entirely taken over by the military. Tighe could see that ledges had been dug through, diagonals had been excavated, narrow crags had been bulked up with planks of what looked like wood (but surely couldn't be!). Doors led into the world and there was a single broad shelf away below him. Presumably the shelf was the reason why the military had been attracted to the place to begin with. But what really caught Tighe's eye was the sheer number of people.

There were more people than he could count; people diminished by the distance to the size of fingers, of insects, all dressed in blue. There must have been hundreds. Tighe had never seen so many human beings in one place together before. They swarmed along every ledge, and congregated in a mass on the shelf.

And there, moored off the shelf, were what – in a flash of understanding – Tighe recognised were the calabashes Vievre had talked about. There were half a dozen enormous spheres, bright blue with red lizard stripes running vertically. They looked like perfectly round pebbles, painted and polished, except that they were so huge. But what was most unsettling about them was the way they simply hung in the air. Like clouds made solid: painted clouds made solid and smoothed by the fingers of God into perfectly spherical shapes.

Tighe paused, and stepped closer to the edge, dropping a little to steady his balance. He wanted a better look at the scene. He could see there were ropes draped from each calabash to the shelf, some drooping, one drawn tight. There were two little wooden (again: could it really be *wood*?) piers poking out from the wall, and there were even people making their way along the precarious walkway. That was because – Tighe could see – there were what looked like pots hanging from underneath the calabashes. Perhaps the calabashes could go up and down according to some method, carrying the people beneath them as passengers. It was breathtaking.

The globes, he could see, were not steady in the air as he first thought. One of them was drifting very slowly towards the wall. It bumped gently into its neighbour, and Tighe saw the skin of the great sphere buckle like flesh. So, they were soft, like big fat bellies hanging in space.

So, that was why the fall hadn't killed him. He shut his eyes, trying to remember. There were only confused images in his mind.

He dropped to his haunches and put his hand out to steady himself. His foot was throbbing, and the prospect of going over the ledge and falling again was horrific to him; but he wanted to take a closer look at these astonishing sky devices. His hand squelched on some of the wild mushrooms growing at the limit of the ledge and he swept away a patch.

'Hey!'

It was the boy Ati yelling at him. 'Hey! Sky-boy! Take care!'

'What?'

Ati was running up towards him. 'Watch where you're stepping.'

Tighe had been so overawed by the sight below him that he had forgotten about Ati. He leant towards the wall and got cumbrously to his feet. 'What is it?'

'What are you doing with those chemmia?'

'What?'

Ati was beside him now, breathing heavily from having sprinted up the ledge. 'Are you crazy? Destroying the chemmia like that is a punishment offence. You want they should throw you off the wall?'

'I don't understand.'

'Understand this, barbarian. You may be the sky-boy, the good omen for this campaign. But they'll throw you off the world as well as anybody if they discover you destroying the chemmia.'

'Chemmia?'

With a little squeal of frustration, Ati gestured at the mushrooms. 'Those!'

'They're only mushrooms,' said Tighe.

'That's right,' said Ati, grabbing Tighe's arm. 'Now leave them alone. They're military mushrooms.' And he hauled him away.

Tighe yelped with pain and it took several steps of this enforced pace before he could slip into his halting limp. 'Wait,' he said. 'They would throw me off the world for a few mushrooms?'

'You don't know anything?'

'Wait,' said Tighe, trying to catch his breath, to get into his stride. 'Why? For mushrooms? Why.'

'They're military mushrooms. Do you really not know?'

'I really not know.'

Ati let go of his arm, and spat over the ledge. 'You're supposed to bring luck, you know. If you don't bring luck, then what are you?'

'Tell me about the mushrooms,' said Tighe.

'They make fire.'

'Fire?'

'The army take the mushrooms and dry them. They have a – a –' he stopped, and then positively shouted with frustration. 'I do not know the Imperial word for it! In my family's tongue it is burzhum. It is, like, earth – yes, Dry? Dry, small, much of it. Plants have it and they put it in the air, and it goes in the air to another place and settles in the earth and new mushrooms grow.'

'I know what you mean,' said Tighe, leaning against the wall on his right to rest his bad foot. 'I do not know the word for it either. It is a kind of *dust*,' he added, using his native word.

Ati shrugged. 'This burzhum, this *dusht*, when it is dry, is packed in boxes and cases. With a flame it makes fire – great fire.' He clapped his hands together and shouted *Bah!* so loud that Tighe jumped. 'It is in the army's weaponry. We have rifette in the army, and they are filled with the burzhum. That is how the weaponry works.'

Tighe didn't follow all of this. But he nodded.

'So,' said Ati. He stretched himself, straightening his posture. He appeared to have used up some of his anger. 'The mushrooms are very important. We grow them everywhere we go, you know,' he said, suddenly speaking confidingly. 'We could not make war without them, you know.'

'And we make war,' said Tighe.

'Soon,' said Ati.

'Who?' asked Tighe, meaning *against whom*? But Ati was off again, down the ledge.

They went down and down until they were on the shelf itself, weaving a way through the mess of people. Tighe was almost hypnotised by the enormity of the calabash bellies. He did not watch where he was going and bumped into several people.

'Watch it,' growled a man, pushing him to one side. The shelf thronged, people coming back and forth, criss-crossing and passing one another in an elegant dance. Tighe tried to concentrate on where he was going, but his eye was snared again and again by the great spheres hanging over him. The sun was rising level to them and throwing enormous patches of shadow against the wall. He could see the pots hung underneath the sphere clearly now; twice the height of a man, like a small house with a doorway and several slit windows. Each appeared to be built of dark wood – the army's use of wood was astonishing, just astonishing. They carried a fortune in wood about them, used it for menial tasks.

Ati was by his side again. 'You're slow,' he said.

'My foot hurts badly,' he said.

Ati shrugged. 'Come over to the wall', he said, 'and rest.' They made their way wallwards and Tighe sat down. Ati took something else from his pouch and chewed it. 'You see that spur?' he said.

He was pointing towards the far end of the shelf. Tighe nodded.

'Just past there is the platon. There are the flatar.'

'OK,' said Tighe. 'We can go there.'

At the end of the shelf there was a man-made walkway set into the spur that led round it: it was a little rickety and difficult to manoeuvre with only one good leg, but Tighe took it carefully and then they were on the other side.

The flatar platon was based on a broad singleton, only reachable by the walkway round the spur. Half a dozen boys were dancing, it seemed, in formation, and stacked against the wall behind them were half a dozen man-sized kites.

6

Ati led Tighe past the boys – not dancing, Tighe could see now, but all going through the same ritualised motions, as if training – to an opening in the wall behind them. This doorway led into a long, narrow space, with grass mattresses on the floor all the way along. The floor was uneven and the walls still marked with the ridges and scratches of spade-work. It had evidently only recently been dug out.

'Ati?' called a figure from the far end.

'Master!' replied Ati briskly. 'Here he is.'

The figure came bundling up through the shadow until, as he approached Tighe and the light from the door touched him, his features came into view.

He was a short man, his torso as round as one of the calabashes that still lingered in Tighe's imagination. The shadows of the room made peculiar patterns on his face; but, no, it wasn't that: he was scarred, the skin twisted and pulled as if in fright. Or caught in a powerful wind; although, as Tighe looked more closely, he could see there was a dead, waxy gleam to the white skin that made it look wrong, frozen in its peculiar tourbillons. The man stared at Tighe, his expression unreadable underneath its disfigurement.

'You're it,' he said. His voice was much more high-pitched than Tighe was expecting.

Ati squirmed, nudged Tighe. 'Say, "Yes Master",' he hissed.

'Yes, Master,' said Tighe.

For long moments this man kept him under his eye. Then he said: 'I'm Waldea. I am Captain here and you are mine. Life and death. That is how the army is. Do you understand?'

'Yes, Master,' said Tighe.

'You speak the language well,' said Waldea, scratching at the folds of skin on his face.

Tighe didn't know if he was supposed to reply. He kept quiet.

'Come,' said Waldea abruptly, stepping forward and grabbing Tighe around the waist. Tighe was so startled he gave a little gasp of fear, but Waldea had him tight round the waist. It was an intimate, unsettling embrace; Tighe's face was crushed into the blue fabric of the man's uniform. Waldea's smell was large in his nostrils, sweat and a smell of the grass-oil, plus something astringent and unpleasant, something bitter like spikenard pieces in a soup.

Waldea hauled Tighe up into the air and held him there. This squeezed the air from Tighe's lungs and he gasped. Then the man put him back on the floor and let go of him. Tighe came down hard on his bad foot and staggered a little bit when released, but he kept his balance. In the light thrown through the door by the midday sun, he could see a tiny dark patch on Waldea's uniform where his spittle had marked it.

'Good,' whistled Waldea. 'You're light – very light.'

'But,' said Tighe and stopped.

'Yes, Master,' put in Ati, and nudged Tighe again.

'Yes, Master,' he gasped.

'You're thin,' said Waldea, scratching his ruined face again. He seemed pleased by this. 'That's excellent for flying. That's the only matter I care about. You're a village boy, I suppose.'

'Yes,' said Tighe.

Waldea nodded his approval. 'Those small villages, there's never enough food to go round. Everybody starves a bit. It keeps the people nice and light.'

Tighe, recovering from the shock of being grabbed, felt a spark of outrage. 'I'm a Prince in my village,' he said.

Waldea wrinkled up his already grotesquely lined face. 'What's that word?'

'It's like *Pope*,' said Tighe, trying to sound self-important.

'Is it? Like *king*? We get all types of people in this army. The army doesn't care if you are *preense* or *king* or *pope*. I am all those things to you. Do you understand?'

Tighe breathed in. 'Yes,' he said.

'Come outside.' Waldea pushed past him and went through the door. Tighe limped after him and Ati fell into step beside him.

'That's your Master now,' he whispered to Tighe. 'Don't make him angry.'

'What's ill with his face?' Tighe hissed back.

Because he was looking at Ati, Tighe didn't see Waldea's fist coming. He had a thundering sensation of impact on the side of his head and a blast of pain and a high, whistling, ringing noise. Then he was on the floor, the trodden dirt of the ledge pressed up against the side of his face. Fiery pain was in his head and everything else about him felt numb.

He became aware of somebody's fingers grabbing at his arm. He lifted his face from the ground and reached round with one hand to touch his throbbing ear. He could see Ati crouched beside him, saying something, his face creased with concern. With Ati's help he sat up and brushed the dirt from the side of his face. His ear hurt sharply, but the screeching sound inside his head was fading. He tried to focus on what was being said. 'I told you so, you barbarian,' Ati was hissing. 'Come on, come up to your feet.'

Shakily, Tighe allowed himself to be hauled up standing again.

Waldea was standing in front of him, arms at his side. 'You do not', he said, his voice high-pitched but calm, 'talk about my face. You do not talk about my face. Do you understand? If you anger *me*, I will *throw* you off the world.'

'Yes, Master,' said Tighe, stunned.

'Shut up and come.' He turned and stalked over to the wall, where the large kites were stacked. Tighe followed him, limping, his hand over his sore ear.

'Now,' said Waldea loudly, turning to face Tighe again. Tighe could see all the other kite-boys. They were staring at him.

'Now,' said Waldea, 'have you ever seen a *kite* before.'

Flatar. Tighe nodded. He knew kites. One of his friends had owned a toy one, back in the village and had flown it in the early morning when the air was rising. It was a toy.

'I'll say this only once,' said Waldea. 'You don't *nod* to me like an idiot baby.'

'No, Master,' said Tighe sharply.

'*Do you know* kites?'

'Yes, Master.'

'Man-kites, like these? Or just the little, cadheo ones?'

'Little ones, Master.'

Waldea nodded. 'These are man-kites. They are war-kites. I have my orders, from the Cardinelle himself, that we are to train you to fly one of these, just like the kite-boys and kite-girls over there.' He gestured with one arm and Tighe followed with his eyes. 'Back to the exercise!' Waldea bellowed at them. 'All of you!' They scurried back into formation. Waldea directed his attention back to Tighe.

'I have orders and we will train you. You will be bad at it because we don't have much time to train you. But I always follow my orders.'

There was a pause, and Tighe didn't know whether to say *yes, Master* or not.

'Your arms are weak,' Waldea said. 'You need stronger arms to fly kites in war. So you will start by carrying stones.' He pointed to a pile of large rocks just beyond the stack of kites. 'Carry them to the other side of this ledge and put them by the wall. Do you understand?'

'Yes, Master.'

'*Carry* them, yes? *Don't* rest them against your hip or your belly. Carry them out – away from your body. You want to make your muscles big. Do you understand?'

'Yes, Master.'

Tighe spent the rest of the afternoon doing the task given him by Waldea. The first rock was not too hard, even with Tighe's bad left foot and his limping gait. He hauled it up, held it away from his torso and staggered away to dump it on the far side. The second was harder, the third harder still. By the fourth his skin was oozing with sweat, his head hammered pain out from his ear, his bad foot blazed with every step. He could see that Waldea was still watching him, so he took care to hold the rock away from his body. But he could only make agonisingly slow progress, step, halt, step, halt.

When he dumped this fourth stone he had to stop. Then he limped his way back over to the original pile. With a relief so acute it was almost like pain itself, he saw Waldea walk away and go back inside to the dorm. Without his new Master's fearsome eye upon him, Tighe hefted another rock, balanced it against his hip and made his way more easily towards the far pile.

He moved twelve in all, by which stage he was so exhausted he could barely stand up. He sat down by the pile and rested, his head hanging between his spread knees, his breath coming in gulps. There were little cuts on the palms of his hands from grasping the rocks, and his hip hurt.

Waldea came back out and Tighe struggled guiltily to his feet. 'How many?' the Master bellowed.

'Twelve, Master,' replied Tighe.

Waldea snorted and went back inside.

Within an hour Tighe's whole body was aching so badly it felt as if his muscles had turned to stone. All the boys and girls in the platon gathered just outside the doorway with the sun high in the sky, giggling and whispering amongst themselves, staring at Tighe. He was too tired to care.

Waldea himself carried out two long, narrow cauldrons with metal handles over their mouths, one in each hand. He dumped them down, and one of the kite-boys followed him with an armful of small bowls. Each of these bowls was filled with the soup from the cauldrons: a grass soup with lumps of meat floating in it: insects, but also chunks of flesh from some larger animal that Tighe didn't recognise by taste.

Tighe felt so weary he assumed he would fall asleep at once. But when Waldea finally shepherded the whole platon into the room and sent them to bed, the strangeness of his environment and his sense of anticipation, not to mention the pain in his limbs, kept him awake.

Once they were all wrapped in their blankets Waldea went back out, closing the tight door behind him. It was very dark. As soon as they were alone in the dormitory, excited whispers from the platon danced through the air, boy and girl passing the hissing up and down along the line. Some of the words were unfamiliar to Tighe, but he understood the bulk of it. Was the new boy really the sky-boy, the boy who had fallen from the sky? Of course, idiot, who did you think? But his hair! The smell! His skin! Did you see how badly he carried the rocks – how weak his arms were? Did you see how the Master beat him on the head? Several people giggled, their repressed laughs coming out as little bursts of *shh-shh-shh*. He must have done something to make the Master so angry. *I* walked him over, hissed Ati. *I* know him. He's stupid, a barbarian. He doesn't know anything. You're a barbarian yourself, Ati-smati, hissed somebody else, you stinking downwaller, and everybody laughed, the giggles more audible and rippling through the room. Shit falls downwall, hissed somebody else, and the laughter started again.

Then the door scraped open and Waldea came back in. 'Quiet!' he commanded and there was silence. Then there was nothing but Waldea fitting the dawn-door against the evening gales, until he too settled down and went to sleep.

7

Tighe carried rocks and practised movements with his body for five full days. For the first of these days every movement was an agony, but by the end he was more used to the exercise and it came a little more easily.

He quickly got used to the routine, to the way the days were harder edged, the way the tasks and the rituals of living were squeezed into a pattern dictated by military routine. It seemed that everything in the army (outside the hospital ward) was run by the clock. But the army clock was unlike the clocks he had known in the village, which divided the day into ten hours, marked out as portions of a circle. The army used a sundial and divided the day into degrees, from small angles in the morning to large ones at the end of the day. Fifty degrees was midday, a hundred meant the sun had disappeared over the top of the wall.

And so the day was organised. At this hour (fifteen) food, at this hour (thirty) exercise, hauling stones to build the muscles in the arms and shoulders. This was a regular exercise that everybody had to do; and after his first week Tighe joined the others. He no longer hauled all day, but only in the morning.

By fifty the sun was level with the ledge and had heated the air enough – so they told Tighe – to produce updraughts. That was the way the world was constructed, they told him. The blaze of the sun heated the air and the heated air went up – seeking God, said Ati, who turned out to be devout, although devout in a religion that Tighe did not recognise. One of the other kite-boys, called Mulvaine, told him that this same principle was behind the operation of the calabashes. Their great sewn sacks were filled with hot air and that hot air strained to move up the wall. Seeking God, said Ati again. Tighe wondered about sharing with the others what he had learned in the village: that God did not sit on top of the wall, but huddled at the bottom, hurling the sun over the battlement. But he didn't trust any of his fellow kite-boys enough to mention something so heretical – he didn't know how seriously the Empire took religious orthodoxy. Sometimes they treated him well, but then sometimes they mocked his accent and his skin, pulled at his hair and punched him.

But the hour was fifty and Waldea was hurrying the boys to their kites.

'Ravielre!' he would shout. 'No evening meal for you, you're too fat – and Bel! . . . too long in the bone now, you've only few months of kite-flying left you, you're getting too big. Nothing to be done, and no use in crying there – some people grow too big to fly the kites. Let's hope the war comes on and you get a chance to fly in combat.'

The other boys and girls flew their kites every day for practice; but in the beginning, after his first week, Waldea put Tighe into a sort of stationary frame. The frame was made all of wood – more wood than Tighe had ever seen before all in one place, just one more example of the army's incredible profligacy with wood. It was like four door frames put together to make a wall-less room, and inside a series of leather and ropes draped over the top and fed down to heavy stones. Inside Tighe was strapped as if to a kite, and made to go through various manoeuvres, to control the kite, to angle it and steer it.

'Tig-he,' yelled Waldea, working his grotesque face, 'you're more the shape. Thin, you see! You're more the shape for a kite-boy! Those village boys who eat nothing but grass, they don't get *fat* like you other city boys and girls.'

Tighe worked and worked in the frame until his every joint ached and there were blisters on his back. At night, in the dormitory with all the others, there would be an hour when Waldea left the platon alone and everybody would whisper excitedly amongst themselves. For days Tighe was too timid to join in, but soon enough he was being asked direct questions. The voices came from all directions.

'Where you from, sky-boy?'

'Why is your skin that colour?'

'Did you fall from the sky – really?'

'Yes,' said Tighe.

'Ooh! Ooh!'

'Fallen from the sky!'

'What was it like?' asked one of the kite-girls, a tangled-haired individual called Mani. Tighe recognised her voice from the chatter in the darkness at night.

'I don't remember very,' said Tighe. 'I fell for a long time.'

'Listen to his *accent*,' hissed somebody on the other side of the room. 'How *stupid*.'

Ati blurted out, 'I spoke to him a long time. He is stupid, he don't know nothing, he speaks funny.'

'You speak funny yourself, downwaller,' shushed somebody.

'You rederen off a calabash,' said somebody else.

'What's rederen?' asked Tighe, trying to be bolder.

There were muffled shrieks of laughter, mockery. 'Don't you know *anything*?'

'Rederen is *boing boing*,' said somebody else.

Soon everybody had joined in. *Boing boing boing*. They were all laughing so hard the volume level was getting higher and higher. Then the door was open and the Master was coming back through. The laughter dissipated immediately.

'Sleep now,' he said.

The kite-girls, five of them, tended to keep themselves to themselves; when they weren't exercising or practising they would sit together and play variations of the same game over and over – slapping their palms together and slapping one another's palms in complicated patterns whilst chanting something. Tighe couldn't catch the words.

The dozen kite-boys were more boisterous, or at least they were when Waldea wasn't looking. They bickered and fought amongst themselves, threw pebbles at one another (as well as at Tighe), taunted each other. Only the presence of Waldea brought any discipline to their group.

One morning as Tighe was extricating himself from his blanket ready for the morning food, one of the boys leapt upon him, pulled down his leggings in an instant and gave his wick a sharp, painful tug. The humiliation of it as much as the pain – although the pain was very real – made Tighe collapse in a bundle with tears in his eyes. Around him the air was filled with hilarity, whooping and mocking. Then it all fell silent. Waldea must have come back in.

'What are you doing Tig he, on the floor?' Tighe could tell, from the proximity of his voice, that he was standing over him. 'Why are your leggings down? It's disgusting, disgusting.'

Tighe hauled himself up, his eyes messy with tears. 'A boy pushed the leggings down,' he said. 'He hurt my penis. It was Mulvaine, I think.'

Waldea slapped him on the side of his head; not hard, but not soft either. 'Don't tell me so! Don't be a putavre! You are in the army, you look after yourself or not at all.'

But Tighe couldn't acquire the knack of looking after himself. He found himself crying most nights, silently to himself when he was wrapped up in his blanket. The other kite-boys took a particular pleasure in making him cry. But the strange thing was that, some days, the other kite-boys would be touchingly kind to him. He didn't understand it. Usually it was when Ati became the butt of sharp comments and practical jokes. One morning, when Waldea stepped out and the platon was supposed to be folding up their blankets and getting ready for breakfast, three boys jumped Ati. They pushed him down, for all his yelling, and squashed something on to his face, trying to get it into his mouth. 'Eat! Eat!' they called. Everybody gathered round, eager, excited: even the girls. Mulvaine put his arm round Tighe's shoulder, 'You see how we all hate the down-waller?' he said, smilingly. With a lurch in his stomach, Tighe realised that Ati's face was smeared now with shit; that somebody must have pushed out a turd in the night, and now they were trying to make Ati eat it. 'Shits falls downwall!' somebody crooned. 'Nice piece of breakfast for you,' called somebody else. Everybody was chattering, laughing. Ati struggled, grunting through clenched teeth. Tighe felt sick, sick from the thought of it and sick at the cruelty, but he also felt excited. It was thrilling in a strange way. He was laughing, just like the others; grinning, waving at the tangled mass of boys. He felt guilty at laughing, but he did it anyway.

Then, as suddenly as it had begun, it was over. Everybody was back at their mattresses, folding their blankets, smoothing down their hair and clothes. You could see which boys had been grappling with Ati, because they were wiping their hands on the floor and on their own leggings. Ati himself stood in the middle of the room in the half-light, his face darkened with shit. His whole body spoke misery, his slumped shoulders, his gash of a mouth.

'Ati,' bellowed Waldea, who had come back in, 'what is it with you? Do you want me to beat you?'

'I'm sorry, Master,' replied Ati. With another lurch in his belly, Tighe realised that the downwaller was close to tears.

'Everybody outside,' ordered Waldea. 'You all carry stones.' He looked at Ati. 'Disgusting! Disgusting! We'll make sure Ati here remembers to keep *clean*.'

And so they all went outside and carried stones. Some of the boys were grinning, squinting in the morning light, but Tighe wasn't. When Ati finally emerged to join in the exercises his face was clean of shit, but there was a large bruise, shit-coloured, on his cheek.

Tighe worked and worked in the frame until it became second nature, and the blisters on his back had broken and healed back over as tougher skin. Then one morning, as the other kite-boys and kite-girls assembled and fitted themselves into their kites ready for another practice, Waldea grabbed Tighe by the shoulder. 'Today you'll fly,' he said.

It was as simple as that.

He was given his kite, the real kite: a wooden cross with other wooden spars, the shape of a teardrop, as tall as Tighe himself and half as tall again.

The material covering the frame was a kind of leather, but a leather thinner, more flexible and tougher than any hide he had seen before.

Every kite-boy and kite-girl assembled their kites before flying them; slotted crossbar into mainbar, fed the smaller spars through, stretched the leather over the frame and pinned it into place. Tighe had done this before many times and now he did it again. Every member of the platon was sitting cross-legged on the ledge assembling his or her kite. Tighe went through the motions.

When assembled the kites were leant against the wall, to catch the sunlight to dry and stretch taut. Whilst this happened the platon went through a series of precise movements with their arms and legs. To loosen their limbs, get their muscles ready. It was these exercises that Tighe had seen when he first came round the spar.

Then he joined the line with the other kite-boys and kite-girls, gathering up his kite and moving to the edge of the ledge. Waldea stood behind him. It was all right. He tried not to think about what he was going to do. And then, there he was: standing on the very edge of the world and about to step off it. His stomach shrunk fiercely, his heart was squeezing and pulsing. He couldn't co-ordinate his limbs properly.

With a horrible sense of realisation he knew that he couldn't go through with this part of it. He just couldn't. He just couldn't. He stiffened, strained back; but Waldea's hand on his shoulder was rock. 'Into the harness, omen-boy,' said Waldea. His voice was thorny, pricking. Tighe slid his arms through the harness, felt the kite settle against his back; but his skin was numb, sweating. He couldn't do it.

Couldn't.

To his right Tighe could see Ati. The downwaller was fiddling with his chest, tracing a complex pattern with one of his thumbs. He caught Tighe's eye.

'Always bless myself before I go out,' he said, speaking loudly so that his words would carry over the shush of the rising wind. His cheek was flushed red, his pupils pin-sharp.

'No,' said Tighe, in a small voice. Then, louder: 'No, I can't.'

But Ati wasn't listening to him any more. Waldea was tying a cord to Ati's kite. He brought it over to Tighe's and fixed it. 'This cord', he said, 'links you with Ati's kite. He will guide you. Follow him, learn how to fly in the air, watch him and follow him.'

'No,' said Tighe. It was unbearable. The world shrank, span outwards. His vision was hollowing out. The wind seemed to have bored into his head, filling his inner ear. 'No,' he said.

'You'll feel different when you're up,' said Waldea, his mouth very close to Tighe's ear. Oddly, he didn't seem angry at Tighe's reluctance.

To Tighe's right kites were tumbling from the wall, falling into the void. The kite to the left of Ati's was hauled into the air by the wind, a figure strapped underneath. It wavered in the air, then ducked down out of sight. It was too much for Tighe to bear.

Tighe felt it all rushing inside him, an overwhelming upward push in his body as if his guts were hollow and possessed by the upward gushing air. Then his gullet convulsed and he was vomiting.

'Puking?' screeched Waldea in his weirdly high-pitched voice. 'Disgusting! Disgusting! Away with you.' But he didn't push Tighe away; instead he grabbed the crossbeam of his kite and pulled him down, tipping him at an angle, letting the stream dribble from the boy's lips to the dirt at the lip of the ledge.

Tighe closed his eyes, the misery of vomiting distracting his attention from the drop in front of him. He heard somebody several arms away down the ledge make exaggerated noises of disgust. Nearer at hand he heard Ati yelling over the rising air, 'Ready to go, I'm ready, I'm ready.'

Tighe's insides felt wrenched and there was a scorching trail from his stomach up his throat, but he felt himself manhandled, pushed and hauled upright again by a cursing Waldea. He opened his mouth to apologise to the Master, but only a moan came out. He still had his eyes shut. The kite straps pressed hard against his shoulder, a deep tug inside him that repeated the clench of the vomiting, and the sound of the wind took on a deeper timbre.

He opened his eyes. He was up, in the air.

Against the background of the gushing noise of the wind was a reedy wail. It was, he realised, his own voice, howling punily. The wind turned, caught him, lurched him to the left.

His feet were dangling over nothingness. All the way down to –

Look up.

The worldwall was there. It reached up for ever and down for ever with an awesome solidity. For an instant Tighe's fears dissolved; the hideous taste in his mouth, the hollow twist in his gut, were shrunken to nothing before the sheer spread of the wall itself. He was far enough out in the air to see the range of it, the slight curve of it away to the left and to the right. The trick of perspective as the eye was drawn upwards, all the way up until the wall itself was lost in haze.

There was a tug on his line and his kite jerked, veered away, pulling him through a half-turn. His vision of the wall slipped to the side, to be replaced by an expansive blue wash with tiny shredded clouds. He saw the line leading away from his kite and Ati's kite in the distance pulling the rope taut.

Tighe's stomach spasmed again at the yaw of the drop beneath him.

The kite strained and creaked at his back and he dipped and swooped down.

He wondered if he were still afraid. He wished he could have some water for his bitter-tasting, burnt tongue. The savour of vomit was still in his mouth, on his teeth, on his lips.

A runnel of sobs came and went, shaking his chest. But here he was. Flying. The kite trembled in the wind, shook noisily behind him as a larger gust took it. Flying. He reached out and grabbed the pull harness, as he'd been taught to do on the frame. With a yank the kite struggled to turn in the roar of the wind. Even above the noise of the air Tighe could hear the leather rope connecting his to Ati's kite creak as it strained. Almost without thinking about it he hauled the other way. The kite flexed, the edges of its wings dipping in, and with a juddery grace it swerved to the left. The line slackened and wind braided and twanged it.

Ati's kite was a fair distance away, growing slowly as Tighe steered his kite towards him. Then, so suddenly that Tighe yelled out in fright, it was right there, huge, close enough to touch. Tighe caught one super-vivid image of Ati's face, mouth open, eyes creased in the effort of yelling – fear – anger – and then Tighe was past him, flying through clear air.

He had passed a hand's width from collision.

Sluggishly Tighe pulled his weight out of the harness's left side and the swoop came to an end in an ungainly turn. For a moment Tighe was upside-down and his stomach lurched again. Then he was rightways again, gasping. The air washed hugely past him. The skin of his kite twitched as if alive.

Ati reappeared before him, controlling his kite with fierce little jerks of his body to keep it facing Tighe. He was yelling, but there was no way his voice could carry in the enormity of the wind's crashing. Tighe stared, dumbfounded, at the anger of the boy's expression.

The wind rattled them, separating them.

Tighe fought the buffeting, trying to bring the kite he rode under control. The frame, rooted as it was to the shelf, had been nothing like the real thing. Besides, he could see that Waldea was hurrying him through the training before they went to war.

He pulled on his harness again and the kite lifted him and swept him round. Setting back into a hovering flight was the tricky thing. His mind alert now, he realised that he would need that sort of control if he ever wanted to land the thing.

There was a sharp, agonising switch against his left leg: the rope was flapping loose, whipping frantically in the breezy air. Belatedly Tighe understood that Ati, angered at the dangerous proximity of Tighe's pass had freed himself from the tether. The slack line curled and snapped, poising itself, snake-like, as if to strike. With clumsy movement Tighe unhooked his end of the tether from the underside of the kite, just by his shoulder. The rope slipped from the bar, coiling through the air as it fell away.

Tighe looked around. The exhilaration of what he was doing was starting to penetrate him. He pulled to the left, then to the right. The whole worldwall, the massy solidity of everything, danced and jogged before him. Away to the left, to the right. He wriggled in the harness the way he had been told to do in the frame back on land: only here, in this new element, the balance of his body and the broad stretch of kite existed in a new relationship. Lean it forward into the push of the wind from below and it hovered and wobbled; lean back and the breeze lifted him up. Angle it far enough and the flat plane of the kite relinquished the hold of air and fell, cut through the air knife-like as he hurtled down. But this fall could be slowed and curved away from with the pressure of his arms or the angling of his body.

The other kites were circling now, drifting downwards in spirals for all the world like birds. Tighe concentrated and started coming down. His mouth was very dry, his eyes were stinging. His legs were so cold he could not really feel his feet. It was not easy to bring the kite under control.

He could understand now some of the snatches of talk he had overheard in barracks. Away from the face of the wall itself the winds were cleaner: not free from all crosswinds, but easier to ride. But near the wall the winds became chopped up and bitty, and the kites tended to vibrate and thrum noisily. It was hard even to see properly because the vibration jarred the eyeballs.

Tighe swept away and curled back. He could see, fairly distant now, kites landing back on the ledge: it was over to the right and a little below him. Suddenly, trembling at the prospect of landing without crashing fatally into the face of the world, Tighe tugged himself back in that direction. He tried to coax the kite into a gentle descent, but a bucking strong breeze knocked him wallwards and a blank stone patch of sheer vertical world sprang up towards him with sickening speed. Terrified, Tighe threw all his weight away skywards and the kite arced round and swung out.

He was scared now and panting. Giving the wall a much wider berth, he tried to swing down to the platon's ledge. But he ended up circling pointlessly in the air. Looking around he could see no other kites. He was alone in the sky; everybody else had landed. He tried another pass, but the terrific rattling of the kite's fabric seemed to convey itself directly into his bones. Terror took root in him. The bitter taste in his mouth intensified.

The ledge swept past and then the spur that separated the platon's base from the main shelf. The calabashes loomed into view and Tighe swerved up and round to leave them behind. He twisted in the harness as he repassed the spur, brought the kite round and tumbled through the sky, picking up speed, falling again. Sudden flash vision of his pashe, her face buckled with anger. And the air howling at him.

With a reflex, by which he surprised himself at a deep level, the kite veered up and all the speed bled away in the sharp ascent. He lowered and toppled forward where the hard dirt of the ledge came banging up against the soles of his feet.

Some of the other kite-boys and kite-girls were there, arms out, to grab at the tips of his wings as his body went limp, his knees scraping the dirt. It took him several long breaths to realise that he was back on the wall. Home. Firmness under foot.

With this understanding came an elation, soaring in the middle of his chest. He wriggled out of his harness, clambered out from the structure of the kite. Waldea would be happy with him. He had flown; he had landed. There was a bright light in his stomach.

Waldea was lumbering towards him, head down. He arrived right in front of Tighe and flashed his fist out. The sideways blow, glancing, caught Tighe unawares. His head jerked to the side as a star of pain burst in the side of his temples.

'You threw that rope away,' Waldea was yelling. 'I stood here and *watched* you. Do you know how much tether rope *costs*?'

The second blow, being less unexpected, hurt Tighe less. He caught a sense of Waldea's arm coming up and let himself go looser. Then, with the impact, he rolled to the left, tumbling over, sprawling in the earth. He landed softly. But despite the throb of pain at the side of his head Tighe felt the grit of the ledge underneath him with a rush of satisfaction. Flown, landed.

Waldea's rage burnt itself out straight away and he hunkered down to check the boy. 'OK? I get no pleasure hitting you,' he said.

'Fine, Master,' said Tighe.

Waldea helped him up. 'Hit a man once,' he said, uncharacteristically communicative. 'Blinded him in one eye. Don't make me strike you again. Can't fly a kite with only one eye.'

'No, Master,' said Tighe. He was on his feet now. His head didn't hurt so bad really.

Suddenly, unexpectedly, Waldea laughed, a single burst of noise. 'Looked like *combat*, God fuck it,' he said, 'like you were *trying* to bomb boy Ati out of the sky.' Then he turned on his heel and marched away.

Tighe put his hand to the side of his head, but there was no blood. Then he looked around. The other kite-boys and kite-girls had disassembled their kites and taken the packages back into the dormitory, so, with fumbling hands, Tighe did that. He felt strange, his head still stinging. He felt alone, uncertain what to do next. Then, angling his head back to look up, he understood that he felt euphoric.

Alive!

Somehow the sky seemed brighter, more soaked in light, than it had done before. The colours of the wall itself had intensified, the browns were richer, the greys more pure, the green more lively.

That evening in the dormitory Ati was stand-offish. Tighe tried to gauge the mood as he wrapped himself up in his blanket.

'Sorry', he said in a soft voice, 'that I nearly strike you.'

Ati mumbled something, looking in another direction.

'In the sky,' Tighe added.

'Fuck,' said Ati. For a while he was silent. Tighe waited on a fuller reply and then gave up, turned on his side and tried to compose himself for sleep. Then Ati's voice came back, peevish.

'You don't *do* that, could have killed,' he said. 'Killed the two of us, you, me. Fuck. Still,' he added, his voice warming a little. 'That was then. No demerat in thinking of the past all the time.'

Silence.

'I guess', Ati said, eventually, 'I figured you might fly better, you being the sky-boy and everything, but you flew badly, you flew like shit. Turd on a kite.' He hissed with repressed laughter. Suddenly, without expecting himself to, Tighe started laughing as well, pressing his lips together with his fingers to try and stop the sound coming out. Waldea would be coming back into the room any moment now. Shouldn't make any noise. But it was so funny – Tighe falling through the sky like a stone.

'You supposed to be the *sky*-boy,' said Ati, laughter eroding the sentence as he said it until it ended in a series of gasps.

'Sky-boy,' repeated Tighe.

'You good omen? You *shit* omen.'

'Yes!'

'You supposed to flown down here to us,' said Ati, his body trembling with the giggles. 'I don't think so.'

'I fell,' said Tighe.

The door opened and Waldea was back in the space. 'Quiet now,' he boomed.

*

The following day at breakfast Ati came and sat next to Tighe. They didn't say anything to one another, but it was the first morning when Tighe did not eat alone.

8

Tighe flew again the following day and the day after that, and the third day as well. Each time he felt the terrors thrum through his whole body as he stood on the edge of the world. He told himself not to look down, but he could barely help himself. His eyesight would drop as if it were subject to the same laws of gravity as physical objects. And there was the world, at his feet, plummeting away for ever until the strong block of hard stone dissolved into the mist of clouds and everything diminished and became blue with the distance. Just looking down like that would make his ribs clench together like fingers in a fist, make his heart pop and rattle, would dry his mouth and make all the hairs on his head tingle and stand apart.

But, each time, he had stepped over the edge into the push of the rising midday air and the kite at his back had filled and soared. And every time *that* happened, Tighe had wept – actually wept – with the euphoria of it.

The more he knew Ati, the more he realised that the downwaller's command of the Imperial language was not as good as he had at first thought. What he had interpreted as smooth expression was actually haphazard in its syntax. But Ati himself, for all his strangeness – his strange look and smell, his peculiar manner and attitudes – began to seem homely to Tighe. Familiar, close.

On the morning of one particularly bright day, as Tighe joined the rest of the platon for the stretching exercises and tyshe movements, he had summoned his courage and addressed Waldea directly. 'Master?' he had said, his voice more quavery than he would have liked. 'Master?'

'Tig-he,' grunted Waldea. He was fixing a broken spar from one of the kites with daubs of glue from an antique plastic pot.

'I want to go, some days,' he said. 'To the field hospital.'

Waldea didn't say anything, his whole ruined faced concentrated on the broken kite. When he had finished glueing and splinting the spar, he said, 'You sick?'

'No, Master.'

'Broken bones?'

'No, Master.'

'That's what the field hospital is for.'

'The man there is Vievre, Master. He healed me after my fall. He a father to me, I love him.'

Waldea looked up at this, his sky-grey eyes settling, unblinking, on Tighe's gaze. 'You love him,' he repeated, in a colourless voice.

'He a father to me, I love him,' Tighe repeated, uncertainly. 'I love him a father.'

'No, Tig-he,' said Waldea, clambering to his feet. 'You cannot go. There is no time in our day when we can spare the time for you to wander away.' He slapped his own oval belly with the flats of both hands. 'I am your father now and you must love *me*. You must love me, or I will have to beat you again.' Then, for some arcane reason that Tighe could not fathom, he started laughing and strode away.

One evening, as the two of them sat apart from the rest of the kite-boys and kite-girls eating the evening meal, Tighe asked Ati, 'Ati, this war?'

Ati was always wholly absorbed in his eating until he had finished every fragment of food. He said nothing until he had run his forefinger round the inside of the bowl and licked it. Then he said, 'What you say, barbarian?'

'This war.'

'What about this war?'

'Who do we war?'

'Don't say *we war*,' said Ati, smirking. He loved being able to correct Tighe's language usage; it made him feel better about his own often halting command of the Imperial tongue. 'Say *we fight*.'

'Who do we fight? In this fight?'

'Who do we fight in this *war*?' said Ati. 'You are a barbarian if you do not know who do we fight!'

Tighe put his bowl to his face and ran his tongue round the inside. His tongue was long, but he couldn't quite reach into the very middle. Ati leaned over and knocked the bowl with his knuckles so that it jarred against the bridge of Tighe's nose.

'Shiteater!' squealed Tighe, dropping the bowl and reaching over to slap Ati on the forehead. Ati was laughing now and Tighe grinning, but they both looked round nervously to see if Waldea was watching them.

'So?' repeated Tighe. 'Who do we fight?'

'You *are* barbarian! – everybody knows who we fight.'

'I am a Prince,' snorted Tighe. 'You shiteater.'

'I apologies, you *preens*,' said Ati, making a grinning obedience with his head.

'Tell me!'

Ati's grin dropped away. 'We are at a holy war,' he said, with sudden seriousness. 'We fight a holy fight. All three Popes have written. To the east alongwall from here is a mighty nation of darkness. They are called the Otre.'

'The Otre,' said Tighe, solemnly.

'They are evil. They pull out the eyes of all boy-children, because they worship an el-daimon.'

'What is el-daimon?' said Tighe, horrified. Their eyes!

'It is an enemy of God, a devil.'

'A devil.'

'Yes, but a woman devil. A woman devil and the Otre worship her. She tell them to put out the eyes of all boy-children of their enemies, to cut off their penis. They take two boy-children, and they cut off the two penis. Then they kill one boy-child, making sing-song prayers to the she demon, the el-daimon.' Ati was rubbing his hands with the joy of telling this story, and leering at Tighe. 'They kill the one boy-child and push his dead-body off the world. Then they take the two penis' – and Ati wriggled his two little fingers in illustration – 'and they put them in the eyes of the other boy-child.'

Tighe breathed out a long, horrified sigh. 'In the eyes?'

'In the eye caves. The eye houses, where the eyes were. In my language we say *gnazh*.'

'Eye sockets,' said Tighe.

'Yes,' said Ati eagerly. 'They put the penis in the *gnazh*, so that the end of each penis sits there like eyes. At the end of penis there is little hole, you know? Little circle. Those are the pupils.'

'Pupils,' said Tighe.

'And the end of penis is like eye. And each woman in Otre is given a boy as slave. They tie tether through the neck, you know,' and Ati pulled the skin away over his adam's-apple to demonstrate, 'and they walk them around all day.'

'Horrible!'

'And if they capture us in war, they do this to us. Only with men, sometimes, they cut off balls – you know? – and do the same in the *gnazh*.'

'Is this true?' asked Tighe, wide-eyed.

'Entirely the truth,' said Ati, leaning back looking satisfied. 'It is a holy war and we bring the Empire to these barbarians, these women devils.'

'We fight their army?'

Ati blew out a long exhalation, expressive of his contempt. 'They have small army. We fight them past the Meshwood.'

'They have only women in the army?'

'What?'

'No men in the army?'

'Well,' said Ati. 'No, the army is men, I think.'

'But they have no eyes!'

Ati coughed. 'Some men have the eyes,' he said. 'Many men have eyes, perhaps. But they are evil people and we will destroy them!'

'Evil people,' repeated Tighe.

'Yes. East of here is the Meshwood.'

'What is that?'

'That is great wood, not trees but – we say *ash*.' He made a gesture with both hands, all the fingers splayed and drawn together as a claw. 'It stretches for many miles over the face of the worldwall. The Otre live on the other side. We march there, through the Meshwood, and fight the Otre.'

The following morning, as the platon worked through its ritualised exercise movements, Waldea came and stood before them all. This was unusual and the platon's movements broke up in uncertainty.

'Children!' barked Waldea. He was holding something behind his back.

The kite-boy standing behind Tighe reached forward and pinched through Tighe's clothing, grabbing a piece of the skin at the base of the spine and yanking it. Tighe couldn't help yelping and immediately reddened and clamped his mouth shut. Waldea's gaze settled on him for a moment and then passed on.

'Today you will fly to the Pause.'

There was an absolute stillness. Tighe had never heard the phrase before, although he recognised the word as meaning a gap in time, a moment of waiting. He had never heard it used as a noun before, never so ponderously, and he wondered what it was. But Waldea was holding up a curiously shaped box that he had been keeping behind his back.

'These are my sight invigorators,' he announced. 'You know them. Through these I can see you, even though you are all the way out at the Pause. Through these I can see every one of you.'

He waved the peculiar shape, black and tattered, in the air. Tighe's eyes followed it, hypnotised.

'Fly out to the Pause, you grubs, you grass-blades!' Waldea declaimed. 'You are warriors! Go to war against your fears! Some of you know it, many do not, but you must all be skilled at navigating at the Pause. It is strange air, out there, and you must be used to it. The sky goes strange there, so you must take care. But you will fly!'

They started towards their kites, and Waldea called to them to stop again. 'Have a care, all of you,' he cried. He seemed unusually agitated, as if scared of something. Tighe felt a thrum in his belly, a fear at this new task. What was the Pause, exactly?

'Go on then,' yelled Waldea, his anxiety turning to anger.

And so the kite-boys and kite-girls, uncharacteristically silent, collected their kites and strapped themselves in. Tighe found himself next to Mulvaine.

'We are warriors,' he said to the lanky boy.

Mulvaine looked at him. 'What did you say, sky-boy?'

'We go to make war with the Otre,' said Tighe.

Mulvaine looked at him. 'You're a strange one, sky-boy. All the wall knows that.'

'They are a women nation,' said Tighe. 'They have evil women there.'

Mulvaine coughed and yanked a leather strap to tighten it. 'Where did you hear that, you disease bag?'

'I heard that they cut off the penis of the men.'

Mulvaine spat. 'That's not what I heard. I heard they make their father and mothers eat themselves. They cut off first a leg, or something, and cook it and leave the fathers and mothers in a prison with nothing else to eat.'

Tighe's eyes were saucers. 'Fathers and *mothers* too?'

'Sure.'

'But the mothers are the Princes in that land!'

'The what?'

'The Popes in that land – the Popes there are the mothers, the women.'

Mulvaine spat again. 'Never heard that. But I *did* hear they lock up their parents, and cut away their legs and arms. Then they cook the meat and leave the mothers and fathers in a prison, like I said. They've nothing else to eat! They have to eat themselves or die! It's muove, really muove, it's bad.'

They were at the ledge now. Tighe's stomach was fizzing with the anticipation of going over the edge of the world again and his head was flickering with images of the atrocities committed by the Otre. Cutting off penises! Forcing their parents to consume themselves! Horrible!

'Mulvaine,' he called over. 'What is the Pause?'

'You'll find out,' said Mulvaine grimly.

And they stepped off the world.

There was the usual rush of agonising euphoria as Tighe fell away and as the invisible muscle of the wind flexed and lifted him into the air. The rushing sound of the wind filled his ears, and the updraught was unusually choppy and vibrated his kite. His vision was blurred by the shaking, but he swam round and saw the ledge below him. Then he circled again and saw his fellow kite-boys and kite-girls flying briskly away from the wall.

He swung in and followed, allowing the updraught to give him height and then angling to sweep down and along. Soon he had caught up with the main flock of the platon and he concentrated on keeping a good distance from the kite nearest him and on flying on, away from the wall.

At one point he circled up and round and saw how far away from the worldwall they had flown. He could no longer make out the platon ledge or the spur amongst the patchwork scattering of shapes; squares and wedges, semicircles and lines, grey and brown and green. He strained his eyes and thought that a tiny row of dots might be the calabashes moored along from the ledge, but he couldn't be certain. The pattern revealed how plain the wall was above the military camp – a speckled, striated stretch of blank grey, a natural upper boundary to the growth of the Empire. A desert. Unless the Empire expanded to the west, or the east, and found another way upwards, a series of angled and connected ledges and pathways that led round this block, Tighe could not see how they would hope to go any further upwall. They might go up in calabashes, but they could surely not raise up a whole people in calabashes – supplies, food, building materials.

With a twist in his chest, he realised that this same desert stood between himself and home. But then (his heart pattered with hope) he could ride his kite away – fly up and up on an endless updraught until he arrived back at the village.

The air was colder around him now. It felt strange and unnerving to be flying so far from the body of the wall. Looking ahead, Tighe saw that the platon was in front of him.

He swirled around in the air and climbed to get the acceleration to rejoin the platon; and he pondered. Go home – but to what? To Grandhe? To beatings and being cheated of his birthright? To a village where people starved, where most of his best friends had left because they were too poor to stay? Most of all – to a place where his pahe and his pashe were not. What was there for him? Only Wittershe. Only beautiful Wittershe, with her elegant face and her body. But she was probably married to somebody else by now – lost to him for ever.

This pathway of thought was leading him to a dead end, to the internal plunge of misery and despair. He wriggled in his harness and manoeuvred back into formation with the platon. He needed not to think about those thoughts. That was what he needed.

And up ahead things were happening to distract him from his pain. The lead kites suddenly flipped back, turning with impossible speed and dropping rapidly away. Tighe's head tingled all through with anticipation.

They were at the Pause.

One by one the kites reached an invisible barrier, flipped back and dropped away. All of Tighe's childish wonderings about the nature of the universe came back to him. He remembered sitting on the ledge back in his village and staring at the sky. Remembered wondering if the sky was another wall, a purer, ethereal wall; a wall of light and air perhaps, raised by the same God who had put brick on brick and clothed it with earth and life and made the worldwall. Another wall to hold in the air, so that it didn't all bleed away, so that God's people could breathe, could live in the space between the walls.

Was he now at the place? Was this what the Pause was – the approach to the pure blue wall of the sky? The air was as cold as ice.

Tighe came up at the rear and angled up to quell his speed. If this was a great blue wall, then he didn't want simply to crash into it. He tried turning a little to the side, wondering if he could fly past it and observe the nature of its surface. But he could see nothing; it seemed only as if the sky went on for ever here – there weren't even clouds to stain the view, and the bright, yellow, hot sun sat solidly over to the right.

Then, abruptly, he was upside down and his stomach lurched. He couldn't see what had happened, how he had flipped over; he seemed to be in the same position in the harness. But then he felt himself – impossibly – slipping *backwards* through the air and he was tumbling and falling and his eyes were dazzled by a tumbling strobe as the sun span round and round his head, and the distant wall lurched up and round and over and came back at him from underneath.

For a second he was stunned; then he strained with his body and pulled with his arms and righted his kite, swerving it into a sweeping dive that pulled round and up. He circled, caught an updraught and made up some of the height he had lost.

He looked around; his fellow kite-girls and kite-boys were round and about, speckling the sky, no longer in formation. He swung by one of them, wanting to reach out and ask questions – *what happened*? – but there was no way his voice could reach across the screaming of the rushing air. Then he pulled up again and had a clear view of another kite heading fast away from the wall. Once again it flew so far and then seemed to be grabbed by an invisible hand, spun round and thrust back.

Tighe found that he wasn't scared; once he was up and flying he felt peculiarly safe – it was difficult to explain. Standing on the extremity of the ledge, with solid earth under his feet, the prospect of the fall gripped at his guts and he was terrified. But once that initial tumble off the world was out of the way everything began to assume the logic of a dream. Only the centrifugal wrenching in his gut, only the chill of the wind rushing past him, told him that his experience was physical at all. Otherwise it was a magical, floating hallucination.

He turned his kite back in the direction of the Pause and braced himself. For a moment there was nothing but his own onward rushing; then with a sudden *whoosh* of air the yank of gravity changed. He was no longer flying on, but somehow, impossibly, flying *up*. For a fraction of time his whole perspective changed; he was on his back looking up at nothing but sky. Then the kite shimmied and fell away, tumbling back, jerking through fifty degrees and falling again.

He struggled to control the spinning kite, hauling his body so hard that he started sweating, even in the chill of the cold rushing air. It took a little longer, but he got the kite under control eventually. When he got his bearings he could see none of his platon, so he flew wallward for a while until he found a strong updraught and rode it spiralling helix-like. After a little while a number of kites came into view.

Soon enough he rose further and gave himself a vantage point from which he could see several kites tackling the Pause. They flew at it, slowed and reversed, fell away. One kite – Tighe couldn't see who piloted it – built up an enormous slope of speed and hurtled through the Pause. The kite continued for a good long way and then turned on its side, as if it were about to nosedive down and away. But, somehow, it didn't; instead it hung for a moment in that impossible posture, and then another moment. Then it slid backwards, as if being yanked in slow motion, inching along and being slowly pulled back towards the wall, towards Tighe.

Tighe circled closer to the kite, and watched as it approached, angled wrongly, as if drawn in by an invisible rope. Then, suddenly, it was falling properly, dropping precipitously away. Tighe started a spiralling descent to try and follow, but the kite soon disappeared from sight.

After a few more passes at the Pause, the platon slowly reassembled and then turned the points of their kites and started back towards the wall. The sun had risen higher and the updraughts were getting more erratic, so the platon formation became scattered and ragged as it came closer to the wall as individuals had to fly further apart to seek out updraughts. Eventually they were close enough to see where they were; and to discover that they were a mile or so westward of the platon ledge. The lead kite pulled round and flew east, and Tighe fell in at the rear of the train.

The wall they flew past was pocked and touched with singleton ledges and odd cave mouths, far from any access. It was much more grown over than the desert above the military base that Tighe had noticed on the way out, but was still inaccessible; a broken and debatable land. At one point he thought he saw smoke coming out of one of the cave mouths, which suggested habitation, but the wall around the cave hole was smooth and bare and access clearly impossible, so he assumed he had been mistaken.

Eventually the lead kite dipped down and the rest followed. They were back at the platon ledge, swooping past the spur of wall and getting glimpses of the military camp, the calabashes still hanging impossibly, the thronging shelf. Then swinging back in, ducking down and rising up at the last minute to kill off as much speed as possible – then legs running as they hit the earth of the ledge, and Tighe hauling himself back to try and stop himself from running flat into the wall.

He clambered out of his kite panting, and looked around. He was still trembling with the sense of having seen something incredible.

'Children!' boomed Waldea, stalking over towards them from the brink of the ledge where he had been watching with his sight invigorators, 'one of you is missing.'

It was Bel, one of the kite-girls. Everybody else was accounted for.

'Master!' announced Mulvaine, 'I saw Bel fly deep into the Pause. It almost looked as if she might break through – but then she was pushed back out and then she fell fast away.'

Waldea swore; drummed his feet on the floor.

He made the whole platon assemble on the ledge in the far-risen sunshine, to wait for Bel's return. 'I will lose no more of you on *training*!' Waldea ranted. 'This is bad, bad.'

The kite-boys and girls were subdued by this uncharacteristic mood. When Waldea turned to go back to the edge of the world and look out, several tucked their heads together and whispered.

'Bel's too fat now to fly kites,' Ati hissed to Tighe, as they sat in rows on the ledge looking out at the sky. Waldea was pacing up and down in front of them, putting his sight invigorators to his eyes to check if Bel's kite was in view.

Tighe nodded. He pictured Bel: as stringy by body shape as all the rest of the kite-boys and kite-girls, but longer in the bone than most, taller, and now at the age where her breasts were showing. She had large breasts, and her hips were spreading; a disadvantage for kite pilots.

'What do you think happened?'

Ati shrugged, watching Waldea to slip his whispered comments in at moments when he could be sure the Master's attention was distracted. 'Two months ago a good flier, named Pegivre, he mistaked the landing. He collided with the wall, with the lip of the ledge.' Ati whistled very softly. 'He almost fall all the way down, if some of us had not grabbed him with our hands and fingers and pulled him up. But he was all broken, all his bones broken, and blood coming out of his nose and mouth. He was carried to the field hospital but . . .' Ati punctuated his account with a sucking noise, a *sheesh*. 'Died, he died. The Master was *very* unhappy, angry. And half-year ago, when we were training in the Imperial City . . .'

But Waldea was stalking back in their direction and Ati shut up abruptly.

*

They all sat there until the sun was disappearing over the top of the wall and the light was growing grey. A few of the kite-boys were fidgeting, when Waldea's eye was not on them; flapping their hands, pinching their neighbours, or drawing up gobbets of earth and shaping them into crude phalluses or balls.

'He'll have to give us the supper I think,' Ati hissed to Tighe. 'My stomach is hungry.'

'Mine too,' said Tighe.

'There!' howled Waldea. It sounded so exactly like a howl of rage that all the kite-boys twitched in fear. But it was exultation. 'There! There she comes!'

And finally, halting, spiralling and climbing with agonising slowness from every drop in altitude, came a kite. It grew larger and larger and finally arrived at the ledge. Bel's face came into view; whiter than white, pinched and exhausted. Without a word from Waldea the whole platon got to their feet and rushed to help her, to gather her in.

That evening's meal was a far jollier affair than usual. Even Waldea seemed happy. He swigged some drink or other from a tiny plastic bottle, disappearing from time to time to replenish his supply. Bel told her tale several times, embellishing it more with each retelling; how she had spiralled miles downwall after emerging from the Pause (or tens of miles, or *hundreds* of miles), until she was able to regain control of the kite. She might even have passed out, she wasn't sure – or she *was* sure, she *had* passed out – or she had slept and dreamt a wonderful dream. Anyway when she finally regained control she was completely lost. She knew she had fallen a long way so she spent a long time, an hour, more, circling up on what updraughts she could find, which grew feebler and fewer as the day went on. She didn't recognise anything and she began to panic – not a single feature on the wall. She had cried, prayed, swung east and west, crawled up on thinning updraughts and wasted her gains in long downward slides trying to find a landmark. Eventually she flew in from the east over a part of the upwall portion of the Imperial City itself! Yes, she had been so far downwall, and further too (far enough to see the bottom, maybe, somebody said, and everybody laughed). From there she knew the way, but the updraughts were so feeble by that stage in the day that she had spent several hours gaining the mile or so of upward wall to come back to the ledge.

Still, she had made it back; and she was so tired that she fell asleep whilst they were still outside on the ledge, still putting away the supper bowls. So Waldea himself carried her in and wrapped her in a blanket. 'Time for bed now,' he announced.

He was readying himself for bed too. Usually he left them alone for a while, going for an evening stroll said some, but not this night. Accordingly it looked as though there would not be the usual dormitory conversations. But then a messenger came and called him away. Waldea pulled on his leggings and hurried away, and everybody chattered about what this could mean.

Tighe inched over towards Ati. 'What is it, Ati?' he asked. 'The Pause – what *is* the Pause?'

Ati laughed. 'You saw today. That's what it is. You fly out far enough, to go out and out and then – suddenly – you reach the Pause. The air go funny there, I think.'

'God put it there,' said Tighe.

Ati made the holy gesture with his thumb over his chest, which he often did when God was mentioned. 'But that say nothing', he declared, 'because God made everything.'

'I think', said Tighe, 'that the sky is another wall. If we fly far enough we fly to the sky wall, but God put the Pause there to stop us from crashing into it.'

Ati pondered this for a while. 'You have barbarian ideas,' he decided. 'You a kite-boy now. You believe what we believe. We believe that one day we fly *through* the Pause. If we get enough speed, maybe – like Bel', he nodded his chin in the direction of the sleeping form three bodies down, 'only more, then we push *through* the Pause.'

'And what on the other side?' Tighe asked.

'Who knows?' said Ati.

Waldea was away a long time. Half an hour passed. People ran out of things to say. The dormitory went quiet.

Tighe dozed, woke with a fuzzy arm that had got bent back under his head. He shook it loose and rubbed it to bring life back to its numbness. Then shifted position. He dropped off to sleep again. He was woken once more by Waldea coming back through the door and stomping over the dormitory floor before settling himself down. Tighe lay quietly, listening to the grunts and struggles of the big man wrapping himself up in his sleeping blanket. Then everything was silent.

Tighe dozed again and then woke with a lurch, with that same sickening falling sensation that used to wake him up back in the village. He was sweating. There was some crazy dislocated dream in his memory (fading as he thought about it) of himself and Wittershe, of stretching himself upon Wittershe in the act of lovemaking, only to realise that they were both falling – to realise that Wittershe was, in the mad way of dreams, actually a kite, a human kite. He had been scared, he remembered, because Wittershe had not handled as his kite handled and he was convinced that they were both falling to their deaths. But she had smiled and urged him on with the lovemaking, and he had thought to himself . . . what had the thought been? The dream slid away, lost coherence in his memory.

For a while he lay still, until the sweat on his body cooled and dried. It was quiet in the dormitory, the silence punctuated only by the breathing of the boys and girls. One set of breathing was out of synchronisation. Tighe turned to follow the sound, and saw shadowy, supine movement. He stared for a while before realising what was happening: there was somebody wrapped up with Bel in her blanket. One of the kite-boys, but Tighe couldn't see who, had crept over and got into her blanket, and now the two of them were lovemaking, their faces pressed closely together, each mouth trying to stifle the moans of the other. Tighe's heart hammered and his wick stiffened. But it was the audacity of it that most impressed him. What if they woke Waldea? He would beat them severely; he could shout out, 'Disgusting! Disgusting!' and make an example of them. They were taking such a risk.

Making himself as still as he could to avoid startling them Tighe lay and listened to the rustles of the blanket, the occasional muted breaths and gasps that came from the pair. Then they were still and after a while the boy disentangled himself from Bel's blanket and crept, in slow stages, away to the far side of the dormitory where his own blanket was.

9

At breakfast the following morning Tighe waited for a moment when he and Ati could talk without being overheard, and said, 'I saw something last night, in the dormitory.'

'What?'

'I woke up and saw Bel's blanket, and inside it Bel, and inside it also somebody else.'

Ati snorted and grinned. 'Oh I know,' he said, nodding vigorously. 'I know this, this is talked about. It is Ravielre. Everybody knows.'

'Everybody knows?'

'They in love.' He bent his head and giggled. 'Such dangerous! They creep together and fuck-fuck, but if Waldea find them he will beat them both good and hard. Dangerous!'

'I never see it before,' grinned Tighe, bowing his head as well, so that he and Ati's eyes were on the same level. 'I never saw them do it before.'

Ati nodded, and reached out to grasp Tighe's hand. 'I know. But before they only fuck when it is Bel's monthly.'

'What is that word, *monthly*?'

'Every woman has that. Always the same time and the blood comes out instead of piss. Everybody knows that.'

'Happens every month,' nodded Tighe, using his own word. He knew about that.

'Monsh?' asked Ati.

'You are stupid downwaller,' said Tighe, tapping briskly on the side of Ati's head. Their foreheads were leaning together now, skin pressing against skin. Somehow it felt good, it felt comforting, the closeness of it. 'Is not *monsh*. Say *month*.'

'Mofe.'

'Month.'

'Man-the.'

'No – *month*.'

'*You* are barbarian,' said Ati pinching him. 'It does not matter, I think.

144

You know that in a month, that every month, a woman pisses blood instead of piss. Ravielre and Bel would sometimes fuck at this time.'

'But why?' asked Tighe, horrified at the thought of this. Was that really how women were?

'You know nothing in your barbarian land,' sniggered Ati. 'It is impossible to build a baby inside a woman at this time. You can fuck-fuck all you want at this time. Obvious, Bel does not want to be fat with child. If she is fat with child she is too fat to fly the kite.'

But Tighe had stuffed his fingers into his mouth in horror at the mental picture of Bel having her monthly bleed and Ravielre putting his wick in amongst all that blood.

'It is not her monthly now though,' said Ati, leaning back.

'How do you know that?'

Ati shrugged. 'I don't think she cares any more about babies. Maybe she hungry for a baby. She is too big to fly kites properly anyway. Why should she care about her weight any longer?'

After breakfast the platon went through its exercises as normal. But after this Waldea lined them all up and made his announcement.

'My children! We are going to war!'

Rumours to this effect, prompted by Waldea's unusually prolonged time outside the dormitory the previous night, had been circulating all morning. Waldea's statement acted as the release to a frantic burst of cheering and jumping up and down. The Master waited, head down, with a smile (or what looked like a smile – it was difficult to tell because his features were so distorted) on his face. Eventually he raised his arms, and the cheering died down.

'This is why we have trained, my children,' he announced. 'This is the purpose of it all – to serve the Empire, to defeat the Otre. To capture the great door they guard! This platon of kite-boys and kite-girls is most important in the war effort, never forget that! I have been hard with you, but only to make you the best, to make you the best for the good of the Empire!'

He paused, looked at the floor for a while. There was absolute silence. Presently he spoke again in a quieter voice.

'Tomorrow the Pope of War will ascend the worldwall from the Imperial City,' he said. 'The Pope in person! He has said that he wishes to meet the noble kite platon, on which so much of the aerial strength of the Imperial army depends.'

Tighe supposed this was a good thing, but looking around at the faces of his fellow kite-pilots he saw awe, shock, even terror at this news. He could see it was more of an honour than he had realised – as if it were more like a divine blessing than a human honour. To meet the Pope himself!

Waldea stepped forward, came towards Tighe. 'The Pope has heard the story about our newest member, about the sky-boy, the good-omen boy.' He grabbed Tighe by the hair at the top of his head and gave him what Tighe assumed was meant to be a friendly shake, although it was really quite painful. 'But he will meet us all. All of us! My children . . .' Waldea stepped back and strolled along the ranks of kite-pilots. 'I am – happy,' he said. His eyes were moist. The glints from the morning sun came up from below and illuminated the glassy moisture of his pupils. 'Proud of you. Today you need not fly. Today we will sing the great Songs of the Empire! Tomorrow we assemble with the Imperial army for the march along the wall. Within the week we will have defeated the enemy! Otre will be part of the Empire!'

Everybody cheered.

'War is a glorious thing, kite-children,' said Waldea. Tighe could see that he was actually crying now, smeary teardrops rolling along the ragged creases of his cheeks. 'War is glorious, although it is terrible. War will make you wealthy! War can find you a wife, find you a husband! War stocks the houses of the mighty with slaves and servants! Thank God, my kite-children, that you have been born upon the worldwall at a time like this!' His face was weirdly contorted, as if the emotions within him were tormenting him in some way. 'You will lose friends and lovers, but you will gain new ones. You may lose – your looks, your health, but the Empire will be stronger! War is a – glorious – thing.'

Tighe didn't catch the meaning of every one of these words, every nuance, but the sheer passion in the Master's voice conveyed his meaning, carried Tighe away. Tears were zigzagging over the creases of his face.

Then, with a growly, raspy voice, Waldea began to sing. Tighe did not know the song, but the majority of the platon joined in, hesitantly at first, then with more gusto. Tighe found himself crying and he was not alone. He felt wonderful, warm somehow; absorbed into the loving body of the whole platon.

They sang songs for an hour or more. Tighe, embarrassed at knowing none of the words, tried to join in; making shapes with his mouth and humming vowels with the rise and fall of the music. Waldea fetched some of his alcohol from the metal jug in which he kept it, and passed his little plastic bottle around so that everybody in the platon got a sip of the acid-burning liquid. By the time the bottle got to Tighe the plastic nipple at its top was slick with the spit of everybody else, and he had to upend the thing to get a dribble of fluid out of it.

Everybody was gathered in little knots, cross-legged on the ledge; laughing and chattering. The Pope himself! They would meet the Pope himself! It was unbelievable.

Tighe found Ati and huddled close to him. 'It is all so exciting,' he said.

'You barbarian, you have turd for a heart,' said Ati, grinning and slouching back. 'You excited by anything, the singing of some songs. I am not excited.'

'Have you ever been at war before, Ati?' Tighe asked, with wide eyes.

Ati waved his hand, as if he had fought too many battles to remember them all. But then he leant forward and said, 'No, in fact, no. But I know many stories about war. Much fire in war, fire and flames.' He made his eyes wide, 0-0, to hint at the horrors he could tell.

'Ati,' said Tighe, tears pricking at his eyes again. 'I am happy to be in the army, and full of happy. But the Otre, they are – fear.'

'You mean they *frightening*?'

Tighe nodded. 'They frightening me. They are strong, you said so.'

'They not so strong,' said Ati. 'Otre is a small land, few ledges, only one shelf. They work with plazár.'

'What's that?'

'Meshwood is wood, but not made of trees, of platán. It is like wood, but is smaller, softer. It grows all over, like a weed. That is the Meshwood. The Otre work with the platán, make things, trade them. They are a weak people and we will destroy them.'

'Do the Otre live in the wood?'

Ati scoffed. 'You know *nothing* at all, barbarian. Nobody lives in the Meshwood!'

'Why not?'

Ati waved his hands. 'Horrors live in the wood! Animals that cut human flesh, that eat and eat human people. Claw-caterpils! Terrible things! Land-lobsters, snakes and uruchai – terrible things.'

Tighe shivered. He didn't want to hear this. 'We don't want to go through the Meshwood,' he said.

'The Meshwood is between us and Otre,' said Ati with a grim smile. 'The army passes through.'

Suddenly Tighe was crying again; not in fear of the horrors of the Meshwood, but for more nebulous, emotional reasons. With a sharp focus he suddenly hated the platon; he hated the way nobody regarded him with the proper respect a Prince ought to have, the way all of them – except Ati – bullied and mocked him. He hated the way Waldea beat him; hated the way Waldea was so ugly and so unyielding. Hated being shoved off the world to tumble through the sky strapped to a kite. Hated facing the prospect of battle, of violence and maybe death. But, and this was the strangest thing, at the same time he felt a joy filling every part of him, a trembly inner-sunshine happiness in his stomach. At the same time as all the fear, the sense of isolation and desperation, he knew that he loved the platon; loved

Waldea; loved the Empire. Ati was sitting in front of him grinning and he knew that he loved him too.

He reached out and touched Ati's face. Ati brushed the gesture aside, with a nervous look in the direction of Waldea; but when he turned his gaze back to meet Tighe's there was an answering glance in his dark eyes.

10

The following morning Waldea woke the whole platon earlier than usual. The dawn gale was audible past the closed door; the Master bellowed to be heard over the roar.

'You will all wash! Today, everybody washes, face *and* hands. When everybody has washed, I will inspect you. If there are any rips in your clothing, you will borrow the platon needle and sew them up. Do you understand?'

This frightened Tighe a little; he had never learnt to sew. It was not something a Prince needed to do. But he went carefully over all his clothing and checked each seam, and everything seemed intact.

Then he joined the queue of happily muttering boys and girls at the sink. It was not a proper sink; but, then again, the dormitory had been excavated only recently. It was a matting-lined space scooped out of the wall at the far end, fed by a piece of pipe. The faucet on the pipe was opened only as the water evaporated; there was no plughole. When he finally arrived at the sink the water was even muddier than usual, but he went through the ritual of splashing his face and rubbing himself with a handful of broad-leaved grass-blades.

By the time this was over the dawn gale had died down and Waldea opened the door. Everybody lined up on the ledge outside and Waldea stalked up and down the line, plucking at the kite-boys' and kite-girls' clothing.

'My children!' he announced. 'Today you meet the Pope himself! If any of you disgrace me, I will beat you bloody afterwards! But you will make me *proud*, proud.' He drew himself up to his full height, so that the weight of his belly rose a little towards his chest. 'Then we shall join the army, and march to battle. To battle! Gather your kites.'

Another line, as each member of the platon gathered up their un-assembled kite and hoisted it over their shoulder or balanced it on the fulcrum of their neck. Waldea checked the line one more time and then marched to the front.

As the sun started rising and the last of the morning clouds faded and dissipated in the air, they made their way round the spur in single file, treading carefully on the man-made walkway.

There was the same confusion of human activity on the main shelf. The calabashes still dominated the scene, swollen and perfectly spherical. From this angle the large pots they carried beneath them were more clearly visible: painted with red and blue patterns, as were the floating bellies of the calabashes themselves. Each of these cradles had one large door that displayed a prominent lock and several small slits. As he watched Tighe saw a thin tube poking through the slit, angling round and being withdrawn.

'What is that? In the calabashes there?' he asked the boy in front of him; but he was ignored.

The line of kite-pilots made their way round and on to the shelf itself. Waldea, who had been following at the rear of the line, came hurrying up at this point and, shouldering his way through the throng of blue-uniformed people who surrounded the platon, took a position. 'My children!' he yelled, over the chatter and noise of the shelf. 'We march to the pier and take our position!'

It was harder to keep the line along the shelf because people were coming and going, cutting through them and jostling them. A group of three tall men in uniform were lounging in the way, leaning on long poles. They stared at the kite-pilots, and started laughing. 'Hey kite-babies!' one of them called. 'Tweet-tweet! Tweet-tweet!' These three men thought themselves hilarious and laughed loudly with their heads angled back. Tighe looked expectantly at Waldea, leading them on, expecting the Master to rebuke these men. But instead Waldea put his eyes to the ground.

Tighe began to feel self-conscious. All the other kite-pilots were marching in step, but his bad foot made it impossible for him to do the same. He kept losing the rhythm and had to make a little hop-skip to get back into it. A round-bodied, bald-headed man pushed against him in passing, so hard that Tighe stumbled and nearly fell. For a moment he caught a whiff of the bald fellow's strange smell, like goat's butter on the turn, and then the man was away, pushing through the crowd to a doorway in the wall at the back of the shelf. Tighe stood, resting his foot, watched him, and then was distracted by what appeared to be a metal crane by the entrance, stacked with metal globes like fruit from a fruit tree. Two men in black overalls stood languidly beside it, occasionally stepping forward to push people away who came too close. A couple of metal poles, oiled but with freckles of rust showing through, were stacked against the wall beside them. Tighe remembered Ati saying something about these: the mushroom dust was put in them and they spurted fire at the enemy. He wished he could have a closer look at one. He hurried and caught up with Ati.

'Ati,' he said. 'There – are those . . . ?'

'Very rare,' said Ati, with awe. 'Very precious, our most deadly weapon.' But the whispered conversation was cut short.

'Here!' called Waldea. Tighe hurried on.

The line assembled itself by a wooden pier that reached out over the lip of the shelf.

'Stand and hold your position here!' yelled Waldea and stood tall himself.

They waited for an age. Tighe felt hideously impatient and it took all his self-control not to twitch and fidget – not to give way to his urge for motion and run up and down the ledge. The unceasing bustle around him filled him with the urge to get busy, to do things. A mighty army! He was part of a mighty Empire now – a small part, maybe, but still a part.

As the wait by the empty wooden pier dragged on, Tighe found his mind running on. It was better to be part of an Empire than a tiny village that nobody on the whole wide worldwall had even heard of! It was better to be part of this great enterprise against the evil of the Otre than it was to loiter around at home doing nothing. He was proud to be here. At the thought, tears squeezed into his eyes again. It was a magnificent thing.

But, as the wait dragged on, this sensation of epiphany and marvel faded and died. He became simply bored. Around him the kite-pilots began to twitch their arms, jump up and down. 'Be still!' Waldea roared. 'Stand in line!' But it got harder to keep people straight as the wait dragged on.

Finally, Waldea cried out. 'Here, now! It comes up!'

The bustle around them took on a more definitive purpose. People hurried on to the pier, a guard of blue-coated soldiers, all carrying the metal poles before them with both hands, lined up along from the kite-pilots. The murmur of voices on the shelf became more pronounced, rose in timbre.

Then, with the astonishing splendour of enormous scale, as unexpected and impossible as dreamwork, the bald red-blue-painted crown of one of the calabashes appeared over the edge of the world. It rose slowly, smoothly, filling out and tapering away until its whole belly was visible and the pot underneath came up into view; it was varnished wood studded with metal spikes. Standing this close to the apparition, Tighe could see all the detail that made it up. The great circle was made of fabric – perhaps the same thin leather that the kites were built with – hundreds of skins stitched together carefully. A network of lines, a web drawn tight around the swollen sphere, led the eye down to the cradle beneath; this was how the large metal-studded pot was attached, hung there in a harp-mesh of lines.

The people at the far end of the wooden pier threw out lines of some kind that snagged in the supporting cables of the calabash. Then four of them grabbed the line and hauled, pulling the great shape closer towards the wall. There was a flurry of action, tethering the calabash, and sliding a plank out to make a walkway with the now-opening doorway of the cradle beneath.

Then three people in brisk military style marched along the pier, up the walkway and disappeared inside the cradle of the calabash. Tighe thought he recognised one of these as Cardinelle Elanne, the high-ranking officer who had visited him whilst he was still in the hospital ward.

There was an expectant hush, but nothing happened. Slowly the murmur started again on the shelf. As minutes stretched and accumulated, the kite-pilots, who had been frozen with the excitement of expectation, began to relax and fidget again.

'Hold yourself!' cried Waldea. 'Be still! Order!'

Tighe's expectancy was intense. He found it extremely hard to stand completely still. With surreptitious glimpses over his shoulder when he thought the Master wasn't looking, he noted the ranks of military arrayed behind him. Somehow the still, ordered strips of men gave an even greater impression of numbers than the usual sight of the shelf thronging with people all moving in different directions.

He had never before realised that there were so many people on the worldwall.

After what seemed a lengthy wait the gilded door of the calabash cradle banged open. A murmur rippled through the assembled crowd and died swiftly: Tighe noticed Waldea glaring at the line of kite-boys and kite-girls, willing them to silence.

The Pope emerged. He was a tall man, grass-blade thin, who had to genuflect forward in order to fit through the small space of the doorway. When he stretched upright he paused for a moment to look about him, before walking confidently along the pier. He was dressed in a bright blue whole-body uniform that bristled with prongs, like blue thorns. Tighe assumed it was some sort of thick-haired animal skin, most of the hairs having been plucked out to leave only a few regularly spaced bristles.

The Pope was, as Tighe could see as he approached, an extraordinarily pale man; his skin was utterly white. As he stepped on to the shelf itself, it became apparent that he had been sweating; presumably it was hot inside the calabash's cradle. But the combination of pure whiteness and the glistening sheen of sweat made the Pope look weird, unpleasant; as if instead of ordinary skin his body was covered with the material out of which the whites of the eyes are made.

His nose was long, flat and bony with a sharp edge, like the shoulder blade of a skinny man; and it poked clear away from the Pope's round white face. But there were several chunks missing from the upper edge of it, crenellations in the line of the nose that started just below the bridge and culminated in a frayed nose tip. The whole thing looked like a leaf whose edge has been chewed by a caterpillar. Whether these deformities were the result of injury or disease wasn't possible to say; but Tighe sucked in a breath, and several possible battle fantasies suggested themselves to him.

Behind the Pope came the senior officers who had gone aboard the calabash's cradle to greet him, and he turned to exchange words with them as they came along the pier. Tighe was close enough to hear the sound of the Pope's voice, but he couldn't quite catch what was said. The Pope turned back to face his army, his huge, strange-shaped nose swinging round like a threatening finger. Cardinelle Elanne said something to him and pointed in the direction of a line of men, all carrying the metal poles over their right shoulders. The Pope stalked in that direction, away from Tighe and the kite-pilots.

He had a strange, jaggedy stride, as if his hip joints were sore.

For a while the Pope and his small retinue passed up and down the line of soldiers. They chatted with a man at the end of the line, and inspected the man's metal pole.

'Riflemen!' hissed the boy next to Tighe in a tiny voice, a touch of awe in the expression. Tighe made a mental note to remember the strange word.

The Cardinelle was touching the Pope's shoulder and pointing in the direction of the kite-pilots. Despite himself, Tighe felt his stomach clench in excitement. The Pope, nodding at something the Cardinelle was saying, loped back across the shelf towards him.

He stopped at the end of the line and spoke briefly to Waldea. It sounded like 'ownership of the air' and some other words that Tighe couldn't catch. 'Yes, sir,' said Waldea, his voice strangely choked.

Then, following another gesture from the Cardinelle, the Pope started down the line of kite-pilots, nodding as he walked. As he came closer, Tighe could see that his wide-spaced eyes gave out glints of red. He seemed to be without eyebrows. The roots of his head hair, as thick and ropy as any Imperial citizen's, were just visible at the base of the blue snood that covered his head and were a shocking white. In Tighe's roiling mind, he wondered if this whiteness was something the Pope had been born with, or was the result of some treatment, some bleaching out of his normal human colours that was a necessary precondition of assuming Popehood.

He stopped in front of Ati, a few boys away from Tighe. Looking sideways at him, Tighe could see that his blue uniform was made out of some odd form of plastic, a matt blue material that creased and squeaked as

153

the Pope moved. It was a shift that fell like a woman's dress from the shoulders to the knees, and the papal legs underneath were dressed in ordinary blue leggings. But the prongs on his blue uniform were not hairs, Tighe could now see, but were rather extrusions of the material of the cloth, poking out like thready fingers and jiggling as the Pope moved. They were spaced all over the blue material. If this uniform was made of plastic, it was of a kind of plastic that Tighe had never seen before.

'This', the Cardinelle was saying, indicating Ati by pointing with the knuckles of his right hand, 'is the boy who fell from the sky, your war-ness.'

'I have heard about your story!' declared the Pope, nodding his head at Ati. 'A remarkable story.'

Tighe twitched his face round to look more clearly. He could see Waldea at the end of the line straining, ready to take a step forward, but holding himself back. There was a furious expression on his face.

'Answer the Pope, boy,' said the Cardinelle.

Ati's eyes were bulging. He spoke, as if forcing the words out, 'Pope Effie.' There was a fractured pause, and he added, 'yes.'

'You are fairly dark on the skin,' said the Pope. 'Not as dark as some I have seen.'

'Yes, Pope Effie,' said Ati, in a strangled tone.

'I have heard it said that the higher up the wall one moves, the darker, because the skin is burnt more by the sun as it goes over the wall. I suppose the people who live on the very *top* of the wall must be as black as the blackest plastics!'

Ati made another strangled noise that might have been a yes.

'But then again,' said the Pope, still nodding his strange white head pleasantly as if he were chatting in the most relaxed of environments, 'there are people downwall who are almost as dark of skin as you are, my brave kite-boy, so perhaps the theory is wrong. Still, you will bring us luck!'

'Your war-ness,' said Cardinelle Elanne, touching the Pope's shoulder to take his attention. 'Perhaps, the arsenal now?'

'Yes, yes, Cardinelle, a moment. This boy has a remarkable story to tell.' He smiled warmly at Ati. 'So you fell from upwall?'

Ati did not take his eyes from the Pope. He looked, Tighe could see, terrified. 'Yes, Pope Effie.'

'How strange! I hear you bounced off one of our half-flated calabashes. That's stranger! And what did it feel like, to fall such a great distance?'

Ati stared, even wider-eyed. But the Pope seemed to have lost interest in the exchange anyway. He turned to face the Cardinelle, saying 'This boy will be a good omen for the campaign.' And then the Pope and the Cardinelle and the small retinue were striding away, towards the back of the shelf. Tighe caught Ati's eye, smiled at him. But Ati was sweating so hard it was dripping from his chin.

The Pope and his retinue disappeared inside a doorway at the back of the shelf and did not reappear for a long time. Waldea made one quick sally up and down the line of his kite-pilots, hissing at everybody to keep still, to keep order. Eventually the Pope re-emerged, and chatting – it seemed – amiably with the Cardinelle, stalked back over the shelf along the pier before disappearing back inside the calabash's cradle.

Almost immediately there was a great cry, an *aahh-ee!*, from somewhere away to the east of the shelf. The march-caller was summoning the men. *Aahh* in a deep voice, *ee!* rising rapidly to a shriek. 'Kite-pilots,' hollered Waldea over the sudden tumult of thousands of human beings bustling and moving away. 'Stand where you are! Kite-pilots stay!'

But all around them the strict, rectangular forms of the army were disintegrating, men hurrying away from lines and squares and streaming eastwards along the shelf. The noise of so many feet running along the shelf made a thunder and rumble that was like a great wind.

The kite-pilot line broke too and the kite-boys and kite-girls huddled into an excited knot around Ati. What did he say? What was it like? What was it *like* to look into the eyes of the Pope himself? I thought he looked ugly, said somebody. There were cries and howls at this little heresy. Well? Go on – well? What was he like? But Ati only stood in the middle, looking dumbfounded, and then Waldea was pushing the little huddle of boys and girls along through the throngs of people to the back of the shelf.

The scene cleared of people rapidly. Tighe strained his neck to get a better view of the flow of people as they streamed off the eastward parts of the shelf on to the ledges that led away towards the enemy. The voice of the march caller could still be heard clearly, even though he was out of sight. *Aahh-ee!*

'Kite-pilots,' declared Waldea, 'we wait until the main army has marched, and then we follow.' He glared at Ati, as if holding him responsible for the papal mix-up.

11

The yelp of the march-caller faded away and the shelf emptied itself of almost all the people. A few older individuals stood patiently in doorways or leaning against the wall at the back of the shelf, watching the streams of humanity leave.

The papal calabash rose slowly until its cradle dangled twenty feet over the ledge.

When there was space, a group of a dozen or more stocky individuals hurried along the pier and fitted ropes to the wall of the calabash. They scampered back to the shelf, spooling the ropes out behind them. Then they took up positions, tautening their cables, leaning forward with the ropes over their shoulders. With a grunt, they all began to pull and the calabash juddered. Three further men hurried forward with long poles, to stop the cradle from swinging in and dragging against the wall.

They got into their labour swiftly, hauling eastwards and dragging the papal calabash behind them. Within half an hour they were out of sight around the spar of wall at the eastern reach of the shelf.

Two calabashes remained.

'What happens to the calabashes at dusk, at dawn?' Tighe asked.

Mulvaine, who happened to be near-by, sneered at him. 'Don't you know anything at all, sky-boy?'

'But they're so light – look how easily they pulled away! When the big winds come, at dusk, at dawn, they must be torn and blown.'

There was general laughter at his ignorance.

Tuvette, one of the kite-girls, took pity on him. 'They pull them on to the shelf and take the air out of them,' she said, in a confidential tone. 'It is only hot air, you know, in the belly of them. Then they are strapped to the shelf. Those ones', she pointed, 'will be carried along the ledge. Only the Pope is important enough to be carried alongwalls in a calabash, you know.'

'My children!' announced Waldea. 'Now that the muscles of the army, its men and rifles, have made their way, we may make ours.'

Everybody fell silent.

'We have to reach the forced-march bolt hole by the time the sun goes over the wall,' Waldea announced. 'We will be travelling along open ledge – some of the ways have been prepared by sappers and that means fragile walkways. You *will* take care, children.' He wheeled on one foot and marched back down the line. 'You'll be walking along *exposed* ledge, so if we are still on the ledge by the time of the dusk winds, some of us will be lost. Do you understand?'

'Yes, Master!' as one voice.

'Shoulder your kite-spars, and bundles! Along this shelf and for a mile or so eastward – that is good way, a strong way. Because we met with the Pope himself we are late – the time is seventy, maybe seventy-five. So we must run the first stage of our journey – run.'

Tighe found the running hardest of all of them. He had built up his arm muscles, but had done little with his legs. Almost straight away his left foot began to burn. His stride was heavily lopsided and with each impact his left leg twinged and stung and his left foot complained. Trying to balance the frame and bundle of his kite over his right shoulder was difficult; with each uneven stride it juddered to the left and smacked painfully against his neck. He halted and shifted the bundle over to his left shoulder, but then it threatened repeatedly to fall off altogether, and his already loping stride was complicated by on-the-hoof attempts to compensate by twisting his torso.

He quickly fell behind the main group. The wall east of the camp was irregular, marked with prominent vertical spars of differing sizes around which the ledge wound its way. The main group would disappear round one of these headlands and Tighe would be alone. Limping and stumbling, sweating, with tears of frustration in his eyes, a fretful fear grew in his heart that he would be left behind. That the sun would go over the wall and the dusk winds would get up, and he would be exposed on the ledge all alone – that he would be blown away, blown off the world.

He struggled on, but he was crying now, sobbing hard, which made his whole body tremble and made it even more difficult to run. Halting along. He passed deserted doorways, occasional habitations spread along the reach of the ledge. He paused, dumping his kite on the ground, sucking breaths so huge they hurt his lungs, at a place where the ledge widened. Old stumps of bamboo rooted in the earth marked out a place where an animal enclosure had once existed. There must have been a village along the ledge here, or the beginnings of one. But the grass inside the worn-out post marks was long now, past grazing length. It was a waste. A good few goats could have been kept going in that space.

His brain, hammering and hurting, started to focus a little more precisely. If the worst came to the worst, and he were trapped out on the ledge as the dusk winds started, perhaps he could find a refuge in one of these deserted houses?

He stood straight, trying to ignore the throbbing of his bad foot. Then he hoisted his kite and started lumbering forward.

Around the next bend of the ledge-way he ran straight into Waldea – almost collided with him outright.

'Deserters are thrown off the wall!' he bellowed. 'Thrown *naked* off the world.'

'Yes, Master!' gasped Tighe.

'Tig-he, run faster!'

'Yes, Master,' said Tighe. And he genuinely tried to put on a spurt of speed, hurrying forward. But his left ankle seemed to liquefy and he tumbled down, sprawling in the dirt of the ledge and almost dropping his kite over the world.

In his panic he threw himself forward, snatched at the end of the kite and skidded in dust towards the edge of the world. His stomach clenched hard. But he stopped short of falling off the worldwall and wriggled round in a panic. The relief at still feeling solid ledge underneath him was so intense it was a taste in his mouth. He lay for a moment, his grip fierce on the spar of his kite. He was shivering. To his left he became aware of the crouching shape of Waldea.

'Little Tig-he,' he said, his voice gentle, 'to fall from the world one time and to survive is a great fortune. To fall again will surely be to die.'

Tighe tried to answer, but was panting too hard.

'You are not a good kite-boy,' said Waldea, settling himself more comfortably on the ledge. 'You tug too hard at the controls and you cannot anticipate the billows of the air. But you can fly and as such you will be useful to the Empire. Do not throw yourself away over the edge of things!'

'No,' breathed Tighe. 'No, Master.'

'Come,' said Waldea. 'I know your foot is poorly formed now. I will carry your kite and together we will jog to the bolt hole.'

Without the burden of his kite Tighe made much swifter progress, although he was wary of straying too near the edge of the world and jogged cumbrously with the wall itself at his left. Waldea himself, though a large man, ran with a slow flowing grace, the kite seeming shrunken against his bulky frame.

They passed along a broad ledge that sloped slightly upwards, open doorways like unfilled eye sockets to their left. But soon enough this remnant village passed behind them and they moved along uncultivated ledges, some of which were little more than crags. The passage of the army had rubbed away all the grass to dust, but Tighe could see that until recently these ways had been rarely trodden by humankind. From time to time the work of sappers was in evidence, planks of wood shoring up the crumbly outwall portions of especially narrow walkways. Tighe gasped to see such extravagance – presumably the sappers would follow up behind the march and gather up the precious wood.

Even with the augmentation, Tighe found these narrower ledges uncomfortable to move along. His heart tripped and rolled in irregular beats. All his instincts told him to slow down, to hang on to the wall at his left, to proceed slowly, cautiously, if at all. But Waldea was jogging fluidly on, and Tighe knew better than to deny him. So he swallowed the bile that rose in his gullet and pushed on too. Not looking to his right, that was the important thing. Not casting his glance into the abyss at his right.

They rounded another spar and Waldea slowed up. They had reached a broader ledge and Tighe could see a scattering of blue-frocked soldiers patrolling. At the far end was a peculiar blue-and-red blob being man-handled by a team of people working with long sticks. It was so far distant that Tighe could not at first make sense of it. Then he realised what was going on: the air had been taken out of the belly of the Pope's calabash and its floppy enormous skin was being piled and folded.

Waldea's stone-heavy hand was on Tighe's shoulder. 'In here, little Tighe,' he said, handing him back his kite. 'This is the bolt hole. Do not tell the others that I carried your kite for you.'

'No, Master,' said Tighe.

'I must have authority, you see.'

'Yes, Master,' said Tighe, incredulous that anything could undermine Waldea's authority, which seemed to him as godlike as the Pope's himself.

'The others would mock you, Tig-he, and think less of me. Never tell them.'

'No, Master.'

And then – miraculously, because Tighe had never seen it happen before – Waldea smiled. The scars on his face wriggled and crinkled like an animated painting of white fire, and his teeth flashed in the high sun. 'You and I share a secret now, boy,' he said.

Tighe stared up at him, goggle-eyed.

'Perhaps I will tell you some of my secrets when the battle is over, boy,' Waldea said, leaning over him. 'You and I are more alike than are the others. You and I are both from outside and both are wounded in the body. And I know some things, my boy!' he said, his voice grumbling with what sounded like a chuckle of laughter. 'I know some things about this war, my boy! I know the stories told in the Officers' Mess about the real reason for the Pope's marvellous action.'

'Master?' asked Tighe.

'Into the bolt hole for now,' said Waldea, standing straighter and his usual stern expression reclaiming his face. 'Into the bolt hole with the other kite-boys, the other kite-girls. The sun has almost gone over the wall.'

The bolt hole was a naturally formed cave, dusty floored but with hard rock for walls and ceiling. Grass-wax torches were pinned to the back wall, giving out a puckering light. The kites were stacked along the far wall and Tighe added his to the rack.

It was crowded inside. The kite-boys and kite-girls shared this bolt hole with a number of other platons from the papal army. There were no riflemen or regular soldiers – they were billeted in a more spacious cavern further along the ledge, it seemed – but there was a knot of sappers talking amongst themselves in one corner, and the kitchen staff with all their potboys and potgirls took up a lot of space. The kitchen workers were serving food out of a clay cauldron at the back, and Tighe grabbed a packet of something wrapped in grass-leaves and wove his way through the mess of people until he found Ati.

'You took your own slow time coming here,' said Ati, licking his fingers. He had finished his rations.

'My foot,' said Tighe. 'Bad foot.' He was still startled by Waldea's sudden intimacy with him, on the ledge outside.

Somebody slammed the door shut and wedged it tight.

A little later everybody fell silent and listened to the dusk gale outside. The wind seemed almost to be singing, a mournful and savage opera of howls and grinds. Somehow the noise was more spooky than usual.

Tighe untied his blanket from his back and unfolded it. 'Ati,' he said, as he wrapped himself up.

'Yes, my barbarian?' replied Ati, in a sleepy voice. He was already swaddled up, ready for sleep.

'Do you think of things?' Tighe asked.

'What?'

'Do you think of the worldwall?'

'You have turd for a brain,' said Ati, shuffling to make himself more comfortable.

'It's a strange place for people to live. Why did God build the wall?'

'God has reasons,' mumbled Ati.

12

The next day the army got moving much earlier. The sappers were up and moving around long before the usual time of the kite-pilots. They woke Tighe up with their laughter and he lay listening to their bustle. There was a gripping feeling in his stomach that was not pleasant. Would they go to war today?

The kitchen staff were up next, dragging their rumbling cauldrons over the dusty floor through the supine figures to the doorway. 'Kite-pilots!' barked Waldea suddenly. 'Up early today! Food and then straight away we march for the Meshwood.'

As they ate, Ati came and huddled close against Tighe. 'Today we'll see the Meshwood,' he said.

'Have you seen it?'

Ati grimaced. 'No, but I have heard stories. Claw-caterpils, terrible things. Like dragons.'

'What are *dracons*?'

'Like snakes, big snakes.'

'Oh,' said Tighe, nodding and looking serious. Then, 'What are *snakes*?'

Ati gasped in exasperation. 'They are huge, the claw-caterpils, with long bodies as long as a ledge. They are thin and long, like ropes, only bigger. And all along their bodies they have claws, like razh – yes?' Ati tapped at his fingernails with the fingernails of his other hand. 'Razh, yes?'

'Fingernails,' said Tighe.

'Yes, but much thicker and like a cat's claw. And there are dozens of these all along the length of the body.' Ati gave a little cry, giving up his attempt at description. 'They will eat you! Cut your body with their claw and their jaws.'

Tighe shuddered. 'They live in the Meshwood?'

'In the depths of it.'

Tighe shook his head sorrowfully. 'I do not understand', he said, 'why we must go through the Meshwood.'

'The Otre are on the far side.'

'But why must we march with the army? Can we not fly with our kites?'

At this Ati laughed hard. 'You are especially ignorant for a kite-boy,' he said. 'You are a turd for a brain. The winds do not flow that way, not along the wall. We cannot fly east – up, down, wallwards, awaywall, yes. But east, west, is hard to fly. Unpredictable.' He laughed again. 'A kite-pilot must know these things!'

Tighe blushed and bowed his head; and then, with a sudden access of energy, he bundled into Ati and pushed him to the ground. The two of them wrestled together, laughing, until one of the other kite-boys, Chemler, slapped them on the back to break them up.

They marched out in line a little later that morning. Waldea strode along at the back.

To begin with the line was straight and marched purposefully in order. Tighe walked ahead of Ati and behind Ravielre. But after an hour or two the discipline began to erode. The ledges they trod were broad and people began hurrying forward to chat to people ahead of them, or stopped to pick things off the ledge. They passed a single doorway, as empty as all the others on the march path, and several kite-boys scurried inside. Tighe waited by the opening; there was something evil-smelling about the opening that he didn't like.

'Come out of there!' bellowed Waldea from behind. 'Keep the line! Kite-pilots, keep discipline!'

They marched all through the day as the sun rose on their right. Tighe's bad foot pulsed with pain. Ravielre chattered incessantly in the morning; and then, when the sun crept over the fifty, he fell silent. He began picking pebbles out of the dust and throwing them as far as he could out into space.

'You should stop that,' said Tighe. 'You might hit kite, or calabash.'

'There's no kites flying, idiot-boy,' Ravielre snapped. 'You are stupid.' Then he grumbled to himself, and burst out with, 'When we go to war they'll be throwing more than stones at us. Fucking barbarian.' He tossed the next few stones over his shoulder at Tighe, but because he wasn't aiming they flew wide. Then he fell silent again.

Eventually, as the sun climbed higher and higher, the train of boys and girls came within sight of the Meshwood.

It was enormous. At first it was only a dark blur in the distance; then, as they came closer, it resolved itself into a vast excrescence, reaching upwall and downwall as far as could be seen. It bulged out from the face of the wall hundreds of yards in some places, a rippling mass like the surface of troubled water in a sink at which somebody washes, ripples frozen in time and enlarged to enormous proportions. It was also a colour that Tighe had

162

never seen before; a green so dark as to be almost blue-black, a much heavier shade than the green of grass.

As they came closer still the shape seemed to billow out into the sky. And then it superseded the sky altogether.

Tighe was overcome by the shape, the darkness that bulged from the worldwall. He was exhausted by the march; hungry and sore, and this shape seemed to give material expression to his own unease. By the way the other kite-boys stalled and meandered, the way they hung their heads, he could see they were also unnerved by the shape. But Ravielre seemed to straighten himself, to push out his legs like a goat stretching in the morning. Tighe understood the forced quality of the jollity, but valued it none the less. The fact of it was more important than its artificiality. He responded to it, as did the others.

Ravielre turned abruptly and poked his fingers sharply at the back of Ati's head. 'You're touched.' Ati started laughing. 'You're touched,' said Ravielre, prodding somebody else. 'You too. You.' He came up to Tighe. 'Hey, I know a question we never asked you in camp,' he said. 'You ever had a woman?'

'Yes,' said Tighe immediately. But his stomach clenched at the question. The kite-boys shrieked, pranced up and down. Several were running cumbrously about now, shouldering their kite-spars or carrying them under one arm, playing the game of tag, reaching out to touch their fellows, ducking to avoid the touch. From further back along the path came a booming order from Waldea, 'Keep order, keep the path.'

'You're tagged.'

'Kite-boys, keep the path!' Waldea boomed.

The boys settled down and fell back into a more regular rhythm of step. Tighe marched on, shifting the weight of his crossbeam over his shoulder. Where the skinny bones of his shoulder blades chafed on the wood it was starting to hurt badly. Up ahead the dark mass, like a titanic outcrop of hair, utterly eliminated the line of the worldwall. Behind him Ati was gabbling in a low voice, the tone too quiet and the language too unfamiliar for Tighe to guess what was being said. The titters of the kite-boys behind him gave him some idea, though.

'What is that?' he asked, casting the question generally into the air. 'What is that up ahead?' He knew the answer, but there was something frightening about the way none of the kite-pilots were talking about it.

The chatter of the kite-boys stopped at this, and the mood fell. Nobody answered him.

Tighe tried concentrating on the ledge ahead of him. The ground was narrower here and had been built outwards by the sappers with unevenly planed boards. They bent and sang under Tighe's feet. He wondered how many others had marched across this man-made ledge since the sappers had laid it down. He wondered how stable it was. His stomach clenched again and he shuffled over towards the wall, making sure to plant his left foot on God's good earth.

There was a sharp prod in the back of his head, so hard and unexpected Tighe cried out. 'Barbarian,' said Ati, his voice close to Tighe's ear. 'You're so stupid. You're so know-nothing.' There was real malice in the voice; not personal animus, Tighe realised, but the fear of the shape ahead infecting Ati's mood.

'I'm sorry,' said Tighe.

'Sorry is a *stupid* thing to say,' snapped Ati. And then, almost immediately, 'That there, ahead, is the Meshwood. Where the monsters live.'

'Sorry,' said Tighe again.

'We'd better get there before sunset too,' said Ati, 'or the big winds at sunset will just *push* us off the world.'

They made it to the outskirts of the Meshwood by sunset. As the sun disappeared over the top of the wall, they filed off the open ledge. The path led straight into a tangle of branches and shadows. Tighe's first impression was of broad, thick tree trunks, although unlike trees these trunks were twisted and curled. Platán wood, not regular timber.

The border was sharply distinguished: from open path and grass, with a dusty pathway worn by the passage of the army, the lead kite-boy led them all under the ribcage curve of a series of meshwood tree trunks and they were in a darker place.

There were sentries posted in a small military eyrie at the crossing place from outside to inside, and they made Tighe and the rest of the boys wait until Waldea came up from the rear. As soon as he arrived they started bickering with him, waving their arms and shouting.

'We've had *hundreds* through in the last few days,' the guards – three of them – were saying. The enormity of this number had clearly struck them because they kept repeating it. 'Hundreds – hundreds. Why should you get treated any differently?'

'I have my orders direct from the War Pope,' Waldea kept saying. 'I have a grandbul in my pack.' He retrieved the paper and flapped it in front of their faces. 'We're to bivuoac near the outskirts of the Meshwood tonight.'

'We have orders too,' said one guard.

'Move everybody through deeper into the wood. The path's clear enough,' said a second.

'There've been *hundreds* up along it,' said the third. 'It ought to be clearly beaten through by now.'

'Ah, I should think so,' said the first.

'We're a *kite* squadron,' shouted Waldea. 'Do you see what my boys and girls are carrying on their shoulders? We're no good in the middle of the fucking Meshwood.'

'Oh,' said one of the guards, as if sorrowful. 'Hardly a need to swear, I think.'

'My orders are to wait by the outskirts until we get further instructions. You can't deny my orders – here's the grandbul.'

'Maybe they meant the outskirts of the wood downwall a way,' said the second guard.

'We have *our* orders, you know,' said the first.

As they quarrelled Tighe unshouldered his crossbeam and peered up the path. It was like being indoors, in that it was murky and felt covered. But there was a strange smell. Tighe tried to picture what a *land-lobster* looked like. He couldn't help but shudder.

One of the other boys slapped Tighe on the back of his head. 'You look like you've never seen a forest before.'

'I never have,' he said. 'At least, never so many trees in one place. I've seen trees before, of course.'

Ati mimicked his voice. 'Oh, I've seen *trees* before,' he said. There was a general laughter, but it was strained. Tighe realised how nervous they all were.

Waldea and the guards were still bickering. With an army so large, clearly, it was hard to keep everybody in harmony. 'How far,' Tighe asked the boys behind him, gesturing with his right arm at the wood they had just entered, 'how far does it go?'

The kite-girls, a dozen or so of them, kept themselves together as a group. Once the bivouac was set up, a few of the more courageous kite-boys sauntered over to them and tried to talk to them: but it happened under the eye of Waldea and the girls made no sort of response, so they eventually gave up. 'My father,' said Ati, to Tighe, as they settled themselves into their pouches to sleep, 'my father is a carpenter. You know what that is?'

Tighe shook his head; the word was unfamiliar.

'It means he worked with wood. This,' and Ati slapped the stem of meshwood that the pouches were tied to with the flat of his palm, 'this is poor wood. You'd think it would be possible to build with it, but no.' He reached down and took hold of one of the smaller limbs of it. It bowed, curved round. 'No, too spongy, too soft.' He released it and the branch thrashed back, wobbled eventually settling.

'Listen, kite-children,' called Waldea, 'we have the shelter of the wood now, but we're near the edge, so we'll still feel the evening gale. Untie your kite-bundles, and then tie them to a branch. Have a care with that! Then you all must all use your belts to strap yourselves to a trunk of a meshwood tree until the wind dies, and then I'll call to a couple to take watch.'

They unbuckled their blankets and unfolded them, talking in short, nervous sentences. The thought of spending the dusk outside was frightening. The proper place to be during dusk, when the winds screamed and bustled up and down the wall, was safely inside.

'I'm frightened,' hushed Tighe to Ati.

Ati nodded sharply, focusing his attention on tying his belt tightly so that his torso was strapped to a trunk.

Tighe tried to tie himself to a trunk next to Ati, but the wood was so spongy that the belt cut into it. Tighe yanked and the squishy stuff inside tore and pulled apart. He needed an older, drier trunk. Anxiously, because everybody else was strapped in now, he clambered up the steps provided by the trees, stepping past his fellow kite-pilots. Eventually he found an unoccupied stiff, dry trunk. It was next to Mulvaine.

He busied himself with tying himself down and then settled himself. When his breathing had calmed a little, he looked round, and caught Mulvaine's eye.

'Hello,' he said.

'You Barbarian turd,' said Mulvaine, without malice.

There was silence. The branches and strands of Meshwood were rustling; the dusk gale was starting up. Tighe chattered to distract himself from his terror.

'Ati's father was *carpenter*,' he said. 'My father was a Prince. What was your father?'

Mulvaine glowered at him through the thickening light. 'You Barbarian turd,' he said again, but there was no passion in his words. 'You're deformed. Your foot is so ugly. No girl would ever fuck with you.' But this was all said in a desultory manner and Mulvaine lost interest in it soon enough. 'What was that you were saying?' he asked. 'My father.'

'My pahe, my father, was a Prince. That is like a Pope, for a village, you know.'

Mulvaine breathed contemptuously through his nostrils. 'Small village nobody. I come from the Imperial City itself. *My* father was a philosopher.'

'A what?'

'A philosopher. A priest of God and a thinker.'

'Oh.'

The wind was getting up and the conversation died. Tighe braced himself, but it was not as terrible as he thought. There was a thrashing sound from below, and soon the trunks were swaying and jiggling; but somehow the roaring of the wind sounded less intimidating out in the open. Tighe wondered how that could be.

After half an hour or so the winds died, and pretty soon it was quiet and calm. It was now pitch black. Tighe wondered what to do. He could hear Mulvaine moving in the darkness near to him. There was a vague apprehension of shadow.

'What are you doing?' he hissed.

'Unbuckling myself, what do you think, you idiot,' replied Mulvaine. 'I want my supper. You think I'm marching all that way and then not eating anything?'

Tighe's own stomach was shrunken with fear and anticipation. But he was, he realised, hungry too.

A little below and away to the right there was a spark that flared into a flame. As Tighe fumbled with his own belt he watched the orange light swell. Somebody had lit a fire. Mulvaine was already climbing down towards it.

Waldea had pulled out branches to clear a sort of chimney up through the Meshwood and was now burning the wood as a bonfire. Tighe marvelled at the wastage – even if it wasn't proper wood, it still seemed extraordinary to burn wood rather than dung. But as the night got chillier he was glad of the heat. The kite-pilots huddled as close to the spitting bonfire as they could.

Waldea made spits of sticks and speared morsels of meat on the end of each of them. Groups of boys and girls cooked themselves supper and then climbed, monkey-like, to seats amongst the meshwood branches to eat. Soon enough everybody had eaten.

After a space of staring silently into the fire, Waldea said, 'I'm going to sleep now, my children. Be sure you all strap yourselves in tightly before you go to sleep, or the dawn gale may pluck you out of the heart of the Meshwood. I do not say to you, go to sleep immediately. I know how excited you must be in your hearts. Only, do not stay awake too long – it will be a tiring day tomorrow.'

'Will we go to war tomorrow, Master?' asked Mulvaine, his voice quavery.

'Tomorrow will be a day of glory, my children!' declared Waldea.

He wrapped himself in his blanket and strapped himself to a broad meshwood trunk. One or two of the kite-pilots did the same; but Tighe was too excited to think of sleeping just yet.

The fire was starting to burn down, but it was still fierce enough.

'War,' said somebody. 'Think of it!'

'The Otre are a terrible people,' said Mulvaine. He was sitting closest to the fire, poking a stick of platán wood into it and drawing it out to stare at the tamed fire at its end.

'I heard', said Tighe, 'that the Otre cut off the legs and the arms of their pas – of their mothers and fathers, and make them *eat their own arms and legs!*'

He looked around, hoping for a horrified reaction from the small group of kite-boys and kite-girls around him. But none of them looked impressed at this information.

'Well,' said Mulvaine, '*this* is what *I* heard.' He looked about him, as if he were about to impart a profound secret and wanted to make sure that nobody else would overhear. The Meshwood was a tangle of shadows in every direction. Tighe didn't like to look at it. He concentrated his gaze on the fire. Flame wriggling upwards like branches.

'What did you hear?' asked Sluvre.

'I heard that when we fight them tomorrow, we had best make sure we are not captured by them. Do you know why?'

'Why? Why?'

'Because of what they do to their prisoners of war. And do you want to know what they do with their prisoners of war?'

'What? What?'

Mulvaine leant closer towards the fire, and spoke in a lower voice. 'They tie you up, in the outskirts of the Meshwood. A place like this perhaps.'

'Do the claw-caterpils get you, maybe?' asked Bel, breathless.

'Worse than that,' intoned Mulvaine.

This was met with cries of disbelief. Worse than the claw-caterpils? Impossible!

'They strip you naked,' said Mulvaine, drawing out each word with a drawling emphasis. 'Then they tie you down straddling a branch of this platán. Do you see this little bud here?' He flicked a tiny nubbin, no bigger than a fingernail, growing out of the platán trunk in front of him.

Everybody leaned in to look at the bud.

'What is it?' asked somebody.

'It's a bud,' said Mulvaine. 'A new branch will grow out of it. So they strip you naked and tie you so that your bumhole is exactly over one of these buds.' There were shouts of disbelief, but Mulvaine raised his voice. 'It's true, I heard this from one of the sapper regiment people, and he said they found some Imperial soldiers who had been captured and treated this way. They tie you over the bud and the branch grows up through your bumhole and up your bum! Yes it does!'

There were squeals, shouts of denial, laughter.

'They feed you a little and they put a wet rag in your mouth morning and evening so you don't die,' Mulvaine continued, speaking even louder to be heard over the tumult. 'And over a week the platán trunk grows up inside you. And over two weeks it grows bigger, and bigger. And eventually it grows and *stabs* your insides.' He pounded his fist against the broad trunk beneath him as he said this. 'It *stabs* your insides until you die.'

Everybody was silent now. Nobody doubted that this horrific treatment was standard Otre business.

'This man from the sapper regiment,' said Mulvaine, dropping his voice, confident now in his command of his audience, 'he said they found one of the Imperial guides, and he was dead, but a branch of platán was growing *out of his mouth*! With leaves and everything!'

Tighe was troubled by difficult dreams that night. In the morning he could not be sure of them, except that they had been unsettling and unpleasant; populated with frightening hybrid people whose limbs sprouted platán leaves, whose wicks were as thick and broad as platán trunks; people who had Mulvaine's eyes and intended to torture Tighe. Tighe had a vague recollection of struggling through the tangle of branches and leaves of the Meshwood with pursuers at his back.

But it was dawn, and the light was coming through the leaves, and a camp potgirl was bringing breakfast slung around her neck.

13

They did not see battle the next day, nor for several days afterwards. When the sun had heated the air and started it rising, Waldea took three kite-pilots to the entrance to the Meshwood and sent them flying out away from the wall. They scouted and returned and reported that there was no sign of anything, except the Meshwood reaching away into the east.

'Are there any crosswinds east?' Waldea wanted to know. 'How far might a kite fly east today?'

But the crosswinds were patchy and treacherous. The last thing a pilot wanted was to be caught out in the sky, blown so that there was nowhere except Meshwood to land – trying to land in the midst of the spiky, curly branches and trunks would be suicide.

So instead Waldea ordered the kite-pilots to shoulder their kite-spars and belt their bundles around their waists. 'You must march through the Meshwood!' he declared. This was not as easy a matter as marching along clear ledgeway. 'At some places', he told them, 'you must pass your kites through carefully and then follow. Have a care for your kites at all times!'

To begin with the path was clear enough, boot-marks still visible in the dust from the strides of riflemen and soldiers who had passed before. But after an hour or so the path dissipated and the line broke up. Each individual kite-boy and kite-girl had to make his or her way as they found best, stepping from trunk to trunk, sometimes finding little paths along truncated crags and craglets, sometimes passing along what seemed to be sheer wall, stepping on wobbly trunks. To Tighe's right the blue sky was visible, though scored over with the arcs of dozens of trunks and branches. At one point he lost track of the rest of his platon and became scared; but on calling out in a high-pitched voice he was answered with several yells and he realised that his comrades were all around him.

By now they had left the ledge far behind and were all picking their way along branch and trunk. The complex patterning of shadows across trunks shifted its design as the day went on. The pools of shade that lay everywhere about in the morning thinned as the sun rose to shine directly in through the tangle. The shadows resolved themselves into a tracery of wickerwork that was beautiful to look at – or so Tighe might have thought if he hadn't been wholly occupied with finding secure footholds whilst hefting his kite over his shoulders.

At some time around midday, or fifty as (he rebuked himself silently) he had to get used to saying, the sun started spotlighting through the branches, blinking into the corner of his eye. The shadows diluted and the detail inside the forest became more apparent.

Tighe paused. The way ahead was not clear and his blistered shoulder blades were complaining. He unshouldered his kite and propped it on the runt-end ledge he was standing against so that the spar rested against a trunk of meshwood.

He stretched. All around him the forest rustled. He thought it was the wind, but as he looked more closely he saw something slithering through the leaves up ahead. He was momentarily frightened, but the thing could hardly be the claw-caterpil Ati had described. It was the thickness of a wrist and the length of an outstretched arm. Coloured shadow-grey, it had wound its way around a trunk of meshwood and was eating one of the leaves. Every now and again it would pulse its body forward and start on another leaf, flowing along on a row of legs so numerous and so tiny as to look like a fringe of cloth. Two teeth poked out from its head, which it used to gather the leaf into its belly-button-like mouth. It seemed to lack eyes.

Now that he had paused and was able to look around him, Tighe could see that the Meshwood was full of life. Normal-sized insects bustled along the branches or through the yellow grass of such crags as there were: beetles, grass-lice, meat-fleas, teardroppers, fireslugs, vivid blue- and green-coloured hoppers with ornately puckered carapaces. There were knuckle-bone-sized ledge-flies, much larger than he had seen before, which drew invisible curlicues lazily through the air. But there were also insects the size of cats or monkeys: Tighe looked below and saw two beetles, as big and knobbed as human feet, which were banging heads together along a trunk. A strange silvery flying bug, looking like a toy fashioned from plastic, flapped cumbrously upwards, landing on a trunk to rest, then pulsing a hat-like section of its back up and down rapidly to flutter up again. Peering into the distance, Tighe thought he could see something the size of a small goat, although greatly elongated, pushing noisily through the branches and leaves.

The awareness of so much wildlife all around him unnerved Tighe; partly the fact of it and partly the thought that he had been blundering through the wood for half a day without noticing it. He had been completely absorbed in himself. He reached over to shoulder his kite-spar again and press on eastwards when there was a tremendous crash away to the west and a little way up.

Somebody was crying out noisily; Tighe recognised Chemler's voice.

Leaving his kite where it was, Tighe scrambled up from stem to stem. He found Chemler easily enough, draped over a branch. He was having difficulty breathing.

Tighe helped him up to a sitting position, with his back against the wall. 'Are you well?' Tighe asked.

'Better,' said Chemler, gasping. 'Got winded. Fell a bit.' He pointed upwards and Tighe saw a ragged chimney of broken twigs. Leaves were still fluttering down and several branches were wobbling gently.

'You fell?'

Chemler nodded. 'Not far. Not easy to fall far in this wood, I'm', he breathed in, 'pleased to say.'

'What about your kite?'

'Don't know,' said Chemler. 'I dropped it. But I think it's still up there.'

When he got his breath back, Chemler climbed up the way he had fallen. Tighe went with him. They found the kite-spar easily, wedged in a V of branches.

'Mine is down there,' said Tighe. Chemler nodded, hefted his kite and started east again. Tighe made his way back down and retrieved his own kite.

He moved on, more conscious now of the variety of wildlife around him. Bugs of all scales slithered and rustled all around him. Once, as he was reaching for a handhold on a stem of meshwood, something slippery touched his hand. He yanked it away with a yelp, and looked up to see another of the grey worm creatures with the myriad legs nosing along the branch. He felt certain it was harmless, but none the less he chose another branch.

On another occasion he saw a monkey. It was so unlike any monkey he had ever seen before that at first he took it for a man in an orange jacket – bright orange fur over its torso and black legs, with two tails and a frond of long hair cresting its head. It swung easily up branches as handholds and came to within ten arms' lengths of him. It had quick black eyes and it gave Tighe a cool up–down appraisal, before swinging further up. Tighe passed it cautiously and looked back up at it when he was further along. The monkey had lost interest in him and had instead captured one of the fat grey worms and was biting chunks out of the thing's back.

A little later in the day Tighe heard a scream, but could not be sure if it was human or animal.

Still later, he heard the unmistakable voice of Waldea, bellowing through the woods. 'To me, kite-pilots! To me!'

Tighe started upwards.

Waldea kept calling out and Tighe picked a way upwards along trunks of meshwood like steps following his voice.

The platon gathered. Mani was crying, her hand bloody. Something had bitten her, she said. Something in the wood. She hadn't seen what it was and she had thrashed out with her hand when bitten – she thought she had dislodged it, but she hadn't heard it fall. Waldea examined the wound and cleaned it with leaves and some water from his own canteen. Then he wrapped it in cloth and told her not to fuss.

When everybody had arrived and was accounted for, Waldea tore twigs and branches from a tall space over a particularly large meshwood trunk. These he gathered in a bundle, tied with a spare belt to a trunk. Then he ordered everybody to strap himself or herself to a trunk as they had done the previous day. They settled there, more exhausted by the day's march than they had been by the ledge-walking of the day before. Deep in the wood now, the dusk gale hardly made itself felt at all, and Tighe was eager to unstrap himself as soon as he could, almost before the gale was over.

Waldea built a fire in the dark and the platon huddled round it, quieter than before. Several people pressed Mani to show her hand, but she kept it wrapped in cloth and clutched close to her body.

They all ate in silence, cowed by the strange environment. Even Mulvaine, usually cocky, was quiet.

'It was probably a land-lobster that bit you, Mani,' said Waldea eventually. He spoke with a dark voice. 'My children, you must be wary of all such things as live in this wood.'

It was remarkable, thought Tighe, how Waldea's manner had changed towards them since the order had come to march to war. He was less distant; it was more as if he were a comrade than a leader.

'Master,' he asked, a little quaveringly.

'Yes, Tig-he?'

'Were you ever in this wood before?'

'I was, my children. I have been through and through this wood before, and I know its terrors. The worst of them are far below us, thank God and the planning of our Pope. But when I was here before I encountered all of them. Worse than any land-lobster.'

He stopped speaking, and the firelight made curious shapes over the scars of his face. Every kite-pilot's gaze was on him.

'Master?' said Tighe again, meaning to ask how Waldea had come to be in the Meshwood. But he started speaking again without the prompt.

'My children, you are young. You know little of the history of our glorious empire. But we have been here before. In my day, I was as tiny as

173

any of you and I too flew a kite. And in my youth I was part of a mighty army, almost as mighty as this one is. We marched eastwards a league or two downwall from where we are; we marched to conquer the heretics of Otre. Those were glorious days, my children! Glorious days!'

The kite-pilots were silent: spellbound. Never before had Waldea been so forthcoming. He seemed to withdraw from his narrative for a while, staring into the fire, his face curiously distorted. But he resumed it without prompting.

'We had a hard march. Downwall from here the wood is plagued with terrible beasts. Beasts with jaws so big and teeth so metallic they'd bite clean through your arm – devour your head in a single snap. Terrible insects, enormous. We lost many on our march and fought harder against these creatures than we ever did against the enemy. But the Popes knew that the Otre had to be defeated. Because the Otre hide a secret in the heart of their evil world.'

He paused again, and Tighe wondered if he was going to share this secret with them all. He was reminded of the gnomic conversation they had had the day Waldea had carried his kite for him.

Suddenly Waldea spoke, 'Do you know this secret, children?'

There was a synchronised tremble as every kite-boy and kite-girl shook their heads together.

'Children, this is what our world is about. There is a Door in the wall!'

Waldea widened his eyes and stared about him, gauging the impact of this news on his young audience. Nobody said anything. The fire grumbled and cracked.

'A Door, do you see?' Waldea said. 'A Door in the worldwall – and it exists in the heart of the kingdom of the Otre. They have laid impious hands upon it and we are sending an army to recover it. To reclaim it for the Popes, the Empire and for God!'

'What, Master,' said Ravielre, nervously. 'What is through this door?'

Waldea shook his head. 'It is a holy Door. God built the wall and lives on the other side of it. This Door will lead us through to Him.'

'I was taught', said somebody else, 'that God lives on top of the wall, from there he can see all eternity.'

'No,' said Tighe, urgently, 'no, God lives at the *bottom* of the wall.'

There was general scoffing at this idea.

'Why do the Otre not step through their Door?' asked Mulvaine. 'Why do they not go to meet with God?'

'It is a holy Door,' repeated Waldea. 'The Otre are an impious people and cannot open it. God would not permit something so wrong. But our Popes will open it when we have captured it. We will meet God face to face. We will see the paradise on the other side of the wall.'

'No!' piped Tighe. 'We must not open the Door!'

Everybody looked at him.

'And why not, little Tig-he?' asked Waldea, with a trace in his voice of his old sternness.

'I was taught in my village by . . . by a wise man,' said Tighe, feeling nervous that the eyes of the whole platon were on him. 'I was taught that God lives at the bottom of the wall. That God is at war with creatures on the far side of the wall – that is why every day he heats a great rock until it shines with heat and throws it over the wall. He wars with the creatures on the far side of the wall.' He was surprised at his own fluency in this foreign language, but he felt an urgent need to convince the others of his insight. 'We must not open this Door in the wall, or these creatures will come in. They are very terrible, God builds the wall to . . .' he wanted to say *to separate us out from them*, but he couldn't think of the words.

'Idiot barbarian,' said Mulvaine. 'God sits on the top of the wall, everybody knows that.' He looked nervously at Waldea. 'Except, Master, that perhaps God lives on the far side of the wall.'

Waldea did not seem to be in a mood to be angry. 'Ours is a holy war,' he said. 'The Popes themselves will decide what is to be done when we have defeated the Otre and captured the great Door.'

'Master?' asked Bel. 'What happened in the last campaign?'

'My child?'

'You said you were part of an army years ago. You came through the Meshwood?'

Waldea lowered his gaze, staring intently at the fire, and squeezed his brows together into a scar-lined crease.

'We came through the Meshwood,' he said, 'but it cost many lives. There are monsters downwall that turn your blood to liquid shit, no matter how brave you think you are; monsters that fret the heart and seize up the legs. I have seen brave men squeal and run like children before them. They fell upon our army, with their blank, myriad eyes and their hungerless, never-ending jaws. Grotesque they are, armoured with plates as tough as the enamel of teeth all along their backs, and each of their many legs is as sharp as a knife blade. Some are as long as two tall men laid end to end, and as fat around their hairy, pulsing bellies as a man's waist. Their faces are the worst; foully deformed imitations of a face, with slimy mouth parts and bristling bulging cheeks, and stone eyes like evil jewels, all faceted. They cut through arms and legs with their jawbones as easily as I pull down a branch from this tree. They might seize a man by the neck and kiss him mouth to mouth, devouring his lips and tongue; and when he would fall they would feed out of his face as out of a bowl. They moved like a tether falling through air, swiftly and undulating and with a silence which was the worst thing of all. We would march fully armed. Sometimes there would be the sound of a rifle discharging and we would stop and listen, and if we heard nothing else we would thank God that another abomination had been dispatched. But sometimes there would be the sound of a rifle discharging and a cry, a terrible cry, as uncontrolled as a baby's scream, and we would know that somebody else had been taken.'

He fell silent again, musing over the fire. He seemed unconscious of the fact that he was running a forefinger over his scars.

'By the time we reached the far side of the Meshwood, we were only a third of the army we were when we came in. But we rallied ourselves and I went out in my kite, and reported to the generals and the War Pope, and we took the holy war to the Otre. Bravely we fought, bravely my children! As bravely as we shall fight again, as we come through. But we were too few and the war was not ours that day. We were forced to flee back through the Meshwood, and then the carnage was worse because we had less discipline and many of us were wounded. The claw-caterpils can smell blood from a long way off and they came in hundreds, swarming over the meshwood trunks from all sides. How few of us emerged on the Empire side of the wood! How few!'

He turned to Mani. 'The land-lobsters are poor things by comparison!'

There was a silence. Eventually Mulvaine spoke what they had all been thinking. 'Master,' he said, 'I'm scared.'

Waldea – deliberately or otherwise – misunderstood the statement. 'Defeat is a frightening thing for any warrior to contemplate,' he said, 'and it is right that you are scared, because that will give you the fire you need to win. To win! And as for the claw-caterpils,' he added, as if in afterthought, 'they are all to be found in the wood a long way downwall from here, my children. The Popes have planned this campaign carefully and this portion of the wood was explored carefully. There may be some land-lobsters to give you the odd nip with their pincers, but you will not encounter a claw-caterpil.'

The fire had burnt low, and Waldea announced, 'To sleep, now, my children. Tomorrow we will march again and perhaps reach the far side of the wood.'

Tighe wrapped himself in his blanket and strapped himself to a branch. He felt nervous and could not help but look all around him at the shadows as the last embers of the fire gave out its last hints of light. Ati had taken a branch close to him. 'I'll not sleep, Ati,' Tighe quavered into the dark. 'The Master has filled my head with nightmare.'

'Horrible,' agreed Ati.

But Tighe, despite himself and with a vague feeling of being somehow cheated, felt himself falling asleep straight away. That sensation of dropping into something; then nothing.

The following day they breakfasted, gathered themselves and struck out east again. Waldea's words the previous night worked a particular sort of effect upon them, however; instead of ranging through the wood, they picked their way carefully as a crowd. That meant that progress was much slower than the previous day, kite-pilots clogged on a small crag waiting to step, one at a time, on to a convenient trunk and file forward. But Tighe was glad to have the companionship of his fellows.

Waldea loitered at the back and seemed withdrawn. Occasionally Tighe glanced back over his shoulder at the Master and wondered if he regretted his confidences of the night before. It had been so unlike him. Because progress was often held up, Waldea took to sitting down on an available perch and staring out into the tangle of branches and shadow, as if reading a special significance in the murk.

At one point in the afternoon Mani started shrieking up ahead. Tighe pushed forward, and saw her being comforted by one kite-boy, whilst another thrashed out with a stick at something amongst the leaves below. With a flash, like a flame in the shadows, a bright red creature two hand spans long scurried away and down. Tighe caught only the briefest glimpse of it: like an animated red plastic shoe with great horns at the front, except that the horns ended in pincers that snickered alarmingly, clicking open and shut.

'Is that land-lobster?' he asked.

'Move along,' called out Waldea from behind.

That evening they made another fire after the dusk gale. Conversation was thinner. Everybody was tired. 'How much longer in the Meshwood, Master?' asked Mulvaine.

'Tomorrow, my children,' said Waldea. 'Tomorrow I believe we will emerge the far side.'

'At least we saw no claw-caterpils today,' said Tighe.

'There are no claw-caterpils this high up the wall,' said Waldea sternly. 'God would not permit evil to come so high up the wall. This is why our Popes have led us this way through. It is their wisdom.'

It occurred to Tighe to ask why, if the Popes were so wise, they had led the youthful Waldea and that whole doomed army through the midst of the claw-caterpils all those years before. But such a question would not be advisable.

'Why', asked Ati, out of nowhere, 'would God create something so terrible as claw-caterpil?'

A murmur went round the camp.

'God', said Waldea, raising his voice to an intimidating volume, 'has His reasons. You should not ask such a question!'

But the curious thing was that this act of vocal authority did not work the way it once would have done. Back when Tighe had first joined the platon, Waldea had needed only to raise his voice to intimidate them all. Now the murmuring went on unheeded.

'Why did God', Mulvaine put in, 'give the control of the Door in the wall to the Otre – to the evil Otre?'

'Yes,' said somebody else. 'Why?'

'Why would God do something so terrible?'

'Wouldn't it be better', Mulvaine pursued, 'for God to blow the Otre off the wall with the breath of his nose? Then we would not have to fight them.'

'Children!' bellowed Waldea. 'Be quiet now!'

'What if God is not on our side at all?' asked Bel, in a quiet voice. 'What if God is on the side of the Otre? Then what chance will we have?'

Waldea yelled again, his voice now so strained as to be almost a shriek. 'Sacrilege!' he called. 'Be quiet, now!'

Everybody looked at him. With a start Tighe realised that he was crying, that actual tears were pipetting from his eyes and weaving amongst the alleyways made by the scars on his face. More than his raised voice, this fact shocked the platon into silence.

For a terrible, embarrassing moment, nobody said anything. Waldea sniffed noisily, scraped the back of his hand over his eyes. He mumbled, 'Do not say these things, my children.' Tighe felt the most acute sort of awkwardness, a passionate wish that this moment would pass. He opened his mouth to say something, but couldn't force a word out. Didn't know what to say.

Waldea stood up abruptly and turned his back on the platon. The kite-boys and kite-girls started chattering amongst themselves in low tones. For several minutes the Master simply stood there, his back to the group. Then he turned back and sat down again.

The following day they marched again. They saw several more of the land-lobsters, scarlet and swift, scrabbling along branches from all directions. They were easily scared away; thrashing out with a twig would usually frighten them off, although one of the kite-girls, Pelis, inadvertently put her hand on top of one of them. The beast snipped deeply through the end of her little finger, half-way down the nail. There was a lot of blood, but Pelis – to her credit amongst the platon – shed no tears. Waldea silently wadded the end of the wound with cloth and wrapped it around until the blood stopped soaking through. Then they marched on. The delay cost them no more than an hour.

They found a dribbling spring not long before dusk and all refilled their flasks.

That evening they camped again in the Meshwood. Once the dusk gale had died down, Waldea lit another fire. Almost at once a blizzard of enormous moths came swirling up out of the branches. Tighe, and several others, were so startled as to cry out, but it quickly became apparent that these insects were no threat. They were larger than any moths Tighe had ever seen before; fat furry bodies like mice with great cloth-like wings each of which was twice the area of a man's hand. Dozens poured through the gaps in the leaves to swirl about the fire.

'Moths!' called Waldea. 'There's good eating on a moth this size. We'll feast well now, my children!'

There was no need to catch the creatures. They fluttered themselves into the fire until their wings caught like paper and they spiralled into the flames. Squealing with delight, several boys picked twigs from the branches and plucked the smouldering bodies from the fire. Tighe got one and bit into it; the meat tasted inky, slightly sour, but he gobbled it down anyway.

After the fire died down and they were all strapped to trunks, Ati said, 'The gugzh here are so large. The insects I mean.'

'I never saw insects so big before,' agreed Tighe.

'Why would God make such ugly things?'

Tighe dropped his voice a little. 'I think I know. Ask yourself, why God build the wall?'

'Why did God build the wall?'

'Exactly. Is to keep *out*. There are evil things on the far side of the wall. Man-eating, evil things.'

'Like claw-caterpils?'

Tighe whistled softly. 'Maybe like, maybe much bigger. If there is Door in the land of the Otre, maybe some came through and came to the Meshwood. That is why they are here I think. If we win the Door, win the war, then we must shut it! Shut it!'

The next day was colder than usual and several kite-pilots wore their blankets over their shoulders rather than fold them and strap them to their backs. Tighe tried this, but found it hard to balance the kite-spar.

As the day went on the crags and ledges became fuller; there was less need to pick a pathway from trunk to trunk, and the platon moved faster. The branches were thinning; more sky was visible to the right. With a tremendous lightening in his heart, Tighe understood that they were coming towards the far side of the Meshwood at last.

At about seventy-five the platon ran into a guard of riflemen. There were six of them, sitting on two trunks and eating what looked like grubs. Each of them had their long metal tubes – or were they made out of plastic? – strapped across their backs: their rifles. They did not react when the kite-pilots emerged.

'Weren't you alarmed that we might have been enemy?' asked Mulvaine, cocky and excited to be so close to a rifle.

'We heard you blundering through the Meshwood from a long way away,' said one of the riflemen gruffly. 'You were no Otres.'

Ravielre tried to reach up and touch the end of one of the rifles, but had his hand knocked away by its owner. 'Keep off there, boy,' said this rifleman.

Waldea arrived from the rear. 'Comrades,' he called, 'how far to the edge of the wood?'

'Twenty minutes,' said one of the riflemen, spitting out the carapace of whatever he was eating.

Their estimate was exactly right. Twenty minutes later the platon arrived at a guard eyrie built into the very edge of the Meshwood.

As Waldea negotiated with the guards there and then went off to report to a superior officer, the kite-boys and kite-girls gambolled along the ledge and threw stones at one another. Their spirits were high. Before them stretched a landscape of open wall, its contours throwing long arcing shadows downwall in the high sun.

They became bored with their game eventually and settled themselves in small groups, squatting on a crag a little above the ledge that was being used as the main thoroughfare. A few people, including Ravielre and Bel, went back a little way into the wood.

Tighe sat with Ati for a while, picking blades of grass and chewing them absently. Ati declared that he wanted something more substantial and went back to the outskirts of the Meshwood to find some grubs to munch. Tighe was hungry too, but he was too entranced by the vista of open worldwall to leave it.

The sun rose higher and faded redder, throwing deeper-hued shadows sharply downwards. Blue-coated soldiers and various army individuals passed back and along the ledge.

Mulvaine came up and sat next to Tighe, saying nothing. For a while they simply sat together. The size of the worldwall, the sheer scale of God's construction, awed Tighe, as it had used to do when he had been a mere child in his own village.

'It's so big!' he said, to Mulvaine.

The older boy spat, turned to him. 'What?'

'The worldwall,' said Tighe. 'It's so big. So big! The majesty of God, that he would build something so big.'

Mulvaine grinned, and then said something that struck very deeply into Tighe's mind; something that later haunted his thoughts. The seed of some great branch of platán that would grow over his consciousness; the key to the mystery of the worldwall itself. He said, 'Is it big?'

Tighe didn't, at first, grasp the penetration of Mulvaine's observation. 'What?'

'Don't say *what* like that you barbarian turd for a brain. I'm senior to you in this platon! Show respect.'

'What was it you said, Mulvaine? Not big?'

'I ask: is it big?'

Tighe shrugged. 'I don't understand. Is it big? Look at it. Doesn't it look big?' The worldwall reached away to the east, like the broad forehead of God himself. The grass on this side of the Meshwood had a purple shade to it, and as the wind tickled the ledges and the wall, this blueness shimmered over the surface. It reached so far east that the detail became hazed by distance. It reached so far down that Tighe could not see the bottom. It was so tall that it took all day for the sun to climb the height of it. Not big? 'What do you mean, Mulvaine?' he asked. 'What do you mean, is it big?'

'Is it big?' Mulvaine repeated. 'Or is it that we are small?'

14

It was a revelation to Tighe; not an instant one, but one that grew within him over the next day. The revelation that there might be – that there was – a mystery attached to the worldwall. And the curious thing about this revelation was that it chimed deeply with Tighe's sense of his own childish life. He had always known, he realised, that there was some sort of mystery to the world into which he had been born. It was only that he had not *known* that he had known this. It had been something like an instinct, a feeling of intensity in his breast when he had looked out over the sky, or lain on his back to look up along the height of the wall.

He spoke with Ati the next day, 'Do you know what Mulvaine said to me yesterday?'

Ati made a grunting noise. 'That thug? I dismiss him.'

'His pahe was a philosopher, you know.'

'His?'

'His father. His father was a philosopher.'

'So?'

'He said to me, *Is it that the worldwall is big, or is it that we are small?*'

Ati looked blank. 'Meaning what?'

'Do you not think about it? Why has God build the worldwall?'

'Why has God *builded* the worldwall, is the proper saying.'

'All right – why has God builded the worldwall? But why?'

Ati shrugged. 'I don't know. Why should I know?'

'But the insects – in the Meshwood. You said yourself they were very big.'

'They were big.'

'And what if they were not big – but we were small?'

Ati barked with laughter, hurried up to Tighe and tried to grab his ears. Tighe wriggled to escape and soon the two were rolling and wrestling together, laughing. But afterwards, and that night when Waldea took the platon back a little way into the wood to strap themselves to trunks during the dusk gale, Tighe found the idea had seized his mind with unusual force. What if the tree trunks around him were not trees but blades of grass? What if he himself were an insect and only he had not realised the fact? Would not a ledge covered in grass look like the Meshwood to a low-worm crawling through it; and would not a low-worm have the dimensions of a claw-caterpil to a human being tiny enough?

One thing above all seemed to him to seal the argument. If he were God, he thought, would he build the worldwall on so enormous a scale? Or would he build it convenient to himself and shrink his people to fit?

Sudden lurching shifts of scale inside Tighe's head made him feel almost dizzy. A religious vertigo.

The following morning the platon was woken by distant rumbling sounds, as if the sky were crumpling and collapsing far away. It was shortly after the dawn gale.

'Kite-pilots!' called Waldea. 'Awake! Unshackle yourselves!'

In the confusion of bustle, Tighe dropped his belt; but fortunately it only fell to the branches of the trunk below and he was able to retrieve it easily. There was a fizzing excitement in the air; everybody knew what the distant thunderous sound meant. War.

At last, war! Tighe thought.

It was almost too exciting.

Waldea led the kite-pilots out of the wood and along the ledge. The guards in their eyrie were the only soldiers to be seen. Otherwise the ledges were deserted. In a matter of minutes, however, the platon worked their way round a spar and ran into a knot of soldiers. Riflemen, bomb-hurlers and sappers were crowded into a short, deep ledgeway.

'Cardinelle Elanne!' called Waldea. 'I have my orders from the Cardinelle! Where is he? I must report.'

But nobody took any notice. The bangs and booms in the air sounded closer now. Waldea pushed on, leading the gaggle of kite-pilots behind him. They were simultaneously intimidated and excited by the scale of the hurly-burly around them.

Up a sloping ledge and along a ragged crag made broader by the sappers, pushing past soldiers of all sorts, they arrived eventually at a broader space: overhung, not long enough to be a shelf, but with a series of dug-out spaces in the wall at the back. Two tall wedges of dirt testified to the recent nature of the excavation.

Waldea told the kite-pilots to wait close by the wall and stay out of mischief whilst he himself went off to find Cardinelle Elanne or some superior officer. Tighe was disturbed at the haphazard nature of the military command. He felt somehow that the process should be smoother, more natural.

The kite-pilots milled around, wound-up and agitated, chattering amongst themselves. Ravielre and Bel were now quite open about their romance; holding hands and talking quietly with one another.

With a cry to clear the path, a couple of soldiers hurried by carrying a blanket between them in which was slung something heavy. They passed through one of the dugout doorways, and Tighe realised with a start that the thing being carried in the blanket was a human body.

He went to the doorway and peered in, hoping to see Vievre, the old doctor. But it was murky indoors and whatever was happening inside was hectic, generating a great deal of noise and fuss. Tighe decided not to investigate further.

After about an hour Waldea returned and wordlessly led the kite-pilots away from the mini-shelf. They filed down some crudely carved stairs and on to another ledge, this one open, at the end of which was a much smaller dugout doorway. 'This is our camp for now,' Waldea announced.

The door was so small that the kite-spars and bundles had to be passed through first, with the kite-pilots following behind. Inside the earth was moist with the smell of recently dug soil. The wetness of the walls suggested that there were streams near-by, and Waldea sent Chemler off to investigate so that they could refill their flasks.

Mulvaine was told to tie up a grass torch and wedge it into the earth at the back of the dugout. By the time he had finished, and Waldea had lit the thing, Chemler was back. 'There are several trickles along the ledge,' he announced.

'My children,' announced Waldea, waving them all into a semi-circle before him with a sweep of his arm. 'Battle has begun! Already we are attacking the evil of Otre at their heart.'

Nobody said anything.

'Soon we shall be called – the generals, the Cardinelle, the Pope himself, have need of us. We are to fly and gather valuable information for the higher command. Soon they will call on us!'

Nobody came for an hour and the kite-pilots became restless. Waldea stalked out of the dugout, bending low to fit through the tiny door. He returned. Nothing happened.

Several kite-pilots napped, curled on the floor. Others went out on to the ledge to see what they could see, but it was no vantage point.

Waldea returned, clearly annoyed. The sun went over the wall and the dusk gale began. There was no door for the dugout hole, so the kite-pilots huddled together at the far end of the hollowed space. The wind sucked the torch out, sang and shrieked, threw clods of earth through the door and tugged eagerly at clothes and hair. But it died down eventually.

The following morning, immediately after breakfast, Waldea departed again. This time he was gone for about half an hour, and came hurrying back in a state of great excitement.

'Now, my children! Assemble your kites! You are to fly! The Cardinelle requires you to fly out and take an overview of the battlefield – report back with tactical information.'

The pilots assembled their kites on the sunlit ledge outside. Nobody spoke. Tighe unpacked his bundle and spread the fabric out; then he fitted the main kite-spar into its crossbeam. The usual sounds of distant booms and crumples made their strange music.

It felt odd to Tighe to strap himself to the kite once more; it had been so many days since he had flown. He was anxious too; uncertain what was required of him and keen not to incur Waldea's displeasure. But the thrum and smell of war was all about him now and distracted him from the usual terror. Ati stepped forward off the world and Tighe followed him quickly, pushing away from the ledge into the burly morning wind.

He dropped until an updraught caught him and hauled him high. He realised he was drifting westwards, the wrong direction, and angled up and over to fall, gathering speed in the descent and sweeping east in the process. He pulled quite a long way awaywall, banked, climbed and turned again. The wall came round into view. Catching a little eddy of rising air, he wobbled his way back in.

The scene that grew before him was chaotic and, in the first instance, unimpressive. The wall was patched and scorched with small areas of black and grey, but was otherwise mostly green and purple with its grasses. Ledges were set at gentle angles to one another and a large shelf was thronged with blue coats. But as he swept in Tighe could see that the grey-coated Otre soldiers were occupying the upper ledges. Occasional glints of light, like a silver surface turning to bounce the sunlight, glittered on the lower ledges. Tighe flew closer still and saw that these bursts of light flew out of the end of the riflemen's weapons, aimed upwards at the grey soldiers above them. He was a little above the central ledge.

Something shiny hurtled past Tighe's kite. For an instant he thought it was some large shiny-skinned insect, but when he turned a little he could see that it was a fireball, arcing downwards now. It narrowly missed another kite – Tighe could not see whose – and fell away.

It took a heartbeat for Tighe to register the significance of this.

He was evidently too close to the wall now. He tried turning, zigzagging to find lift, but there were no updraughts. He drifted closer still to the wall, on a level with the Otre-occupied areas. Gasping with fear, he swung in close enough to make out enemy faces, pale and helmeted. One tall soldier pointed out at him with an outstretched arm; his colleague lowered a rifle and there was a flicker.

The noise of the wind was so huge in Tighe's ears as to drown out most of the sounds, but he certainly heard a breathy whistling sound and a *ploc* that made his kite shudder. He wobbled, turned and fell away, picking up speed that enabled him to swerve away from the wall. When he pulled out of the dive and swept upwards again he had time to look over his shoulder. There was a fist-sized hole in his kite.

His mind still did not register that he was in danger. The adrenalin of flying blotted out more refined appreciation of his situation. He circled round and tried to make a more concerted survey of the battlefield. The Otre occupied all the higher ledges and seemed to have built some sort of fortification along the overhung ledges further east. The Imperial army was concentrated on the central shelf; but Otre soldiers directly above were throwing things down on them. These objects flew out and then – improbably – swerved back in. As he flew lower to gauge their strength there was a spectacular explosion of red and orange and a wash of heat over Tighe's face. The kite shuddered and lifted, and without controlling it Tighe was carried up and away from the wall.

He circled again, but the kite was awkward and stubborn, difficult to steer with a hole in its fabric. He pulled westward and flew in a trembling downward trajectory back to the launch ledge.

He landed awkwardly. Waldea was hurrying over to him as he picked himself up. 'Well?' he was calling. 'Well? Is there something important?'

'My kite, Master!' said Tighe, breathless, unhitching himself from it. 'Look at my kite.'

'What? Kite? That's no damage, hardly any damage. Report, Tig-he!'

'Master, the Otre command the upper ledges. They are throwing fire upon our soldiers.'

'And?'

Tighe couldn't think of anything to say. Waldea pressed his hands into fists in frustration, and repeated himself: 'And? And?'

'And nothing, Master.'

'Idiot! We know the Otre have the upper ledges. But what about further east? Did you not fly further east?'

'My kite was damaged, Master.'

'Repair your kite and go out again,' snapped Waldea. 'Fly east! We must know about the fortifications further east.'

*

Tighe, bewildered and scared at feeling so uncertain, rooted out a patch of leather, needle and thread from platon supplies in the dugout. He made his way back to the launch ledge to sit and repair the kite as best he could. He had never learned to sew, but was too ashamed to tell anybody.

He sat cross-legged and poked uselessly at the torn cloth with the needle. It was difficult making the plastic needle push through the leather and he hurt his thumb trying to force it. There was a rush of air and Ravielre landed a few yards from him.

'My kite caught fire!' he gasped, unbuckling himself. 'I was struck by fire from the wall and the material caught. But I beat it out with my arm. Look at my kite!' The material was singed and ragged on the left side.

'Ravielre?' shouted Waldea, hurrying over. 'What have you to report?'

'Nothing Master, only that my kite was on fire.'

'Repair it,' yelled Waldea in frustration. 'Fetch materials from the dugout like Tig-he – repair it and go out again. Don't return until you have something to report.'

Ravielre hurried away, leaving his still smoking kite lying on the ledge. Feeling increasingly awkward, Tighe poked ineffectually at the material he was trying to patch over the hole. When Ravielre returned, he was glad to have somebody to have a conversation with rather than work at the stitching. 'You were on fire!' he said.

'It was a dizzy-bomb,' said Ravielre, brushing the charred pieces free from the wing of his kite. He was in a state of excitement.

'What is dizzy-bomb?'

'You are an ignorant barbarian,' said Ravielre automatically. 'They are bombs, with metal blades attached by a cord. Throw them away from the world and the blades spin and pull the bomb back in towards the world downwall.'

'Bombs!' said Tighe, amazed and impressed.

'They are bags of leather really,' Ravielre confided. 'They have a fuse and are full of powder. But they explode with a mass of fire!'

Deftly, Ravielre patched over a stretch of leather, stretching it taut and stitching with dextrous fiddling motions of one hand. Tighe watched in amazement. He was ready to go out again in minutes.

Waldea had come back. 'Tig-he! You are still waiting? Fly again, go out and fly again.'

'I have not yet patched the hole in my kite,' Tighe murmured, ashamed.

'What? I cannot hear you if you speak so small. There's no time to waste – I have to report your intelligence directly to Cardinelle Elanne. Get out again!'

'My kite . . .'

'You can fly perfectly well with only a small hole – that is only a small hole.'

He manhandled Tighe upright and would have physically inserted him into his kite if he had not been distracted by the arrival of another kite-pilot at the ledge, a girl called Stel. Tighe had time to overhear the beginning of their conversation as he strapped himself in. 'What will you report?' snapped Waldea. 'My shoulder,' whimpered Stel. 'It is hurt, popped I think.' 'Shoulder?' bellowed Waldea. 'Shoulder?' shouting in an enormous voice – and that was the sound Tighe had in his ears as he stepped off the world again and flew away.

The kite was wobbly and unpredictable, but could be flown. Tighe circled and circled, and made his way very slowly eastwards against what were now difficult contrary winds. The battlefield was clearer to him now because he was more used to the logic of the vista. He could see the soldiers crammed along their ledges, trying to kill and dislodge their enemies above or below. He could see where one stairway, which had evidently once been used to link the central shelf and the higher ledges, had been destroyed – the actual steps kicked and blasted featureless on the wall. Sappers, from which army Tighe could not tell, had attempted to build another stairway to provide access either up or down: spars poked out of the wall, some of them still burning, most blackened and cracked.

The pattern of lines and diagonals was emphasised by the flurrying action of men moving back and forth, and picked out with sparkling flashes and occasional belches of smoke. Grey puffs, like tiny clouds, swept across and upwards, dragging their shadows over the undulating surface of the wall.

Tighe struggled for several hours, making slow progress eastwards, his repeated circles drawing the attention of snipers from the upper ledges. Several projectiles whispered past him, one catching the sole of his shoe and unzipping the leather so that the cold grabbed his right foot. He was straining to look east, to look carefully at the fortifications of the Otre, but eventually the sun rose too high and the updraughts began to die. There was nothing for it now but to fly back to the base ledge: if he stayed out too long he would lose lift altogether.

The ride back was a great deal easier than the ride out had been; Tighe coasted all the way, the air whistling a pure note of music through the hole in his kite.

15

That evening, in an angry tirade, Waldea berated the entire platon. They were useless; they had given him no information that was of any benefit to the War Pope – it had been humiliating for him to have to trot back and forth between the base ledge and the Cardinelle's eyrie like a pet monkey with nothing to say, nothing to report. As soon as the dawn gale died down the platon would go all out, would all fly east, and would fly so close to the enemy ledges that they could count the *teeth* of the Otre soldiers – and if anybody did not, then he, Waldea, would personally eject them from the world and they could fall all the way to the rubble at the foot of the wall.

The platon sat, heads down, in aching silence. Tighe felt devastated; he felt has if he had personally betrayed Waldea, the Popes, the Empire itself. But he was so exhausted that he fell asleep almost at once.

The next morning, they all expected to be sent out flying straight away, as soon as the updraughts started. But instead Waldea disappeared and came back an hour later to tell them to stay where they were.

It was a warm day, with the sun climbing slowly and pushing light and heat at the wall in generous heaps. The usual sounds of battle were stilled; and a plump silence edged the occasional gust of wind.

The platon lounged about their little ledge, chattering nervously. When would the order come? The hours advanced, fifty, to sixty, to seventy, and it began to look as though they would not fly at all that day. Tighe was restless. When Waldea left, as he did from time to time to hurry upwall and check on the latest orders from the higher command, Tighe itched to go roaming about, to see what was happening. But he was afraid of leaving the ledge, afraid that if he stepped upwall for even a few minutes it would be at the time that Waldea came barreling back down and ordered them all into the air. Other boys were not so inhibited, particularly as the sun rose and the air cooled and it became clear that there would be no flying that day. Mulvaine and a few others darted away and scrambled upwall, returning breathlessly after a short while.

'There are whole lines of men, riflemen and other soldiers,' Mulvaine reported to the kite-pilots, who gathered eagerly around him. 'They're queuing up there, preparing to go forward.'

'It's a big push,' said somebody. 'They're going to push through and capture the Otre fortifications.'

'They're going to use darkness to get into position, I think,' said Mulvaine. 'Tomorrow will be the day of victory.'

The excitement of this intelligence buoyed Tighe up for a while, and there was a certain amount of high-spirited darting about and boys grappling and wrestling. But this died down and soon enough Tighe was bored again.

He curled up on the purple grass of the ledge and fell asleep, napping for no longer than ten minutes; but it was sleep filled with the most vivid dream-sense of flying, of pulling back away from the wall as full battle raged. The Imperial soldiers pushed forward, sweeping away the Otre, and Tighe caught a glimpse of the Door, the Door through the wall that was the purpose of the whole campaign – an enormous door like the front door to a house in his old village, complete with latch and storm-covering. People swarmed up and down it like ants, and then, impossibly, Tighe could see the top of the wall – could see the cloud-snaggled upper rim of the world. An enormous head, a head as big as the world, rose above it like the belly of a calabash. The head of an old man, and Tighe realised it was God, and at the same time realised that it was Grandhe, his old Grandhe. Grandhe opened his titanic mouth and bright light began spilling out.

He woke up, gasping, a sweat on his face.

Next to him a couple of boys were sitting opposite one another, playing a game with pebbles. Each boy had a pile of awkwardly shaped pebbles in a pile in front of them. Each took turns and put a pebble in a circle drawn in the turf: a pebble could be placed anywhere, so long as it touched another pebble. If it touched only one other pebble it could not be moved by the opponent, but if it touched two or more it could be nudged sideways by the other player's move so long as it stayed in contact with at least one stone. If any pebbles strayed outside the circle the player concerned lost the game. This game was called *jazua*. It was sometimes played as a passtime by the kite-pilots.

Tighe watched the gameplay for a while until his pulse calmed and the sweat dried from his skin. Then he grew bored and sought out Ati.

'Ati,' he said, 'will you help me stitch the hole in my kite? I do not know how to stitch the hole.'

'You are an ignorant barbarian,' said Ati automatically.

Together they fetched Tighe's kite and Ati showed him how to work the needle through with pressure from the thumbnail and how to do a rough lock-stitch. As he worked he talked.

'It is most exciting,' he was saying. 'They say tomorrow will be the big push. Tomorrow we can fly free and watch the Otre being pushed off the ledges. By the next day we will have the Door and we will have won the war.'

'Ati?' asked Tighe. 'Do you ever look at the wall when you fly; and think it small?'

'How do you mean, small?'

'You know you see ants on a patch of earth? What if the wall is small and we are ants? The whole worldwall small and we are ants.'

'What a philosopher you are,' said Ati, grinning. 'Would it matter if we were ants? We are still bigger than *our* ants, bigger than other bugs. We are big enough, I think.'

Tighe shook his head. It was hard for him to convey the hollow sense of falling away within his breast that this concept produced. It was as if the entire world had been trivialised, as if the epic conflict between the two mighty nations were nothing but insects bickering over a blade of grass. It diminished existence, corroded the sense of meaning in being. 'Bigger than ants,' he said, mournfully, 'but not bigger than claw-caterpils.'

Ati made a *chch* sound in the back of his throat. 'There,' he said, 'your kite is made whole, I think.'

Later that day Waldea gathered up three of the boys, Mulvaine, Oldievre and Mocghe, and took them upwall. When this little party returned, the boys were swinging grass-weave sacks full of something.

'Now,' said Waldea, 'we fly tomorrow. And each of you, my children, will carry a wax-bomb. You must carry it inside your trousers, at the top of your trousers, children, and hold your thighs tight and cradle them in your lap not to drop them. They are lit, with a grass fuse that will smoulder – the fuses are tarred, so they will smoulder even when you fly and the wind will not put them out. And you will fly up and release the bombs at the soldiers on the upper ledges. Do you understand?'

The pilots eagerly gathered around the three boys as the wax-bombs were brought out. Fist-sized spheres of wax, they were hollow. 'Filled with mushroom powder,' explained Mulvaine, cocky and knowledgeable. 'You throw them and when they strike the wall the wax breaks and the fuse here flames up the powder and *boum.*'

'Handle them carefully!' fussed Waldea. 'You are only to look at them today and we shall pack them away tonight. Tomorrow morning is a big push and you will assist.'

Tighe, almost trembling with the excitement of the thing, cradled a bomb in his open palms. The wax had been mixed with grass filaments, drawn out of the finer blades, to form a rough circle. The wax was dark red, almost black, and there was a little tar-covered nipple at the top. A weapon! Explosives!

Waldea gathered every one of the precious bombs and stocked them at the rear of the dugout. Then he had the platon spend an hour practising throwing stones. Since one of the favourite passtimes of most of the boys and some of the girls was precisely this, the platon proved adept. Waldea set up a target by scrawling the shape of a man into the mud of the wall and everybody took turns hurling pebbles at it.

After the dusk gale, at supper, Waldea was in an expansive mood again. 'Tomorrow will see a great victory over the wickedness of the Otre,' he said. 'And this platon will play its part. We will play our part! There will be no shame.'

After the day's idleness, Tighe found it difficult to go to sleep that night. He was not alone. Whispered conversations rustled around the dugout like the wind at dawn, mostly speculating about the Door that the army was sure to capture if not tomorrow, then surely the day after tomorrow. 'It must open on a corridor,' said somebody. 'It is a mile high,' said somebody else. 'I was speaking to a soldier,' said Ravielre, 'an old soldier, and he knew somebody who had actually seen the Door.'

Hissing astonishment. No! Really! What was it like?

'Sleep, my children,' grumbled Waldea, turning over and pulling his blanket more tightly about him.

This quietened the exciting hissing for a moment, but it soon started up again. 'It seems that the Door is ten miles high,' whispered Ravielre. 'Nobody has ever been able to open it because it is so big.'

'How will we ever do it?' asked Ati. 'It is impossible to open so big a Door!'

'Impossible for a shit-eater like you,' hissed Mulvaine, 'but not for decent Imperial citizens like us. We'll open it, won't we, boys!'

There was a babble of sounds, rising above a whisper now, until Waldea barked out in the darkness, 'Be still! Be quiet! Sleep, or I'll light a torch and begin by punishing every boy in turn.'

They were quiet after that and eventually Tighe fell asleep.

16

The morning after the dawn gale was quiet, but everybody was excited. Tighe could barely manage his breakfast, his stomach was so agitated with the thrill of anticipation.

The kite-pilots all took positions on the ledge and assembled their kites. Then nothing happened. An hour passed, while Waldea paced up and down. Tighe felt the excitement wane in his belly and he began to believe that they would spend another day waiting pointlessly.

Without warning there was an enormous explosion from the east. All the kite-pilots shouted and cheered in unison, and Waldea hurried through the dugout to fetch the wax-bombs. 'This is it, my children,' he called out to them, going amongst them and handing out the bombs. 'Wait till I have lit your fuse and then fly off – fly away and bring the proper wrath of God upon the Otre. Fire from the sky! Fire from the sky! Now it is their judgement.'

There was a series of regular booms in the heavy mid-morning air, and Tighe, straining his ears, even thought he could hear a sound like cheering as (he imagined) the Imperial troops surged forward. Or was it a sound like screaming? – as the Otre soldiers plunged from their ledges, fell through the air, to be dashed to fragments against the boulders at the foot of the wall?

The kite-pilots were gathering at the edge of the world as Waldea went amongst them, bending forward with his flax and lighting the fuses. First Mulvaine, and then a procession of boys and girls stepped into the air and flew away. Tighe stepped up to the edge.

'Keep the fuse free, give it air. Don't stifle it with skin or clothing – it'll burn your skin, Tig-he,' said Waldea. The old man was panting, the scars on his face gleaming with sweat. 'Tuck it, here, into the top of the trousers. That's right. Now, fly – pick your target carefully! Do not merely throw it away!'

Tighe nodded, gasped excitedly, and stepped into space. He was so intent upon not dropping the bomb, and not stifling the fuse, that he barely noticed where he flew. He swept rapidly away, looking up just in time to see another kite circling back, and hauled to the side to avoid colliding with it. His heart was really hammering now.

The winds were good; clear and with strong lift. Tighe circled and pulled round and cleared the spar. The battlefield came into view.

He had been expecting there to be something decisive marked on the face of the wall – lines of blue-coats marching along, grey uniforms falling – but the scene was much as it had been the day before yesterday. There was a mess of action, scattered bursts of flame or light, rags of smoke drifting up or being yanked to nothing by the wind. The central shelf was still occupied by the Imperial forces and they seemed no closer to the Otre fortifications.

Tighe whirled through the air and made a pass at the ledge directly above the central shelf. Not close enough. He swung round again, as the air was tracked with smoky threads all around him. On the return he had lost height and was closer to the central shelf. A knot of blue-uniformed Imperial soldiers swelled into view. He swooped close to a group of them; two were kneeling and firing upwards with their rifles, a third was standing and reloading. Their attentions were distracted for a moment by Tighe's approach, and he struggled to turn his kite without wriggling his body too much and risk dropping the bomb.

For an instant their faces seemed close enough to touch, eyes wide. Then something buzzed through the air and the standing soldier opened his mouth, closed his eyes and toppled forward. Tighe pulled away, turned and angled back in time to see the body of the soldier twisting and falling through space. A lengthy string of red beading stretched up from the figure as it fell and dissipated into red mist. In a moment the body was gone.

The wind was shushing in Tighe's ears as he dropped down, hit a strong updraught and began a wobbly ascent, spiralling tighter and tighter. A shining orange blob hurtled past his face and he found himself abruptly confronted with a line of Otre snipers. Most had their weapons angled down, but one or two were firing out into the sky, aiming at kites. With a rushing sense of power, Tighe plucked the still smouldering wax-bomb from his lap and threw it.

His fingers slipped a little as he jerked his arm, and the sphere spun upwards as it left his fingers. He just had time to see it collide with the overhang of the ledge and scintillate into flames before he banked and fell away. Rifle bullets zzed past his body.

It was a disappointment not to have hit anybody with his bomb, but his heart was hammering anyway. He had a clear view of blue sky and squeezed his eyes flat in the glare of the sun; then he banked, and the worldwall slewed round into sight. Half a dozen kites were framed against the vista. They were all swooping diagonally down, closing in on the wall.

One kite flickered, dimmed, and was suddenly on fire, flames flapping like streamers against the fabric of the kite. The kite-pilot – Tighe, mouth wide in horror, couldn't see who it was – flapped with one arm in what appeared to be an attempt to put the fire out. But the flames slid easily along the arm and the body of the pilot was soon twitching and jerking in harness. The whole structure was alight, hundreds of tiny flames wriggling on the broad plane of the kite itself like grass in the wind. For a while, freakishly, the kite rose, lifted on the cushion of hot air it had itself created; then a pole, burnt through, broke, and the kite crumpled with a puff of ash and an intensification of the fire. It dropped straight down, falling like a meteor and leaving only a streaky column of black smoke behind it. Tighe, circling again, couldn't be sure if the kite had been struck by some weapon from the wall, or if the pilot had mishandled their bomb and set themselves alight.

The other kites in view swept close against the wall and Tighe could make out the actions of throwing arms. Pimples of flame started at various points above or on the main Otre ledge and the kites wheeled away.

Back on the base ledge, Tighe unharnessed himself as Waldea hurried over. 'A kite,' he babbled. 'Burn! Burn and fall . . .'

'Be quiet!' snapped Waldea. 'This is war. No time for that. Strap yourself in. Take another bomb and go again. This is the great push!'

Bewildered, blinking, Tighe took another bomb. He felt miserable with his cargo now; its burning tar fuse smelt to him of death, the little parcel of wax could burn him and kill him as it had done to whoever it was who had fallen to their fiery death.

As he stepped off the ledge, Tighe resolved to get rid of the wax-bomb as soon as possible. It did not occur to him until afterwards that he could just have flown out of sight of Waldea and dropped it. Instead he worked round and up on the rising air and flew hard at the Otre ledge. He hurled the bomb with a newly inspired vigour, but he was travelling so fast that he had to bank immediately and he did not see where or whether the bomb struck home.

After this he pulled away from the wall and circled, uneager to go back to the base ledge and be armed once again. He watched waves of kites circle up, swoop down and throw their bombs. Mostly they would strike bare wall or explode next to soldiers, and Tighe could see that they were remarkably ineffectual; scattering nothing more damaging than shortlived fire and hot wax. 'They're more dangerous to us than to the enemy!' he said aloud to himself.

One bomb, thrown from another kite, hit a soldier in the chest and the fire rapidly claimed his grey tunic. He was struggling to pull the clothing off, as far as Tighe could see from his distance. Then he stumbled and fell off the world. The rush of air kept the flames close to him and he was soon gone.

Eventually Tighe decided he could not loiter much longer in the air without incurring Waldea's anger, so he returned to the base ledge to be armed once again. For the third time that day he flew out, flew over the battlefield, swept straight up and lobbed his bomb. This time he yelped with pleasure to see it glance off an upraised rifle and slide along the shaft to explode directly in the face of an Otre soldier. The fellow dropped straight to the ground rolling back and forth in the dust to put out the burning wax. His hair had caught fire. Tighe passed and circled round, anxious to see whether he had actually killed somebody, but on his return it looked as though the soldier's comrades had put out his flaming hair.

The Otre had armed themselves with a new weapon. From several points on a number of ledges they released birds; to these birds they had tethered a mesh filled with tarred grassblades. Set alight, this globe of fire would terrify the birds to which they were attached, and the creatures would fly fast and straight to try and escape the flames. Blur their wings in flight and hurtle away.

At first Tighe only saw the burning circles, tracing a thread of smoke away from the wall, speeding out in an impossibly straight line. The first of these missed its aim, but the second struck a kite away to Tighe's right and spread its burning load over the wind-dried leather. It flamed and dropped in seconds.

As more and more of these fiery parcels shot out from the Otre ledges, Tighe could see the birds that preceded them, and realised what the weapon was. A ball of fire came straight for him and he twitched his kite aside.

He span, losing control for a moment, and then pulled round and flew west. He cleared the spar and left the battlefield behind. As the base ledge came into view he could see Waldea standing there. There were two kites on the ledge next to him, one warped and broken. Two kite-pilots were sitting at his feet.

Tighe came in to land and unshackled himself. 'Master!' he shrieked. 'I saw two kites destroyed! Two! It's terrible!'

Mulvaine and Mocghe were the pilots sitting at his feet. Mocghe was nursing his left arm.

'This we know,' said Waldea in a strange tone.

'They have a new weapon!' Tighe said, as other kites came whooshing down around him. 'I think it bird, with fire tethered. Flies straight to us. Two kites!'

'This is the glory and the pity of war, my children,' said Waldea, in a musical voice. 'There are no more bombs or I would send you out again. Again and over again until you destroyed every Otre soldier!'

Tight's stomach was crossed with conflicting senses of horror and excitement; the image of the kites crumbling in flame and falling to the bottom of the world kept flashing over his mind; but there was a thrumming in his blood so intense and exciting that his hands were trembling. He had thrown a bomb! Brought down an enemy soldier! 'I struck an Otre,' he told Waldea. 'I hit one! His head flamed!'

But Waldea was distracted now by the return of the remaining kites.

The upwinds died as the afternoon went on and the kite-pilots huddled together on their ledge. Four were not present: Stel, Mani, Tolo and Chemler. The talk amongst those who remained was subdued, and avoided all mention of the dead companions. Each kite-pilot in turn related his day, the accuracy of his bombs. 'I threw three,' said Tighe. 'The first two went bad, but the three was good. It struck an Otre on the head and his hair went on fire.'

Murmurs went round the circle.

'I threw four,' said Mulvaine. 'Two of those claimed Otre lives. I am glad to have killed two of the enemy!'

Murmurs again.

'My kite was struck twice by riflemen of Otre,' said Ravielre. 'There was such a rattle! Such shaking when their bullets went through my kite! But I threw two bombs and they both landed on ledges.'

'I threw four,' said Oldievre.

'Three,' corrected Waldea, in a deep base rumble. He was sitting, head down, silent for most of the time. 'I only gave you out three bombs, Oldievre.'

Oldievre blushed. 'Three, I say,' he said. 'They all struck at the ledges and I saw grass on fire under the feet of several Otre soldiers.'

There was a silence.

'You have done well, my children,' said Waldea, after the pause had extended long enough. 'We shall be heroes of the war!'

'Did we push through?' asked Mulvaine tentatively. 'Did the army capture the fortifications?'

Nobody replied.

Tighe slept poorly, and kept waking sweating. He had nightmares about fire, dreaming he was flying his kite as fire sprouted spontaneously from all around. Then he was falling and he woke up crying aloud as he had done as a child, with a gut-wrenching sensation that the ledge beneath him was tilting and that he was falling all over again.

He must have woken half a dozen times, each time blubbing and sweating. Finally he woke to the sound of the dawn gale through the open dugout doorway and could not sleep further. He felt exhausted in every part of his body. There was a clench of terror at the back of his throat, a palpable sensation of horrified anticipation. But at the same time he was eager to get back out into the air, to throw more bombs at the enemy. It was them; it was the Otre. They were devils.

Over breakfast, Ati came and settled himself next to Tighe. 'We're soldiers now,' he said, in a quavery voice. 'We fight in the war.'

'Yes,' said Tighe. 'I am hungry to fight again.'

Ati nodded, as if he understood exactly the complex of eagerness and terror that informed Tighe's statement. 'We always be soldiers now,' he said. 'All through the future. We will always be soldiers now after this.'

'I am hungry to fight again,' repeated Tighe. But, as he thought about what he was saying, he realised that his real eagerness was to get back to his village. He remembered his pashe. He remembered being held in his pashe's arms.

Waiting on the ledge in the low, early sunshine, the kite-pilots could already hear the sound of battle from beyond the spar. Waldea stood before them. 'We have no bombs now,' he declared, 'but we will have bombs soon. The higher command is very happy with the work you have done, my children! The Pope is pleased! You harassed the enemy, you distracted them from their attacks upon the Imperial comrades. Today our glorious army will push hard and break though; and you can repeat your heroism. You can distract the Otre from our attack. Each of you will gather stones in a grass-weave sack.' He held out an empty bag as illustration; it was big enough for half a dozen stones perhaps, no more. 'Fly, my children! Pelt the enemy with stones! Today will be a great victory!'

Tighe, agitated and unhappy, eager to get out in the air and fight, or eager to spring up the stairway and run back to the Meshwood – he could not even decide which thing he wanted to do more – got down on all fours with the rest of the platon. They all searched the ledge and even up the stairway for stones to gather into their sacks. 'Barbarian,' said Mulvaine, crawling close to him, 'this is an idiot idea.'

'Hush,' said Tighe.

'What harm can we do to soldiers by throwing stones at them? It is a children's game. It is an idiot idea. How many of us will die?'

'Hush!' said Tighe in a louder voice, his panic rising inside him.

He fitted six stones into the bag; any more and the extra weight would start to interfere with the flying. But he couldn't have fitted many more in. He tucked the sack inside his trousers and started strapping himself on to his kite. Ati's kite was next to him. 'Today the army will push through,' said Ati, his voice wobbly with fear. 'They will – yes?'

'Of course,' said Tighe. 'Today.'

He was glad for the clench in his stomach as he fell off the world, glad for the rush in his head as he banked and climbed.

The battlefield looked as it always did. If anything, the central shelf looked less thronged with blue uniforms than it had done before. It was impossible to see how the battle was progressing, whether the Empire or the Otre were prevailing. The whole thing looked static. Tighe's eye for detail had improved a little: so that he noticed, now, when a blue- or grey-suited individual tumbled from the ledge. He distinguished between the blossoms of flame that resulted from dizzy-bombs and those from cannon fire; he could start to pick out individual kites and distinguish them from the differing patchwork patterns of their construction.

He swept down and then pulled in towards the enemy ledges. Snipers turned their attentions from firing down to firing out at the incoming kites, and Tighe felt the blended sensations of thrill and fear. His free hand was groping in his trousers, pulling out a graspful of stones and flinging them desperately. They rattled down harmlessly, and Tighe pulled back and away.

He flew away from the wall and passed several other kites coming in. By the time he circled round for another pass each of these was returning, flying awaywall again. Tighe saw Mulvaine pass, then Ati, and then Bel. He passed close enough to Bel to see her face, which was caught in a rictus of fear, mouth open. She looked as though she was yelling, screaming, but with a twinge Tighe realised she was dead; dribbles of blood were falling away from her feet, her clothes were black and glistening, soaked with blood, her free arm and her legs dangled slackly. He turned, followed her kite for a while and flew in behind her close enough to see the perforated hole in the exact middle of her back. But even in death, with her right arm wedged under the cross-spar, she flew a good kite; she flew, following the ups and downs of the morning air, out and out. Tighe turned back. Perhaps she would fly all the way to the Pause.

He had time, as he rummaged in his grass-weave sack for the last few stones, to wonder about Ravielre. What would he do, now that Bel was dead? Would he be unhinged by grief? He felt tears himself and then he remembered: the wall was not an enormous, epic environment; it was no giant world filled with heroic souls. It was an ant-hill, a small-scale structure built by a small-minded God. He, Tighe, was nothing but an ant; Bel had been an ant; Ravielre was an ant. How stupid it would be to grieve for the loss of an ant! This thought, hollow and grief-tasting as it was, gave him a strange strength. What did it matter? What did anything matter?

He almost didn't realise that he was screaming as he swept in towards the Otre ledges. He banked fast and late, sweeping within a few hand spans of the enemy, and flinging down stones. Pray God, at the bottom of the wall, that these stones fly true! Pray that one strikes an enemy soldier in the eye, blinding them so that they stumble off the world and die!

And then, before he even realised what he was doing, Tighe had landed on the enemy ledge.

It was a wide ledge that was about a third overhung, and the Otre sappers had constructed a rim along the outside edge of its floor that was a hand-span high. The ground was panelled with stems of planks of wood and the wallside was regularly marked with windows. Tighe hopped over the rim and ran a little way down the ledge to kill the last of the speed of his kite. Up ahead were four Otre soldiers, all crouching down and aiming weaponry below them. With a start, one of them looked up at Tighe and fell backwards in what appeared to be sheer astonishment, collapsing on his back. His three fellows looked up.

For a fraction of a moment Tighe could see straight into their eyes. They were afraid at this apparition, and then their fright blenched to anger. In unison the three of them levelled their rifles, as their fourth comrade struggled to get himself upright again.

'Hello!' Tighe said, loudly, in the Imperial language. Then he said it again, 'Hello!' this time in his native language. He couldn't think of anything else to say. Then he started to laugh, the laughter just bubbling out, unstoppable, inappropriate, as he stepped smartly to the left. His bad foot struck the rim of the Otre ledge and he fell sideways off the world.

His head went down and the blood flushed into his face. Then the blade of his kite, cutting through the air, caught and swirled round. He was instantly righted and then he pulled hard left to fly down and away from the wall.

He had only two stones left now, so he scooped them both out and threw them vaguely in the direction of the wall to his right, uncaring now whether they hit friendly or enemy troops. He was still laughing. It all seemed ridiculous to him.

A series of yawing tumbles and a rising spiral on a strong updraught brought him into a position where he could see the battlefield. It looked as chaotic as before. Some blue-suited soldiers were trying to climb, like flies up a sheer surface, from the central shelf to a tiny hummock half-way between the two front lines. They moved slowly, picks attached to their wrists and ankles, digging one pick into the clay of the worldwall before removing another and creeping up. Dizzy-bombs swirled out and round, exploding close to them; sniper fire rained down. Each time Tighe circled through the air and round another one of them had been picked off by the enemy.

He flew back to the home ledge as the morning winds began to lose lift, and discovered that he was one of the last to return. Ati came running up to him as he landed. 'We thought you'd been killed, you stupid barbarian,' he said, embracing Tighe whilst he was still unbuckling. Tighe felt strange; mostly he felt annoyed that Ati was interrupting him getting himself unbuckled from his kite. The laughter had all dribbled out of him now and had left a residue of bad temper, like a petulant child. He couldn't understand why Ati was acting the way he was; couldn't understand the tears. All through supper, Ati chattered, hyperactive, fidgeting and repeating himself over and again. Tighe sat sullenly, glowering around him, and brushing Ati's arm away whenever the downwaller tried to embrace him.

After eating, Waldea stood up to address them. 'Today I spoke with the high command,' he said. 'We are close to victory, my children. Think of it! Victory will be ours soon! One more day!'

Nobody cheered; but when Waldea led them all in singing patriotic songs they all joined in.

17

That night Tighe lay for a long while awake, staring up into the darkness. He became convinced, as his restless mind circled round and round, swooped through the same thoughts like a kite marking time in the air, that his pashe had once told him something that was terribly important, something that would serve him well at this time. But he couldn't remember what it was. And he searched and searched through his memory for the thing that his mother had told him, hoping it would come back to him.

His head was itching, as it sometimes did, where the scars ran over his scalp. He scratched at them with dirty nails, thinking again of his pashe.

Eventually he fell asleep.

He woke in the dark, shoved awake by somebody pressing a foot against his shoulder and rocking him back and forth. 'What? What is it?'

'Out of your blanket, you one,' came Waldea's voice. He was holding a grass-torch, which threw queer shadows over his face, doubling the ridges of his scars with dark lines, hollowing out his eye sockets.

Tighe sat up. The sky through the dugout door was still tar-black; it was long before the dawn gale. There was the sound of shouting from outside, and a hectic bustle all around.

'What's going on?'

'Outside, my children!' shouted Waldea. 'Outside and up the stairway!'

Several of the kite-pilots were still evidently half asleep as they climbed out of their blankets. Mocghe stumbled over to his kite and began to pick up the main spar. 'Leave that!' bellowed Waldea. 'Leave your kites here, my children. Straight through the door and up the stairs.'

Out of the dugout it was bitterly cold and Tighe pulled his blanket around his shoulders to keep his neck warm. With only starlight the ledge looked murky, alien; Tighe followed the boy ahead of him and soon was stumbling lumpishly up the stairway. Still wondering if he was dreaming, he lined up with the rest of the platon on the broad shelf at the top of the ascent. Soldiers passed and returned. The dugout doors on this level flickered with the orange light of grass-torches inside. There was a general commotion, shouting and knocking noises from inside the dugouts and from further east along the wall.

'What's going on?' asked Ati, breathless with the night climb.

'I don't know. Mulvaine! Mulvaine, what's going on?'

Mulvaine looked around. 'Where's Waldea?' he bleated.

A man emerged from one of the dugouts; a short, pouch-bellied man with a great mane of hair. 'You!' he screamed. 'Who are you?'

Nobody dared answer until he had screamed again, 'Who are you?'

'Kite-pilot platon, sir,' answered Tighe. 'Command of Waldea. Ordered to come up here, sir, in the night!'

The little man grunted, a high-pitched noise like a pig. 'Get in this dugout and take a pike each – you know what a pike is?'

The platon stared at him, until he started screaming again, and they hurriedly filed through the door. Inside, the dugout was a chaos of people and flickering lights; the floor over to the left was piled with blue-coated bodies, blood patched over their clothes and skin. Some still trembling. The dust of the floor had been turned into a sticky mud by what Tighe realised was probably blood. The sight did not shock him, but he turned his eyes away. It was, somehow, untidy. People in the dugout were hurrying in all directions and there was a stench of something unpleasant. Tighe followed the other kite-pilots to the far wall, where a jumble of poles had been stacked. They were all of wood, with tarred fire-hardened points at one end. Each member of the platon took one and made their way back outside.

The little man was still there. 'Hurry! hurry!' he screamed. 'Come along now – all of you.' And at a jog he led them east, up a slope, a series of steps and through a short tunnel. On the far side of this was a view of the battlefield, a dark expanse of mostly flat vertical worldwall, lit with the jewel reds and oranges of fires.

'How,' shouted the little man. 'How many?' He started counting in threes, running his eye from pilot to pilot. 'Twelve and one is thirteen, very well. That will be enough.'

'Please sir,' offered Mulvaine. 'Our commander is Waldea . . .'

'Be quiet!' the little man shrieked. 'Your orders are to hold this ledge. Use your pikes. If any of *us* come, any Imperial, they will call friend and you must let them past. If any enemy come, you must use your pikes and *not let them past*! You understand! Desertion is cowardice and you will be thrown off the wall. The glory of the Empire is at stake! The life of the Pope himself! You must *not let them past*.' And without another word he hurried off west, carrying his torch with him.

For a while the platon stood, a little stunned, in the absolute darkness. Eventually Mulvaine said, 'Well, we have orders, I suppose.'

'What must we do, Mulvaine?' asked Ravielre.

'Form a line – be careful in the dark, though. Form a line and then a line behind it. I suppose we do that. Do we do that?'

'Yes,' offered Tighe. Then Pelis said, more forcefully, 'Yes.'

They shuffled into position on the ledge and held their pikes out at an angle before them, with the points facing away. For a while everything was quiet. Tighe felt his breathing calm a little. He looked around himself; the blotches of orange and red visible from this oblique perspective all over the night-time wall seemed a crude imitation of the pure sharp light of the stars.

'What are we doing here, do you think?' asked Ravielre.

'Holding this position,' said Mulvaine. But his voice was trembling.

'Are the Otre coming, then?' asked Ati.

'Shut up,' said Tighe, with feeling, 'you shit-eating idiot.'

But they all knew it must be true. For a while Ati was silent, stung by Tighe's rebuke; but eventually he couldn't contain himself. 'But if they come what will we do? They are a terrible enemy – they will eat us, kill us.'

'We were breaking through,' said Mocghe, but there was no real conviction in his voice. 'Victory is almost ours.'

They stood for a while; it was hard to know for how long. Tighe's forearms began to ache with the load of holding the pike out. His foot twinged. As the time dragged on, he began to feel a little absurd. Somebody coughed and the boy next to Tighe shuffled.

'This is stupid,' muttered Mulvaine.

Tighe didn't say anything, but the sensation of ridiculousness was spreading through him.

Somebody appeared at the end of the ledge, a tall man carrying a rifle. 'Stop!' warbled Mulvaine. 'Stop!'

'Who are you?' grunted this figure. 'Fuck it, what's this?'

'Are you friend?' insisted Mulvaine, wobbling his pike in front of him.

'No time for this, you idiots,' said the man, pushing past. As he brushed past Tighe smelt on him the odour of fresh blood.

After he had passed by, the platon chattered nervously.

'What's happened? Have the Otre broken through?'

'You saw how it was on the battlefield – we all saw how it was from the air.'

'Yes – yes – it was chaos.'

'The enemy had the higher ledges.'

'Oh God,' wailed Ati. 'They're coming.'

'Hush!' called Mulvaine. But his own voice was breaking with fear.

'They'll be here soon,' said Mocghe.

'Oh God,' wailed Ati.

'These pikes will be no use,' said somebody behind Tighe. 'We'll all die – all of us.'

'Be quiet,' whimpered Mulvaine. 'Please – be quiet.'

There was the sudden, piercing sound of an explosion somewhere in front of them and a clamour of voices; the platon fell silent. Further explosions followed, like giant footsteps percussing the wall closer and closer to the ledge where the platon cowered behind their pikes. Tighe could see the bulges of white and yellow light spilling out from the wall below them.

The voices were suddenly very close, and a gaggle of soldiers appeared at the end of the ledge. Two of them had torches fixed to their helmets, but the light was low. Their uniforms looked dark, might have been blue, but that might have been only shadow colouring the grey darkly. Tighe's heart was hammering.

Mulvaine started saying something, but the soldiers were upon them in an instant. They took no notice at all of the pike-guard and swept right through them.

Almost as soon as they were past, Ati threw down his pike. 'We're dead if we stay here,' he cried and suddenly everybody was dropping their pikes and starting backwards along the ledge, Tighe losing his weapon just as eagerly as the others.

They swarmed back through the tunnel and hurried down and along. They quickly caught up the guards who had passed them earlier. Behind them the sounds of the explosions boomed and every blast made Tighe twitch in his skin.

Somebody collided with Tighe in the darkness and sent him spinning. For one horrible moment he thought he was going to fall off the world, but his chest and face slapped hard against the dirt of the ledge and his relief was almost strong enough to drown out the pain.

Feet were thudding past; somebody trod on his hand and he yelped with pain. Rolling aside and getting himself up on his feet again he found himself in the midst of a jostling crowd. He elbowed his way back to the wall, gasping with the general infection of fright, and made his way along to the opening of one of the dugouts. As he stepped forward to go inside somebody slammed into him in a hurry to get out. Tighe was knocked back, but not over, and abandoned himself. There was no hope. It was all over.

He started running westward along the ledge in the same direction as the bulk of people. Shouts filled the air. Pools of light passed as he hurried along. The only thing that mattered in the world was to get away – to get away from whatever unseen horror was approaching from behind.

He ran into a blockage, a tight huddle of people all trying to squeeze down a narrow defile. Initially he felt a terrible panic at the thought of being blocked in his path and he threw himself against the back of one of the soldiers at the rear of the ruck and slapped with his fists. 'Let me through! Let me pass!'

Somebody's voice rose clear above the hubbub. 'To me! For the Empire! To me!'

There was a moment's hesitation in the knot of bodies, and then, with a palpable sense of something turning about a hinge, the flow of people shifted. Tighe was being jostled the other way now, as people pushed past him to stream eastward along the ledge. The voice receded, *To me! For the Empire!* and with a sense of something clicking Tighe's fear switched to courage. He was hurrying eastward along the ledge, actually pushing past people in his eagerness to get to the front. A group of kite-pilots were with him.

They ran back along the shelf, past the flickering lit holes of the dugout doorways. The voice carried them along. *To me! For the Empire! On to the Door! Let us capture the Door!*

The flood of people slowed, clogged, up the stairs and back into the tunnel. This pause gave Tighe time to catch his breath and wonder what he was doing. Rushing into battle? Without a weapon? His pike was probably where he had dropped it, but even if he could find it in the darkness, did he really want to come up against a terrible, fearsome Otre warrior armed only with a pike?

He doubled back with the vague intention of finding the stairs back down to the kite-platon base ledge, and almost at once he ran straight into the small fat-bellied man who had screamed at them earlier.

'You!' screeched this fellow. 'Where are you going? The battle is *eastward*, you!'

'Kite-pilot, sir,' gasped Tighe.

'There's no kite flying at night!' howled the man. 'Deserters are thrown off the wall! That way – that way!' He gave Tighe a huge push and propelled him eastward along the ledge. Tighe almost fell, picked himself up and ran along the ledge. At the end of the shelf was the stair up.

'Tighe?'

It was Mulvaine. 'Tighe what's going on?'

'*Empire!*' bellowed a tall man, hurrying past them up the stairs. He was pulling his rifle from his shoulder as he ran.

'Tighe what's *going on*?' repeated Mulvaine. Tighe pulled him hard against the wall, out of the way of the intermittent stream of soldiers hurrying up the wall. He saw that Ati, Ravielre, Oldievre and Pelis were also huddled there.

'It's chaos,' said Tighe, breathlessly. 'I think the Otre are trying to break through.'

'Should we fight?' Mulvaine asked nervously. 'We could go up the stair and join the others.'

'We have no weapons!' moaned Ati.

'We should fight!' said Oldievre. 'We are soldiers!'

'We're kite-pilots,' countered Ati, hugging himself and rocking a little back and forth, so that the back of his head bumped against the wall behind him. 'We fight already.'

'Well, we can't stay here,' said Tighe. 'It'll be dawn soon.'

He was right: the sky was beginning to pale and the hurrying soldiers had a weird, spectral quality to them.

'Through here!' shouted somebody from up the stairway. 'Through here!' A group dashed past, carrying between them three or maybe four bodies slung in blankets.

'We should go back to our dugout until after the dawn gale,' said Mulvaine, looking around himself.

'That man,' said Tighe, 'the fat man who ordered us take pikes – he is that way.'

'We'll be trapped on the ledge in the dawn gale!' said Ati. 'We'll be pulled off and die!'

'Stay quiet!' snapped Oldievre. 'We must fight. We are soldiers.' He was extremely agitated.

'The soldiers will be trapped by the dawn gale like the rest,' Mulvaine pointed out. 'If we find shelter, we can come out after the dawn and fight.'

'No,' said Oldievre, stepping away from the wall. 'We must go now.' He sprinted up the stairs, two at a time, and was gone.

The sky was getting lighter all the time. It did not seem to bother the other soldiers, who still hurried up the stairs, or else came clattering down carrying bodies between them.

'If we stay here,' said Tighe, firmly. He meant, *We cannot stay here*, but the others understood his actions as he took Mulvaine by the arm and pulled him away, westward, hurrying down the shelf.

They quickly caught up with a party lugging a body wrapped in a blanket and trailed them, following them into the first of the dugout doors on the shelf.

Inside the air was smoky from the grass-torches and crammed with people. There were several people screaming, or shouting in pain, and a level of piercing hubbub. Tighe and the other kite-pilots ducked and wove their way through the mass of people and pressed themselves against the wall. Squatting down, each holding hands with each in a line against the wall, they panted, getting their breath back.

The five kite-pilots seemed unnoticed where they were. Legs pressed against them, feet trampled over them, but nobody questioned their being there. After a while Tighe found himself becoming used to the noise and even to the buffeting from people pushing past them. He closed his eyes.

When he opened them again he wasn't sure if he had slept or not. The tumult in the dugout seemed a little less. Through the legs of the thronging people Tighe caught glimpses of piled bodies.

His memory was already a jumble of strange images; the darkness, bright fire hurrying past, a crush of bodies. Was this what war was?

Mulvaine, squatting next to him and still holding his hand, seemed asleep. Tighe poked his shoulder. 'Mulvaine!'

Mulvaine twitched, woke. 'Have we reached the Door?' he asked, blearily.

'It is day, Mulvaine,' said Tighe. 'We go back down to the platon base ledge. Wake the others.'

Mulvaine pulled at his hair with twin fists. 'They will know that we ran from the fighting,' he said, moaning. 'They will throw us off the wall.'

'Be quiet!' snapped Tighe. He looked around him. Nobody in the dugout seemed to be paying them any attention. 'Come, come.'

Tighe woke up Ati, rubbing the sides of his head gently with his hands until he opened his eyes and smiled. Mulvaine woke Pelis, who immediately stood up. 'It is quieter now,' she said.

Ati gave Ravielre a kick. 'Come,' he said, as Ravielre groaned. 'We must rouse ourselves.'

Tighe led the way, and the line of them wove a path through the people thronging the dugout. Tighe made sure to keep his eyes down, to avoid making eye contact with anybody. He stepped through the door of the dugout and nervously glanced up and down the ledge outside. It was a bright morning.

'Tighe?' asked Mulvaine, coming up behind him. 'What shall we do?'

'We must find Waldea,' said Tighe.

'Yes. But will he be cross?'

'We must find him,' Tighe said firmly.

Mulvaine put his eyes down and nodded. The gesture bothered Tighe obscurely. Something difficult to define, as obscure and smoky as the light in the dugout, something had changed. Mulvaine was deferring to him. It seemed wrong, somehow. But there was a sense of some catastrophic change in the air. But he took a deep breath in and decided to ignore his uneasiness. 'I am a Prince, after all,' he said.

'We go down to the platon base ledge,' he told the other four. They were all looking at him seriously; Mulvaine nodded. The events of the night had taken away his arrogance; he did not look at Tighe in the same way, did not call him an ignorant barbarian.

There were half a dozen riflemen lined along the ledge eastwards, but otherwise the ledge was largely deserted. Tighe approached the nearest of the riflemen. 'Hello, in the name of the Popes!' he said, following the polite form of address he had heard others using. The rifleman looked round with bleary eyes.

'Scrap?' he said. Tighe wasn't sure if he heard this correctly; it seemed to be the food word. 'What you want?' The speaker was clearly not a native of the Empire; his accent was thick, difficult to place. His pale skin was mottled all over with red threads.

'We wondering, sir,' said Tighe, ducking his head politely, 'how the war went last night?'

'Hard fighting,' said the rifleman, turning his attention eastward again. 'Hard fighting.'

'What you want?' hissed another of the riflemen, with the same accent.

'Nothing, sirs,' said Tighe, backing away a little. 'Nothing.'

'Platon?' demanded the first rifleman, hoisting his rifle about to point it at Tighe.

'We are kite-pilots, honoured sir. Hello, in the name of the Popes!'

'Kite-pilots,' grunted the rifleman, swinging his rifle back around again. 'Useless. Scraps.'

Tighe hurried back to where the others were standing. 'He said it was hard fighting last night. We go down to the platon base ledge.' He took Ati by the wrist and pulled him urgently.

In a line they filed rapidly along and down the stairwell, arriving back on the base ledge in a matter of minutes. The ledge was deserted. It took only a moment to check the platon dugout, but it was empty except for the dismantled spars and bundles of the platon's kites. No other pilots; no Waldea. 'Where is Waldea?' Ravielre asked, several times, tears tinting his voice. 'Where is Waldea?'

'Waldea would tell us what to do,' observed Pelis coolly. 'What shall we do, Tighe?'

'What shall we do?' echoed Mulvaine.

Tighe scratched feverishly at the back of his head; his scars were itching again. 'We must find him.'

'He is dead,' said Ati in a sepulchral voice. Ravielre started whimpering; his eyes were moist.

'Come!' barked Tighe, trying to remember Waldea's intonation, the manner he had used. 'No crying! We are warriors now – we have fought for many days. Remember!'

'Yes,' said Ati, hurrying over to stand beside him. 'Warriors!'

'If Waldea is dead, we shall report to the Cardinelle and he will tell us what to do. I met the Cardinelle one time and he knows me I am sure. I will speak to him.'

'*I* spoke to the Pope himself,' Ati reminded them all. He seemed agitated, hopping from foot to foot. Tighe recognised the anxiety in him.

The sound of an enormous explosion bounced through the air and all five of them looked east. A plume of grey was spreading into the air from beyond the spar, sagging and drooping; an enormous cloud of dust. Distantly, muffled by the cloud, the sounds of people crying, yelling, shouting, could be picked out.

'What is that?' asked Ravielre.

'Perhaps we have broken through,' suggested Pelis.

'Perhaps we have broken through,' echoed Mulvaine, his face wide with excitement. 'Perhaps we have done that!'

'We have broken through!' shouted Ati, bouncing into the air.

'We should make up our kites and fly to see what is happening,' suggested Mulvaine. 'Let us fly round and see what is happening.'

'No,' said Tighe.

Everybody stopped and looked at him.

'No,' he repeated. 'That is not the best. We must go back up to the main shelf here and find Waldea.'

Mulvaine looked at Ati and for a moment Tighe was aware that matters were on a hinge. But Ati was nodding and Mulvaine started nodding along with him. 'Very well,' he said.

'Come,' said Tighe, not wanting to lose momentum. He had a bad intimation about the explosion to the east. As he put his left foot on the lowest step of the stair that led up to the main shelf there was another enormous cracking sound, and then another. It sounded like rifle fire, only much louder. All five kite-pilots turned, their jaws dropping. There was a high-pitched whine, like a clockwork motor whirring but on the same enormous scale as the cracking noises, and suddenly the bone-jarring cracking noises multiplied: there were dozens of them all following hard upon one another, like a drumroll.

Then there was silence.

'What is that?' asked Pelis, in hushed tones.

'Come,' said Tighe, tugging at Mulvaine's shirt and grabbing Ati's hand, eager to get them up the stairway. 'Come!'

He hurried up and they followed. His bad foot ached with every step.

At the top of the stairs the shelf was in chaos, people running in both directions. Tighe paused a few steps below the top so that his head was at ledge-level. The other four gathered behind and beneath him. He looked up at the scene from his lowered perspective. A dancing flurry of hurrying legs, rifles trailed unceremoniously along the floor; bawling and shouting too loud to be distinct except for the swear words. One man – tripped or pushed – sprawling in the dust of the shelf, his face sliding up close to where Tighe was watching. But his eyes were unfocused with the pain of the fall and he was picking himself up and hurrying on before he noticed Tighe.

'What does it look like?' Mulvaine called from the end of the line, several steps below.

'Ants,' said Tighe, more to himself than the others. 'Ants.'

To his right he heard the sound of rifle fire; not so monstrously loud as the sounds they had just heard, but much closer. The crowd of dancing legs twitched to a faster rhythm.

18

In an instant the scene on the shelf transformed from one of frantic passage back and forward to one of battle. Tighe pressed himself close against the stairway, only his face poking above the level of the floor. The soldiers directly in front of him were yelling, screaming, pressing themselves tightly against the wall at the back of the shelf. A dozen or so had gone charging forwards, their rifles lowered ready to fire, and Tighe watched their progress; and saw, at the far end of the shelf, what they were charging towards. A file of grey-suited Otre soldiers was kneeling at the foot of the defilade, aiming their own weapons: an almost-simultaneous blasting sound of the weapons being fired, a steamy blurring of the rifle ends, and several of the charging Imperial troops stumbled and fell.

What happened next wasn't clear to Tighe because his eyesight was poor and because trails and puffs of smoke wove in front of the grey soldiers; but it seemed to him that the kneeling soldiers dropped their rifles and drew out knives from their belts. Except that they were not knives because the Otre riflemen levelled them at the approaching charge as if they were aiming miniature rifles and the air was stunned again with the sound of bullets being discharged.

Several charging blue-coats sprawled in the dust of the shelf; one threw up both his arms and staggered backwards, his foot missing the edge of the world and his body toppling lurchingly away. The remnant of the charge stopped, turned, and began running back.

Tighe could see now that Otre soldiers occupied the stairs at the eastern reach of the shelf, all the way (it seemed) up. Rifles were being reloaded and volleys rattled out. The Imperial troops, pressing themselves as close as they could against the wall for cover, returned the fire.

Mulvaine was pushing into the small of Tighe's back. 'I want to see!' he called. 'I want to see – they are fighting.' His head appeared beside Tighe's and his mouth went circular.

'Keep down,' called Tighe, having to shout over the roar of the almost continuous gunfire. The smell of spent mushroom powder, a burnt and charcoal-dense odour, was reaching his nose. He sneezed.

'The Otre!' gasped Mulvaine. He started up, so that his head and shoulders poked fully up from the stair, but Tighe caught hold of his shirt and tried to haul him back down again.

'No!' he shouted. 'Stay!'

Mulvaine seemed hypnotised by the rattle of gunfire. An Imperial soldier, not far from the stair, was crouched over his rifle, aiming it carefully. He stood up abruptly, dropping his weapon and reaching with both hands for his throat. Then he toppled backwards.

'Look at that!' called Mulvaine. He sounded thrilled in a deep way.

A bullet cracked into the shelf floor half an arm's length from where Tighe and Mulvaine were, spitting up dust and lumps of dirt. Tighe gave a harder pull and dragged Mulvaine down by main force.

'Idiot!' he called.

As if snapped awake, Mulvaine was suddenly terrified. 'We cannot stay here! We must go back down to the base ledge below.'

Tighe hazarded another look over the top of the stairway. His mind was running, sprinting. If they went down to the base ledge they would be in a dead end; they would be captured by the Otre for sure. Unless they could use their kites to fly away – but it was already fifty and the winds were dying. The best way was along the shelf, west, to run back to the Meshwood and safety there. That was the best thing. But it was dangerous, obviously it was dangerous. The gunfire was severe.

Another bullet gouged into the shelf near Tighe's face, making an odd popping noise and blowing out a hand-sized pit of dust.

'We must go down!' insisted Mulvaine, from below. 'We must!'

But, Tighe noticed, they did not go down. They were waiting for him to tell them it was the right thing to do. They were waiting for his instruction.

'We will be captured by the Otre if we go down there. Down there is no other way out.'

Ati was cowering, trying to press himself into the earth of the stairwell. 'We will die here!' he warbled.

'We need to run back along the shelf. Run to the Meshwood.'

'No, no, no,' said Mulvaine, slapping his own head with the flats of his hands. 'No, it is dangerous.'

There was a yell of several voices from above and Tighe looked up. Imperial troops were charging eastward again: eight or nine blue-coats lumbering up the shelf with their rifles lowered. They were only a little way past Tighe's vantage point when the first Otre bullets hit them. Tighe heard the dull slapping noise, like the wet, clicking noise that is made by bouncing the tongue against the roof of the mouth. Two men stumbled, one turning right around to face the other way as he came down on hands and knees. His eyes were all white; Tighe could see no pupils and blood was blurting from his mouth. Then the man fell forward, as if kissing the ground with his open lips. The charge faltered and the remaining soldiers turned to run back along the shelf, away from the Otre. Immediately one of them was struck in the head by a bullet: there was a scattering of droplets of blood that drummed down upon the dirt in front of Tighe's face and upon Tighe's face itself.

The blood felt warm, a sprinkling of warm points on his cheeks, his forehead.

Tighe was frozen by the ugliness of the sensation. He couldn't even cry out. The shot man stumbled forward and then stopped. He was still standing. Tighe looked up and saw that his head had been cracked open like a clay jar; there was a chin, a mouth, two wide eyes and a sharp-edged nose that ran all the way up to its bridge, but there was nothing more above that. The head simply stopped in a ragged line. But the soldier did not fall. He stood, swaying a little, his eyes unblinking staring directly west. A bullet hurtled so close to his arm as to rip the cloth of his blue tunic. He simply stood there.

Run, thought Tighe, trying to force the words out of his mouth. Run. 'Run! Run!'

But the man simply stood, swaying a little bit. Tighe reached up to touch his own face and the stickiness made his stomach lurch, clench. He was trembling. 'No!' he shouted. 'No!'

'Tighe,' called Mulvaine from below. 'Come on!'

But Tighe's mind was in some form of spasm. It occurred to him that he might be dooming his companions to death, but he could not move his muscles. The horror of what had happened was too great. There were flashes, bright white light, gathering at the corner of his eyes. His brain was hot, sparkling. He could smell a strange smell, exotic and strange but also frightening; it overlaid the smell of blood and of burnt mushroom powder. His hand was trembling. Sunlight was swelling in the middle of his head.

He was moving his mouth, but no words were coming out.

Everything began to bleach white: the blue uniforms of the soldiers fading, the tones of dirt colour and the pastels of the wall greying. The sounds of battle seemed to recede. He was held by the intensity of the moment.

Flashes pulsed in his brain, whiting out everything in time with his heartbeat. And, precariously, he had a sense of tremendous insight, of powerful meaning in everything. It was a sensation he had known sometimes as a child, but here it was so powerful as almost to overwhelm him. He felt close to understanding everything; to unpicking the mystery of the worldwall itself. Its size, its scale. What would be seen through the Door.

Somebody was slapping him on the small of his back; one of the kite-pilots from below trying to get his attention.

Dreamlike.

And, dreamlike, the shot soldier standing before him swayed, infinitely slowly, but managed to stay, impossibly on his feet.

Then, with a sound that started as nothing and built rapidly to a swoosh, the spell was broken; and the sound was the rushing towards him of an Otre bullet, closer and closer until it, *ploc*, powered into the back of the standing man, directly between his shoulder blades. The force of the impact pushed the soldier forward as if he had been a man of clay and he clattered in the dust.

But the sound, the impact, shook Tighe free of the spell. He twitched, looked round. Below him the faces of the other kite pilots were looking up at him, terrified. Ati was slapping him on the back, trying to attract his attention.

'What happened to you?' Ati was calling to him. Bullets keened and shushed through the air. The cries of soldiers and screams of pain were again loud in Tighe's ears. He heard and comprehended Ati's question, and it was in his mind to answer it, if he had the words in Imperial language; to say that he had been frozen, half drawn out of the reality of the battle, taken away. That he had been on the verge of being able to understand the worldwall itself, its scale, its mystery. Why God had built it and – no, that was not it; to understand who God was, and what it would mean to meet Him. On the edge of a revelation, like standing on the edge of the world ready to jump.

Tighe looked around himself slowly. It all seemed less real than it had been before his episode, or whatever it was. The yelling, the hurrying, the bullets firing past. He put the palm of his hand against his forehead and smoothed it slowly over the top of his head and round to the back. There was something not right. Dreamlike.

'There!' Ati was yelling. 'There!' He was pointing down the stair, out at something in the sky.

Tighe followed the arm. The dreamlike purity of his senses buoyed him through comprehending what he saw.

It was a calabash, smaller than the Imperial calabashes, entirely silver and of an odd shape and construction. It was not a sphere, but rather an elongated cylinder tucked in at the waist, and it appeared to be made out of metal rather than woven leather. This was impossible; it was impossible to believe that metal could float, or that it could be beaten thin enough to contain the hot air. At the base of the strange calabash was no basket, but instead an insect-like confusion of legs and pincers.

The silver calabash floated a few hundred arms' lengths from the wall, wobbling a little. Tighe glanced back up at the shelf; none of the battling troops seemed to have noticed it, which added to Tighe's sense of being contained within a dream of his own. A series of loud crashes sounded from above. There was a groan, which Tighe assumed to be from a dying soldier. But the groan resolved itself, musically, into a single pitch that kept an unnaturally steady level and volume.

'That noise!' Tighe cried out.

The sound grew in intensity, shrieked and then was still. The blast of it left Tighe with a humming in his ears. Then it started again, a low grumble that resolved itself and began climbing the scale of pitches.

'What machine – ?' howled Ati, tears dribbling from his eyes, his arm outstretched and pointing at the silver calabash. It was lifting itself slowly through the air, upwards and diagonally.

A thunderous voice boomed out of the sky.

'Tighe!' called the voice. It caught Tighe completely off guard because the mysterious, elemental speaker pronounced the name in the old style of Tighe's village, not with the consonantal tripping mispronunciation of Imperial speakers. He was so unused to hearing himself called by that name, pronounced in that way, that he almost didn't realise what the word signified. Then the thunderous voice spoke again.

'Tighe!'

As he realised the personal specificity of this act of naming out of the sky, Tighe also realised how precariously related to reality all these events were. A tiny wall, no bigger than three arms' lengths high; ants running along all its miniature ledges thinking they were men. It was none of it real. His heart was hammering. Lights were flickering at the corner of his eyes again, as they had done before when he had found himself frozen and had felt his consciousness start to pulse and withdraw from things. He decided he did not like that experience.

He started drawing air in through his nostrils, filling his lungs, like somebody preparing to shout at the top of his voice. For the third time the enormous voice named him.

'Tighe!'

'Come,' exhaled Tighe, speaking to the four kite-pilots on the stairway. There was the slightest internal sense of a thread being snapped and he was standing up.

'Master,' shouted Ati, in confusion. 'Down . . .'

'No,' yelled Tighe, leaning forward and snatching at Ati's hair with his fingers' ends. 'Up. Come. Come.' And he bolted up the last few steps on to the shelf.

The elements of the picture did not quite coalesce in his head. He saw the pathway ahead of him, the broad shelf bounded on the right by the wall (along which blue-coats stood, or lay motionless) and on the left by nothing but the sky. He saw the faces of soldiers, some distracted by this sudden apparition, glowering or staring astonished at him. He saw the little bulges, like instantaneous mushrooms that faded as soon as they flowered, as the bullets flicked into the ground at his feet. 'Come,' he said, uncertain and uncaring whether the others could hear him. 'Come. God is testing us.'

He started walking along the shelf.

Almost at once he was passed by Mulvaine and Ati, who were running with their heads down, weaving from side to side. Ravielre and Pelis followed, almost bent double, Ravielre with his hands folded over the back of his head. It was almost comical.

'God is testing us!' Tighe called to them as they rushed by, but with a laugh he realised that he was speaking his village tongue, and that they would not be able to understand. He was drunk with the strangeness and the intensity of the occasion. Running, ducking, weaving, all seemed like attempts to cheat the test. The only thing to do was to walk calmly, straight, to dare the experimenter God to harm him.

A soldier, close against the wall, was screaming something at Tighe and ran forward. His left arm cradled his rifle and his right hand was outstretched, to grab Tighe. Tighe smiled at him. The soldier went down on one knee, in comical mockery of an obeisance. His chest was hollow. A large hole there. Ends of ribs poked out, like twigs. He toppled forward, face falling hard against the ledge.

Tighe started running. He was not sure why he started running, except that the dream had suddenly taken on an unpleasant quality. He had the sense, nightmarishly, of being followed, of being chased. Of being pursued by something monstrous.

An enormous hand, God's hand, reaching down to pluck this one ant from the wall. Would the others even see God's hand? Would it be an invisible force to them, the fingers gently pinching Tighe's torso nothing more than a focusing of winds, or the magical levitation of a calabash? Maybe he would fly up in the air and the soldiers would put down their weapons in amazement at his transportation.

Tighe was not running well; his bad foot hindered smooth sprinting. He loped a little way down the shelf and his good foot struck something other than smooth ledge, a spongy hillock of something. Tighe threw a leg out to stop himself falling, but his bad foot could not keep him upright. His ankle bent over and he slid down to his knees.

He was panting. He looked back to see what he had tripped over. Mulvaine was lying face down on the shelf.

Still weirdly dissociated from his experiences, Tighe first thought the kite-boy was dead. He pulled himself upright and limped over to the fallen body. Mulvaine was whimpering. Tighe dropped to his haunches.

'Mulvaine?'

'Oh, it hurts,' Mulvaine was saying. 'It hurts.'

'You have shot?'

'It hurts,' howled Mulvaine, twisting over and clutching at his shin. The leg of his right trouser was dark with wetness.

'Your knee? Your knee have shot?'

A clutch of Imperial soldiers hurried past. Tighe flicked a glance up the shelf. There was a huddle of blue tunics up ahead.

'Come,' he said to Mulvaine. 'Get up.' He slid his hand under the wounded boy's shoulder and tried to lever him upright.

'But it hurts, it hurts,' said Mulvaine.

'So', said Tighe, 'we must be up.' He pulled with all his might and Mulvaine's body came off the floor. Mulvaine put out a hand to support himself, and then slowly pushed himself into the sitting position.

'I cannot walk,' he said, through gritted teeth. 'My leg.'

'Come,' said Tighe, trying to inject his voice with an urgency he did not feel. He put his arm under Mulvaine's armpit and round his back, and pushed up with his legs. Slowly the two rose to a standing position, Mulvaine leaning heavily on Tighe.

The two of them began limping down the shelf, westward, in the direction of the Meshwood. Mulvaine was limping more markedly than Tighe.

19

They made slow progress along the shelf. Mulvaine repeated over and over, 'It hurts, it hurts,' in time to the steps, as if he was speaking some form of mantra. At one stage he said 'No, no, put me down, put me down,' and Tighe was compelled to lower him to the ground. It was a relief not to have the weight of him pulling down his shoulder.

As Mulvaine sobbed and clutched his leg, with his back against the wall, Tighe peered up the shelf. They were out of the range of the rifle fire now, but he could see up ahead how the dust kicks of bullet impacts peppered the shelf, and how most of the blue-coated soldiers in view were horizontal and dead rather than upright and fighting.

'Come,' he said to Mulvaine.

'Leave me here,' said Mulvaine, petulant and agonised at the same time. 'My leg, my leg. Leave me here.'

'If I leave you here,' said Tighe, 'the Otre will take you when they come along. You want that the Otre take you?'

Mulvaine looked up into Tighe's eyes; his pale Imperial eyes as strange as gemstones. His face was whiter than before, so pale it looked like a particular sort of plastic that Tighe had once seen when he was a boy; so white that it was almost transparent.

'Come,' said Tighe.

'All right,' said Mulvaine through his closed teeth. 'All right.' He held out his arm for Tighe to help him up and Tighe had to lean backwards away from the wall to apply enough force to raise the larger boy from his sitting position.

They resumed their slow stumble along the shelf. Soldiers hurried past them in ones and twos, rushing eastward along the shelf to join the fighting. Then first one and then several soldiers hurried past them in the other direction, rushing away from the battle towards the shelter of the Mesh-wood.

'They', said Tighe, taking a breath after every syllable because of the effort of carrying Mulvaine, 'leave. War. Lost.'

'*Don't* say it, you – you barbarian,' said Mulvaine in an agony of physical suffering and mental anguish. 'We'll – we'll rally, push through, they'll – they'll *beat* back the Otre.'

Tighe didn't say anything. They were coming to the far end of the shelf now and there was a ledge that sloped away down. Ati was waiting there, crouched close against the wall with his arms tightly crossed. He leapt up when he saw Tighe and Mulvaine approach.

'What happened? What happened?'

'Mulvaine,' said Tighe, gasping. 'Hurt.'

'My leg, my leg,' moaned Mulvaine. 'Shot through the knee, I think. It hurts, it hurts.'

Ati pushed up against Mulvaine on the other side from Tighe and helped to carry his weight. 'The others are near, Tighe,' he said. 'They are close to the entrance to the Meshwood. We will find shelter there, won't we Tighe?'

'We will find shelter there,' said Tighe.

The three of them limped on. The noise of battle was distant behind them now. Meshwood loomed ahead: the sun was high in the sky and it carved shadows out of the irregular surface of the wood that made it look more extreme in relief patterning. The leaves were darker in the late daylight, and as the three of them made their way along the ledge they could see the entrance to the tangle of meshwood trunks. It stared at them, a black oval like the socket of a skull.

Pelis and Ravielre came running up the ledge towards them. 'The guard eyrie is deserted,' shouted Ravielre.

'We saw six soldiers run along the ledge and go into the Meshwood,' said Pelis.

'The war is lost,' said Tighe. 'We have lost.'

'It hurts, it hurts,' moaned Mulvaine in time with his steps.

'We must hide ourselves in the Meshwood,' said Pelis, firmly, 'or the Otre will capture us.'

This thought silenced all five of them. They knew what was likely to happen if they allowed themselves to be captured by the Otre.

'Come,' said Tighe. 'Help me with Mulvaine.'

He passed the weight of Mulvaine's sagging body on to the shoulder of Ravielre and staggered before them, down the ledge towards the Mesh-wood.

The guard eyrie was empty, as Ravielre had said. There was a part of Tighe, an older part, that responded to the wealth the eyrie represented: all that wood! But more pressing was the need to get off the ledge, to get out of the way of the oncoming Otre army.

Once they were in the shade of the Meshwood they paused, leaning Mulvaine against a trunk. He was no longer chanting, 'It hurts, it hurts,' with every step. He appeared to be on the edge of drifting off to sleep, or losing consciousness.

'The Otre,' said Tighe. 'They will come this way. We cannot stay on this path.'

Mulvaine's eyes were closed now, his breathing was shallow. But the eyes of Ati, Pelis and Ravielre were all focused tightly on Tighe.

'What shall we do?' asked Pelis.

'We cannot climb up,' said Tighe, gesturing with his right arm at the canopy of interwoven Meshwood trunks over their heads. 'Mulvaine is too ill. We must drop down – find some quiet place and be still. The Otre will pass us by.'

He locked gaze with each of the three of them in turn to underline his words. 'Come,' he said, 'we must help Mulvaine down through these trunks.' Ati took one arm and Ravielre the other, and together they started the laborious process of lowering the now unresponsive body of Mulvaine from trunk to trunk, away from the overgrown ledge and into a more hidden place. 'God is testing us,' Tighe said to them in both his native tongue and in the Imperial language.

3

Through the Door

1

Through the Door, creaking wide on its enormous hinges. Stepping up to the face of God, an enormous face, large as the world. Carved like a gargoyle visage in the side of the wall, massive, marmoreal, except that a great rumbling low breath escaped from between its lips, that its eyelids closed and opened like the passing of day and night.

The silver calabash: strange apparition, more dream than reality. Floating through space.

Somebody's face: his pahe's, except that the face was that of an Imperial soldier and that the face disappeared in a splutter of bloody droplets.

Tiny droplets marking Tighe's skin. Dew from the Meshwood leaves.

Tighe woke with a shiver. Mulvaine was there, next to him, breathing shallowly. Pelis was pushing handfuls of leaves into her mouth, sucking off the moisture. Ravielre was grunting.

Tighe's stomach was hurting. He was hungry and he had wedged himself in the coign of a double-stemmed meshwood trunk to avoid being blown off the world by the dawn gale – none of them had their belts or their blankets. When he lifted his shirt to look at his stomach he saw bruises, like patches of shadow, running round the lower part of his torso. He had evidently been wedged in too tightly.

'We have no food,' said Ati, dropping down from above. 'I thought we might fetch some insects, but there are no insects here.'

'We must have food,' said Pelis, wiping her mouth.

Tighe reached for some leaves from the branches at the end of his trunk and crammed them into his mouth. The moisture soothed the inside of his mouth. He bit, tentatively, into the leaves themselves, but the flavour was savagely bitter and he spat the leaves out.

Mulvaine moaned.

'Tighe,' said Ati, swinging down and settling on his haunches on Tighe's branch, 'what shall we do?'

'What shall we do?' repeated Pelis.

Tighe looked from face to face. He did not know what to do. Ravielre looked worn, as well as distracted; as if the brute fact of Bel's death – a fact

225

only days old – was ageing him, minute by minute. His eyes were sunk in his skull, resting on a grey ledge of skin, overhung with eyebrows. Pelis had scratches on her pale face and her large hair was tangled and matted. Everybody looked exhausted. Only Ati had anything of the bounce, the elasticity of spirit, of the platon from weeks ago.

Tighe's mind was hurrying with memories of the previous day; the tumult of battle, the strange apparition of the silver calabash. Something, with a voice that sounded like God, had called his name; *Tighe, Tighe*. None of it felt real. Nothing felt real.

He took a deep breath. He had to say something. 'First we find food,' he said.

Ati and Pelis looked intently at him.

'We look for food and find it. Do you have flasks? For water?'

They both shook their heads.

'Well, we must travel from spring to spring. Or find spring and stay. Find food.' He gestured over at Mulvaine. 'He must become well and then we can travel through the Meshwood to the west. Yes? We can go home.'

'Home,' said Ati, dubiously.

'Pelis. Your home?'

'The Imperial City,' said Pelis. 'Ravielre comes from there too.'

'Then you can go there. Ati, your home is downwall?'

Ati nodded.

'Then you can go *there*. I will go back and speak with the Pope,' said Tighe, his head fuzzing with the excitement of the thought, a sense that was something like sudden inflation at the prospect of his resolution. He would go to the Imperial City, would call upon the Cardinelle who had visited him when he was back in the hospital; would call upon one of the Popes themselves, and would persuade them to take him up the wall in a calabash. He would go back to the village, a hero, with his adventures to relate.

'Speak with the Popes?' said Ati dubiously. A grin ran across his face. 'You are mad barbarian! Why would the Popes speak to you?'

Tighe stiffened. 'They will speak to me.'

'The War Pope thought *I* was the boy who fell from upwall!' said Ati. He started laughing. Pelis was chuckling too. The noise woke Ravielre, who groaned and rolled over.

'Stop,' said Tighe, although the laughter was affecting him. He tried for a stern voice, 'Stop this!', but his mouth was widening into a smile against his will. He struggled to shrink his lips to a severe purse, but then he was laughing and reaching forward to slap Ati on the side of his head. Ati was laughing so hard now he could barely evade Tighe's blows.

'What's the laughter?' asked Ravielre.

Mulvaine gave a sudden shout and trembled violently. All the laughter

226

stopped. Tighe, Ati and Pelis gathered round his sweating figure. He was not awake; his eyes were wrinkled tightly shut and his fists were squeezed hard, but he was moving, jerking from side to side. The night before the four kite-pilots had wedged him into a cradle that was half-formed by a series of smaller branches but now he was shaking so hard it looked as though he might dislodge himself from that.

'He'll fall,' said Pelis.

Tighe took hold of Mulvaine's shoulders. The force of his trembling transmitted itself through Tighe's joints up his arms, and made his teeth knock together. 'Mulvaine! Wake you! Mulvaine!' He gestured to Ati with his chin, 'Take his legs, his legs.' Ati grasped each ankle and the two of them pressed Mulvaine down.

He woke at this, from the pressure on his wounded leg, screaming. His arms flapped, and his mouth opened more widely than looked possible. 'Ahh! Ahh!'

Ati let go of his legs.

'Mulvaine,' shouted Tighe. 'Mulvaine. Hello, in the name of the Popes! Wake up!'

Mulvaine's eyes spun like pebbles flicked by fingers, his pupils arcing round. They fastened on Tighe, and he said, 'Thirsty.' Then he closed his eyes and was still.

There was a pause. 'Mulvaine?' said Tighe.

Mulvaine's breathing was very slight, his chest hardly moving at all. 'Thirsty,' he said again.

Tighe grabbed a handful of leaves and pressed them against Mulvaine's mouth. Their moisture, carried up and deposited upon them by the dawn gale, was drying off, but there was enough to wet Mulvaine's lips. He groaned as Tighe removed the wad of leaves. 'More.'

'Shall we take you to a spring?' Tighe asked, leaning close to Mulvaine's head. 'A spring?'

'Spring,' groaned Mulvaine.

'Then you can drink all you want. Ati and Ravielre, take him gently. Is there a spring?' Tighe aimed the question at Ati, who had been around exploring earlier that morning. Ati shrugged. He had a panicked look in his eye; Pelis had the same look. Mulvaine's injuries were alarming.

Tighe looked from face to face. 'He will be well again,' he said, insistently, 'if we move him to a spring so that he can drink. Drink and food.'

But it was no easy matter shifting Mulvaine's trembling, sweating and complaining body through the tangle of the Meshwood. Tighe put his arms under the injured boy's shoulders, Ati and Ravielre grasped him each side

227

of his torso. But if anybody touched his injured leg he screamed and writhed, and he could barely be held in one position let alone moved if he did that. So his legs trailed behind, which meant that when the three carriers made the precarious step from one trunk of meshwood tree to another, his legs flopped and banged and he screamed even more.

Tighe told Pelis to go on ahead and seek out a spring. She made her way westward, straight through the tangle of branches and soon vanished. When she re-emerged it was with a glum expression on her face. 'I can find no spring. Maybe we should go down?'

Ati groaned. 'Not down, that is where Waldea said the claw-caterpils live.' Tighe nodded.

'Perhaps upwards?' Pelis suggested. 'There might be a spring upwall from us?'

Tighe shook his head. 'We cannot carry Mulvaine upwall. It is impossible. Look again.'

Pelis hurried away. Tighe hauled again and they moved Mulvaine's whimpering body on to another trunk. There was a short ledge, a little overhung and shadow-filled, which made it easier to carry him along. Mushrooms grew in the crevices of this space. 'Should we eat them?' Tighe wondered aloud.

'Perhaps they are poison,' said Ati. 'Do you know poison mushrooms from healthy ones?'

'I am hungry,' was all that Ravielre replied.

'It would be foolish to poison ourselves,' said Tighe, uncertainly. But he was hungry too, his stomach clutching in his belly with little stabs of pain.

At the far end of the little overgrown crag was a long step to a broad meshwood tree trunk. Tighe took a breath and reached out with one foot; he could only just span the distance. He was straddling the gap. 'When I speak,' he said, straining through his teeth, 'push with me, and I will complete the step.'

'What?' asked Ravielre.

'Now!' said Tighe and lurched to try and haul Mulvaine over on to the trunk. Something high in his groin twanged and pain shot down his leg and up his spine. He howled and his grip on Mulvaine's body loosened. He was still spreadeagled, straddling crag and trunk with his legs wide apart, but the posture was now causing him the most extraordinary pain. He fumbled, felt Mulvaine slide from him, scrabbled to regain his hold. His bad foot went over. He stumbled, letting go Mulvaine altogether and reaching out blindly with both arms.

He struck the trunk and grasped instinctively. Behind him he heard shouts, and crashing sound, but his own eyes were shut. He clung to the trunk, his burning legs dangling free. For a long moment he hung there, clutching desperately and then he started pulling himself upright. His chest and belly rasped up over the curve of the trunk, and he swung himself round to lie face down panting.

His groin spat and bubbled with pain, pulses of agony that tremored down his thighs and up his abdomen. He had done himself some injury. For a lengthy moment all he could do was lie and be taken by the agony. Then, with a nauseous feeling at the pit of his throat, he turned to see what had happened to Mulvaine.

Ati and Ravielre were standing on the crag, a little over an arm's length away from Tighe. There was an expression of horror on their faces.

'We dropped him,' said Ati, in a weird, high-toned voice. 'He swung down when you let go,' said Ravielre. 'His legs came up.'

'He was bloody,' said Ati. 'He slipped.'

'Pelis!' called Tighe, through the trees. 'Pelis! Come here!'

When Pelis made her way back up to their position, Tighe was sitting upright rubbing at his groin with both hands to try and reduce the fierce aching pain. Ati had begun climbing down to see what had happened to Mulvaine.

'Mulvaine fell,' said Tighe, by way of explanation to Pelis's horrified expression. He couldn't bring himself to say, *We dropped Mulvaine*. That sounded so appallingly clumsy. The pain in his groin was distracting him. Rubbing it seemed to be reducing it a little.

Pelis leaned over to look down, and Tighe lay down with his face over the side of the meshwood tree trunk. There was no sign of Mulvaine, and no indication of where he might have gone – no chimney of broken leaves. Ravielre was sitting with his hands pressed against his face, a posture of abandonment.

After a short while they heard Ati's voice calling up out of the darkness. 'He is here! Come down!' Pelis and Ravielre immediately started clambering down from trunk to branch. Tighe, getting gingerly to his feet, discovered that the pain in his abdomen was a vague burning unless he strained or put pressure on his pelvis joint, when it screamed and stabbed out. Climbing down was almost impossible. He tried sitting down again and lowering himself over the side, but it was slow and uncomfortable, and because he couldn't see where he was putting his feet it was also dangerous. He didn't want to fall.

'Ati!' he called down. 'Pelis! I am injured!'

'Come down,' called Pelis, vanishing beneath him.

Tighe thought of responding, but thought again. It was probably better not to admit to the pain. He was a warrior, he had fought in the war. He closed his mouth and ran a forefinger along the line of his lips symbolically to seal them. Then he reached down with a leg, grunting at the pain, and lowered himself.

2

It took him a long time, perhaps an hour, to make his way down to where the others were. Mulvaine had fallen through a series of bushier, younger meshwood trees whose springy branches had cushioned his fall; and had come to rest in the canopy of a grand old meshwood growth. He was face down, his arms hanging limply, but Ati confirmed that he was still breathing.

The shock of the fall, however, had started his leg bleeding again; in fact bleeding more severely than it had been before. He was completely unconscious. Blood dropped in threads and globs from his bad leg spattering regularly through the leaves beneath, oozing out in pulses. Tighe pale with pain and effort, sat and recovered his breath, whilst Ati crouched close to him.

'Ravielre and I tried to move him from the branches,' he was saying excitedly, 'but the branches have some manner of thorn there and he is stuck on the thorns.'

'Thorns?' gasped Tighe.

'Thorns – so high,' said Ati, illustrating the dimensions of the thorns with his little finger by clutching the second joint and holding the finger up. 'They are not many, perhaps six to each branch, but Mulvaine is stuck on some of them.'

Tighe winced at the thought. 'We must lift him from above.' He pulled himself upright and he, Ravielre and Ati positioned themselves on foothold branches around the supine figure of Mulvaine. The dripping of his blood on the leaves below marked time.

'He will die, I think,' said Ati.

'Don't say so,' said Tighe, making a sour face because the pain in his groin flared and twisted. 'Take hold and lift up – all, all. Ravielre?'

'I'm hungry,' said Ravielre sullenly.

'After we have settled Mulvaine,' Tighe chided, 'then we find food.' His own stomach squeaked with hunger, but the pain in his pelvis was greater. 'After we have settled Mulvaine we will find insects. But not before!'

'How can you scold us? *You* dropped him,' Ravielre observed sharply.

'Lift him!' barked Tighe feeling his temper corrode. 'Lift him up!'

The three of them heaved and tugged, but Mulvaine's body seemed stuck fast. It shifted minutely, and released a gout of blood from the shot leg that splashed through the leaves like a long piss. Tighe was sweating with the effort and the pain.

'Again!' he ordered. 'Again!'

They heaved and Mulvaine rose slightly, sagging in the middle. 'Take his legs,' Tighe ordered Ravielre. 'Lift him.'

Mulvaine was too far gone to make any complaint as they manhandled his leg. Slowly they raised his body up and pulled it to one side. Ravielre's pale face was dark with the effort. 'There!' gasped Tighe. 'Over there.' They staggered, but managed to transport Mulvaine over to where the trunks of meshwood sprouted from the wall. There was a point of intersection where one fat trunk split into two and they lowered Mulvaine on to this truncated platform. 'Turn him over,' said Tighe, panting, settling back and clutching at his groin. 'Turn him over.'

Ati and Ravielre did as they were told.

When Tighe had recovered his breath and the pain in his groin had died a little, he shifted over to Mulvaine's body. His chest was still inflating and deflating, if only a little; and his eyelids pulsed with the movement of the eyeballs underneath. But there was a piece of twig sticking out of the wounded kneecap, and his clothing was pierced and bloody in three places; two on the thighs, one in the stomach, where he had fallen on the thorns. A lengthy scratch, dry but fiercely red, ran from his chin over his lips up the side of his nose and up his forehead. Tighe pulled the twig that was sticking out of Mulvaine's wounded knee; it caught, but with a more vigorous tug it came free. The blood started flowing again.

'He's so white,' said Pelis, peering at him. 'So pale.'

'He's sleeping,' said Tighe, uncertainly. 'When he wakes he will feel better.'

'He will be weak.'

'Weak but better.'

'Should we tether him somehow?' said Ati. 'What about when the dusk gale comes?'

'We are deep enough in the wood to be protected I think' said Tighe. 'We must find food.'

'I'm *hungry*,' said Ravielre in a pained voice.

'He thirsty too,' said Tighe, gesturing at the unconscious body. 'We cannot carry him to a spring. We must find a spring and bring water back to him. We look for a spring and for water.'

*

The shadows were thickening in the Meshwood as the four of them roamed through the trunks. Tighe could only move slowly and awkwardly but Ati, Pelis and especially Ravielre hopped from trunk to branch with an air of hungry desperation. 'Find some insect and bring it back,' Tighe told them. 'Find some spring and call out.'

Ati found a spring and they all made their way over to him. The water was gushing from a cleft in the wall and running over a moss-smothered trunk of wood. After the four of them had drunk their fill, Tighe instructed them to cup their hands and carry the water back to Mulvaine. 'He thirsty,' he pointed out. 'We must help him.'

But carrying the water in their hands was not easy. It dribbled through the seam where the two palms were pushed together, or slopped over as the carrier hopped from trunk to trunk. It was doubly difficult negotiating the branches without having a hand to steady oneself. By the time the four of them arrived back at Mulvaine they had little left but wet palms; and they pressed these against Mulvaine's dried and blistering lips.

'He will die,' said Ati mournfully.

Tighe felt terrible. The pain in his pelvis was making him sick in his stomach. He settled himself with his back to the wall and spoke in a quavery voice. 'Go back to the spring, you three,' he said. 'Fill your mouths, not your hands. Fill your mouths, but do not swallow. Bring the water back and Mulvaine will drink that way.'

They went off immediately. Tighe sucked in deep breaths, tried to focus his attention away from his pain. The throbbing died down and he found his eyelids slipping down. A terrible weariness. Slipping down, falling into sleep like falling off the world.

Rustling in the leaves meant that Pelis had returned; Ati and Ravielre came quickly behind her. Tighe's eyes were sticky; it was hard opening them fully. He waved his hand in the direction of Mulvaine's body and one by one they leant over his face and kissed the water into him.

'It is no good,' fretted Ati after he had loosed his mouthful. 'It dribbles away over his cheeks. Not in his stomach.'

'It is better,' said Tighe. 'Better.'

Ravielre and Pelis went out by themselves looking for food. Tighe fell asleep straight away, so although they were gone over an hour it seemed to him that they returned immediately. They carried between them one of the grey worm-beasts that Tighe had noticed on coming through the Meshwood with the platon. Its head had been pulled off and purple-grey chunks of meat extruded.

'We should cook it,' said Ati. 'We should start a fire.'

'Do you know how to start a fire?' asked Ravielre.

'Mulvaine knows,' said Pelis. Everybody looked at Mulvaine. He was trembling slightly in his sleep; his lips were looking black and puffed.

'We can eat food raw,' said Tighe.

'We will be cold again tonight' said Ati. 'Without our blankets. A fire would help.'

'First we eat' said Tighe, his mouth watering with hunger. 'After, we can think about fire.'

The Meshwood worm was a little under an arm's length and as thick as a man's wrist. A series of finger-thick tendon-like threads reached from top to bottom at regular intervals, like the pieces of some antique plastic machine; and there were some stringy organs too tough to chew. But the bulk of the thing was dark blue meat that started to grey quickly when exposed to the air. Tighe chewed this meat desperately; it tasted bad, inky and stale, but it was at least food.

When the four of them had picked the worm's body clean, Pelis wondered aloud whether they should feed Mulvaine. They all looked at the shallowly breathing body. 'If he did not drink,' said Ati, 'how can he eat?'

It was getting very dark now and for half an hour or so Ravielre and Ati tried to make fire. Without Waldea's tinder-box it was no easy task. Ravielre claimed once to have seen soldiers make fire by squeezing leaves together between flat palms very quickly and for a while all four of them tried this; but the leaves only turned to mulch and stained the palms green. 'Perhaps they used dried leaves,' Ravielre conceded.

Then the dusk gale started up. They all huddled together, clustering around Mulvaine's body, whilst the forest thrashed and howled around them. Eventually the wind settled and it was tar-black.

Ravielre and Pelis clung together and fell asleep. Ati came and clasped Tighe, although the pair of them had some difficulty in finding a comfortable position when every fidget caused Tighe to grunt with pain. But they settled eventually.

Tighe could not sleep. The evening meal sat unpleasantly in his stomach and his pelvis was throbbing. 'Ati?' he said.

Ati breathed out; the warmth of his breath touched Tighe's neck. 'Yes?'

'Back on the shelf – the battle.'

A long pause in the darkness. 'Yes.'

'What was that calabash? That silver calabash that floated through the air?'

Ati mumbled something, nuzzled Tighe's neck. Then he spoke more distinctly. 'I do not know. The worldwall is cluttered with wonders.'

'I think it was a war calabash of the Otre' said Tighe. He had been considering this. 'Instead of the soft leathers of the Imperial calabashes with their wooden cradles they have constructed machine with metal belly, so that it resists rifle fire. It is a terrible weapon.'

'Terrible,' agreed Ati, non-specifically.

'With such a weapon, maybe the Otre will defeat the whole Empire.'

Ati stiffened a little in Tighe's embrace. 'Never!' he said. 'They will be unable. The army will . . .', and he tailed off. 'I do not know,' he said vaguely. 'Perhaps the Pope has led the army into the Meshwood. Perhaps they will ambush the Otre when they attempt to come through the Meshwood.'

There was silence. Eventually Tighe spoke again. 'Ati?'

'Yes.'

'Did you hear the voice?'

'What voice? Now? There's no voice but yours.'

'When the silver calabash flew through the sky,' said Tighe, shivering at the memory, 'I heard a voice. A loud voice.'

'There was the noise of battle,' said Ati indistinctly.

'It sounded as if it was calling my name.'

Ati snorted. 'I heard a great rumble, but it was explosions from the war I think.'

There was silence again. Tighe heard rustling noises in the Meshwood around them, but they settled to silence again. 'Ati?' he said. 'Ati? What do you think is through the Great Door that the Otre guard?'

But Ati was asleep.

3

They were all woken by the dawn gale and lay huddled together until the air cleared and the purer light of the morning began filtering up through the branches. Ravielre and Pelis got up and went off together to search through the Meshwood for more food. Ati grinned stupidly at Tighe when they had gone. 'They go off to be lovers, I think,' he said and made gulping noises in his throat to express his ridicule.

Tighe felt aches all over his body and his legs were particularly stiff, but the fiercer pain in his groin had damped down a little. He made his way awkwardly over to Mulvaine. 'Ati,' he said, 'bring me some leaves with dew on them.'

Together they squeezed the leaves so that the fluid dribbled over Mulvaine's mouth. His lips were alarmingly swollen and as black as night-time. His eyelids had bulged out as well, puffed to jammed globes of skin; a green crust had formed at the join and in the corners. The sweat on Mulvaine's brow felt slimy and cold. His head was pushed back a little way because there were lumpy swellings in his throat, at the junction of jawbone, ear and neck. Tighe tried prying apart his black lips to let the water dribble in, but they were glued together somehow.

'He is ill,' said Ati, making a sour face.

Tighe shuffled down to look at Mulvaine's wounded leg. The blood had stopped flowing and was now as black and sticky as tar. A crust was forming over the top of this jam-like mass, but it was thin and scattered with cracks and lines. The holes left by the thorns seemed to have dried up.

His breast was still rising and falling, but only a very little.

After an hour or so Ravielre and Pelis returned empty-handed; they came scurrying through the foliage. 'Where is the food?' complained Ati, throwing his hands in the air in mock anger.

'We saw a claw-caterpil, I think,' gasped Pelis. 'We ran and scrambled up here, but that was what we saw.'

'No!' cried Ati.

'I do not know,' said Ravielre, hurriedly, 'that it was a claw-caterpil. I saw something, but it was small – no bigger than the worm we ate yesterday.'

'But it was coloured differently,' insisted Pelis. 'I know it was a claw-caterpil. We must leave – we must go back up.'

'No,' said Tighe. It came out quavery, so he restated it more firmly, 'No. We cannot carry Mulvaine up. We will wait until he is better.'

'What?' said Ati severely, turning on Tighe. 'He will die.'

'He will be better in a day or two days,' said Tighe. 'When he is better we can help him climb back up.'

'But the claw-caterpils!'

'I think we are too far upwall for claw-caterpils,' said Tighe. 'Remember what Waldea said? They were in the Meshwood, but downwall a long way. That is why the Popes led us through the wood so high up.'

'The Popes,' snorted Pelis.

Ati turned on her. 'Do not mock the Popes!' he squealed. 'Do not!'

They squabbled amongst themselves for a long time and Tighe gave up trying to intervene, closing his eyes and retreating into a meditative state. The pain in his groin was definitely starting to ease a little, provided he didn't jar it at all. When the bickering had died down, he opened his eyes again. 'We will stay with Mulvaine. Ravielre and Pelis, you must go again and look for food. You can go upwall to look, if you are bothered by the thought of claw-caterpils. Ati, you and I must go again to the spring we found yesterday and bring some water back for Mulvaine.'

Returning with a mouthful of water, Tighe tried to prise apart Mulvaine's lips. He had to dig his fingers into the unconscious boy's mouth until he felt teeth, and then tear the flesh apart. As he did so dark brown blood started seeping out of the corners and tracing lines down the cheeks. It looked disgusting. It took a considerable effort of will on Tighe's part to force his own mouth down to touch the scabby, discoloured, bleeding lips of Mulvaine. He released his amount of water and pulled back to check whether Mulvaine was swallowing it, but it was very hard to tell. 'You, Ati, now. Your turn,' he said, but Ati swallowed his own water himself and made loud noises of disgust. 'His lips are unclean, revolting,' he said. 'You say he will wake up – he can drink for himself when he wakes up.'

Tighe could not think of a proper way to express his exasperation.

An hour passed in sullen silence between them before Ravielre and Pelis returned. Ravielre had a couple of stringy, finger-length worms clutched in his left hand and was carrying the lapis-lazuli shell of a fist-sized beetle under his arm. He held the beetle out to them, shell down, and its myriad eyelash-like legs all around the rim wriggled and twitched. Pelis had an array of smaller insects tucked in the fold of her shirt.

The problem with small insects is that the eater must discard most of the beast – shell, legs – and is left with only a tiny morsel. The four of them picked their way through the array of food, but the feast lasted only minutes and left each of them feeling unsatisfied and still empty. The blue-shelled beetle was too foul-tasting to eat, although Ravielre, more hungry (he declared) than the others, tried for longer with this. The worms were good, but there were few enough of them.

Afterwards they sat listlessly and chattered amongst themselves, Ravielre and Pelis in one another's arms quite openly. 'Shall we really go home?' asked Pelis.

'We shall all go home,' said Tighe, his head humming with the thrill of what he was saying. 'Every one of us. Including Mulvaine, I promise it.'

'You will come to my home then,' said Pelis, reaching up and running her knuckles gently under Ravielre's chin. 'You will come and meet my mother and her consort, and my grandmother also. How they will admire you!'

But Ravielre said nothing to this. With a small start, Tighe realised that his eyes were full of tears. As one, the others realised that he was mourning Bel.

There was an awkward silence. Ravielre said nothing, only turned away, putting his face towards the wall.

The mood had deflated.

Later all four of them went out searching for more food. Tighe had recovered enough to be more agile in the hunt, hopping from branch to branch. He came back with a fist full of ants and an enormously long worm, as long as two men's height, but thinner than the smallest finger. This was wriggly and difficult, so he tore off the head; it remained wriggly so he tore off the tail. Even then it was difficult to hold, twisting and shuggling, so he tied it around his waist like a rope or a tether and made his way back to Mulvaine's sleeping body.

The others returned with similar pickings, except for Pelis, who had captured another of the fat grey worms. They all ate fully, laughing and chattering, until they felt their bellies bulge with food.

That night Tighe slept well for the first time he could remember in a long time. There were no strange dreams, no pains woke him; only the cold pressed itself on his consciousness, so that he was aware of being half awake, half asleep, and not comfortable in the dark before the dawn gale. When the dawn gale started, Tighe pressed himself closer against Ati. He felt a strange sense of comfort; that he was close against the warm body of Ati, that the anger and tumult of the dawn winds were out there, out past the forest. That he was safe.

The winds were particularly wet this morning and he felt the moisture pricking against his body. He unhooked a hand from its position around Ati's body and ran his palm over his own side and leg, over his forehead, scooping up some of the moisture and pressing the wet skin against his lips. It felt cool, refreshing. The thought of Mulvaine's blackened puffed lips occurred to him, but he consoled himself by thinking that the dawn gale was probably blowing moisture against Mulvaine's sleeping lips, perhaps filling his belly with water. Precious water; the thought of it was almost like drinking.

He lay, his eyes closed, listening to the sounds of the dawn gale receding, until the larger roar vanished and he could hear the shuddering of all the leaves, the sucking and rustling noises of branches trembling, droplets falling and settling. It was a pleasant, musical sound.

Tighe opened his eyes. The sounds were amazingly suggestive. It was strange to think that something as simple as water settling and leaves rustling could sound so human. It was like a baby suckling at breast. It made Tighe think of life in the village; he remembered when a girl called Intershe had given birth to her baby, she used to feed it on the market shelf and it had made a sound like that. Or goats at teat, snuffling and slurping. He thought of his pashe. He had a vivid picture of her face in his mind; her smiling at him, warm and loving.

Grandhe Jaffiahe had killed her. Pushed her off the world. Tighe felt misery tangle in his stomach. He had forgotten that fact; it had simply fallen out of his mind. He had squeezed the memories away like milking a goat. And the old refrain returned to him; the littleness of it all. After all he had seen, the great battle clash between two empires, war that shook the whole wall – the stakes so enormous. The idea that Grandhe would murder his own daughter just to claim a few goats, just to consolidate his own position as head of the village! It was absurd, petty. It was tiny-minded. And this in turn recalled Tighe to his sense of things. Perhaps that was nothing more than appropriate because the whole towering expanse of the worldwall was nothing more than a miniature, an experiment by a limited god.

These thoughts soured Tighe's mood. He disengaged his embrace from Ati and sat upright, concentrating as he did so on the pain in his groin. But that seemed more or less to have gone away.

He rubbed his eyes and looked over towards Mulvaine.

The origin of the sucking, gobbling noise became apparent.

A beast – evidently a claw-caterpil, although it was much smaller than Waldea's descriptions had led Tighe to expect – was grazing on Mulvaine's leg. It had chewed its way through the knee completely, so that the lower part of the leg was now detached from Mulvaine's body and dangled below him held up only by the material of his trousers. The claw-caterpil was now munching its way up Mulvaine's thigh, grazing on Mulvaine's flesh as its tiny counterpart might do upon a leaf.

'No!' screamed Tighe. 'No!'

He jumped up and leapt towards it.

The claw-caterpil was grey-green, as thick around the waist as Tighe himself, although stood on end it would not have been quite as tall. Its segmented back was bristling with thick pale-brown hairs and shorter blacker hairs sprouted from between the plates. At the side fleshier skin was pulsing and heaving as the beast sucked in the flesh its black twitching jaws were breaking off from the exposed surface of Mulvaine's leg. The sucking was interspersed with a crunching noise as bone was ground down and sucked up.

Tighe grabbed a branch and tugged violently, pulling several times before it broke free. Then he launched forward and started beating the claw-caterpil. The foliage softened the blow and it was hard to bring it down with any force. The claw-caterpil ignored Tighe's assault as if nothing were happening.

The others were up now, crying and calling out in horror. Tighe felt some part of his mind go very clear. He ripped the leaf-bearing thinner branches from the body of his meshwood club, tearing frantically. In moments it was nothing more than a naked spar of wood.

He stepped up to the enormous insect and began striking it hard across its bony plated back. For the first time the claw-caterpil stopped what it was doing; the hideous slurping noises ceased and the thing curled its head round to fix Tighe with a stone-like glare. Its eyes were two clusters of tiny balls, like millions of tiny black insect eggs fixed to the sides of its head. Beneath these eyes its mouth parts, messy with threads of flesh and smeared with blood, worked open and shut.

Momentarily Tighe experienced a spike of fear, like a moment of clarity in the middle of a temper tantrum. The monstrosity of the creature was fearsome. It regarded him with an appalling purity of expression. Tighe felt an almost irrepressible urge to drop his stick and run, as far and as fast as he could. This was unbearable, the gaze of the monster was unbearable. But his arms were acting almost without the control of his mind.

They used the stick as a form of lever, digging it underneath the softer belly of the claw-caterpil and hoiking it up with all the strength in Tighe's muscles. The claw-caterpil reacted with terrifying speed, curling round and snapping with its jaws; but the motion of the branch was already pushing it away and the jaw parts clicked shut on nothing. Then it was in the air, twisting and curling upon itself as it fell.

There was a crash and a rattle of leaves and the monster vanished down-wall amongst the branches of the Meshwood.

Tighe was gasping; there were tears in his eyes, he realised; tears thick on his cheek. He had to sit down on the trunk because his legs were wobbling so violently with the shock. His heart was hammering.

The others were all about him. 'Tighe!' Ati was saying, over and over. 'Tighe! Tighe!'

'I knew I saw one,' wailed Pelis. 'I knew they're here.'

Tighe's breathing was settling a little, although the tears were still coming out of his eyes. He wiped them away with trembling fingers and climbed to his feet, leaning on Ati until he was properly upright.

'What shall we do?' asked Ravielre. 'What shall we do?'

Tighe went over to the body of Mulvaine. He looked grotesque, less and less recognisable. His face was distorted so utterly that he no longer looked like Mulvaine. He barely even resembled a human being. His cheeks and mouth were massed up and the skin was cracked and broken; there were boils of some kind clustered around his tight-shut eyes. His hair was a messy tangle. The missing leg looked less deforming, in a strange way, because of the way he was lying, which gave the impression that he had tucked it underneath himself.

Tighe leant over him. Astonishingly he was still breathing, his chest still rising shallowly.

'He is still alive!' Tighe announced. 'He is still alive!'

They all gathered round. 'The wound – his leg,' said Ravielre. 'It is not bleeding. How can it not be bleeding?'

'I don't know,' said Tighe.

Pelis kept looking about her, expecting more of the claw-caterpils to come sliding out of the leaves. 'We can't stay,' she said.

'No,' said Tighe. 'That is right.'

'How horrible it was!' said Ati, wrapping both his arms about his head to hide himself from the Universe. 'How horrible! That God would make such monsters!'

'The worldwall is cluttered with marvels,' said Tighe drily. 'Mulvaine is still alive. We must carry him upwall.'

There was a chorus of moans. 'No, no,' said Ravielre. 'He is too ill. He is dead already.'

'*Not* dead,' said Tighe. He felt a powerful intensity in him now, after the initial panic had settled. The incident had cleared his head. There is something purgative about fear – after the event, at any rate.

'We cannot carry him!'

'He is half-devoured!'

'He will attract more of the claw-caterpils,' said Pelis.

'We will carry him,' said Tighe. 'This we will do.'

'He only has *one leg*,' said Ati, whining.

'Then he will weigh less to carry,' said Tighe sharply. 'Come, Ati, you and I will start. We will carry him between us. When we are tired, you and you, Ravielre and Pelis, will carry him.'

4

They made slow progress going up.

Mulvaine, who had slept through the experience of being half eaten alive by a claw-caterpil, started moaning and shifting as soon as they moved his body. He tried to turn over, muttering. Tighe examined the wound at the end of his thigh; it was covered in some sticky saliva-like substance, which was presumably what prevented it from bleeding out. Perhaps the monsters especially relished blood, Tighe thought; their spit kept their victims from bleeding dry. Tighe then – although it made his stomach turn over – plucked the severed bottom of Mulvaine's leg from the cradle made by the material of his trousers. He held it in both hands: a naked human leg, bloody at one end. There was a strange smell to it, not merely the blood, but a fiercely pungent and foetid smell at the wound. The skin near the top looked green and was starting to decompose, although the foot looked so exactly like a human foot, down to the horny toenails and the tiny hairs growing out of the tops of the toes, that it was somehow deeply saddening. Tighe took it by the ankle and hurled it as far as he could, hearing it rattle through the leaves in the distance.

They carried Mulvaine up and along to the spring, where they all drank. It took them most of the morning and they twitched or cried out in terror at every rustle in the blanket of leaves.

At the spring Tighe had the idea of laying Mulvaine under the flow of water, so that it washed down over his swollen face. Tighe reached into the splashing to lever apart his lips to make sure water was going into his mouth, and with a lurch Mulvaine started coughing. So they pulled him out of the line of water and he shuddered and thrashed back and forward.

They sat him up with his back against the wall. He mumbled something, but the words were lost amongst the sloppiness and mess of his lips. Then he fell asleep again and they could not rouse him.

'Should we wash his wound?' suggested Pelis. 'In the spring, perhaps?'

Tighe considered: 'I think the claw-caterpil spit keeps the blood from coming out,' he said. 'I think we should not disturb it.'

'It is a monster,' said Ravielre, his voice full of loathing. 'Its spit is poison. We should wash it away.'

'If it is poison,' said Tighe, making sure to fix each of them in the eye with his glare as he spoke, 'then it is already in his blood, and washing will do no good. If it is not poison but healthful, then we must leave it. We will carry him up.'

'He is dying,' said Ati. 'We should leave him here and go on ourselves.'

'He is not dying,' said Tighe. 'We will carry him.'

'He has only one leg!'

'He is not dying. We will carry him.'

Ati grumbled and the others looked crossly at Tighe, but nobody defied him. They spent an hour by the spring, finding and eating what insects they could, although chancing upon none of the larger kind. Then Ravielre and Pelis took up the burden of Mulvaine.

They made a slow and precarious way up from trunk to branch. At one stage they discovered a gouge in the worldwall that was backed with some manstone in slabs, and which ran diagonally upwards. It was heavily overgrown, but Tighe and Ati went first, clearing a path, and Ravielre and Pelis followed carrying Mulvaine.

They decided to stay inside this ledge for the night and spent the rest of the light scavenging for insects. Tighe sat expectantly beside Mulvaine, thinking he might wake up at any moment, but he slept on uneasily.

In the morning they were lucky enough to find a grey fat-worm nosing its way through the moss and bracken of the ledge, and they all enjoyed a good breakfast. 'We must try and feed Mulvaine,' said Tighe.

'He is now an obsession of you, I think,' said Ati sourly.

But they all lent a hand, holding Mulvaine's mouth open and popping in little gobbets of meat. 'He is not swallowing,' Ravielre pointed out.

'Perhaps the meat will dissolve in his mouth,' said Tighe. 'Then the goodness can run down his throat like water. Come!'

'I hate the way you say *come*!' Ravielre growled. 'As if we were pets. You are only a barbarian, a turd for brains, after all. *I* was born in the Imperial City.'

Tighe looked hard at him. 'Do you think it a good idea to move on now?' he asked. 'Or should we stay here all day?'

Ravielre was silent for a time, glowering sullenly at Tighe. 'Perhaps we should go on,' he said, eventually.

'Ravielre says come!' Tighe announced loudly. 'And so we must.'

They hauled Mulvaine out of the trench and up through the forest. By ninety they reached a fairly broad ledge, hardly overhung at all. It marked a path away both east and west and the grass was well trodden. 'I do not remember this ledge,' said Pelis.

'It is easier than making our way through Meshwood,' said Ravielre. 'We should walk along this ledge, perhaps to the far side of the Meshwood. Then we would be away from the claw-caterpils at least.'

'For now', said Tighe, 'we can rest at any rate.'

They deposited Mulvaine on the ledge, sitting up with his back to the wall, and sprawled themselves out. Ravielre and Pelis had undertaken the majority of the day's carrying and were worn out.

Ati lay on his stomach for a while, but soon grew restless. He paced up and down the ledge a little way, never going out of sight of the others but exploring as widely as he could. 'I think', he said, coming back to them, 'that we might go west along this ledge. That is, back towards the Empire.'

'We are on the eastern side of the Meshwood,' said Pelis. 'We are closer to the eastern side.'

'But the east is controlled by the Otre.'

'Perhaps the west is controlled by the Otre as well.'

Ati bristled. 'What do you mean?'

'Perhaps,' Pelis explained laboriously, 'perhaps the Otre have conquered the whole Empire by now in war.'

'Don't say that! Don't say so!'

'I only mean that it would be better to get out of the Meshwood sooner rather than later. It would be better not to have to encounter any more of the claw-caterpils, that is all I mean.'

'You are only a girl and you are scared,' said Ati, puffing up his chest. 'I am a warrior and I am not scared. Besides,' he said, sagging down and sitting cross-legged on the ledge. 'I want to go to my home and my home is westward not eastward.'

Ravielre said, 'I am hungry.'

'Perhaps this ledge runs all the way through the Meshwood to the west,' Ati continued. 'Perhaps it would lead us easily and clearly out of the Meshwood to the west.'

'More likely it peters out a little way in that direction,' said Pelis, pointing west.

'What shall we do, Tighe?' asked Ati, tugging at Tighe's raggedy sleeve. 'Shall we go eastward or westward?'

'We'll rest for now,' said Tighe, looking west along the ledge. The tangles of meshwood sprouting over the ledge hung down in weird patterns, casting interlocking shadows over the backing of the wall.

'There,' said Pelis, pointing eastward with her arm outstretched.

Everybody looked. Half a dozen grey-suited figures were advancing up the ledge, all holding either a rifle or one of the short-barrelled rifles that looked a little like stubby knives.

They were, very pointedly, looking directly at the four kite-pilots.

'Otre,' hissed Pelis.

'Go!' called Ati, hurling himself forward up to his feet and sprinting westward away down the ledge.

Ravielre, Pelis and Tighe followed almost at once.

'You there!' called the nearest of the Otre soldiers, in a voice that carried powerfully. 'Stop running, surrender. Surrender, or we shall shoot.' His Imperial was heavily accented.

Tighe's groin-hurt was not bad, but he rapidly fell behind the others because of his bad foot. He limped with a desperate stride, pounding down with his right foot and trying to skim over the step of his left, as the first shot rang out.

Pelis was directly ahead of him. There was a second shot and a hand-sized wet red mark splattered out of her shoulder. She stumbled and fell hard to the ground.

Tighe had to leap awkwardly to avoid tripping over her. He skidded, span, and saw her lying face down on the ledge. Then, surrendering himself to the urge to run, he picked himself up and simply sprinted.

'Down!' he called ahead, at Ati and Ravielre. 'Down into the Meshwood!'

Ati looked back over his shoulder and Tighe signalled to him with an arm gesture. Down! They could lose themselves in the Meshwood and evade the Otre soldiers.

Without slowing his pace Ati ducked to the left and slid off the ledge, landing easily on a broad meshwood trunk. He called out as he did this and Ravielre skidded to a halt. There was another rifle shot from the soldiers behind Tighe; he sensed the bullet whizzing past him.

Ravielre was scrambling down after Ati. Tighe, sweating now, ducked as another bullet shot through the air. There was a scream from up ahead, although Tighe couldn't be sure if it was Ravielre or Ati screaming.

He pulled himself down and swung from a branch; on to a broad nexus of meshwood tree roots, all tangled in together. From there it was a series of easy hops down and away from the ledge through the leaves. He chanced one glimpse over his shoulder, but the ledge was invisible through the cloud of foliage overhead. He heard no more shots either.

For a little while he concentrated on making his way as quietly as possible, moving cautiously from trunk to branch. After a while he decided it was time to hazard a cry; he called out to the others. 'Ati! Ravielre!'

There was a moan from close ahead. Tighe hopped awkwardly through the leaves and found Ravielre sitting astride a trunk clutching his head. Tighe's heart sank. Blood was oozing from between his fingers.

'Your head!' he cried.

Ravielre groaned again. 'It's my ear,' he said. 'They shot my ear! I felt the bottom of the ear hurt and now it's all blood. The shit-eaters!'

'Let me see,' said Tighe. He pulled Ravielre's hand away and examined the sticky wound. 'You have most of your ear still,' he announced.

'It hurts,' said Ravielre, sulkily. 'It hurts and I am hungry.'

'Where is Ati?'

'I don't know.'

Tighe stood up. 'Ati!' he called. 'Ati!'

'Shush,' whined Ravielre. 'You will call the Otre to us.'

'We are far from the ledge now, I think,' said Tighe, 'and they will have moved on.'

'They shot me,' said Ravielre, squirming with misery. 'They shot my ear and they shot Pelis. Pelis and I were together. But my ear! It stings, it hurts!'

'Come,' said Tighe. 'We will wrap your ear in cloth. Tear some from your shirt.'

'Tear some from *your* shirt.'

'It is your ear, after all. Ati!' he called. 'Ati!'

'I am here,' came a reply through the leaves.

'Come to us,' Tighe called out. He bent down and picked at the stitching of Ravielre's shirt to rip free a strip of cloth. Ravielre grumbled that now his stomach would be cold at night, but Tighe ignored him to strap the cloth around the bleeding ear and the top of Ravielre's head, like a headscarf.

Ati's head popped up from below. He looked serious. 'What happened?' he said. 'What happened to Pelis?'

Ravielre grimaced. 'I am hungry.'

Tighe shook his head to warn Ati off the subject. Ati sat himself down and clutched his knees to his chest. 'And Mulvaine,' he said. 'What about Mulvaine?'

Tighe said, 'Ravielre hurt his ear, but I have bandaged it now.'

'With my shirt,' grumbled Ravielre, 'and I am hungry.'

There was a rustling in the leaves, like a shower of dew falling early in the morning. The three boys fell silent, looking around them.

'Otre soldiers?' hissed Ati.

'Or worse?' said Ravielre. 'Claw-caterpils perhaps?'

Tighe looked about himself. 'We must move. Come, we have started going west and we should continue to go west.'

5

They moved west. The way was not easy and all three of them were feeling the pain of hunger. An hour or so into their journey they chanced upon a grey fat-worm. With Ravielre chiming over and over how hungry he was, they started after the beast, but it slid away, half wriggling and half falling downwards. They had to drop from branch to branch a fair distance before they could catch up with it. Ravielre and Ati gripped it and held it between them. Then the three of them started biting pieces from its side whilst it still twined and struggled.

'We should find a spring,' Ravielre said, his mouth full so that he spat out fragments of half-chewed worm. 'I want to wash my wound, my ear.'

Tighe looked at him, wondering whether he had now made himself forget Pelis deliberately, or whether his mind genuinely had slipped away from that subject. It was similar to his attitude to Bel; he had barely said anything about her death. There was a blankness about his expression. 'Wash your wound,' he said. 'That is a good thing.'

'We should find a spring,' said Ravielre. He took another bite.

The tail of the fat-worm curled round and thrashed at the leaves. Tighe caught hold of it and pulled it back, but the thrashing of the leaves continued. The head of a claw-caterpil emerged rapidly from the foliage. Ati shrieked and Ravielre shied quickly backwards, loosing his grip on the worm.

The claw-caterpil emerged fully and lunged forward at Ravielre.

'Your blood!' cried Tighe. 'It smells your blood!'

But the three of them were already scrambling up from branch to branch.

Tighe fell to the rear again because of his bad foot. He had to tear his eyes from below to spy out handholds in the meshwood trees above; and the thought of the claw-caterpil drew his glance back down. 'It smelt Ravielre's blood,' he muttered to himself. 'It smelt his blood.'

From above came a shriek and Tighe started climbing more rapidly. Almost at once a body came crashing through the branches, clipping Tighe as it passed and tumbling on. The jarring shock almost knocked Tighe loose, but he clung to his branch.

From higher up came Ravielre's high-pitched squeal of terror. 'They're all around! There's hundreds! Hundreds!'

Tighe hung, bruised and a little stunned. He could see Ati below him, come to rest in a net of branches; but he had consciously to command himself to start to climb down. The claw-caterpil was down there somewhere.

'Ati?' he said, coming down to him. 'Ati? How are you?'

'My shoulder,' said Ati, in a dim voice. 'My arm is numb and my shoulder hurts. And it hurts when I breathe.'

Tighe looked at the shoulder, but could see nothing wrong, except that when he took hold of it Ati screamed with pain.

Up above there was a ferocious rustling in the canopy of meshwood leaves.

'Ati,' he said, 'we must climb up. Do you see? Come!' He reached round to Ati's good side and pulled him upright.

'We can't go up there,' said Ati in a tight voice. 'There are many claw-caterpils up there. They are all around up there – huge ones, hundreds of them.'

Tighe looked up. The motion in the canopy was becoming more and more agitated. A leg appeared, and then the whole of Ravielre's body; part falling, part clutching to the branches as he struggled to slow his descent.

He collapsed into the network of branches that had broken Ati's fall. Only then did the others see that a small claw-caterpil was fastened to the side of his head; the bandage was gone and the monster's jaws were chewing at the wound.

Ravielre's eyes were wide, stupid with terror. He struggled ineffectually, bringing his arms up and dropping them in spastic movements.

Despite its relatively small size, this claw-caterpil was a horrifying creature. Tighe blenched and forced himself forward. He reached out with both hands and circled the thing's abdomen. The bristles stung his skin, and past them he had the sense of touching something unspeakable, something mucus-slippery but dry, something profoundly and physically repulsive. The claw-caterpil took its jaws from Ravielre's head and swung them round with alarming speed to snap at Tighe's hands.

Tighe let go with a yell and stepped back. The monster slipped, gripped at Ravielre's body with its many legs and pulled itself back up.

Ati was howling now; he had fallen back over and was struggling to wriggle clear; each motion that banged his shoulder made him cry out louder.

The claw-caterpil began grazing again on the side of Ravielre's head.

Tighe looked around for a branch or stick he could use to pry the ghastly insect away from Ravielre, but all he saw was a weave of springy branches thick with leaves. There was no piece of meshwood he could rip free. In desperation he aimed a kick at the monster, but this involved standing on his bad foot and his ankle dissolved under his weight. He sprawled backwards, landing partly on Ati, who shouted with pain and surprise.

Something large dropped from the canopy above. A blur of legs and bristles. It landed on the cradle of branches, its tail falling across Ati and Tighe, its head near Ravielre.

This was a much larger claw-caterpil; twice as long as a man's height, fat and taut around its midriff, its jaws glistening and black as plastic. It shimmied up to Ravielre, mounting his body and struggling on top of the other claw-caterpil. It began pinching its rival between its larger jaws. The smaller monster wriggled, turned and tried to bite back, but was so obviously outmatched that it gave up and rolled free.

Ravielre was staring directly into Tighe's eyes, his hands fluttering. He might have been trying to push the beast away, but the only action he was managing was to slap weakly against its underbelly, where its many legs fluttered. Tighe moved his eyes a little and saw the enormous jaws close in the mess of blood that was the side of Ravielre's head. Ravielre's whole body jerked and twisted and then went stiff.

The smaller claw-caterpil curled and straightened like a finger, and then it lunged out at Tighe. Tighe strained backwards, trying to push himself away from the thing, with Ati beneath him howling and screaming. The beast paused, curled back round and latched on to Ravielre's exposed midriff. It scraped at Ravielre's belly, raising blood, and then gouged in.

Ravielre was still staring, unblinking, straight at Tighe and Ati. Tighe met his gaze again, and was held by the intensity of the look.

It was a physical effort to break the connection of eye to eye.

'Come,' Tighe said, gaspingly. He struggled upright, and tried to haul Ati upright too.

Another claw-caterpil was crawling down a trunk of meshwood in the direction of the feast.

'We have to go now,' said Tighe urgently. 'We have to go now.'

'Ravielre,' said Ati, weakly. The colour had vanished from his face, and his lips were almost white.

'We cannot help him,' said Tighe. 'We need to go. They smelt his blood. We're not bleeding, so they will not smell our blood.'

Ati looked at him.

'I'm bleeding,' he said. 'I'm bleeding, look.'

He used his good hand to hold up his numb one; it was cut deeply across the palm and blood was coming out.

Tighe looked deeply into Ati's eyes. Ati's head was trembling with pain and terror.

'We must go anyway,' said Tighe. 'Come.'

They backed away from the tangle of claw-caterpils, Ravielre's eyes following them the whole way. As the two of them retreated Ravielre swivelled his eyes to follow them. His body was entirely motionless now, stiff and straight. The smaller claw-caterpil had buried his jaws and eyes in a hole at Ravielre's stomach. The skin around the wound was clean and torn; it looked like ripped cloth. The larger claw-caterpil lay alongside him like a shadow, its head almost exactly the same size as Ravielre's, its jaws moving in a steady rhythm excavating the space.

'Come,' said Tighe, breaking the tether of Ravielre's gaze by purposefully looking away. 'This way.'

They started along the trunk and Tighe made the jump to a second. Ati followed, but cried out with pain on landing. 'My shoulder!' he called. 'The pain is too much.'

'You *must* come along,' said Tighe. 'Come now.'

'You don't know what it's like,' complained Ati, sobbing. 'You don't know what the *pain* is like.'

'Come *now*,' shouted Tighe. 'There's no time – think of the claw-caterpils.'

This was the wrong thing to say. Ati started shivering, a series of spluttering moans coming out of his mouth. Tighe gripped his good shoulder and hauled him onwards by sheer strength. Ati resisted every step.

Tighe was reaching out to grasp another branch of meshwood tree when he put his hand on something dry and squelchy. He whipped his hand back with a scream, pushing Ati backwards. Ati started screaming too. The two of them collapsed against the wall at the base of a tree trunk.

But it was only a grey-worm. It poked its stupid pin-eyed head round the branch to look at them.

Ati was screaming with enormous gusto. Tighe knew how he felt; the shock had been so terrible. Except that Ati was overdoing it a little. He was howling like a baby.

Tighe tried to calm him. 'It's only a fat-worm,' he said. 'Ati! Ati!' He was having to shout, to be heard over Ati's howling. 'Ati, be quiet, it's only a fat-worm, it's harmless, it's harmless. Ati!'

He gripped the sides of Ati's head, and fixed his eyes upon the other boy's, trying to will him not to panic, to calm himself, to stop screaming. 'Ati,' he said.

Ati stared back at him, screaming and screaming. He twisted his body, so that his limp hand dangled a little before him. Tighe looked down. A claw-caterpil had fastened on to the hand.

Tighe couldn't control his first reaction, which was to let go of Ati and back away. Then he rebuked himself with a yell and launched back towards his friend. The claw-caterpil had fixed itself on Ati's wrist with two crop-haired forelegs and its relentless jaws were chewing at Ati's hand. Tighe watched as a finger loosened from the hand and dropped away.

Tighe grabbed Ati round the shoulders, so that the terrified boy's screams howled directly into his ear. He put his own shoulder to the wall to balance himself and started kicking out with his good foot. He landed several blows against the beast's back. It continued chewing placidly. Ati's hand was a stump now, like a bloodied fist that was too small for the arm to which it was attached.

'Get away with you,' howled Tighe in his native tongue, ecstatic with fear and rage. 'Foulness, foulness – get away, away!'

A second claw-caterpil head appeared over the rim of the meshwood trunk. Then a third.

Ati had screamed himself hoarse and was now breathing heavily and hard. Tighe shifted himself and let go his hold of Ati, thinking to free both his hands and find some weapon against the creatures. But Ati reached round with his good hand and gripped him, his face close to Tighe's.

'Don't leave me,' he rasped, straight into Tighe's ear. 'Don't leave me like we left Ravielre. Please.'

'Ati,' barked Tighe, feeling sick and uncomfortable, feeling the fear chewing him, his mind racing. 'Ati,' he said again, when what he meant was, *Don't distract me, I'm trying to think what to do.* But there was another part of him that thought, *I'm not bleeding as you are, I can get away even though you can't.*

He shouted again, trying to drown out that voice inside him. They were close to the wall and Tighe pulled a wedge of turf from behind him. He stuffed the clump of soil and grass directly into the path of the first claw-caterpil's jaws.

'Don't leave me,' whimpered Ati. 'Please don't leave me.'

The other two claw-caterpils were clambering up the long body of the first one, their jaws clicking like scissors.

Ati hauled another lump of wall-turf free and rammed it between the jaws of the first monster. Its chewing clogged for an instant on the stodge of earth and grass-roots and Tighe gave a frantic kick with his right leg. The claw-caterpil slid backwards a little way. A second kick and, with its two snaky wriggling fellows, it toppled away and down.

Tighe hauled Ati up, reaching for a branch above their head. 'Help me, Ati,' he said. 'Reach up with your good hand!'

But Ati had passed out.

Tighe was expecting a swarm of wriggling claw-caterpils to come out of the foliage all around him at any moment. 'Wake up, Ati!' he called. 'Wake up!' He dropped Ati back to the trunk, his back against the wall. What to do?

'Ati,' he said, pleading, begging. On instinct he reached out and slapped Ati's face, but that had no effect.

With a desperate malice, he grabbed Ati's hurt arm, thinking that the pain might startle him awake. He even jostled it and it moved loosely within its sleeve. There was an audible click and it went stiffer in the joint. But Ati was still unconscious.

There was a rustling below him. Peering over the ledge of the tree, Tighe saw a terror of claw-caterpils, half a dozen or maybe more, twisting and wriggling along the lower branches and through the foliage. Their mouth parts were all snapping together. They could smell Ati's blood. Tighe knew it; he could almost see it in their actions. They were smelling Ati's blood.

Tighe was away, scrabbling up to the next meshwood tree before he even knew what he was doing. One step up and a handhold within easy reach to the next one, but he looked down. Ati looked calm, as if asleep; only the mess that had been his hand spoiled the picture. *Don't leave me, like we left Ravielre.* Tighe shuddered. He was crying, the sobs so sudden and hard they felt like hiccoughs. He could not grip the branch tightly enough because his hand was trembling so much.

He looked up at the climb ahead of him; then he looked back down at Ati.

He jumped, landing on his bad foot which punched pain up through his leg. But there was no time for that. He backed against Ati, reaching round to draw the unconscious boy's two limps arms forward and round his neck. Then he stood up, with Ati a limp backpack, and started forward. He could only hobble; the pressure on his bad foot was almost unbearable.

He could not climb with this weight on his back and it took both his hands to grip Ati's arms and stop him falling back. Below to the right of the trunk was swarming with claw-caterpils. Below to the left there were more, but there was nothing else to be done.

Tighe leapt down, hoping for a good foothold. He landed on the back of one of the claw-caterpils, a large one; the bony plates on its back provided surprisingly good purchase. It whipped its head round and snapped its jaws, slicing through Tighe's trouser-leg and scratching against his calf. But Tighe was away, leaping down to the next trunk, and down again to the next one.

Each leap was a terrifying tumble through space; he could easily have missed his footing, particularly with the added burden of Ati on his back. He had to land on his good foot, or he would have crumpled over. And without his hands free he could not steady himself. Stride followed stride until his foot slipped and he slammed down painfully across the trunk. Somehow he managed to keep Ati on his back and with an enormous heave he deposited him over the body of the trunk.

6

It took him a while to calm his desperate sobbing, and his head twitched back and forth, checking every tremble of leaves for an emerging claw-caterpil. But he also knew that they couldn't stay where they were. The monsters would come sooner or later. They were probably coming now.

'No,' he moaned to himself. 'No.'

He could hear water shuddering through leaves a little way below him, and after checking his way carefully he dropped down and swigged a draft from the cold spring. Then, filling his mouth, he clambered back up and spat the stuff all over Ati's face.

'Wake up, Ati,' he pleaded. 'Wake up.' He started rubbing Ati's face, chafing the forehead, the cheeks. Ati's eyes flickered and opened.

'We cannot stay here,' he said.

'Oh,' said Ati. 'Oh, oh. My arm hurts. My shoulder and my hand.' But he was at least moving his hand now, waving the wine-red stump in front of him. He started crying. 'Look at my hand!' he said, through chokes. 'Look at it! Oh, it hurts.'

'We have to go now,' said Tighe. 'Use your left hand to help you climb. All right, Ati?'

Ati's crumpled face uncreased, and he looked straight at Tighe with an innocent openness. 'Your face looks funny,' he said in a childish voice. 'Have you been crying?'

'Yes Ati,' said Tighe. 'I have been crying.'

Ati nodded. 'What about Ravielre?' he asked. Then his face creased up again and the tears started. 'Ravielre's dead,' he said with a strained voice, crying freely. 'We'll all die.'

'Come,' said Tighe, 'we must climb away to safety. Ati!'

'My hand,' moaned Ati, waving the stump in front of himself. 'Look at it!'

'You have another hand,' Tighe pointed out. He gripped Ati by his shirt and pulled him up. 'Come on.'

It took a little more chiding, but eventually Ati got into a rhythm of going up from trunk to trunk. It was an awkward, slow procedure, but they were climbing up and to the west. Tighe found himself pondering their position. They were presumably still far to the east of the Meshwood. If they hoped to go all the way through to the west it would take them several days.

Ati had stopped and was sitting on a trunk sobbing to himself.

They rested soon, both hungry. The intimacy of their terror had receded a little, but they still both felt overwhelmed by the horror of their surroundings. But at least they had seen no more claw-caterpils during their climb.

The dusk gale started with a tremendous shaking and rustling of leaves that made both Ati and Tighe cry out and hug one another. But it was only the wind disturbing the leaves and they found a place to wedge themselves in. They held each other very tightly as the wind thrashed about. 'Maybe this wind,' said Tighe, trying to think of things that would console Ati, 'maybe it blows off all the claw-caterpils, blows them all off the wall.'

Ati laughed sobbingly. 'But they would have been blown off this morning,' he said. 'Or during last night's dusk gale. Or some other time.'

'No, no,' soothed Tighe. 'They live in a big cave downwall from here. But they were tempted out by us and now they are too far from their cave and are all out on the branches. All blown into the air! All blown away for ever!'

Ati laughed again and for a while they were silent whilst the wind raged. As it died away they both fell asleep, but Ati soon twitched awake again. 'We can't stay here,' he said, feverishly. 'We can't stay here or they'll come and devour us. Oh, my hand hurts!'

'We'll be all right, I think,' said Tighe. But he wasn't certain.

'No, no, we must go away.' Ati struggled up, pulling himself away from Tighe's embrace. 'We must climb.'

The night was thoroughly black, a complete darkness which made climbing much harder to manage. They had to feel their way up the wall at their side, reaching for a branch. 'Ati,' said Tighe after less than an hour of this. 'Ati, can we stop? We must rest, we must.'

Ati mumbled something.

'Ati,' said Tighe firmly, grabbing him round the waist. 'This is idiot thing. Come, stop. We might as easily put our hands on a claw-caterpil in the dark as escape them in this manner. Stop!'

That thought gave Ati pause and he curled himself up, crying. Tighe knelt down and embraced him and then positioned him gently so that he was lying across the trunk with the wall at his back. He curled in behind him, pressing his own body close. 'We'll be warm and safe,' he promised. 'It will be all right.'

Ati sobbed for a while and then it seemed he fell asleep. To Tighe, he felt like a baby in his arms. But Ati could not sleep long. He would come awake abruptly, shouting, 'They are coming!' or 'My hand! No!' Sometimes he woke with a mere yell. Each time it took him longer to get back to sleep.

Tighe felt hungry and exhausted and found himself resenting Ati's constant interruptions. By the time the dawn gale started they had neither of them slept for more than half an hour.

Come the morning, they were both so tired they could barely co-ordinate their limbs. It was much harder climbing in this state, particularly with Ati's added handicap.

'I'm hungry,' he said. 'I'm hungry and my hand hurts.'

They had climbed only three trees up. Tighe left Ati propped against the wall and stumbled along looking for some kind of food. His eyes kept closing themselves and once his foot slid and twisted away when he thought it had been properly planted. The jar to his chest winded him and he had to lie on the trunk until he got his breath back.

He saw a grey-worm, a small one, and pounced on it. But when he brought it back, Ati began shuddering and he turned away. 'I can't eat it,' he said. 'It's too repulsive. I can't eat it.'

'Come!' said Tighe. 'It is food.' He took a bite and chewed it enthusiastically.

'I want grass-bread,' said Ati, tearful.

'Where could we possibly find grass-bread here in Meshwood? Don't be silly. Come.' He pulled free a lump of the worm's flesh and passed it towards Ati, but he mimed disgust and buried his face in the crook of his left arm.

Tighe ate on alone.

When he had finished they resumed their climb.

At eighty, or thenabouts, they made it on to a brief grass- and moss-covered crag. This led up and shortly past its end there was a longer ledge, partly overhung and growing with fresh meshwood tree shoots. At the end of this was another one. This was much easier going and the two of them soon reached the far end.

Before them was a long vertical chimney, backed with tiny slabs of manrock and so straight up and down that no meshwood grew there. Five arms' lengths upwards there was a curious metal grille, deeply rusted, and a slab of smoother manrock beside it. The faint impression of a single yellow line, the paint flaked and over-mossed, could just be made out going straight down. Grass clung to the lip of this gash and moss lined the innards. On the far side another almost wholly overhung ledge carried on up.

'It is too far to jump,' said Tighe, 'but we might make a bridge.'

He pulled a branch of meshwood tree from below and broke it off. This reached over the space easily, filling the hole with its leaves.

'It is not strong enough to support us,' Ati pointed out.

'We will need several. Come, help me.'

But Ati, with only one hand, could not pull and sever the branches and Tighe worked on alone. After a short while he had laid four over the gap and tentatively tried the structure for load-bearing ability. 'I think it is all right,' he said, inching forward. 'I'll go over and you can follow – that way I can catch you and help pull you up.'

The soggy branches of meshwood bowed under Tighe's weight, and the far end arched up; but they jammed under the overhang and did not come loose. When he was across the gap he motioned for Ati to follow him. 'It's safe,' he said, 'really it is.'

Ati was whimpering with fear, but he pushed himself out along the precarious structure. 'Think!' Tighe told him, to encourage him. 'If we find it hard to cross this chimney, then the claw-caterpils will surely find it impossible.'

With a big tug Tighe pulled Ati up the last bit and the two of them lay hugging one another on the far ledge. Then Tighe made sure to kick the makeshift bridge away, and they continued their upward trek.

At the top of this angled trench was a dog-leg, and the two of them doubled back on their track, still ascending. Then the ledge ended, with an easy step to a meshwood tree trunk and up to a clear and lengthy ledge. Branches in easy reach spread up and to the west. Their way was easy, straight before them.

'There!' called a voice.

Tighe and Ati looked round together. Three grey-uniformed Otre soldiers were standing, a little more than twenty yards away. One was pointing with an outstretched arm and the other two were raising their rifles.

'Quick!' squealed Ati. 'We can clamber into the trees, and lose them.' He ran quickly to the western edge of the little crag and leapt, reaching out for a broad, horizontal branch to use it as a swinging-bar to the next crag along.

'No!' called Tighe, starting after him. But it was too late. Ati was in the air, reaching out for a branch with a hand he no longer possessed.

His stump scraped along the branch, and his left fingers scrabbled at the bark. Then he was falling, tipping through the air to plummet straight down.

Tighe, ignoring the shouts of the soldiers, clambered down from the crag and hurried along the downward ledge. He found Ati at the bottom, lying on his back, his head bent so far round that it was practically upside down.

Tighe crouched beside him, weeping fully. Because Ati's head was at such a weird, horrific angle, his scowl was transformed into a grin. When the soldiers came up behind him, placing their huge hands on his shoulders, Tighe was still crying.

7

The three Otre soldiers tied Tighe's right hand to his right ankle with a plastic tether just short enough to force him to stoop awkwardly as he walked. They needn't have bothered. Tighe was too stupefied to think of trying to run away.

He loped along between the lead soldier and the second in line as they retraced their steps, moving awkwardly between ledges. At one point they helped him, hauling him unceremoniously up a series of trunk stepping-points one above the other. Then they reached the broad ledge, possibly the same one that Tighe had been on the previous day when Mulvaine, Ravielre, Pelis and Ati had still been alive. The thought made Tighe cringe into tears and cry with his mouth open. The tears smarted and stung in his eyes. The soldiers ignored him until they became annoyed by the incessant noise and shut him up with a series of sharp knocks from their rifle butts.

They marched east along this ledge at a leisurely pace. All this time the three soldiers chatted amongst themselves in their odd, guttural language. They seemed completely at ease and laughed often.

Within the hour they emerged from the Meshwood at its eastern border. The guard eyrie which had been built by Imperial troops was now occupied by grey-uniformed Otre soldiers and the shelves beyond were busy with Otre military activity.

Tighe walked with the soldiers, making his way awkwardly up the ledge and on to the shelf, loping and snivelling. 'Here,' said one of his captors in atrociously accented Imperial, 'you go here.' They were standing at the doorway to one of the dugouts.

Tighe lurched through and fell forward. The Otre had erected a wooden door and it was dragged across the opening when Tighe was inside. Light gleamed in four thin lines through the gaps between the planks of wood.

There were perhaps a dozen people in the shadow-coloured space; all tethered, either with a wrist tied to an ankle like Tighe or else with their hands strapped together behind their backs. They all looked up as Tighe stood there, but nobody said anything.

He limped over to a wall and sat down. It was all equally irrelevant. What did any of it matter?

One of the others hobbled over towards him. 'What were you?' he asked in fluent Imperial. 'Sapper? Potboy?'

'I don't know,' said Tighe. 'I don't know.'

'Forgotten, eh?'

'And the only thing', said Tighe, looking at the floor, 'is why they all had to die. All of them and not me?' He looked up and caught the other's eye. 'Does that make sense to you?'

'Me?' said the other, a startled-looking, pale-faced man. 'I was a regular soldier. Not one of your riflemen me.'

'And as for Ati,' said Tighe, reaching out with his free hand, 'he endured so much. Had he not earned his life?'

The pale-faced man looked suspiciously at Tighe's outstretched hand. 'As I say,' he said, backing away a little, 'I'll admit to surprise that they captured me rather than just throwing me straight from the wall. It's slaves they'll sell us for. That's our future: we're to be commodities, do you see. And grown men like me don't reach a good price as slaves, as commodities. But here I am, anyway.'

'He fell twice,' explained Tighe. 'The first time he fell further and was all right; the second time he fell not so far and it was his death. Is that fair, do you think?'

'Nice young one like you,' said the man uncertainly, retreating against the far wall, 'you'll get a better price. Strange-coloured skin like yours, that's rarity value. But I suppose I should be grateful that they kept me alive at all.'

He fell silent, and for a while there was no sound in the enclosed space except Tighe weeping discreetly. He lay on the floor curled tight up on himself and wept. The light faded from between the slats of the door and the dusk gale began. After it died down Tighe slept; but vivid dreams of Ati, up and walking around although with his head at an impossible angle, disturbed his sleep.

In the morning the Otre opened the door and pushed through some stalkgrass and a crude clay bowl of water. Tighe lay motionless, watching as the other prisoners bickered around this insignificant treat.

Another day passed. A second batch of stalkgrass was pushed through the door in the afternoon. Once again the other inhabitants of the cell bickered amongst themselves over the meagre provision. Tighe lay motionless and watched them. His belly was hurting with the hunger, but he welcomed that sensation. It was right that he should be hurting. It was appropriate. He valued this physical manifestation of his pain.

After all the food had been eaten, the prisoners settled themselves back into their usual positions. One of them, a dolorous-looking woman, stared at Tighe.

'All sorts in this army,' she said eventually. 'I've seen all sorts. But I never saw somebody as dark as you.'

Tighe didn't reply. He stared at her.

'You're a freak, with that skin,' she said, passionlessly. 'That'll fetch a good price I guess.'

That night Tighe slept deeply. He woke with a start in the darkness, with somebody hunched over him. Hands were rummaging through his clothing. With a yell he kicked out and pushed up with his hand. The individual fell away, whimpering. It was the same pale-faced man who had spoken to him when he had first been brought in.

'What are you doing?' Tighe cried.

'Just checking to see if you had anything valuable about you,' said the man, with a catch in his voice. 'I'm sorry, I really am.'

Tighe sat himself up and tried to watch for movement, but it was too absolutely black to see anything. Eventually he nodded off, and woke after dawn with a pain in the bones of his neck.

This time when the jailers pushed food through the door Tighe struggled with everybody else and grabbed himself some food. He chewed his two fistfuls of grass and licked the dampness off the walls.

'What's your name?' asked the pale-faced man, hunching down next to Tighe. It was as if his attempted robbery the night before had established some bond between them.

Tighe looked at him. 'My friends died,' he said, eventually.

'Sure,' said the man. 'I know. I know. We all lost friends. I lost friends.' There was a pause. 'It's hard,' he added.

'Hard,' nodded Tighe. 'Close friends.' He didn't seem to feel any tears coming. He thought of the inside of his head, which ought to be stuffed with grief. It felt empty, as if the claw-caterpil had excavated it as efficiently as it had feeding on Ravielre.

'I'm called Trose,' said the pale-faced man, nodding at Tighe.

'I feel nothing,' said Tighe, as if testing the phrase out to see how it sounded in his mouth.

'Really?' said Trose. 'I was a regular soldier. I did speak to my commander, you know, about training for rifle duty. But that's a hard billet to get into. Mostly, it was pike-work with me.'

Tighe looked at Trose, at the energy and positivity of his manner. His life was finished, and he didn't seem to mind. He had fallen off the world, but it didn't bother him. There was a sublime power about so banal a philosophy. What happens when the world ends? Well, perhaps you just carry on.

'How long you been here?' Tighe asked.

'Oh, some days, some days,' said Trose, scratching his face. 'My beard's starting through. The Popes tell us – shave. That's God's will. I look on it like this: the worldwall, see, is the face of God. That's where we live. Where things grow out of it, like that Meshwood, that's where evil lives. So we need to shave, really, to keep our faces clean. Pure. That's how I look on it.'

The mention of the Meshwood brought no reaction in Tighe. It already seemed an age away.

'Which part of worldwall you come?' Tighe asked. He felt weary, unable to work out a more correct form of words.

Trose laughed briefly, amiably. '*If* you don't mind me saying,' he said, 'your Imperial's pretty ropy. You're no native, are you?'

'No,' said Tighe.

'I can always tell,' said Trose, leaning back expansively. 'I tend to think –'

But at that moment there came the rasp of the door being drawn back and an Otre soldier came stooping into the space. He stood up to his full height.

'You!' he said, pointing at Tighe, 'come with me.'

Tighe was led out of the space and hobbled his way along behind the Otre officer. He was led along the shelf, up the stairs and through the brief tunnel that opened a vista out on to the former battlefield. There were no fires, but much of the wall was scorched. Tighe caught a glimpse of hundreds of Otre uniforms before his guard pushed him, urging him down and along.

Ten minutes later Tighe and the Otre officer were making their way up a newly constructed stairway and on to the upper ledges. As he hobbled along, Tighe could see the forts that had been the fruitless object of Imperial military ambition.

Soon enough, Tighe passed under a gateway, wooden but pinned with sheets of plastic. The wood of the building was holed and dotted with bullet marks, and Tighe caught a glimpse of a long blackened patch, like an enormous mural of black hair, where the fort had burned briefly. Then he was inside.

*

The corridors and stairways inside the fort were many and all were crowded with the comings and goings of grey-suited Otre military staff. Tighe's escort grabbed him by his free arm and hauled him through the complex; along, down, up a steep flight, round a dog-leg and then further along. Abruptly he turned off and passed through a low doorway into a room set in the wall.

Inside was a perfectly square room. An Otre officer sat cross-legged on a board that was suspended from the ceiling by chains. He peered down at Tighe from this elevated posture.

Tighe peered up, but his guard kicked his legs away and he sprawled on the dust of the floor.

The man on the board above began speaking without preliminary.

'You're an unusually coloured one,' he said. Tighe could tell that his Imperial was fluent and unaccented; but he spoke with a lazy drawling tone.

There was a pause. Tighe wasn't sure how to respond.

The guard who had brought him kicked him sharply in the small of his back.

'Yes, Master!' Tighe barked at once.

'You're not from Imperial City?'

'No, Master!'

'Don't draw this out, I request you. It makes it tedious for me and will be awkward for you. *You're not from Imperial City* is one way of asking you *where you are from*?'

Tighe started gabbling. 'From a small village upwall, Master, I was a Prince there you know, but my parents were murdered and then I was chased off the wall – I fell, you know, Master, but I survived and so . . .'

The guard kicked him again. There was a squelchy burst of pain at the base of Tighe's spine. He shut up.

'What did you do in the Imperial army?' asked the man from above.

'Kite-pilot, Master.'

'How interesting,' drawled the man, although he didn't sound very interested. 'Did you fly many sorties?'

'Many what, Master?'

'Did you fly often?'

'Yes, Master. No, Master. I'm not sure, Master.'

'I watched a number of aerial attacks,' the man said, as if talking to himself. 'There were some pretty gymnastics out there in the sky, but their military use was slim. Boy! Do you know why you're here?'

Tighe's terror was starting to paralyse him. 'No, Master! I was captured, Master.'

'Of course you were captured. You're not very *bright*, are you? Either

264

that, or you are indeed senior staff pretending to be idiotic. Could you be that, I wonder?'

. Tighe didn't really know what the Otre man was talking about. 'No, Master!' he called out. 'Yes, Master!'

'I might think so,' slurred the man above, 'if you weren't so young. I certainly have the sense that you are overdoing your imbecility.'

'I'm sorry, Master,' said Tighe. He was crying now, snivelling. Dust from the floor had gone up his nose and tickled his sinus uncomfortably. His spine burned with pain where he had been kicked. He felt miserable.

'Are you *crying*?'

'Yes, Master.'

'What manner of warrior are you?'

'I'm scared, Master,' said Tighe. 'I have heard stories.'

'Stories?' For the first time in the interrogation, the man above sounded vaguely interested.

'I have heard that the Otre – do bad things to their prisoners.'

There was a heartbeat's silence and then a babble of laughter. The man above sounded genuinely amused by this. Tentatively, his heart still pumping with fear, Tighe tried lifting his head a little to look upwards. The guard's foot made contact – gently enough – with Tighe's forehead and pressed his head back down against the dirt.

The man above had finished laughing. 'My dear boy,' he said, 'we heard those same stories about the Imperial army. "Don't be captured by them!" we were told. "They do such terrible things to their prisoners," ' He laughed again, more briefly. 'That is the way in war, I suppose. We try to discourage our troops from wanting to surrender. Fight to the death, that's a better strategic philosophy.'

There was a pause. Tighe could make out the creaking of the chains that supported the board on which the man sat.

'Anyway, I haven't all day. You've been brought to me because somebody somewhere along the chain of command wondered if you might be significant to the Imperial army. Do you know why?'

'No,' said Tighe miserably. At this moment he felt utterly insignificant.

'Well, to be honest, neither do I. I assume it's because your skin is so darkly coloured, but that doesn't signify to me. Somebody must have thought that your dark skin marked you out as perhaps special in the army. I don't think so. You come from some village on the outskirts of the Empire. You're a kite-boy. You're nothing. It is time to conclude our little talk; goodbye. I hope you fetch a good price.'

Tighe's arm was grabbed and he was hauled upright. 'Price?' he repeated, dazed.

'Well, yes,' said the man above, meditatively. 'The market is depressed at the moment. A lot of goods come to market all at once in war, so we can't earn as much as we would like. But that's the nature of things.'

8

Tighe, bewildered and disoriented, was led back through a warren of wooden corridors. The insane proliferation of wooden structures and devices, the extraordinary wealth seemingly squandered, was even starting to lose its power to shock him. Everything in the world seemed to have fallen away.

He was half marched, half dragged along more corridors and locked in a room. There was another individual in that space, but he – or she, Tighe couldn't be certain – was puffed and bruised with beatings and lay motionless and quiet. The light from between the slats of the door died and it was dark. Tighe nursed his stomach. The fear and agitation had wound up his hunger to a stabbing, acute level.

Just when he thought that he would not see food until the next day, if then, the door opened and a parcel wrapped in leaves was tossed through.

It was grass-bread; it even had insect bodies worked into the dough. Tighe bolted several large mouthfuls and then stopped as his stomach spasmed with the unexpected bulk. He nibbled more cautiously. The other person lay on his, or her, side without making a sound.

'It's food,' Tighe said, eventually. 'You want some? Like some?'

The other person didn't respond.

This presented Tighe with something of an ethical dilemma. He could hear the hissy breathing of the person, so he knew they were still alive. But Tighe was so hungry he could have easily eaten the piece of grass-bread three times over. An inner voice told him that he had offered the food and if this person had wanted any they could have said so and Tighe would have shared the ration. But since they said nothing, it was perfectly right for him to eat it all himself. But, still, there was the hissy breathing. Tighe tried again.

'Are you all right? Did they beat you? Are you hungry, I think.'

Nothing.

'I can give you the food to eat later perhaps? To keep and eat later?'

Nothing.

'Is it that your voice is hurt?' That idiom didn't sound right to Tighe, but

267

he couldn't think of another way of expressing it. 'Is it that you cannot speak? Make a noise, any noise, if you are hungry.'

Nothing.

Tighe gave up and devoured the rest of the grass-bread, and then lay on the floor until the pains in his stomach passed away. Then he fell asleep.

He didn't know how late it was when he finally awoke, but there were lines of light coming through the boards of the door and the wooden walls around. The other person was in exactly the same position they had been in the day before; curled on their side, their blackened, puffed eyes peering at Tighe through slits.

'Good morning,' said Tighe, carefully, sitting and rubbing his stiff limbs. 'Are you good?'

After a little while this individual's silence became part of the rhythm of the conversation between them. Tighe would say anything and then pause, leaving space for a reply that never came. He started telling his own story, from the time with the platon at the battle through their adventures in the Meshwood. He found he could relate the story of everybody's death except Ati. When he came to that part, his throat contracted, a warning of grief to come. So he cut the story short and stared in silence for a while at the wall. So much wood.

After several hours the door was hauled open. Tighe expected food, but instead a single Otre soldier came through. He said nothing, but he leaned down to grasp the ankle of the other person in the room. Tighe watched in silence as his cell mate was dragged out through the door along the floor. The rhythm of their breathing changed, but otherwise they seemed trapped in the same stasis they had been in the whole time.

The door shut and Tighe was left alone.

There was more bread that evening and then Tighe spent another night by himself. In the morning the door opened and Tighe was called out.

Still tethered wrist to ankle, Tighe made his way out of the room and followed his latest Otre guard along the wooden corridor. They passed down some stairs and into a broad atrium of some kind, with sunlight shining through the planks of the floor. Here he was made to wait with half a dozen listless others, all shackled with tethers in the same fashion as Tighe.

Tighe, tired by his strange exercise, tried to sit down against the wooden wall, but a guard snapped loudly at him in Otre language and he stood up.

There were seven in all and they stood silent, sullen, for many hours. People passed and repassed, came and went. Most were dressed as Otre soldiers, but there were others in leather coats and cheaper fabrics. One tall individual was wearing nothing but a headdress, a great bolt of cloth that curled up from his head and then draped down in four broad strips to cover his body, the strips being fastened to his two ankles. He paused in front of the seven Imperial prisoners, and peered closely at them. He seemed especially interested in Tighe.

'You!' he asked in grotesquely accented Imperial. 'Speak Otre?'

Tighe shook his head.

'Speak Tanaha?'

Tighe shook his head again.

'You only speak Imperial?' screeched this figure, waving his hands in disgust. 'What use that?'

'I also speak my native tongue, the language of my village,' said Tighe levelly, in his own tongue. The stranger shook his head and went on.

Another hour or more and two soldiers arrived, armed with sharpened metal pokers which they waved over their heads to intimidate the prisoners. 'You all march now,' they said. Their Imperial was not very good either.

The shorter of these two tied tethers to tethers, linking each of the seven into a chain of people. Then, one at the front and one at the back, they led the captured Imperials out of the fort and east along the ledge.

It was late in the day by the time they left the fort and Tighe was so hungry and thirsty that he barely registered his surroundings. The sun was high and the sky bright. They trudged along a sequence of connected ledges, very little overhung. By the time of the dulling of the sky they had reached a pen, of the sort used for animals. It was already crammed with people, most sitting on the ground looking down with heavy and miserable heads.

'Here!' barked the guards. 'In.'

There was a gate, complete with a small guardhouse. As each of the prisoners passed this station, one of the guards pressed a block against their necks. Tighe could see that they were being printed with some coloured device.

Inside, they were tied to a post, at which a dozen others were also tethered. There were several of these posts poking up in the compound.

'Here you come,' said one of the prisoners already present, with a weary sigh. 'More of you.'

9

When the dusk gale started up, the guards vanished inside their guard-house, but the many prisoners clustered together about their poles. There was something frantic about this struggling knot of bodies; many of the prisoners were whimpering with fear.

Tighe found himself crushed between a fat man and a skinny, sharp-elbowed woman. He could hear the ferocious dusk winds rise in volume and could feel the air twisting and tugging at his clothes. It was fearful. He was sobbing, quietly, to himself. Others were howling. It was the wrath of God, hoping to pull them off the wall with the power of His breath.

The dusk gale howled, raged and finally died down. When the air stilled, the knot of people loosened and Tighe was able to separate himself out, to lie down.

He slept poorly because the crush of people was such that he was frequently jostled and shoved. When the pre-dawn winds started up, people started shifting uneasily and a general moan of misery rose from the assembled people. Tighe was caught up in the crush again and again was shielded from the brunt of the winds by the others who were around him.

The winds eventually died away and the crowds of people disentangled themselves with something approaching a collective sigh.

Tighe licked the moisture left by the morning wind off his free arm.

After an hour or so guards went amongst the people and distributed food: small portions of grass-bread with insects and larger ones of plain stalkgrass. Tighe ate in silence.

Later still the guards returned with the first of a series of strangers. This was a tall, bulky man dressed in fluffy patches of cloth that adhered to sections of his body by some inner traction: around his loins, his chest, his knees and elbows. They looked as insubstantial as clouds, but the pink material rustled heavily as he moved amongst the crowds.

'Who's that?' Tighe asked, of the person sitting next to him.

'A manmonger,' his companion replied.

'What's that?'

'Don't be stupid,' said the other, wearily. 'You don't know what a manmonger is?'

'No.'

'Watch and you'll see,' was the reply. The other person lay down and curled up in a ball, rubbing at the chafed skin around wrist and ankle where the tether had left a mark. After a while he spoke again. 'A manmonger buys and sells people. Didn't you know that?'

'No,' said Tighe, catching his breath. 'I'm sorry.'

'Your accent is strange,' said the other, but he said nothing more and soon seemed to be asleep.

Tighe watched the manmonger go amongst the crowds of people, picking out a dozen or so. Then he retreated inside the guardhouse with one of the Otre soldiers. When they both emerged they were grinning and the manmonger untethered eight individuals, retying them after his own fashion and leading them away.

After this, people came amongst the individuals regularly. One, a man with unusually long legs and unusually short arms, a slightly freakish combination, paused for a while beside Tighe.

'I like your skin,' he said, paddling his stumpy fingers over Tighe's forearm. Tighe, uncertain what to do, sat motionless. 'You'd make an interesting commodity.'

The guard, standing beside this manmonger, looked bored. He said something in Otre to the figure, who wrinkled his face in displeasure and looked back. There was a brief exchange and the manmonger stood up.

'Do you speak Otre?' he asked.

Tighe shook his head.

'It's so stupid. None of these commodities speak Otre. That'll lower the price.' The manmonger turned and bickered with the guard for a while, and then moved on.

Later that day another manmonger came by. The guard made a great show of pointing out Tighe from the mass of individuals and ran his hand over his own face several times. Tighe guessed he was referring to his skin colour.

The Manmonger squatted down to examine Tighe more closely. He was a slender man of indeterminate age; there was a starburst of fine lines from the corner of each eye and his neck looked older than the rest of him. His skin was pale brown and looked sunburnt and extremely dry. When he spoke, his voice sounded dry too, as if all moisture had been dried out of him by the sun.

'How old?' he said softly.

'Eight,' said Tighe.

The Manmonger shook his head. 'Older,' he said. He felt the meat of Tighe's forearms for thickness, and peered into his eyes. Then he stood up and started into a lengthy discussion with the guard.

Tighe watched, feeling disengaged from events. There seemed to be some disagreement. The guard kept gesturing behind him at the guardhouse, perhaps suggesting that they should go inside to negotiate terms. But the Manmonger merely shook his head, letting his lank hair flop, and folded his arms. He unfolded them several times to point to one or other commodity in the pen, but each time he refolded. After ten or fifteen minutes of this incomprehensible chatter, the Manmonger put out a hand and touched the guard's elbow, stopping him in full flow. He turned his head to look at Tighe.

'You speak Otre?' he asked, in his dry-leaves voice.

'No,' said Tighe faintly.

This precipitated another lengthy discussion between the two men. The Manmonger would shake his head gently from side to side and the guard became more and more agitated.

Suddenly, abruptly, the talking stopped. The Manmonger was down at Tighe's side, unlatching the complex knot of the tether at his ankle. With pressure under his arm, he pulled Tighe upright and then pulled his free arm behind him. It felt good to have the pressure relieved from his sore ankle, but the Manmonger almost straight away tied Tighe's left wrist to his right one behind his back. He tied the tether tightly and then ran the spare length of tether up to Tighe's neck, fixing the rope around and under his chin. It meant that he couldn't pull down with his hands too far without choking himself.

The Manmonger was carrying a leather satchel and reached inside to pull out a number of small objects, handing these over to the guard. Then he led Tighe away, towards the gateway and the guard house.

He tied Tighe to the gateway post next to a red-haired girl and a scrawny-looking boy with a tiny, circular nose. Both were tied the same way as Tighe, hands behind their back and the tether running up and around their necks. The red-haired girl was staring into space. Tighe offered a tentative hello, but she ignored it. The young boy was sniffing loudly; there were boils on his skin and his pebble nose was dribbling snot. Tighe said hello to him; but he seemed so caught up in the misery of his illness that he didn't reply.

Soon enough the Manmonger returned to them with another commodity: a dark-haired girl with a wide dark mouth and narrow features, tethered the same way. The pebble-nosed boy with the sores was sneezing intermittently. The Manmonger stood back from his purchases and examined them with a passionless eye.

The boy stopped sneezing. There was a moment of quiet.

'You belong to me now,' he said in queerly accented Imperial. 'I take you east, trade you for goats maybe. You give me trouble, I give you pain. Maybe death. You understand?'

Nobody said anything by way of reply. This seemed to suit the Manmonger, who pulled Tighe forward and started marching eastward along the ledge.

They walked for the rest of the day and at the dusk gale they pushed altogether into a crevice in the wall. After the wind died down, the Manmonger took some food from his sack and ate it. He offered nothing to the four commodities.

The following day he marched them quickly along eastward-leading ledges and crags. To begin with the ways were busy with other people: grey-suited Otre soldiers, other manmongers leading short or long trains of commodities, ordinary people passing to and fro. By ninety or so, however, they had passed on to grassier, less-travelled ledges. The day went on and the Manmonger and his four commodities were soon alone.

That night they slept on an open ledge, albeit one quite heavily overhung. The Manmonger drove four short stakes of wood into the turf and tied the commodities to them. When the dusk gale came, Tighe hung on to this post desperately. But the winds did not seem as severe as he remembered from his childhood.

Soon there was the starlit dark and a perfect quiet, broken only by the sniffing of the sick boy. Tighe, achingly hungry, was so tired after his day's marching that he fell quickly asleep.

10

The following morning, the Manmonger untied the four of them from the posts, pulling the stumps of wood from the ledge and stowing them in his sack. Without a word he started them marching again.

Nobody said anything. The only sound was the incessant noise of the pebble-nosed boy sniffing and coughing. He had to stop when a particularly severe coughing fit took him and this slowed the progress of the four of them.

Nobody said a word. With each delay the Manmonger would come and stare at the sick boy.

Tighe was still limping. The Manmonger stopped at midday and drove one of his stumps into the ledge. Then he looped all the leather leads from the commodities' necks round one another and tied them all to the single stump. When he had finished, he sighed and sat down on the lip of the ledge, chewing stalkgrass and staring out at the sun. Its white circle was hazy, blurred by a shifting bulk of cloud. Further out from the wall the wind was falling so hard that the circle of the sun appeared to deform in the twisting airwaves, to shudder and give little spurts of dancing.

The four commodities sat together. Tighe rubbed his hands against one another. Tethered behind his back, his wrists burned. His calves ached with the constant tramping up and down along the ledges and crags. His mouth was uncomfortable, his lips dotted with chips of dryness. If the Manmonger would unbind his hands, he could chew some of the stalkgrass and moisten himself a little. Maybe that and some food. If the Manmonger had any food for them. It was hard watching him eat his own food, the neat strips of dried goat and small portions of grass-bread in his knapsack. But he would presumably feed them soon. He had to look after them, surely, his commodities – they'd hardly be worth anything at his destination thin and ill with hunger. Tighe looked at the others, but they all had their eyes cast down on the ground. The dark-haired girl was rocking backwards and forwards a little. The pebble-nosed boy was sniffing loudly. The sores around his nose were bulging and more were appearing around his mouth. His smell was urgently bad.

'I'm thirsty,' Tighe said, suddenly, not even looking at the Manmonger.

The silence seemed to intensify. Tighe felt his heart speed. *I've done nothing wrong,* he told himself. Surely the Manmonger didn't want his commodities to degrade? Surely he didn't want them to degrade by the time they reached the point of sale?

Look at the man. Meet his gaze.

Fighting himself, Tighe turned his head. The Manmonger was looking directly at him. His blank eyes were motionless, focused on Tighe.

'And the Sun?' he said, in a rasping voice.

Tighe didn't know what to say. His stomach was clenching horribly. There was some powerful emotion roiling inside him, though he kept his face straight. With the shock of recognition he realised he was terrified. He had been too scared to realise he was scared. The last week, or however long it had been since the Meshwood, had been a damped-down, numb time. He had forgotten he had the ability to feel. But he was feeling now; feeling scared. He continued looking directly at the Manmonger.

'You think She cares? She is strong. She is strength.' He turned back and pulled out another handful of stalkgrass. Tighe couldn't take his eyes from the Manmonger's back. His own heart was jerking enormously in his chest. He was breathing hard. 'The winds drink up our water,' the Manmonger was saying, his voice more difficult to follow now he was facing away from them. 'They are male, the winds, and so they are weak, and they get thirsty and they lick up the water that lies on the crevice. And they get hungry so they pull people from the ledges. But She is greater than that. She will drink up the whole world as fire soon enough.'

There was a silence. Tighe rubbed his hands against one another again behind his back, trying to calm himself. Breathe deeply. Breathe. Again, breathe. The Manmonger said something else, but a sudden buffet of wind took the words. When the noise faded, he was chanting, apparently reciting something. 'The Sun was the first of all things. She floated from ledge to ledge. But the rudeness of the winds, tugging at her clothing, pulling her skin free from her perfect body, drove her away.'

He stopped and there was only the sniffing of the sick pebble-nosed boy.

The Manmonger got to his feet so slowly that his knees clicked. The noise reminded Tighe of Grandhe Jaffiahe; his old joints had pocked and cracked with every motion. The Manmonger was standing over him. 'Still, at least you asked. Some courage there.' He sighed, looking down at his commodities.

'I was only thinking,' said Tighe, his voice popping a little with the fear of speaking, 'that we'd make more valuable commodities if cared for a little.'

Silence.

'Valuable,' said the Manmonger after a while, as if testing the concept out.

'I'm hungry,' said one of the girls, the one with the red hair, in a tiny voice. Her Imperial was heavily accented.

Tighe cleared his throat, ready to say something else, emboldened a little; but, behind him, the sick boy sneezed enormously, and something wet struck the back of Tighe's neck. He shuddered and cried out in disgust. The red-haired girl was chuckling and the sick boy's sniffs increased in depth and frequency.

The Manmonger came over to the group of commodities in little steps, a strange expression on his face. A strand of stalk-grass projected from his mouth. With a little dextrous fiddling he unloosed the sick boy's tether and dragged him out from the group. The boy came willingly, a miserable but musical note in the back of his throat. The Manmonger pushed him down and then squatted in front of him. 'So what's the matter with you, then?' he asked, his dry voice like an old man's.

The sick boy sniffed, and wriggled his hands behind his back. He tried to wipe his dribbling nose against his own shoulder.

The Manmonger pulled up another blade of stalkgrass and used it to prod a little at the sores on the boy's face. There was something almost tender in the way he did this. Then he caught his own leather sleeve up with his thumb and front finger, and used the resulting stretch of leather to wipe the boy's nose for him.

'He'll get better,' said Tighe, on a sudden rushing impulse. 'By the time we get to where you're going, he'll be in a good condition to sell. Maybe only a little drink and perhaps some food.'

The Manmonger seemed to be ignoring him, staring hard into the sick boy's face. 'Food,' he repeated, softly. Tighe did think he ought to say something like 'Yes', to agree with him to keep his mood good, or at least keep the conversation going. But something in the Manmonger's manner put him off.

All four of the commodities were staring at the Manmonger.

Tighe was suddenly very certain that the Manmonger was going to hit the sick boy; to beat him for being sick. There was an ever-present hint of violence to come in the softness of the man's voice. That was it, Tighe realised. The promise of violence, like the winds being held back just before dusk, ready to come roaring out and pull things from the ledge. Tighe realised he was holding his breath, waiting for it to happen. A voice inside his head was scolding him for having spoken out at all.

Then, with a release of the tension inside him, Tighe saw that the Manmonger was untying the thong from around the boy's neck. With careful fingers he picked open the knot and then opened the noose and slipped it up over the kid's head. A puckered line of red marked the boy's white skin where the thong had been.

The sick boy was staring up at the Manmonger's face as he did this. His eyes were wide with hope.

The Manmonger slapped the boy's legs, pushing them together, and retied the tether around his two ankles. It occurred to Tighe to wonder how the sick boy was supposed to walk, with his feet tied together. Wouldn't it be better to tie only one ankle?

Without getting up, the Manmonger reached over and retrieved his pack from the lip of the ledge. He unhooked it and picked out another stump, which he forced into the turf in front of him. Then he tied the sick boy's tether to this new stump. He reached again for the pack and this time brought out a knife. For a moment Tighe didn't register what this artefact was. Thought it was a flask, perhaps something medicinal. There was the edge of misunderstanding about the whole sequence of events. The Manmonger was settling back on to the floor in front of the boy. Tighe didn't have time to be shocked, couldn't quite process what was happening. The Manmonger sank his fingers into the mass of the sick boy's hair and angled the head back. With a swift flick he pushed the end of the knife through the stretched neck, a little above the adam's apple. Almost as part of the same movement, the Manmonger shifted his sitting weight back and kicked out with both his feet. Scattering blood in a glittering arc, the sick boy's body lurched to the side and over the edge. The tether whickered and tautened suddenly, heaving at the stump.

Gone, over the edge of the wall.

It still didn't quite register. Tighe couldn't quite grasp it. Some extreme remedy, folk medicine, somehow. Something. But the shine of midday sun through the red rag of falling blood refused to fit.

The dark-haired girl was sobbing, swift, stifled bursts of air. The red-haired girl was staring at the floor. Tighe wasn't sure she had even seen. But no, of course she had seen. They had all been watching the sequence of events with minute attention.

Tighe realised his own eyes were wet. Why? His breath seemed to be coming in slow draws.

The Manmonger went back over to his seat on the lip of the ledge. His knife, blood still on it, sat on the grass. The sick boy's blood made a mark like a dark slug trail to the edge. Presently the Manmonger got to his feet and began gathering some snatches of stalkgrass. He went further along the ledge and climbed up a little to pull down a withered old ledge-bush. Three pairs of eyes followed his every movement. He came back with the kindling and the woody tendrils of the bush and lit a small fire, chiming sparks from a flint until the old grass caught, feeding the little fire and eventually making a smouldering heap of stalks. Then, still watched by everybody, he hauled the sick boy's body back up to the ledge and laid it down on the grass.

The clothes were mostly vegetable cloth, rotten, and were ripped away easily. The Manmonger examined them, checking if anything was salvageable, but it was junk, so it went on the fire. Then he crouched over the nude corpse, peering minutely at the skin – checking it, Tighe realised with a lurch, for sores. But, apart from the face, the skin seemed clear.

The sun was high in the sky now and the ledge was filling with shadow. Tighe was shivering, but not, he thought, from the cold. He watched, blinking rarely, as the Manmonger butchered the boy as deftly as he might a goat. He turned the body over, where strands of grass were sticking to its white back and narrow buttocks. Then he cut briskly through the spine at the back of the neck and sawed round to the front. With a heaving cut the head was free. The Manmonger picked it up and looked more closely at it, peering at the sores. They had lost of lot of their raging colour when the body had been drained of blood, but they were still obvious and disfiguring. The Manmonger seemed to be considering if there were anything that could be redeemed from the head, but it didn't take long for him to make up his mind and he tossed the ball carelessly over the edge.

Tighe wasn't looking at the Manmonger now; he was mesmerised by the headless body lying on the ledge. The bony body of the boy, with shoulder blades poking up like rocks and the bumpy line of the spine drawing the eye up towards the neck; only there was no head, nothing to complete the picture. There was something monstrous here. The Manmonger was retrieving something from his pack. A smaller sack, also made of leather, that unpeeled and opened up into a flat piece of skin. Inside was a pile of grey powder that Tighe only belatedly realised was precious salt; bought from the pans of the canyon ledges away to the west.

Then the Manmonger was back at the body, cutting away first the right arm and skinning it expertly; then the left, then the legs, the buttocks, the small of the back and the top of the torso. He turned the dismembered body that remained over and carved some more from the belly. Finally he cut free some of the ribs and poked his knife end amongst the viscera. Blood was leeching out all over the grass. He had worked quickly. Had it been a goat, Tighe would have spent several hours salvaging good meat from the carcass before giving the rest as fodder for village pigs. But the Manmonger seemed easily satisfied, and he kicked the remainder over the edge in a desultory fashion.

He cut prime pieces from the arms and legs and wrapped the fillets in the salt bag, stowing it back in his pack. Then he fed the fire with some of the bush twigs, so that it chuckled and threw up flames. He picked up the bones and dumped them on the fire to cook up the marrow. Then he took some of the lesser cuts and packed them in mud to stop them singeing. By the time he put them on the fire they were shapeless lumps of brown.

The smell of cooking meat made Tighe's hungry stomach inside him twist. He felt sick.

Soon enough the Manmonger was pulling out bones with a stick and cracking them open with his knife. He scooped out the bubbling marrow and ate it still hot, slapping his lips together noisily and panting with satisfaction. Then he chewed a mouthful of grass, presumably for the moisture. He pulled the mud balls out of the fire with a stick and cracked them open with his knife. The meat inside smoked, and the smell was so like freshly cooked goat – that sweet luxury – that Tighe's mouth watered. More than watered: saliva dribbled down his chin. He hated himself for that.

The Manmonger seemed to be in a better mood now. That made some sort of sense. He had been eating nothing more than a few strips of salted goat's meat and some pieces of grass-bread. He was a thin man, stretched, used to meagre rations. Here was a sudden, luscious feast of tasty meat and fat. He sat cross-legged and devoured one portion of meat from the mud, absorbed wholly in the meal. By the end he was grinning. Then he picked out a piece of meat on the end of his knife, and got to his feet. It was the red-haired girl he went to, holding the little piece of cooked flesh in front of him.

He sat down in front of her, only holding the morsel in front of her mouth. She stared at him, not with horror or fascination but with a kind of dumb blankness; but she did not open her lips. After a while he laughed, a deep growly sound. 'Not hungry yet, not there yet,' speaking almost to himself and he popped the meat into his own mouth. 'Give it a couple of days, give it a week, you'll be different. You'll watch me feasting like an Emperor every night and you'll start to thinking why should I go without?' He got up again and returned to the fire.

For a long time he simply sat, finishing off his meal. Then, as the shadow crept down the wall, he lay down with his knife still in his hand and fell asleep.

His three remaining commodities stared at him. Nobody moved; nobody tried to free themselves from their tethers, although it would have been easy enough to do. It was (the thought rose in Tighe's head) as if he had fastened them with a more than material tether.

The Manmonger twitched in his dreams.

After a period, some hours, he woke suddenly and lurched upwards with his eyes wide. It took a moment for him to orient himself. The fire had burnt itself out. He held his knife out in front of him. Then he rubbed his face with his clear hand and breathed noisily in and out through his nose.

He prodded the fire with his foot to check that there was no more heat in it, and then he went and sat on the lip of the ledge one more time. His head was back now, as if (Tighe thought) in sleep; but, no, he was only looking up after the swift rising sun. There was a pink tint to the white-blue of the sky that Tighe could see, which must mean that it was nearly time for the sun to go over the wall.

Then, without saying anything, the Manmonger got to his feet and paced over to his commodities. He still had his knife in his right hand, but he put it into a pocket of his leather jacket as he unfastened the tether of (Tighe's heart pummelled, he couldn't immediately see which one) the red-haired girl (despite himself, Tighe felt a rush of relief). She was rigid as a wooden woman, but he yanked her and pulled her away from the group.

The sick boy's free tether was lying on the ground and the Manmonger hooked it around her ankle (only one ankle, Tighe noticed), and tied her to the other stump. Then he retrieved his knife and simply pushed her to the ground, himself on top of her. With his knife he reached down to cut through the cheap cloth of her trousers before pressing the blade against her neck. Tighe couldn't see clearly what was going on. He could see that the red-haired girl was lying completely motionless, her left leg trembling slightly. Her pink flesh was visible now through the rips in her trousers and Tighe could see the tremor that passed up and down it. But otherwise she held herself completely still as the Manmonger loosened his own trousers with his free hand. Then his form was juddering over hers, a weird pulsing motion as if he were seized by convulsions. It didn't last long and then he seemed to be asleep again, lying directly on top of her, his knife still at her neck.

Tighe watched; the motionlessness of the scene seemed more terrible than the action. His own wick betrayed him. He shuddered. He tried to fix his eyes on the colour of the sky, trying to trace with his eyes the subtle gradations of colour. He rubbed his hands against one another behind his back, as much as he was able. But his eye was caught by movement; the Manmonger's body was in jerky motion again, heaving and bouncing. On, on, stop. Then he was adjusting himself and climbing off her.

Later, during the dusk gale, the three commodities were forced to huddle together with the Manmonger, pressing in against the back of the wall to avoid being blown off. Tighe was so revolted by the stench of the Manmonger's skin that he hardly noticed how feeble the dusk gale was. But as it drained to nothing he did feel surprised; it seemed to him that the gale had somehow got stuck in a preliminary phase, as if it had not developed its proper ferocity.

The Manmonger removed himself from his charges, checked their tethers in the darkness, and curled himself up in his blanket.

It was not that night, but rather the following day, that Tighe realised – with a sickening sense of belatedness that made the realisation more painful to him – that the Manmonger had never intended to sell them as commodities at a near-by village. He could sell the three of them and maybe have enough for one goat; but why would he want to eat one goat when he could feast on all of them and eat three times as much? Tighe realised that, from his own point of view, this was a special time for him, a time to indulge himself, a sort of holiday.

In the morning the Manmonger took out one of his pieces of human flesh and ate it, wiping a rag over the dewy grass and chomping on it to relieve his morning thirst. There were no rags for the others. Taking his cue from the other two commodities, Tighe fell to the floor and licked the wet grass. For a while his thirst was satisfied, but that only made his hunger more acute.

The Manmonger sat grinning at them. 'Hungry?' he asked them in Imperial. 'Hungry?'

The three of them sat and stared at him. Tighe had a sudden flash of Ati, of Ati's head twisted round through a terrible angle. It forced a spurt of anger up through his chest and he coughed. 'You'll devour us all,' he said. 'You are evil man.' Twist *his* neck, the way Ati's neck had been twisted!

'I am reputable Manmonger,' the grinning man said. 'Evil? I have a full belly. That is the difference. There is no *good* and *evil*, there are only full bellies and empty ones. We have a long march today.'

'Where are we going?' asked Tighe, emboldened. It hardly seemed to matter any more; if he was going to die then he would die, and cowering and being frightened would not avert the destiny.

The Manmonger pulled back his lips to show off all his teeth all the way to the roots. 'You are bold,' he said, 'bold. Perhaps I eat you next and that way I digest your boldness into me.' He laughed.

'Where are we going?' persevered Tighe.

'East,' said the Manmonger.

'To your home?'

'My home is with the Goddess the Sun,' said the Manmonger, as he busied himself packing up his belongings and tying up his clothes.

'You are not Otre, I think,' said Tighe.

'And you are not Imperial,' returned the Manmonger, 'though you speak the language. We come from all different portions and levels of the wall, but we all return to the One.' He turned to the sky and made a complicated

281

obeisance to the sun. 'Now,' he said, returning to his commodities and untying their hands, 'there, you are free. It is time to march I think.'

The going was much easier with free hands. That day they marched in line along a series of mostly untrodden ledges, few of them overhung at all. Some were so virgin that their slope had not even been levelled, and they angled sharply away at forty or fifty degrees, which made them dangerous to traverse. The Manmonger himself crossed these spaces easily enough, but the two girls, miserable, hungry and scared, whimpered and clung together.

'Don't do that!' chided the Manmonger. 'If one of you falls then you take the other with you! You Imperial types are so stupid. Why should I lose both of you at once?'

'Leave them be!' snapped Tighe. 'They are scared. You have scared them. Can you not see they are scared?'

The Manmonger, smiling broadly, stepped up to Tighe. 'The day when I find your spirit entertaining,' he said, 'and the day when I find it irritating are often the same day.' He reached up and grabbed Tighe's hair in a sudden, snake-strike movement, holding the head steady, and then he pressed a grimy finger against Tighe's eye. With a heart-trilling moment of fear Tighe felt certain that the Manmonger was going to gouge the eye out altogether. It all happened too rapidly for him to struggle; but with a twist of the finger the dirty nail wormed its way into Tighe's eyelid and then with a focus of pain the whole finger's end went under and pulled the lid away from the eye.

The girls gasped. 'Now,' said the Manmonger, straining Tighe's eyelid painfully away from his eye. 'I could snap this out with a flick of my finger. You want? Then you'd have no eyelid, and your eye would quickly go blind in the excess of light. The sun would drink your eyesight as a sacrifice. You want that? I could do it with both eyelids, perhaps?'

Tighe could feel the grains of grit on the Manmonger's finger grinding minutely against the inside of his eyelid; he had instinctively shut the other lid, but light flooded in through the pain of his other eye.

'Then,' he said, gasping, 'I would be a less valuable commodity to you.'

The Manmonger pulled his finger down and out and Tighe's eyelid snapped back into place. He clapped both his hands to his sore eye. 'You are a freak anyway,' the Manmonger said, 'with your black skin. A freakish eye would only add to your resale value. Come on, all of you,' and he led them over the sharply sloping ledge.

Even more fearful, the girls hurried after him. Tighe, clutching his eye, peered with his other one and stumbled along at the rear.

*

The day wore on. They made their way from crag to ledge and in the afternoon along some more thoroughly worn ledges and into a small village. The people there peered out at the Manmonger and his commodities from their doorways. He greeted them as he passed along their central shelf, but none of them seemed interested in buying people.

They left the village and an enormous spur running directly up and down the wall came closer and closer. They passed through another village and settled themselves down on the central shelf in time for the dusk gale. The Manmonger ate and drank, and then sat silently by himself as the winds roared. But Tighe could see now that the dusk gale was much less violent here than it was back in his own village. They barely had to clutch at the grass under them; and half-way through it Tighe saw a door in the village open and an old woman make her way along the shelf to a second door.

After it had died down and the Manmonger was tying the knots that bound their hands together, Tighe spoke up again. His eye still stung. 'The further east we go,' he said, 'the less violent is the dusk gale.'

'Observant,' said the Manmonger.

'Is there a place, far enough east,' Tighe asked, casting his eyes meekly down so as not to anger the man, 'where there is no dusk or dawn gale?'

'It lessens the further east we go,' said the Manmonger. 'And it gets stronger the further west. That's curious, isn't it?' But he wouldn't say any more, and shortly he was asleep.

In the morning he used the red-haired girl again, and then he left the three of them tied up and went from door to door in the village. Eventually he returned with a red-faced elderly man. This man's skin was flushed like a baby and even his old-man wrinkles had the just-pressed look of the very young; but his nose was a bulbous mass of age tumour and his white hair was close cut against his knobbly head like turf. He wheezed as he walked.

This old man and the Manmonger had a lengthy conversation in a language Tighe could not understand, accompanied by hand gestures and elaborate noddings and duckings of the head. After an interminable amount of this posturing and arguing the two of them retreated in through one of the doors, and the Manmonger re-emerged carrying a small leather sack. It chinked as he carried it.

'You,' he said, pointing at the red-haired girl. 'You belong to him now. He wanted you,' he added, grinning, indicating the dark-haired girl, 'but I said I hadn't tried you yet myself, so I wasn't about to give you up yet.'

The red-haired girl was sobbing now, her head down. The Manmonger took her and loosened her bonds, with a surprising tenderness, and led her unresisting to the doorway of the old man.

'There are no more sales here, I think,' he said when he came back out, 'but beyond that spur of worldwall', he said, indicating the mass that obscured the eastward journey, 'is a great city and we'll find buyers for you yet.'

11

The Manmonger took his two remaining commodities out of the village to the east and along a series of well-trodden overhung ledges. The spur grew and grew until it bulged enormously out in front of them and filled most of the eastern portion of the sky.

They paused in the afternoon and everybody chewed grass. Tighe felt ravenously hungry, but it seemed unlikely that the Manmonger was going to give them any proper food. When he thought of the succulent, tasty-smelling strips of boy-meat that the Manmonger occasionally popped into his mouth, he felt a sick mixture of disgust and desire. He started calculating how long it would be before he starved to thinness, thinking of the itinerants he had seen in the village in his youth. Death could not be much further away. There was even something comforting in that thought.

The Manmonger himself sat cross-legged with his back to them, chanting something to the sun in a strange voice. It occurred to Tighe to rush at him and try to push him off the world, but something stopped him.

They stayed the night and in the morning they started eastward again. They finally reached the spur by eighty in the morning, arriving at an enormous and strangely hooped gateway that led inside the bulge of worldwall.

Beside the gateway was a house and as the Manmonger and his charges approached a middle-aged man emerged from the doorway. The Manmonger greeted him as if he were an old friend, and they embraced and talked for a long time. There were several posts set into the ledge just outside the gateway and the Manmonger tied Tighe and the dark-haired girl to this before going inside the gatekeeper's house.

Tighe peered along the ledge, through the gate. It was a tunnel through the spur, but so long that he could not see light at the far end. A damp, unpleasant exhalation wafted out of the space. 'I suppose he will take us through there,' said Tighe to the girl. She looked at him with unfocused eyes. 'Do you speak Imperial?' he asked. 'Are you not of the Empire?' Nothing. 'Perhaps you are Otre?' Still nothing. Tighe shook his head, speaking aloud in his village tongue, 'It is difficult for me to understand such a one as you, I'm afraid.'

Eventually the Manmonger returned with the gatekeeper. They both smelt of liquor and the Manmonger's grin was more intense than it had been before. 'He wanted you,' he said as he untied the dark-haired girl. 'His wife wasn't happy about it because there could be no confusion as to *why* he wanted you, let's be honest. He wanted you as the toll price for going through his tunnel. I told him – toll price for a *hundred* journeys through his stinking tunnel! But he was insistent. There's something about your looks, my pretty, that appeal to the people this far east.' The dark-haired girl was free now and the Manmonger turned his attention to Tighe. He was still talking to the unresponsive girl. 'He said that if I paid him with you, my pretty, then I'd have free toll for the rest of my life. Imagine! I was tempted, I'll not pretend, but I haven't tried you yet myself, have I? I can't let him have you before myself, can I?'

With both his commodities free, he hauled them up and waved a final goodbye to the surly-looking gatekeeper. 'I had to placate him with several of the trinkets I earned in the village,' he said sourly. 'And I hope that you're worth it, my pretty. I hope that, at any rate.'

He marched them to the mouth of the tunnel.

'Now,' he announced to them both. 'I don't like this tunnel. It is hidden from my mistress, the Sun. I cannot pray to her, I cannot feel the heat of her pleasure on my skin. So I do not like to stay in the tunnel. We shall hurry through, you and you and I, and we shall emerge into the sunlight on the other side. Do you understand?'

They stared at him.

'Do you?' he barked.

'Yes,' said Tighe. 'I do not like this tunnel either. It smells funny.'

'It does that,' said the Manmonger. 'And worse than that. But there is no other way around this spur of worldwall, so through we must go. Jog all the way – do not let up. There are fleas the size of your fist in here. And rats; did you ever see a rat? I have seen rats as big as a man, and they are nasty, nasty. Come along!'

He turned to the sun one last time, closing his eyes to let the late-morning rays bathe his face. Then, with a shove, he hurried his two objects into the mouth of the tunnel.

The ground underneath was soggy and Tighe with his bad foot found running particularly difficult. The light behind them faded and soon they were in darkness. It smelt of decay, although it was not entirely black. As soon as the pale light from the gateway behind them faded a spot of light appeared before them. They hurried on, Tighe's stomach clenching with a stitch of hunger and exhaustion; but he had no more desire to stay in this dank place than had the Manmonger.

As they struggled on the dot of light swelled and expanded. An ashy light brought the shapes of the tunnel out of the gloom; strange contortions of rock, an enormous bulge of manrock to the right that was freakishly shaped like a giant brick, like a house excavated out from the side of the wall, complete with puckered indentations down its side that even resembled tiny doorways.

They hurried on until the shape of light had grown large enough for them to jog through it and out into the sunlight again. At the far end was a short shelf, on which a number of people were sitting. The Manmonger and his two commodities collapsed on the grass here and lay, panting and gasping, until they had their breath back.

As soon as he was able, the Manmonger settled himself down to perform his religious duties before his goddess, the Sun, now high in the sky. He did not even bother to tie up his two commodities. Tighe, sitting upon the grass as the pain in his chest and stomach receded a little, looked around him. There was no gatekeeper's house this side of the tunnel; presumably people paid at the far end. Tighe wondered about what happened to those who, entering the tunnel from this side, did not have enough for a full fare; were they sent back along the tunnel?

The other people on the shelf were all dressed in striped dresses that fell from a tight neck collar down to the ankles; their heads were wrapped in scarves and Tighe could not even be sure whether they were male or female. There were perhaps a dozen of them, sitting together with their backs against the wall. They observed the Manmonger and his possessions with impossible-to-read expressions for a while and soon enough they all stood up together and filed into the tunnel.

The Manmonger was left alone with his commodities.

'This shelf', he said, 'is too close to that terrible tunnel. Come, we shall walk a little way.'

He led them along and up through a series of short interlinked crags, each one less well trodden than the one before, climbing and climbing until they came to a semi-circular platform covered in tall grass. Here he hammered in a peg and settled himself down. The sun had almost settled over the top of the wall and the light was dimming, but there seemed almost no motion of the air around them. Had they reached the place where the dusk gale was no more?

'Now,' said the Manmonger, fiddling in his pack. 'If I don't give you food you will die – as you, my black-skinned possession, have pointed out several times. So I traded some of my trinkets for grass-bread and ratmeat from the gatekeeper and you two will eat. Only do not eat too much, or your stomachs will rebel. Here,' he handed out some small portions of bread and two or three knuckle-sized pieces of meat.

Tighe was too ravenous to think of anything else. He gobbled the food down straight away and felt his stomach clench and stab with pain. He felt extremely thirsty. 'Drink?' he asked. But the Manmonger only laughed.

'You'll have to wait until the dew tomorrow,' he said.

The sun had gone now and it was getting darker by the minute. The Manmonger's pale face flashed as he turned from side to side. 'My pretty,' he said, shuffling over towards the dark-haired girl. 'Do you feel better with some food in your belly? With some food inside you?' He chuckled to himself. 'Would you like something else inside you?'

She moaned and seemed to be trembling. It was difficult to see in the half-light.

'You wait a moment', said the Manmonger, 'whilst I tie up this boy.' He came over to Tighe with a thong in his hands. The dark-haired girl was sobbing in a most pitiable manner. 'We wouldn't want to be disturbed, now, would we?'

Tighe felt his stomach knot and clench again; although that could have been just the food. His throat was so dry it was painful. He thought he ought to say something, but was not sure what.

The Manmonger tied Tighe's wrists together tightly and then drew his knife. He turned back to the girl.

'Now, my pretty!'

As he moved towards her, she gave a little yelp and darted to the side. In the increasingly dense darkness it was hard to see exactly what happened. The Manmonger lurched to the side, his free hand outstretched to grab her, but she ducked and put a burst of speed on, slipping past him. Tighe angled his head to follow, twisting his body to follow. The Manmonger grunted and lurched towards her again, this time holding the knife out.

One moment the dark-haired girl was there, crouched, her pale face just visible in the darkness. Then she was gone. The Manmonger dashed to the edge of the world and crouched down. 'Are you there?' he called. 'Are you there? Where have you fallen to? How far down?' There followed some words in his own incomprehensible language. He hurried back to Tighe and fixed him to the peg he had driven into the platform earlier, then he left, making his way down and away.

'She flies, you fool,' said Tighe, in a quiet voice, speaking at the Manmonger's retreating back.

He was gone for only a few minutes, but when he returned he was in a foul mood. He ranted in his own tongue for a while, and then said in twisted Imperial, 'Idiot, stupid girl, how would she think? How would she think that? She is fallen to the bones that litter the base of the wall and good riddance. Disease, she was; darkness and disease. Her hair was darkness and my Goddess despises darkness, dispels it. Idiot! Idiot!'

Tighe kept himself very quiet, lying still on the platform.

12

In the morning the Manmonger was still in a bad temper, although he no longer ranted. 'It is the waste,' he said, as he untethered Tighe. 'The waste is the most provoking thing of it. I could have given her to the gatekeeper and had free passage through the tunnel for all my life. But now I have nothing! Not even her body! She has angered me. I should have given her to the gatekeeper.'

He ate some more food from his satchel, although he offered Tighe none. Then he smacked Tighe a few times to get him moving, and together they continued their climb along the crags and ledges of this section of worldwall.

'We are going to a great city?' Tighe asked, eventually. He felt strangely numb about the loss of the dark-haired girl, perhaps because it had happened in the night-time and so felt unreal. But then again, so much had felt unreal since the death of Ati.

'What?'

'Is it your city? Your home?'

The Manmonger snorted. 'I come from a long way away from here, my black-skinned possession. But, yes, we are going to the City of the East. This trip has been unprofitable, mostly. I must reclaim what little I can from the situation.'

At ninety, as was his habit, the Manmonger settled down on a broad grassy ledge, overhung about a third, to pray to his goddess. He crossed his legs and made his strange bodily movements, and chanted in his strange tongue. Tighe sat, clutching his own knees, watching him.

After he had finished, the Manmonger came over and fished some food from his pack. Tighe looked dolefully at him as he ate, hoping to prick his conscience into giving him a snack. But the Manmonger was in a snappish mood.

'No food for you today,' he said. 'You ate yesterday, it is enough. You could have had that girl's food, if I'd known she would throw herself off the wall! What a waste of food. Could she not have left the food, at any rate?

What difference does it make to her bones, bleaching at the foot of the wall, whether she had a full stomach or an empty one when she died?'

He sat for a while in silence. Tighe said nothing more.

After a little while, he spoke again.

'Great reaches of bones,' he said. 'That's what is at the bottom of the wall.'

Despite himself, his hatred for the Manmonger, and despite his hunger and discomfort, Tighe felt his interest piqued. 'Have you seen them?' he asked. 'Have you been to the bottom of the wall?'

'Yes,' returned the Manmonger. 'Or, if not, then at least I have spoken to men who have been down that far. There's nothing there, nothing on the lower portions of the wall, I can tell you. And the bones are scattered as far as the eye can see. It is like a giant ledge, all busy with bleached bones and rubbish. Everything that falls from the wall ends up there; it is death. Every day my mistress, my Goddess,' he pointed at the sun, 'leaves such death. That is why the morning is death, it is the death of night. And She leaves death and climbs to life. Life is on top of the wall.'

There was a pause. Tighe said timidly, 'I never met somebody who worshipped the Sun before.'

'It is the true religion, my boy,' said the Manmonger heartily.

Tighe tried looking at the sun, but his eyelids closed automatically at the glare. 'It hurts my eyes,' he said.

'She does,' said the Manmonger, and laughed to himself. 'Not all can bear her beauty. But I can!' He stood up and flung his arms wide, facing directly into the bright midday sun. 'I can! Her heat! Her light! Shall I tell you what I pray for?' he said, turning back to Tighe.

'Pray for,' echoed Tighe.

'I pray for the end times. This is how it will be: when the end comes, She will approach the wall more closely. She will come close a *flame* and burn all the liars. Only the pure will be able to bear Her beauty up close! There is a door in the sun and I shall step through it.'

'A door in the sun,' said Tighe. 'A door?'

'Through that door is light, is life.'

'There is a door in the wall, too,' said Tighe.

The Manmonger looked at him. 'A door in the wall,' he said. 'I have heard those stories, but I never saw such a thing.' He laughed, turning back to the sky. 'I pray,' he said loudly, 'I pray that You will come soon, my Goddess!'

Then he gasped in pure astonishment. Tighe, winking and blinking and shielding his eyes with the flat of his hand, looked out at the sky.

A blob of bright light was dropping from the base of the sun; like hot white wax melting and dribbling down.

'There!' screeched the Manmonger in an immediate ecstasy of excitement. 'My mistress! There!'

The blob hung for a moment, like a radiant teardrop, and then detached itself from the circle of the sun. Tighe clenched his eyes, letting his eyelashes act as a crude filter, trying to see what was happening. This second miniature sun, like a particularly bright star, dribbled slowly down the wall of the sky. Tighe felt his own heart struggle rapidly in his chest. There was a tremendous sense of expansion inside his head, as if the epiphany were here. The sun!

'My mistress!' howled the delighted Manmonger. He began a peculiar nimble-footed dance, hopping from foot to foot. He gabbled something in his own tongue and then hurried over to Tighe, gripping him by the shoulders. 'As I said, no? We have travelled through the darkness, we have lost the dark girl, and now we are in the light, and my Goddess rewards us! As I said! The door in the sun has opened and a being of light has come through. Look there – !' He stretched his arm out with manic energy, his finger trembling with excitement. 'Look where it comes towards us.'

The blob of light did seem to be growing, as if it were flying through the air towards them.

'Coming straight for us!' announced the Manmonger. He let go of Tighe and resumed his odd dancing, chanting in his own tongue as he did so. When balanced on his right foot he twitched his left through a bizarre pattern; then he shifted his weight on to his left foot and waggled his right one in the air. He hopped back and forth with enormous gusto.

Tighe was hypnotised by the growing fragment of light. It wobbled a little, dropped. Then it rose. By the time it had grown to the size of a hand's span, Tighe could see what it was.

It was a floating calabash of some sort; bright shiny silver, curiously shaped, an elongated cylinder. It might have been made out of metal; three spindly pincers protruded from its underbelly; but its hourglass-shaped body possessed no marks or windows except for a band around its waist and what seemed to be three small portholes immediately underneath this. It floated, sweeping up through the sky.

Tighe recognised it: it was the same silver calabash he had seen during the battle on the Imperial ledge, the thing out of which the booming noise had issued that he had interpreted as his own name. The memory was sharp as lemon-taste in his mind; he could remember everything about that last encounter – Ati tugging his shirt from below him on the stair, urging him to keep his head low: the crack and volley of rifle fire up above and the stench of burnt mushroom powder.

He had thought this strange apparition had called his name; and now here it was again and this time the Manmonger seemed certain it had come specifically in answer to his prayers. 'It has come, it has come!' he cried aloud, singing the words. 'As I prayed! It has come to me!'

13

The silver calabash came through the air, unerringly, until it was close against the wall at the lip of the ledge on which the Manmonger and Tighe were standing; it hovered, and settled so that most of its shape was below them and they could see the top of it. Up close it was even more startling than it was when seen floating in the middle distance. Unlike calabashes, which displayed the stitching and the leather panels that constituted their skin, this structure was utterly smooth and clear, pure unsullied silver all over. Now that it was nestling against the wall Tighe could see that it was the size of a small house.

The Manmonger was running up and down the ledge in little spurts of excited activity, gabbling something. Tighe stood motionless.

There was a slight popping noise and a swirl of air directly over the smooth crown of the machine, a dilating spot of dark, and a figure emerged, elevated from within until it stood on the top of the device. A man, it seemed, dressed in a black cloak; or perhaps a boy, because it was a small figure.

This person ran down the gentle slope of the device and hopped over on to the ledge. He hurried up to stand next to Tighe.

He was a strange individual; almost as short as Tighe himself and much smaller than the Manmonger. His head was bald and his skin was very dark brown. He was much darker than Ati had been, although not as deeply coloured as Tighe himself, but the strangest thing was that his skin had something uncanny, even unpleasant about it. It creased in a fatter way than normal skin at his neck and it moved far less over his face than ordinary skin would. It appeared to be more of a mask and of a strange, inhuman consistency. The man's face was wrinkle-free, although there were patches of vague discoloration at the corners of his mouth and eyes. His nose had a shrunken, mummified look to it. Only his eyes looked fully human; lively, brown eyes that darted back and forth, checking Tighe over.

Although there was this odd, inhuman look to him, Tighe had the strangest sense that he had met this short, dummy-like individual before. There was something familiar about him.

The Manmonger hurried up to Tighe and the newcomer and stopped, uncertain what to do. 'You have come!'

The man looked over at him briefly and then turned his gaze back to Tighe. 'Evidently,' he said. His voice was queerly high-pitched, almost like a child's.

'How should I call you? You have come from the Sun!'

'The sun?' repeated the man, not removing his stare from Tighe. 'No, just the sky. Just out of the sky. Here!' He reached out and grabbed Tighe's chin between two fingers; his skin felt very peculiar against Tighe's own, leathery and dry. The man moved Tighe's head to the left, to the right.

'Should I call you Master?' asked the Manmonger. 'Should I call you Wizard?'

'Wizard,' repeated the man, in a distracted voice. It was not clear whether he was answering the Manmonger, or just echoing him without thinking, but the Manmonger assumed the first.

'Wizard! You are so brown! Your skin!'

The newcomer looked over at the Manmonger again. 'Eh?'

'You are an emissary from the Sun, O Wizard! Your skin is brown because it has been burnt brown by Her magnificence! Burnt brown and leathery by the Sun!'

The Wizard grinned briefly, his face creasing into thick, unnatural-looking lines. When he stopped grinning the lines vanished. 'What are you saying?'

'You have come with a message for me?' panted the Manmonger.

'You? No, no. No!' This last word was almost a shout, almost a laugh. 'Not you, but this boy. I have come for this boy.'

The Manmonger looked nonplussed. 'I don't understand.'

The Wizard turned his attention back to Tighe, reaching out with his oddly wizened-looking hands and grabbing Tighe's arm. 'Under-eating, I think,' he said. 'Hungry, are you boy?'

'The boy?' asked the Manmonger. The expression on his face shifted as he reappraised the situation. 'You come in a curious craft, Mister the Wizard.'

'Curious,' repeated the Wizard, apparently caught up in the business of scrutinising Tighe closely.

'You are a man, though,' said the Manmonger, scratching his own head. 'A man like any other, perhaps. Your skin is strange.'

'Strange,' agreed the Wizard, absently.

'Still,' said the Manmonger with sudden decision, 'if you are interested in the boy, he is for sale. Do you hear, you strange fellow? The boy is for sale.'

The Wizard stepped back and regarded the Manmonger. 'For sale?'

'That's right. He's a curious example, I know; his skin is darker than any

I've seen. Darker even than yours, although perhaps you and he are kin, given the darkness of your own.' The Manmonger smiled broadly and showed off both his empty hands, a salesman's gesture. 'If you're interested we can agree a price, I think. But I had high hopes for a very high price in the City of the East – they'll pay a good price there for curiosities like this one with his dark skin.'

'You know the City of the East?' asked the Wizard.

'I've traded there for ten years or more,' said the Manmonger. 'What don't I know about the City of the East?'

'Then you should know', said the Wizard, rummaging through one of the pockets in his coat, 'that they have enough curiosities there already. You'd get a poor price for an underfed boy such as this.'

'Perhaps,' said the Manmonger. 'But you're interested, I can tell, and that'll drive the price up. If you don't offer me enough, well perhaps I'll take him there anyway and try my luck.' He rubbed his face and reverted momentarily to his former astonishment. 'Such an entrance! I really thought you were from the Sun, my Goddess!'

'No, no,' said the Wizard, still rummaging through his pockets.

'Well,' said the Manmonger, 'that's a fancy craft you fly about in. I've seen calabashes west of the Meshwood, but I've never seen one of that design. I dare say you have strange and electronic things aboard and perhaps we could trade one of those for this boy.'

'This boy!' said the Wizard, in his reedy voice. 'Tighe!'

Tighe was startled out of silence. 'You know my name?'

'What I propose', said the Manmonger, 'is you offer me something and I tell you whether that's an acceptable price for the boy. What do you say?'

'This,' said the Wizard, bringing out a handful of fluff from his pocket. 'This.'

The Manmonger took a step forward. 'A joke? That looks like fluff.'

'Fluff,' said the Wizard. 'Yes. Come, Tighe, come and see.'

'How do you know my name?' asked Tighe, stepping forward despite himself. 'How do you – what is that?'

The Wizard held out his left hand flat; on its palm was a small pile of fluffy threads. With his forefinger and thumb of his leathery right hand he picked a single thread up and held it in the light.

'What is that?'

It looked like a piece of dandelion seed. Tighe peered closer. There was a peppercorn-tiny silver speck, and out from it came two or three, maybe four, gossamer threads, each of which ended in a tiny black knot. The threads could only be seen because they glinted in the sun.

'You intend to buy the boy with *that*?' asked the Manmonger, incredulous.

'Buy? Yes, yes. Do you see? Do you see, Tighe?' The Wizard let go of the tiny piece of mock-dandelion fluff. Instead of drifting to the ground, it hung in space. Tighe's mouth dropped open. It was the most tiny, most delicate thing he had ever seen.

'Why doesn't it fall?' Tighe asked.

The Manmonger took a step forward, creasing his brow. 'What is that?'

'It's in the kernel,' said the Wizard. 'That tiny thing in the midst, where the threads are anchored – do you see? That's the trick of it. The same principle by which my craft floats through the air. Clever, clever. Look!'

Slowly the tiny thing was starting to rotate in space. The dangling threads flopped up and over, and then, as the spinning kernel gathered speed, they began to be stretched out by the torque. Soon the thing was a cartwheel, or miniature windmill; its various threads were pulled taut by the rotation.

'How does it *do* that?' asked the Manmonger.

'Now,' said the Wizard, 'Tighe. Do you see?'

Tighe looked up into the eyes of the Wizard, the deeply human, moist brown eyes in the heart of the odd, mask-like face. With a sense of the dream deepening, intensifying, he realised why this strange leather-skinned individual had seemed so familiar to him. His voice, his intonation, was like a warbly, high-pitched version of Grandhe Jaffiahe's. Even his weird, mask-like face had something of the smack of his Grandhe.

'You seem to me', said Tighe, in a near-whisper, lapsing into his native village tongue, 'like my Grandhe alive again.'

The Wizard smiled, exactly as if he understood. 'Now,' he replied, speaking the village tongue fluently, 'you must watch this part very closely.'

The dandelion-fluff device, spinning leisurely in the air, suddenly increased its rate of rotations. The individual threads became a blur. It started drifting through the air in the direction of the Manmonger.

'The threads are what we call *monofilament*,' said the stranger who so unsettlingly resembled Tighe's Grandhe, still speaking Tighe's native tongue, although the last word was not one Tighe understood. 'They are amongst the toughest of things on the worldwall. The kernel in the middle is a *pollenmachine*, for although it is small it is complex and advanced. Now – watch!'

The Manmonger, completely beguiled by the floating thing, watched its shimmering light-flickering approach, held up a finger as it floated towards him. He reached as if to touch it. The spinning blob simply sheared through his upheld finger – as if the spinning dandelion fluff had been made of the hardest stuff, of rock or diamond; and as if the Manmonger's finger had been made of the most evanescent material. There was a fluttering sound and the end of the Manmonger's finger was no more. The floating device simply powered through the flesh.

It happened so quickly that the Manmonger did not even have time to cry out. He was still holding out his hand, still upraising his finger, except that the end of the finger was not there. Blood pulsed from the end, like ink from a pen.

The twirling monofilament device floated on, not rapidly but evidently not to be pushed aside. The look of astonishment on the Manmonger's face was almost comical. The blurry bubble was in front of his chest and then with another short-lived burr it was gone, carving through the shirt. A perfectly circular hole had opened up in the Manmonger's chest. Almost at once it filled with blood; pink, frothing blood poured out of the hole. The astonished Manmonger opened his mouth and an amount of bubbling blood came out. He toppled forward, and lay face down, twitching.

Behind him the spinning monofilament device was still floating through the air, heading now towards the wall. Tighe looked down at the body of the Manmonger, and then at the Wizard, and then at the Wizard's floating device.

It approached the wall. Tighe felt a surge of fear. 'What will it do?' he asked the Wizard. 'Will it eat right through the wall, like it ate through the Manmonger? Will it go through to the other side?'

'Dear me no,' said the Wizard, carefully replacing the rest of his handful of fluff back in his pocket. 'It'll lose its energy quickly enough in hard stuff like the rock of the wall. Don't worry. It'll bury itself in, perhaps an inch. But it's not a magic thing, it's only a machine; it obeys the same laws of energy conservation and entropy as everything else. Now!' He looked around him.

The Manmonger was stretched face down on the ledge, motionless. The Wizard walked over him as if he had been nothing but a mat and retrieved his pack. He spent a moment going through it, but quickly became bored. 'There's some food,' he said. 'What meat is this?'

Tighe was staring at the dead body at his feet. He pulled his gaze up. 'Some of the meat is goat's meat,' he said, his mouth watering as he spoke the words. His stomach clenched again and reminded him how hungry he was. 'Some of it is – is human.'

The leather man wrinkled his strange face and dropped the food. 'That meat is too strong', he said, 'even for me. There's grass-bread here though, which I think I'll take. Come, Tighe,' he said, 'are you hungry?'

'I am hungry,' said Tighe. 'How do you know my name?'

'Know lots about you,' said the Wizard, 'but come aboard my machine and I will give you some food and drink. And answer your questions. I have been looking for you, Tighe.'

'Looking for me?'

The Wizard was hurrying away from him now. With practised ease he hopped from the ledge on to the roof of his craft. Tighe followed, sparing a single glance back for the stretched-out body of the Manmonger. There was a momentary sense of panic at the prospect of stepping off the worldwall, like his old kite-flying fear, but he was carried along by the much stronger sense that all this was a sort of dream, a nothing. He hopped from the worldwall on to the top of the Wizard's floating machine, his feet slipping a little on the polished metal. It felt warm. The Wizard beckoned him over and grasped his hand as they stood on the exact top of the craft. The touch of his dry, leather fingers was strangely upsetting.

Just as he had arrived, although in reverse, the Wizard and Tighe descended through the roof of the machine. The world rose up, and then they were in blackness and the roof irised shut over their heads.

They were in a room, furnished like no room Tighe had ever seen before. The Wizard led him down a ladder and they entered a second room, directly beneath the first. And in the corner of this room there was a human being, crouched down, clutching her knees. With a jolt, that was only partly cushioned by the sense that he was still experiencing some sort of trance-like dream, Tighe realised that this person was his pashe.

4

The Wizard and the Ice

1

Inside the Wizard's craft were two spaces, each the size of a large room, one on top of the other. The top room was green; its walls well wadded with fabric, each bolt of the dark-rich material pinned in its middle with a fabric knot that was hard like a pebble, which gathered the curves and folds of the surrounding material to a point. There were dozens of these points, constellating over the wall. The fabric itself was a deep green. Set against the wall of the room in the midst of all this opulence was a bed – or, rather, a strange cross between an elongated chair with a padded backboard and a bed. The bed-chair was of a giant size: half a dozen people could have sat on it in comfort and three could have lain on its spongy fabric base to sleep.

The Wizard and Tighe descended from the roof and through this room on a small platform. The gap in the ceiling closed over their heads and they came to stand on the floor.

The floor beneath this chair, or bed, was of metal studded with a hundred knobs, like silver pimples in a grey skin. A small sink, just the size for a man to stand in and as deep as Tighe was tall, was fixed to one wall. There were other devices fixed to various places on the circular all-round wall and on the side opposite the bed was a space in the floor, through which a ladder led down to the lower room. But most marvellous of all was the brightness of candle fixed in a plastic cup-shape hanging off-centre from the ceiling. It threw a powerful yellow light into every crevice of the room.

The downstairs room was crowded with sculpture in metal and plastic, a fortune's worth, although the shapes and figures meant little to Tighe. After the Wizard had taken Tighe down to this lower room, he settled himself into a skinny metal chair in front of a number of netscreens. Tighe's pashe sat in the corner.

For a while Tighe simply stood and stared at her. The leather-skinned Wizard looked over at him. 'Why not say hello?' he offered in his squeaky voice, speaking Tighe's native tongue.

'Pashe?' offered Tighe. His heart was pulsing hugely. He could hear the sound of his blood rushing through his head.

His pashe sat silently, staring past Tighe's head.

It made no sense to Tighe; he tried again, leaning forward a little. His head was a swirl of thoughts. He was about to cry; about to fall. About to laugh.

On an impulse, Tighe scrambled back up the ladder to the upper room, to look again at the giant chair, or bed – to prod it, to sit on it, to jump up and down on it. None of it was real. The worldwall was a tiny model, a vicious god's small-scale experiment, populated with real-size insects and rats and miniature people. It was all insane. But his pashe was alive! Down the ladder again. The Wizard sat in his cradle fiddling with controls and Tighe's pashe still squatted in the corner.

'Pashe? What is this place? Are you all right? Pashe, I thought you were dead.' Tighe was crying now, but his pashe still wasn't looking at him. She cradled her knees and looked directly at the wall opposite her. It was as if Tighe did not exist.

He went over to the Wizard. 'She won't look at me,' he said, plaintively, his eyes wet.

'No?' squeaked the Wizard. 'Perhaps she'll speak later.' The room gave a fluid lurch and Tighe staggered on his feet. He hurried over to his pashe again and squatted next to her. Tentatively, half expecting a rebuke, he lowered his head until it was resting on her shoulder and put an arm round her neck. She tolerated his embrace, but she didn't say anything to indicate that she recognised him or even knew he was there.

For a while Tighe simply stayed in that rather awkward position. His tears stopped coming. Soon enough he started to feel uncomfortable and he withdrew his arm and stood up again.

'What's wrong with her?' he called over to the Wizard.

'Wrong?' repeated the Wizard. 'Nothing, nothing.'

Tighe mooned about the room. The circular wall of this lower room, in contrast to the upper one, was hung with a blood-coloured fabric. The cloth was like nothing Tighe had seen before. It was covered in tiny soft bristles, thousands of them per hand's width. Tighe became fascinated by them. Thousands of *tiny* little soft red hairs, all poking out of a red cloth backdrop. 'What is this cloth, Wizard?' he asked. 'I have never seen anything like it.'

'*Not* easy to clean,' said the Wizard. 'But harder wearing than you'd think; each tiny strand is micro-coated. But *not* easy to clean. There's a device in one of the cupboards.'

'Wizard,' said Tighe, meekly, 'it is magic, I think.'

The Wizard laughed. 'I wish, sweet boy,' he said, in his strangely high-pitched voice, 'that you wouldn't, truly, act the primitive so crudely. What cliché!' And he laughed again.

Tighe came over and could see that the Wizard was absorbed in his screens. He hunched, wandered over to his pashe again, and squatted down, touching her leg. 'Pashe,' he said, 'are you well?' When she said nothing in reply, he said, 'When you were gone I was so sad. I missed you so much.' He could feel the tears coming again.

'I think,' whispered his pashe, and stopped. 'Yes,' she said, shortly. 'That's it. I think I am most comfortable here.' She folded her arms more tightly about her own knees as if clutching them to her breast, as if they were her own babies. Tighe thought she had stopped speaking because she closed her eyes and rested her chin on her arms, but as he turned away she spoke loudly. '*This* is where I belong.'

Tighe twitched at the unexpectedness. He turned back to her and reached out to touch her again; a finger brushing her naked knees, touching her hair. But she didn't respond and he gave up.

'I'm hungry, Wizard,' he announced.

'Yes,' said the Wizard. 'Yes, you are. Here.' He swivelled his cradle, and brought out a small portion of something and a vial of water. The vial was plastic, but the plastic was pure and unscuffed, the finest material, fit to make jewellery out of. 'I'll give you more later,' he said, 'but if you eat too much now you'll be sick.'

Tighe took the two gifts with an expression of awe and then settled himself on the floor with his back to the cloth-padded wall and drank deeply. The water tasted empty, almost metallic; the food on the other hand was a grass-bread of a delicacy and taste he had never experienced before. It was delicious; instead of the crushed bodies of insects, it contained chunks of pure meat. Instead of the rough texture of grass-dough it was smooth and a cold salty jelly surrounded the whole, wrapped in turn in a moist crust. It was the most delicious thing that Tighe had ever eaten. When he had finished he drank some more of the water.

His stomach was throbbing with unusual use and he curled up on the floor and fell into a brief sleep. When he woke, his pashe was still sitting hunched up on the floor over the way and the Wizard was still in his cradle.

Feeling immensely revived, Tighe got to his feet and went over to the Wizard, standing directly behind his bald, leather-skinned head. His screen was showing four separate images, one in each quarter. Top right was the sky: bottom right and bottom left were the wall to the left and right of their position. Top left was the wall directly ahead, with a large head-shaped blot of silver in the middle of the picture. With his sense of dreaming becoming more acute, Tighe realised that this impossible image was of themselves – as if a bird had carried a screen-eye out into the air and was looking back at them with it.

'Wizard!' he exclaimed, pointing at the picture. 'That's us.'

'Perhaps', replied the Wizard without looking round, 'you expect credit for stating the obvious?'

'But how can such a picture be possible?' Tighe had seen screens before. From time to time screen-tinkers would pass through the village and charge a small fee to show off their stained and battered toy. Older people were usually not interested in such stuff because they had seen it all before and it was a kind of entertainment that swiftly went stale. But there were always children for whom it was a new thing, and the tinker, on his long loops around villages, would return after years to scratch out a little more of a living from showing the screen to these youngsters. *Look at the screen!* he would say – *Like a picture, but, magic! Your own face in the book! Your own ledge in the picture!* And as the children huddled round the old cracked stretch of plastic trying to make out the image the tinker would pull the screen-eye from his pocket and carry it in his hand. First he would angle the thumb-sized eye at the children themselves and – miracle! – their own faces, their *friends'* faces would appear on the screen. Pictures that smiled when they smiled, bulged their eyes when the giggling children bulged theirs. Then the tinker would swoop his hand up to show the sky, angle it at the ledge, walk along with a bored expression. The image, as Tighe remembered it, was dark and often puzzling. Anything that moved trailed a thin line of blur immediately behind it; and the edges of the screen cut off the image, which sometimes made it hard to understand the relationship of line and line, of patch of light and darkness. But the wonder of it! Tighe and other children had stared as if hypnotised at the tinker's screen, snatching occasional glances at the direction of the tinker himself to confirm that the landscape of ledge, wall and sky at which he was pointing his screen-eye was *just the same* as the magic shifting pictures on the screen in front of them! It was breathtaking and all the children whined when the tinker turned the screen off and packed it up. 'You get your pas', he said gruffly, 'to pay me a little more in cheese or cloth and you can see some more. Yes?' So they had hurried off to badger their pas – all except Tighe, who hadn't dared bother his pashe with the request.

But the tinker's screen he had seen as a child had been tiny, dark and marked. It had to stand in the sun for an hour before the dimmest, bleariest picture emerged; whereas the Wizard's screen was enormous, bright and clean. There was no blurring of the image with movement, every detail of the world outside was clearly defined. And there was that impossible perspective of the Wizard's craft itself, which looked as though it had been taken by a screen-eye two hundred yards outwall. Tighe touched the Wizard's sleeve, and said again, 'Wizard, how is such a picture possible?'

306

'I wish', said the Wizard, 'that you, my bright boy, would speak the Imperial tongue, which is so much more elegant than your village language.'

Tighe felt this as a rebuke. He swallowed and began to rephrase the question in Imperial language.

'Master Wizard,' he began.

'Now,' said the Wizard, still speaking Tighe's native tongue for all his expressed preference for the other, 'perhaps it is time we departed.'

The floor lurched and Tighe tumbled over. His stomach pulled uncomfortably at the base of his torso. He felt momentarily sick and then the sensation stopped and he was able to stand up again. The images on the screens were of wall spinning past; except for the top left which showed the silver blob that was themselves hanging stationary in the middle of the screen whilst the green-brown blur behind showed the speed at which they hurtled to the east.

'Wizard,' said Tighe, in his native tongue, 'you did visit the battlefield. You were looking for me.'

The Wizard spun his cradle around. 'I did indeed, my sharp boy. I did indeed. My dear boy. I was looking for you and you were hard enough to find.' He smiled and the stiff leather of his facial skin creaked and creased awkwardly.

'Why?'

'The most profound question in the philosopher's store of questions,' said the Wizard.

'You called my name.'

'I did. I amplified your name. It did me no good because you went off running, running along that ledge. Bullets sped past. I was worried, I will confess to you; my heart was in my mouth. At any time you might have been killed – killed! Imagine it. Still, these things have turned out for the best, I believe. I believe things turn out for the best more often than they do not. You ran and I tried to follow you, but then you disappeared into that Meshwood and I lost the ability to track you.'

Tighe was unfamiliar with the phrase. 'To what?'

'To follow you. To find out where you were, on all this enormous wall we call the world.' There was something grating about the Wizard's high-pitched voice when it went on at length. The resemblance Tighe had spotted with his Grandhe seemed clearer the more Tighe looked at his bizarre leathery face.

'You followed me in this machine?'

'There are things in your head – your head – ' and he leant forward to pat the top of Tighe's head with his dry, unreal hand. 'Things that enable me to tune into you. It's not easy because the wall is crammed with things and

307

people. But I spent a great deal of time looking. I returned to the village and found you gone. Gone!'

Tighe's heart flushed sore at the thought of returning to the village. 'You returned? To the village?'

'Indeed I did, my handsome boy. And such stories! I almost despaired. They said you had run mad and fallen off the world. Of course, I assumed you were dead; but sometimes fate intervenes – don't you think so? Sometimes fate intervenes.'

'The village . . .' wavered Tighe, uncertain how to frame the question that filled his breast. *How is it? How are things there? Does life continue as it always did? Do they miss me – do they talk of me?* But the Wizard was pursuing a different angle.

'I tracked for a while, but without much hope. Then I had other business. When I returned I tried one last time – and there you were! There you were! It was luck – no, no, let us call it fate, *please* let us use that word – that I found you. And at such an inopportune time! *Such* a poor occasion. The middle of a war, I *ask* you! Then you were lost in the Meshwood and I lost your tracking. But once I realised that you were still alive I could pursue you. And so I did! Until I found you! And here you are.'

'Why were you looking for me?' asked Tighe.

'Why? Because of how important you are, dear boy. You know how important you are. You've always known it.' He smiled his hideous smile once again. 'You are precious harvest, dear one. Precious harvest. As was your pashe here.'

Tighe gasped. Each answer the Wizard gave him seemed to make the business more mysterious, not less. He felt a loss of control; an increasing discomfort in the presence of the leather-skinned Wizard. Something was wrong. He went back over to his pashe and put his arm around her unresisting neck.

'There is something wrong with pashe,' he said, in a cracked voice. 'Why is there something wrong with pashe?'

The Wizard inclined his head. 'So many questions! Well, pashe has things in her head too. They are like the things in your head, if not quite as refined. Sometimes they make her – how shall we put it? – emotionally uncertain. Unstable, sometimes. The fact that you have had so much more *stable* an emotional development informs me that the things I put in your head are that much more refined. But your poor pashe. Ah,' he said, shaking his head slowly, 'ah, I sense your unhappiness, my sweetheart boy, your unease with me. But you shouldn't be uneasy! I am your rescuer, after all. I rescued you from the slave-man, didn't I?'

Tighe's hand went, almost involuntarily, to the scars on his scalp. 'What things are these in my head, in my pashe's?' he said, shutting his eyes. He had a sudden, unbidden, horrible flash of memory, of Ravielre's head being devoured from the side by a Meshwood claw-caterpil. 'Who are you? Who are you anyway? What is all this – all this magical machinery? Is it yours?'

'*That*', said the Wizard, nodding, 'is a whole bunch of questions all at once. What can I say? Things are not as you have been taught. There is a mystery about the world which you do not comprehend.'

'I know about the mystery!' flashed Tighe, suddenly swelling with courage. He leapt to his feet. 'I know that the wall is not what people think it is!'

'Do you really?' said the Wizard languidly. 'What an amazing, intelligent boy you are.'

'You have my pashe,' said Tighe. 'Where is my pahe? Where is he?' He took a step towards the Wizard, his eyes flashing.

With startling, unbelievable rapidity the Wizard was standing by the ladder. How he had got up out of his cradle and moved across the floor so quickly was impossible to determine. Tighe's eyes widened.

'How?' he gasped.

The Wizard smiled another of his repulsive smiles. 'One of the things you will learn about me', he said, 'is that I require more than the average amount of sleep. I don't mind this fact; I enjoy sleep. But I fear it may become dull for you. For this I apologise. But there is nothing that can be done.' He started climbing the ladder.

'How did you move so fast?' asked Tighe, his voice slipping into a whine. 'What have you done with my *pahe*?'

But the Wizard had vanished into the upper room.

2

Tighe tried the hatch that led into the upper room, but it was fixed tight. For several minutes he heaved and banged. 'My pahe!' he yelled. 'Explain! Where! My pahe!'

From above, muffled by the layer of metal that separated them, came the querulous voice of the Wizard. '*Please* be quiet, my dear boy,' he said. 'I'm trying to sleep.'

'Master Wizard!' shouted Tighe, banging furious.

'That *doesn't* help.'

Tighe gave up and slid back down the ladder. He went over and sat next to his pashe, cuddling up against her as best he could. Everything was so bizarre, so unbelievable, that he felt his mind heave as if to reject it. Like a stomach that had taken poison, it clenched and tried to expel it. 'Pashe,' he said, 'what has happened? What has happened?'

'He came for us in the night,' said pashe unexpectedly.

'What?' replied Tighe, excitedly. 'Will you speak to me now, pashe? Pashe?' But no matter how he prompted, she would say nothing else.

After a while he began to get cramp in his arm, so he disentangled it and stood up. He paced about the space, examined the Wizard's cradle, the curiously shaped control mechanisms, the images of blurring world-wall on the screen. He tried sitting in the Wizard's cradle, but the device ejected him with a metallic spasm and he nearly collapsed face down on the floor.

Soon enough he became thoroughly bored. He thought through all the things that the Wizard had said; his strange, oddly accented delivery, his high-pitched voice. *There is a mystery about the world which you do not comprehend.* Everything was connected. Somewhere was the key.

He tried lying down and going to sleep, but he wasn't tired. Images from the day hurtled round his mind. The Manmonger, with a perfectly circular hole carved cleanly out of his chest, tumbling forward in death. The way the Wizard's craft had seemed to fly right out of the sun. His pashe.

He got up and went over to his pashe, and hugged her again. 'You and me, pashe,' he said, 'together we are strong, I think. Together we will . . .'

310

but he broke off, looking around himself nervously. Who knew how the Wizard worked? What if he were eavesdropping on them at that very time?

Hours passed. Tighe occupied some of the time staring intently at the controls of the Wizard's machine. There were a number of identical-looking protrusions, like metallic thumbs, and a series of star-crossed indentations in the smooth metal. He tried fiddling with the levers, prodding his fingernails into the indentations, but it had no effect.

He sat for a long time on the floor. What he had taken to be merely decorative metal studs, fixed into the floor, were in fact something else. With a mesmerising slowness they moved over the metal. As Tighe watched he could see that they all changed position together, so that the regularity of the pattern they formed stayed the same. He tried prising one up from the floor with his thumbnail and it flipped up easily. Underneath was a tiny hole, with several striations leading into it from the rim. It felt like a slightly humped metal coin in his hand. Tighe replaced it on the floor, deliberately out of pattern with the others. Slowly, over a period of about an hour, all the other nubbins adjusted themselves until the pattern was restored. Tighe had no idea what the function of these tiny machines might be.

Soon enough he became hungry, and thirsty. There were several doors that opened out from the metal podium underneath the screens, and inside one of these Tighe found a metallic flask with some fluid inside. He tasted it tentatively, and swallowed it. It was faintly bitter, but fairly refreshing. He rummaged through the cupboard, but found nothing else to eat or drink.

He offered the flask to his pashe and she took it without a word, swigging and returning it to him.

He paced around the lower room; tried the upper hatch again, hung from the ladder like a bored monkey. After a while he lay down on the floor and slept.

When he woke, nothing in the tiny room had changed. His pashe was sitting in exactly the same posture, staring into nothing. He paced around again, checked the images on the screen, and felt his anger grow. Climbing the ladder he started banging on the hatch. 'Wizard! Wizard! Wake yourself – how long must you sleep?'

This produced no reaction. Eventually Tighe's arm grew tired. He sat on the floor and swigged from the metal flask, offered it again to his pashe. Then he tried sitting in the Wizard's metal cradle, but it ejected him again. He flew up and landed on his feet – more elegantly than before, this time, because he had been expecting the thrust. He tried once again. It was not painful and even had a pleasant aspect to it. He peered closely at the seat of the cradle, and sat in it again. The metal itself deformed and buckled to throw him off. It was remarkable.

He turned his attention to the screens again, and started fiddling with the controls. The whole craft shuddered and skittered left-right, yawing and pitching. Tighe threw himself backwards, away from the controls, terrified that he had accidentally done something that would destroy the whole machine and them all along with it. The floor rocked more gently and the images on the screen slowed. Then it stabilised and settled. Tighe felt a tight pressure in his bladder, but he controlled himself. He sat down or rather half collapsed; his heart was thundering. Sweat had oozed out of the skin of his face. His hand was trembling.

With a squeak the hatch opened and the Wizard's black-clad legs appeared, fumbling their way down the ladder. His high whistly voice followed. 'Ten hours! A little less! Really not *enough*, though I'm not one to complain.' He stepped on to the floor and stalked over to the screens, his uncanny leather face blank. The images on the screen showed that they were stationary; a view of rocky wall patched over with white was in every corner.

Tighe's breathing was settling. He was still startled, but not so much as to miss the slight pressure the Wizard applied to a point on the underside of one of the back bars of his cradle. He settled himself down and fiddled with the controls.

Tighe debated with himself and decided that it would be better to be honest from the beginning. 'I touched the controls, Master Wizard,' he said in Imperial, looking bashfully at the floor.

'Of course you did, my beautiful youngster,' said the Wizard, without looking over. 'I would expect nothing less. But you are locked out, so your touch counts for nothing.' He looked round with his grotesque smile. 'Did you think you interrupted the flight of my machine with your tinkering?' This idea seemed to amuse him, for he grinned to himself. 'Nothing so dramatic. No, the craft responds to the fluctuations in the gravity. As we approach the East Pole, gravity lessens and the flow tightens. My beautiful machine functions so smoothly in a conventional gravity, but it is calibrated to operate with a ninety-degree interface. Digging its gluon-expression into the flow-lines at exactly ninety degrees for absolute stability. This far east, the angle closes and we will find our platform less solid.'

Almost all of this went over Tighe's head, but he picked up the one phrase. 'East Pole?' he asked, standing unsteadily. His breathing was still sharp and shallow, but the fright had focused his mind more acutely. 'Is this our destination, Master Wizard?'

'Well observed,' said the Wizard. He spun his cradle around and looked at Tighe. 'Yours is a fine intelligence, my beautiful one.'

'Is this *pole*', said Tighe, uncertainly, 'the eastward limit of the wall?' He had a hazy notion of an enormous flagpole, towering into the sky marking the furthest extremity of the wall itself. And beyond? The blueness of infinity, reaching for ever. 'Is there a pole at the western edge as well?'

'You are amusing,' said the Wizard, although he didn't sound amused. 'You picture, perhaps, a giant trunk of wood, stretching up hundreds of miles.'

Tighe couldn't think of a reply to this.

'The worldwall', said the Wizard, with an airy gesture of his right hand, 'is not as you think it is.'

The superior air of the man, with his distorted face and eccentric manner, sparked a feeling of resentment in the exact centre of Tighe's head. He felt his eyeballs heat up with annoyance. 'I know the secret of the worldwall!' he blurted. 'You think I am a boy, that I know nothing. But I am not! I have been a warrior and I have fought monsters. I have learned the secrets of the wall.' Tears were pricking his eyes now and he fought them back with a furious inner self-chastisement. To cry, in front of him? No! 'I know more than you think.'

There was a strange moment of silence.

'So', said the Wizard slowly, 'you know the secret of the wall, do you? But, do you really? You are a remarkable boy. Your beauty is matched by your ability to say the surprising things.' He inclined his head. 'And what is the secret that you know?'

Tighe felt, suddenly, inhibited from saying anything more. He wasn't sure why; he didn't regard what he knew as a *secret* exactly. But there was something menacing, something that might have been an edge of ridicule, in the Wizard's manner. He turned and went over to where his pashe was sitting on the ground, to sit beside her.

The Wizard was watching him, waiting for him to reply. The silence stretched uncomfortably.

'There is a Door in the wall,' Tighe said eventually. 'It leads through to God.'

'Really?' said the Wizard. His leather face was beyond expression.

'No,' said Tighe, stung despite himself. 'There is. The Imperial Popes put together a mighty army to capture this Door. That was the army in which I fought.'

'I saw your fighting', said the Wizard, his leather lips stretching to the merest smile, 'on one of my screens.' He gestured over his shoulder.

Tighe understood that the allusion was to his flight away from the battle and towards the Meshwood. He ground his teeth together. 'I know more,' he said. 'God lives at the foot of the wall, not on the top at all. Every morning he hurls the sun over the wall to combat his enemies.'

'To combat', repeated the Wizard neutrally, 'his enemies.'

Saying this, in so many words, was making Tighe uncomfortably aware of how thin his explanations sounded. He struggled to find a means of conveying the potency of the idea; of the way the thought of God lurking at the base of things, of God hurling the flaming boulder with main force of his strong arm, of the eternal war between cosmic forces separated only by the thinnest of walls – to make the Wizard understand how intoxicating this notion was. He hummed, tried again. 'The wall is there to separate out good and evil,' he said. 'The wall is . . .' But he stopped.

'Go on,' prompted the Wizard.

'The wall is small,' said Tighe, in a cowed voice. 'That is the secret I have come to comprehend. It seems big, but it is not big. It is we who are small. The wall is a toy, built by a small-minded god – by a child god, perhaps. Populated with miniatures.' He stopped. He had spoken the mystery of mysteries.

'What ingenuity!' declared the Wizard. 'But quite, quite wrong. The wall is not tiny!'

Tighe looked up at him. 'How do you know?'

'Believe me, I know. I have travelled widely over the wall. And I remember, I remember because I am older than you can imagine. But I am always impressed, my philosophical fruitling, at the perplexity people wrap themselves in when contemplating simple matters.' He sucked in a large breath.

There was a silence for the space of seven heartbeats.

'Now,' said the Wizard, 'shall I tell you what the wall is?'

3

The floor wobbled and Tighe cried out in fear. The Wizard swivelled his cradle around and began fiddling with his devices. 'No requirement for alarm,' he squeaked. 'These are merely the manner of perturbations we must expect this far east. We'll have to proceed much more slowly from here. But we shall proceed! Let me show you the East Pole, my charming one. Few humans have seen it; fewer still have seen it and lived.'

There was a dry hiccoughing sound in the Wizard's throat; it took a moment for Tighe to realise that this was laughter.

'Who are you, Master Wizard?' Tighe asked, feeling a profound sense of discomfort. 'What have you to do with me? With my family? Why . . . ?' but there were so many questions that they collapsed together in Tighe's mind. There was no way he could ask all of them at once.

'Your skin,' Tighe said shortly. 'Why is your skin, so . . . so . . .'

'So what? So unusual? Or were you about to say something like *so grotesque*? It is a good skin, my delicate-complexioned boy. A strong skin. It is tanned leather, laid over a network of fine-woven filament wire and genbonded underneath with vital carapace that connects it to a living subcutaneous layer of fascia. But these words mean nothing at all to you, do they? Eeh, poor ignorant boy. My skin. My skin is a good place to start, I think. It is stronger than your skin; and much more durable. It suits me better. But it can only be because of a command of pollenmachines, and a sense of the workings of technology, that derives from an earlier age. You have heard of this earlier age?'

Tighe was rolling his lower lip between his thumb and forefinger; one of his expressions of nervousness. He did not reply.

'But of course you have heard of this age!' said the Wizard. 'The evidence for it is all around; the old machines, the screens and pieces of time-stained electronics that are traded back and forth. The structures, the manrock, the archaeological evidence. The very metal out of which are made the tubes for military rifles – nobody actually *makes* metal any more. It all derives from the past, great age. How could you not notice these things? Or did you notice them and ignore them? The stories are of an age of wonder and then a fall. Always a fall. Humanity always thinks of itself as balanced most precariously on the edge of things; as already falling, already defined by the Fall.' The Wizard chuckled his dry, spooky laugh again.

'Fall,' said Tighe, in a thin voice.

'Did you ever wonder about that past age?' asked the Wizard.

'They built this,' said Tighe, with a sudden burst of understanding, 'your machine.'

'They did. Well, not exactly; but this machine does indeed derive from their antique technology. Many of the parts are old; and the décor,' he gestured at the richly hung walls, 'that too. Once every man and every woman had the skills to make such machines as this. Once *we* all had those skills.'

'Why did we lose the skills?' asked Tighe.

'*We* did not. *You* did, I concede. You and your people, not I. But that is a function, I think, of population. A degree of technological advantage can only be maintained in a large enough population base. How many people inhabit the world today? Some few thousands? It is insufficient – and you,' he said, gesturing at Tighe with one hand, 'you do not understand anything I am saying, do you?'

Tighe fiddled with his lower lip, put his eyes to the floor.

'You are talking about pollenmachines,' he said, sulkily. 'The bolts on the floor – they are pollenmachines.'

'Dear me no; they're much too large. They are simply cleaning devices. They keep everything spotless inside here, crawling back and forth, very simple machines. Pollenmachines are much more intricate. But I can see this is going to be harder than I thought. Tell me this, my dazzle-eyed young man. How tall do you think the wall is?'

'How tall?'

'Yes. Hundreds of miles, perhaps. Thousands?'

Tighe had often pondered exactly this question when he had been younger. 'From its base to its top?' he said. 'Thousands.'

'We could travel upwards,' said the Wizard. 'In my machine, if you would like to undertake the journey. We could travel upwall thousands of miles. I have done it.'

Tighe caught his breath. 'Have you been to the top of the wall?' he gasped. 'All the way to the top? And is it true – does God live there, or below?'

'There is no top to the wall,' said the Wizard. 'You can travel up for ever; you can travel down for ever, if you wish.'

Tighe digested this. 'The wall goes on for ever,' he said. Somehow that sounded somehow right, somehow appropriate to the mystery of the wall. 'But how can you know it is endless?' he asked. 'You cannot have travelled up the wall for ever. And', a second objection occurred to him, 'if the wall has no top and no bottom, then where does God reside?'

'Ah,' said the Wizard. 'God. But I think we are all three of us hungry.'

He pulled out a parcel from a pouch by his belly and unwrapped some more of his delicious meat-cake, followed by a metal flask identical to the one Tighe had discovered in the cupboard under the control panel. He swiftly divided the food three ways and handed the smallest portion to pashe. She munched it absently.

Tighe devoured his portion in a few mouthfuls and drank deep of the bitter tingly fluid in the flask. It made his thoughts blur a little, but he soon refocused himself. The Wizard himself picked at his food without energy, breaking off tiny fragments of meat-cake between thumb and forefinger and popping them delicately between his black leather lips.

'What is wrong with my pashe, Master Wizard?' Tighe asked, reverting to Imperial again, to express deference. 'She is not herself.'

'You speak more truth than you know,' said the Wizard. 'There has been a – shall we say, a cortical diminishment. Unfortunate, but necessary. She does not suffer, that is the important thing; but it would take me too long to explain to you the precise nature of the cerebellar microplaque operation that obtains in her skull.' He lifted the flask to his own lips and let a tiny dribble pour into his mouth. 'Where was I?' he asked, picking again at his food.

'I do not know, Master Wizard,' said Tighe. 'I find it difficult to follow your explanations.' He was speaking the Imperial tongue, thinking this would find favour with the Wizard, but his leather face creased momentarily.

'Don't chatter so in Imperial,' he said, crossly in the village tongue. 'It's hard enough explaining these things to you in the first place, without your having to translate them into a foreign language in your head! Speak your native tongue, boy!'

He nibbled another morsel.

'Let us talk about gravity, my son,' he said. 'Gravity. What else is it that makes the world so precarious a place? And precariousness is, after all, the condition of existence. It has been my struggle to escape the precariousness that defines the rest of humanity. Most of the rest of humanity, I should say, for neither I nor my Lover are defined by our precariousness.'

Tighe looked up. The thought of so grotesque an individual having a lover made him queasy in his stomach. 'Your Lover, Mister Wizard?' he asked.

The Wizard nodded. 'You are surprised because you find my face hideous. Your failing, my pretty one, not mine. I have several Lovers and they are all myself. We go to the East Pole because that is the best place to hide from them. From one in particular, who has devoted himself to destroying me. As if he can destroy me! It would be destroying himself. We are the same. But', he said, waggling his head with annoyance, 'we are not talking about my Lover, fascinating though I find the topic. We are talking, my dear boy, about gravity.'

'Gravity,' said Tighe.

'You understand gravity?' prompted the Wizard.

Tighe swallowed. The taste of the meat-cake was fading from his tongue and he mourned its passing. 'I understand the word, Wizard,' he replied.

The Wizard seemed to find this amusing; he scraped out his dry laugh and nodded. 'An excellent answer, my young monkey,' he said. 'Worth a philosopher's salary. Yes, human beings have spent their lives trying to understand gravity. And yet it defines us. Who built the wall?'

Tighe thought at first that this was a rhetorical question, so he didn't answer. He was busy running his tongue into the coign of his mouth, where the last crumbs of meat lurked behind his teeth. When the Wizard stopped, and Tighe realised that he had directed the question at him, he looked up.

'I'm sorry, Wizard?'

'Who built the wall, boy?'

'God,' said Tighe, automatically.

'Man,' returned the Wizard. 'Man built the wall. *We* built it.'

Tighe thought about this. 'Not possible, though, Mister Wizard,' he returned. 'How can man build something so high that it goes on for ever?' He had, none the less, a sudden, piercing sense of the enormity of such an undertaking. Hundreds of people, hauling enormous blocks of stone together one after the other, building a wall on such a scale. Hundreds and hundreds. How many generations would it take? What now-lost skills of engineering? But it was a false image; it was nonsense.

'I never said', replied the Wizard, 'that the wall was infinite in proportions. That was your contribution. I said that the wall has no top, nor bottom; and neither has it.'

'I do not understand,' said Tighe.

'When I say that man built the wall,' said the Wizard in gentle tones, 'I mean that he altered his world and turned it into the worldwall. It is gravity, do you understand?'

'No, Wizard.'

'Of course not. Let me explain. Gravity changed. You know what gravity is – it pulls us down. If we step off a ladder, it pulls us down to the floor. If we step off a ledge, it pulls us down through the sky. I hardly need to tell you this! You fell!'

'I fell,' said Tighe.

'Gravity pulled you down. Do you see? Gravity runs parallel to the world and that is what defines the world we live in. But it used not to be that way. Once, and it was some hundreds of years ago, gravity pulled in a different direction.'

Tighe pondered. 'What other direction could there be?' he asked.

'Not parallel to the world, but at a ninety-degree angle to it. Imagine that!'

But Tighe could not imagine it. 'I don't understand,' he said.

'Before worldwall there was flat-earth,' said the Wizard. 'Try to enter imaginatively into such a place, my bright boy. The wall was not up, nor down, but a huge shelf, a never-ending shelf that stretched flat on all sides. That was because gravity in those days ran at ninety degrees to its way now. This is, in fact, the way gravity runs most elsewhere in the Universe; on other worlds, on other stars. And our world, that we call the worldwall – our world still orbits around the sun, and the sun still pulls us inwards with perpendicular gravitational attraction, or we would not so orbit. This is physics, my sweet-smelling child; please pay attention.'

'Yes, Wizard,' replied Tighe, baffled.

'Once, our world was a sort of sun; it shone with the light made by its people and glittered out into the void. Like the sun it had its own planet, orbiting the world, which was called moon. After the gravity changed we lost the moon, which ran its own way. These days the place of turbulence, the point at which gravity starts to angle away from its universal direction, is only a few thousand yards out. But it seems that immediately after gravity changed this boundary fluctuated; it spooled and whirled, like water that is unruly, and the boundary whirled outwards in a great Van Eder pattern. It caught the moon, and the moon fell suddenly and sped away. But, according to my Lover – who has many interesting theories about this time of change – it was the vastness of the impulse required to accelerate the moon out of its orbit, the orbit it had maintained for so many millennia, that reined the Van Eder pattern back towards the earth. Instead of spreading ever outwards in every-weakening spirals, the pattern of changed gravity shrank back to this world. It might have shrunk wholly to the centre of the planet and we would have had the old world restored to us. But this was not the way things happened. Instead it settled into its current pattern.'

'This', said Tighe, with a hazy sense of what the Wizard was talking about, '– you mean, the Pause.'

'The Pause,' said the Wizard. 'Is that what you call it?'

'Kite-pilots know this,' said Tighe. 'You can fly only so far from the wall before you reach the Pause. Then you can fly no further.'

'Well, exactly,' said the Wizard. 'That is the Pause, then. A good name for the phenomenon. How exciting, my witty adventurer! You bring tales from the boundary of the world. This is the boundary between the spiral of gravity that surrounds our world and the perpendicular force that applies elsewhere. As for the moon, it fell away from us, and in the vacuum of space there is none to slow its fall and it sped so fast it ran clear free of its one-time owner. Now it is out there on its own, and my Lover – who has examined it – says that its orbit is erratic, sunwards. Like as not, it will become a moon for another world, for Venus most say; and Venus is a foul world, acid and hot. Perhaps our moon will calm the world of Venus. Ah, the telescopic view of it makes it seem severely beautiful, fine and silver, etched with delicate patterns and designs like art-ware! I can imagine that having the moon will shake up the stagnant acid of Venus's world and maybe bring about a better place. Maybe a place for a new life, so perhaps the changing of gravity will bring great good in the universe.'

The Wizard stopped, as if musing. But Tighe had lost track of what he was saying. 'Master Wizard,' he said, in Imperial, and then stopped himself. 'Mister Wizard,' he said in his native tongue. 'I do not understand. How can gravity change? How was the world before?'

'Like,' said the Wizard with a hush of irritation, 'like a never-ending shelf that stretched flat on all sides. Do listen! Handsome, but not so bright, not so bright.' He shook his leather head. 'Now, I am telling you about the change in things, and they changed a little before I was born; but this is a true history none the less. The world stretched flat on all sides because gravity ran perpendicular, as is its way. *Millions* lived on the world – *billions* – and you cannot even imagine such a word. Your language does not even possess such a word because you have no call for numbers so large.'

'Gravity,' said Tighe. 'Did it change often?'

'No, no, you don't understand. It changed once, catastrophically. That is the true history I am telling you. Please listen! This explains the world – no small-scale model, no mythical doors through the world, but the way things actually are. It is hard because you have never thought of these issues before.'

'I have!' retorted Tighe. He remembered his childhood on the sunny ledges, staring out at the sky, pondering the nature of things.

'Be quiet, my dear one. Now: gravity. Think of gravity, I request you: think of a great fabric, which is the fabric of space. Bodies such as the sun, the planets, make dents in this cloth, and the lines of force of space-time run down towards the centre of these dips. In the rest of the universe this is the way; but on our world gravity twisted. The earth still makes the same dip in space-time, still orbits the sun in its old path. But a traveller from outside coming along those lines of force will find herself suddenly jolted to the side; in the heart of the gravity well the lines of force run circular about the bottom point. It is like water running down a plug-hole. Well, that is a crude analogy, but it is the best I can manage. If only you possessed a proper physical education.'

'Physical education?'

'An *education* in *physics*, my silk-haired young darling. It changed, suddenly. And the changing of gravity brought about great suffering on this world, on our world. There were *billions* living here. And that word means thousand of million, such that a *million* means thousand of thousand. Your mind rebels against such profusion of people, I can see, but think! If the wall were flattened and ran all the world about, would there not be space for billions? Those places where the wall is smoothest were the most populous, and those places where we now live, the bumps and crevasses, were the least. So it was that this event has turned the world upside down.'

'Upside down?' asked Tighe, genuinely confused now.

'A figure of speech,' snapped the Wizard. 'Please don't feel compelled to be so literal, sweet one. I meant: turned the world through ninety degrees.'

He leant forward to peer closely at Tighe and then settled back in his cradle, apparently satisfied with what he saw.

'You want to know', he said, softly, 'how this great change happened?'

'Yes,' said Tighe hesitantly. He was uncertain what to say.

'Human beings generate energies for their uses. In the more distant times, and mostly today, energy generation was mostly heat, mostly the burning of materials; sometimes heat is converted into electricity by under-efficient means. *Underefficient power-source* is one where more power is fed into the system than is derived from it; and such was the way for many years. *Overefficient power-source* is one where more power is derived from the system than is fed into it. When overefficient power was lighted upon, the people blessed it. They called it Power-at-Zero, and it depended upon the oscillation of electrical current at high frequency to create electro-magnetic harmonics that bled power from the fabric of space-time. Machines were converted, mostly to use the P-at-Z to take apart water into *Oxygen* and *Hydrogen*, and use the one to combust the other, and so were machines powered. It is a P-at-Z machine that powers my engines here, that moves my craft about. But there was a great danger in the ubiquity with which these machines were once used. For gravity is part of the space-time fabric; it is dents in that fabric – remember I explained that to you? Down-pulling dips and holes. When power is taken from the fabric of space-time for a small thing, the whole fabric distorts very minutely, to accommodate the loss. But with sudden large power drains the fabric can suddenly ripple, flex. This is what happened with us. The fabric was distorted, it rippled and shifted. The flow of gravity changed in the dip in space-time caused by the weight of our world. Before it had flowed from the outer boundaries of the dip, where it was weakest, to the middle of the dip, where it was strongest – do you see? The inverse square law? After, it flowed turnways, rotating around the dip as the world turned. All that had been down before became to-the-side; all that was then called west became upwall. That which used to be called east became downwall. The old North Pole and the old South Pole became the left-most and right-most reaches of the wall; became called east and west by many peoples. Now, am I reaching you at all with any of this? Am I getting through to you?'

Tighe paused. He didn't want to offend the Wizard. 'I think so,' he said, slowly. 'Only, I do not understand the fabric you are talking about. What is this cloth? How does it fit into the story?'

The Wizard whistled and span through three hundred and sixty degrees in his cradle. 'No, no, no,' he said. 'You misunderstand. I apologise, the analogy with the fabric was ill judged. Let me try again. Have you ever wondered what gravity *is*?'

Tighe shut his eyes. 'It pulls us down,' he said.

'Yes, yes, that is what it *does*. Shall I tell you what it *is*? Well, all things are made of atoms. You have heard of this fact?'

'Of course,' said Tighe. 'Atoms are very small. The smallest thing.'

'Not the very smallest, as it turns out, but yes, for our purposes. Mass is the accumulation of atoms. But even where there is no mass, even in the vacuum of space, there is subatomic activity. Particles even smaller than atoms come into being and wink out of existence in a turmoil of subatomic creation and cancellation; particles and anti-particles. This is the real nature of the universe at the most fundamental level, this seething and boiling of primal matter, creating and destroying.

'Where does this happen?' said Tighe. He didn't like the sound of this description: it sounded violent, like the boiling of water over a fire. Scalding. Was this how the Wizard saw the universe?

'All around us! All through the universe – it's too small for you to *see*, you literal-minded beauty. But this is what space-time *is*, this constant seething of subatomic activity. The important thing to realise about this constant activity is that it is not random, not swirling around in no particular direction. It has a larger pattern to it, it has a *grain*, shall we say, like the grain in wood. These subatomic events all happen in a certain way following a certain grain, and this grain is what we call gravity. Where there are more atomic structures – which is to say, where there is greater mass – the trajectories of this subatomic foaming become shorter and passage along them becomes quicker, which is another way of saying that gravity becomes greater. Away from atomic massing, the trajectories become longer and gravity is weaker. Yes? Yes? Now, the point about Power-at-

322

Zero technologies is that they derived their power from this quantum foam. Gravity is a weak force, but it accumulates; and it is possible to steal billions of quanta of energy from the foam and accumulate as much power as you like without much difficulty. But there is a price to pay in the long run; there always is. Humanity discovered this. Eventually the drain on the subatomic foam was so intense in one place, one concentration of atomic mass we call the world we live on, that it sheared the grain of the subatomic flux right around through ninety degrees.'

The Wizard sat back, looking pleased with himself. Then his leather face shifted expression minutely and he looked cross. 'This means nothing to you, does it?' he barked. 'Nothing at all!' He ran a hand over his leathern face. 'Never mind. Never mind. It's not your learning I want you for, not your *education*. It is your *capacity* for learning, well yes, that's the truth, the truth. And for the sake of that, please tell me that you understand something of what I've been telling you.'

Tighe swallowed. 'Gravity changed,' he said.

'Yes. Hundreds of years ago now, that's right.'

'It used to be upside down, but the fabric was torn.'

'Well,' squeaked the Wizard. 'In a manner of speaking. Ninety degrees, boy! Ninety degrees.'

'Ninety degrees,' gabbled Tighe quickly.

'Well, anyway,' said the Wizard. 'I'm older than you can imagine, but I'm not old enough to remember those events *exactly*. Old enough to get tired; and on only ten hours' sleep you can't expect me to be the most cogent of teachers.'

'No, sir,' said Tighe.

'Don't call me sir,' said the Wizard languidly. He stretched himself out, like a monkey stretching after a meal.

4

There was a silence for a long while. Tighe sat, motionless, overawed by the incomprehensible narrative the Wizard had just spun out.

'Wizard?' he asked, softly. 'Wizard?'

But the Wizard seemed to have fallen asleep in the cradle. There was a faint snoring sound coming from his mouth.

Gingerly Tighe got to his feet. He had the feeling that this was some sort of opportunity, but he didn't know what to do. Perhaps if he were able to bind the Wizard up somehow? To hold him hostage? Force him to fly them all back to the village. Yes, that was a plan.

He took a step towards the sleeping figure.

At once the Wizard woke up. 'Where was I?' he demanded immediately.

Tighe pulled his foot back and sat down. 'Master?'

'What was I saying before I fell asleep there?'

'The world turned upside down,' said Tighe, his heart hammering. 'The catastrophe.'

'Oh, yes,' said the Wizard. 'Oh yes! Oh, the terrors of days immediately after gravity changed! You must understand the world. It was flat – flat – it lay flat in all directions. It was mostly covered with water, water that lay as it were in pools, pools that stretched for thousands of square miles. Two-thirds of the world was covered by water, imagine that! After gravity changed, this water all went into the air and fell downways. It rained for years. Much more than rain at first; great shire-sized sheets of water falling, resolving itself eventually into a never-ending downpour of fat raindrops. People had built houses, built cars and machines, and all were resting flat on the ground. Most things went into the air and fell downways. Some people were out, doing their people-things, when the change happened: they were walking on the flat, or sleeping in houses that could not stay fixed to the wall after gravity changed. Most people went into the air and fell; they simply fell. They fell and crashed against the other flying debris, or were smashed against the wall like rubbish, or were simply plucked to pieces by the ferocity of the tempest winds. Most of all the rain fell; it was rain muddy with all the loose earth and sand that was also in the air. Rain that was heavy, falling as fast as it could fall round and around the world. Raindrops like bullets, rain that killed many of those who had managed to avoid falling by clinging to the new crags. Rain that shredded up those few up in the air in aircraft that were able to fly on and not crash into the wall. And the wind howling like a beast. The rain fell for years and the wind howled for years. Clouds that moved fast as falling boulders filled the sky and blocked out the sun. And it grew very cold.'

As if in response to his words, the floor of the craft shifted and trembled. The Wizard paused and checked his screens. They showed a slow passage of worldwall now, a stately procession of white-marked rock. They were moving much more slowly, still going east. He turned back to face Tighe again. 'Nothing to worry about,' he said. 'There will be these hiccoughs, my young one.'

Tighe inched closer to his pashe and put his arm around her.

'Catastrophe,' said the Wizard, gesturing in the air with his arm. 'Apocalypse. People believed it was the ending of things. And indeed it might all have ended there as many survivors thought it would. Many threw themselves into the void with prayers to their gods on their lips. Many starved, huddling in the caves formed by cellars from which the housetop had been ripped away. Some survived for a time, in subterranean tunnels living off ratmeat and micemeat, in government bunkers eating the metal-tinned food laid by for emergencies. Some found themselves somehow on one of the ledges, not fallen off or blown away, and were able to dig themselves into crevices. Sometimes food would fall against the wall and wedge there. Water was so plentiful people could drown breathing the air, but it was salt water and not drinkable. But then, as now, there were springs and spouts of water from the wall. By all accounts, the first year was the worst and the second year lessened the suffering. Rain and snow.'

'Snow?' Tighe asked. He was following few of the details of this latest narrative of the Wizard's, except to glean a sense of terrible disaster and people falling off the world.

'Oh, you won't know that. It happens almost never towards the equator of the worldwall, where the winds are too warm – heated by the sun, sinking when they cool.'

'Equator?'

'The centre line of the worldwall,' said the Wizard quickly. 'It runs from bottom to top at the very centre. The fattest portion of our twisted globe. But out near the West and East Poles, where we are going, there are still squalls of snow. *Snow* is where frozen water falls in drops and flakes from the sky.'

'Oh,' said Tighe, little illuminated.

'Well, anyway, it rained. Perhaps the rain would have fallen for ever;

perhaps the wind would never have relented. But the water was slowly taken out of the atmosphere by freezing. It settled on the far-eastern and far-western ledges as snow and ice, and much water was held there; but more found its way to the graveyard of water at the Poles. Before gravity changed, the Poles had been frozen, the coldest parts of the world because those parts were furthest from the Sun. But before gravity changed the Poles had been flat, and gravity had worked there just the same as it worked all over the world, pulling people flat against the ground. Now, the nature of the Poles has changed. At the East Pole and the West Pole the flow of gravity is weakest. The downward flux is least. To begin with, this meant that snow and ice from the Poles were continually being ripped by the speed of the more equatorial winds and thrown into the atmosphere, but with time the system began to approach an equilibrium. Water settled at the Poles as snow and ice and accumulated there. Before gravity changed, our world was an almost perfect sphere, and indeed was a little flattened at the Poles. Now – as we shall see when we arrive there – there are two great Polar Promontories, oceans' worth of water frozen into two massive mountains. There in the cold, where the pull of gravity is the least. Earth, which was orange-shaped before gravity changed, has become lemon-shaped now.'

'Orange?' asked Tighe, completely confused.

'*Orange* is a fruit named for its colour, which is also perfectly spherical. It grows on the trees, you know. A *lemon* is another species of fruit, shaped like the world. But why am I telling you this? This means nothing to you. The important thing for you to realise is that the rain did stop. So much of the water in the atmosphere was frozen out that, although the rain fell for a decade, the air did eventually clear. Most of the animals had died, along with most people, but different ledges had preserved different livestock, a little here, a little there. Life started again. So many challenges! The atmosphere – that's very different now.'

'Is it?'

'Yes, it tends to pull down with gravity. It used to rest on the ground, now it rests only on itself. But it heats in the day and starts to rise, or at least stops falling. But then it chills at night and falls faster. Where day and night meet – dawn, dusk – there are ferocious gales, *very* dangerous. Of course, those become less the further towards the Poles one travels. Life manages, somehow.'

5

Tighe scratched at his head. The story was so ornate, so full of inexplicable terms and so ungainly, that he had difficulty even remembering most of it, let alone believing it. Something bad had happened, that much was certain. It was a punishment, perhaps; God's punishment for crimes committed by humanity. The world had been an enormous shelf, nothing but shelf all around; and now God had condemned everybody to the precariousness of the worldwall.

'I think,' he said, 'I think I understand.'

'I think you're lying,' said the Wizard, without heat, 'but it matters very little, I'm afraid. The important thing to keep in mind is the fact that the world was once flat and might be again.'

'Might be again?'

'Oh, yes,' said the Wizard. 'We have to relinquish command to the laws of thermodynamics, to the essence of the universe. That is simply the way it is, my bright-toothed beauty. If a man were to fall from a ledge he might fall for ever, passing round and around the world. Well, he would probably be dashed against the wall into pieces, or torn apart by winds, but you see the point I'm trying to make. It violates the law of physics that a body might fall for ever; accordingly, logically, there must come a time in the future when gravity will change again. This will probably mean the wall tilting flat again and humankind resuming its old way of living. Things will again be flat. Or perhaps some further change will come, something we cannot anticipate – a further twist in the contorted rag of space-time, something beyond our comprehension. When will this second apocalypse come? That is the biggest of questions. That is the question that my Lover is most centrally concerned with.'

'Your Lover,' said Tighe.

'The chief amongst my Lovers,' said the leathern man, 'at any rate. He understands that every action of any mass in this system is draining energy from somewhere. Energy is not free, my pretty child. Every person who dips their cup into the never-ending flow of gravity that circles our world draws energy from the greater fabric of space-time. One theory of physics suggests that when this drain on the larger fabric becomes too great for its balance to be maintained, then, as before, change will flip our world into some new gravitational permutation. But this could happen in one hour's time; or one year's; or a thousand years from here. The calculations are rather ambiguous, I'm afraid to say.'

'What will happen in an hour's time?'

'Almost certainly nothing, my child. I speak only in a general way, as an example.'

There was a silence, broken only by the sound of pashe noisily scratching her shins.

'Well,' said the Wizard, ruminatively. 'I suppose it's a lot to take in. And I haven't slept enough. I need more than ten hours' sleep, I can tell you. It's my age. Something to do with the material with which I've been augmenting my own cerebral cortexes; it needs a lot of serotonin to integrate itself. That's one of the prices for eternal youth.'

He rose from the cradle, his hand sliding surreptitiously under the bar at the back as he said, 'Enough for now.' He crossed the floor and starting climbing back up the ladder. 'You think about what I've said, my young beau,' he said as his head disappeared. 'You'll forgive me for shutting the hatch behind myself. It's not that I don't trust you, as I'm certain you realise. But I sleep better with a certain degree of security.'

The hatch shut and Tighe was left alone with his pashe.

Tighe waited a moment and then stood up and went over to the cradle. Groping under the bar at the rear, he found a tiny scratch that tingled a little as he touched it. Was it a switch? He lowered himself gingerly into the cradle, but was not ejected from it.

He felt a glow seep through his face; joy. In this one small thing he had outwitted the Wizard, he had mastered one of the Wizard's tricks. If in this, then why not in other things too? Perhaps he could learn to fly the device himself – unlock the controls, to use the Wizard's phrase. Perhaps he could find some way of sealing the Wizard upstairs and then take over the device and fly it back to his village. Take his pashe back home. Surely in the familiar surroundings of the village she would return to her full senses. He looked over to her. She sat, perfectly still, staring into space. 'Pashe,' he said, his success with the cradle emboldening him. He didn't care if the Wizard was eavesdropping: let him eavesdrop! 'Pashe, I shall take you home. I shall, I promise.'

His pashe said nothing; stared ahead.

Tighe turned all his attention to the screens and the controls. The images on all four screens were now of white rock and bulging shapes. Tighe ran his finger round the rim of the control, looking for a switch such as the one that had operated the cradle. He pulled a fingertip all the way along the underside of the panel and then repeated the manoeuvre, but found nothing. Finally he started fiddling randomly with the knobs, hoping that by chance he might strike some constellation of positions that unlocked the panel. But nothing happened.

Eventually he gave up and searched instead through the cupboards underneath the panel. There were some circuitboards, apparently discarded, and plastic-laminated sheets of paper. Tighe brought each one out, but it was impossible to decipher the diagrams on them. Then there were various plastic nobbles and stumps, and a long fluffy piece of thread. Tighe experimented with the idea of using it to garrotte the Wizard – to threaten to strangle him, perhaps, force him to fly back to the village – but when Tighe gave it a sharp tug it snapped. Finally, in the far corner of the cupboard, his groping fingers lighted upon what it took to be a piece of fluff. His heart pulsed with excitement. Drawing it out, he could see that it was one of the dandelion-puff devices with which the Wizard had killed the Manmonger. He held it between his fingers, trembling with excitement. He could use it as a weapon against the Wizard! Perhaps hurt him, or even kill him. Threaten him with it, maybe. Excitedly he held one of the tiny strands so that the miniature kernel dangled, and let go. It drifted slowly to the floor. Disappointed, Tighe picked it up again and peered closely at the centre. Was there a switch somewhere about the device?

There was a loud honk from the control panel.

Startled, guilty, Tighe stuffed the dandelion puff into a pocket, and quickly replaced all the rubbish he had pulled out of the cupboard. The floor wobbled and jerked and the control panel honked again. Tighe looked up, alarmed. The picture on the screens had settled: the image was almost pure white.

He could hear the hatch opening behind him, and he pulled the doors of the cupboard shut and scuttled over the floor to where his pashe sat.

The Wizard descended ponderously, grumbling. 'That wasn't even an hour. It's hardly any use sleeping at all if I only get an hour.' He marched over to his cradle and spoke directly to Tighe – to distract him, Tighe could now see – as his leather fingers fumbled for the switch on the back. 'At least you'll not grow bored, I hope, with all this noise and excitement.' He stopped, stiffened, and turned slowly to face Tighe directly. His brown face was expressionless, impossible to read. 'You are a *quicker* learner than I have given you credit for, my elegant-fingered handsome one. You have discovered the trick with the cradle, I see.'

Tighe looked up at him. 'Wizard,' he said. 'I have.'

'I'm impressed. It pleases me, to be honest. Your brain is a valuable thing and I'm glad to see that it's not a dull one. How many other tricks have you picked up I wonder? But there's no point in dwelling on your triumphs, or you'll grow vain. Do you know what that alarm signifies?'

'No, Wizard.'

'It is my Lover. Or one of them.'

'Your Lover, Wizard.'

'He is not far. I have a proximity alarm. I don't believe he knows about it or he would have done something to cancel it. To disguise himself, perhaps. But it is sounding now, so he is somewhere within fifty kilometres.' The Wizard settled himself easily into his cradle. 'Still, he is not within visual range, so that's something.'

'Is he hunting you, Wizard?'

'He hunt me? Or I him? Well, no, no, to be truthful. He hunts me more than I hunt him. For the time being, at any rate. At least until the harvest in your sweetly shaped head can be drawn out!' The Wizard chuckled to himself, a dry, scraping sound. 'Then perhaps the boot will be on the – on the – my!' The Wizard sat back. 'We're almost there!'

'Almost there?'

'At the East Pole, my lovely.'

'Why is your Lover hunting you, Wizard?'

The Wizard scratched at his ear with a sudden and intimidating ferocity. 'I don't often get *itches*', he said, 'in this particular skin. But when I do get them, they take some serious scratching, let me tell you. No, no, I'm not ignoring your question. It's a good question. I ask it myself sometimes, but with a slightly different inflection. Shall we say that I am too *individual* for his purposes?'

Tighe put his arm around his pashe's unresisting neck.

'You could ask him, were you ever to meet him,' said the Wizard. 'And I can tell you what he would say. He would say that he made me and therefore I am his. Can you believe it?'

'Slavery?' offered Tighe, thinking of the Manmonger.

'Oh, more intense, more intense. It is true, I suppose, that he made me; but he was in his turn made. These squabbles amongst us are misdirected. We are all Lovers, after all. He and I. I and you.' The dark face turned to Tighe. 'We are the same, after all.'

'Wizard,' said Tighe, trying hard to control his breathing. 'Where is my pahe? You must have picked him up when you picked up my pashe, after all.'

'I do not believe', said the Wizard, 'that my Lover will find us just yet. And in half an hour I can position myself over the Pole and we'll be safer than we were.'

He touched one of the knobs and the craft dropped and turned slowly. For several minutes he stared intently at the screens, shifting the angle and position of the craft. The whole thing wobbled and jerked; Tighe began to feel sick. Suddenly out of nowhere, his pashe spoke, loudly, 'Coming to get us, wake up, wake up!' Her eyes were wide. But when Tighe hugged her and spoke soothing words to her, she calmed down and settled back into her usual placid staring.

'What will this Lover of yours do, Mister Wizard,' asked Tighe, 'should he ever catch up with us?'

'Oh, he'd be cross,' said the Wizard. 'There's no doubt of that. Cross with me. He'd take you, and probably extract things now without waiting, which – in my opinion – would be a mistake. There are large stakes being played for here! The whole world! He'd be cross and he'd take it out on us. For instance, I don't believe he'd have a use for your pashe, there – that woman there you're so fond of. There's nothing in her to interest him now; he'd discard her. So you should be grateful to me. My Lover and I, we are identical in so many ways; but yet I am superior to him. Kinder, stronger, better. I keep your pashe alive, you notice. You must be grateful; you must be loyal.'

With a sudden, painful intensity of realisation Tighe knew then that the Wizard had killed his pahe. Whatever mysterious use he had for Tighe, or for pashe, had not been the case with pahe and he had disposed of him. Tighe clamped his teeth into the flesh of his inside lower lip to prevent himself from calling out with the shock of the revelation.

The craft slewed and slowly turned. Tighe felt queer inside; sick, lighter. There was a hazy dislocation in his sense of balance, as if he were about to fall over even though he remained upright. He put his hand out to steady himself. Nauseous.

Things seemed to be slowing down. The patterns made by the Wizard's cloak as he fiddled with the controls fell limply, in slow motion. Everything swam. 'What's happening?' Tighe asked, his own voice warbling with fear.

'Nearly there,' said the Wizard. 'A little more by way of adjustment.'

There was a bang and the whole room shuddered.

'Fine!' barked the Wizard, apparently pleased with himself. 'That's good. It's always exciting to come to the East Pole. I always feel so exclusive – so few people have been here.'

He leapt from the cradle and walked over to the stairs. With the ghastly distortions of dream logic he leant back as he approached the stairway, until standing by the stair he was at an angle of twenty degrees. Yet he didn't fall over. 'Shall we go out, my sweet one?' he called over, from this impossible posture.

Tighe stared at him.

'Come along. We'll leave your pashe here I think; she's in no state for explorations. But I have some things stored in the snow out here and I think you'll be interested. Stand up, boy!'

In a daze, Tighe got to his feet. As he was rising he got the sudden, horrible sense that he was going to fall forwards; he lurched backwards and banged the back of his head against the wall behind him. The Wizard chuckled in his dry way.

'Take your first steps. This is a strange, rotational gravity situation. The pull shifts from footstep to footstep, but you'll get used to it. Come upstairs.'

Still leaning back the Wizard faced the stairway and pulled himself upright on it, climbing more slowly than usual up the hatch. Tighe rubbed his eyes. The whole thing was too bizarre. He took one step and his stomach heaved. Another step and the whole room around him seemed to distort, the walls looming in drunkenly. By the time he had walked over to the stairway everything was out of alignment; the stair that had seemed straight from where he had been sitting with his pashe now leant away at an angle of twenty degrees, and curved towards the top. He reached out to grab a rung and missed, clutching at air. A second attempt and he still couldn't co-ordinate. The third time he held his hands in front of him and waved them upwards until they connected with the metal of the ladder rung. It all seemed so unreal that Tighe half expected his hands to go right through the material of the ladder.

'At the Poles,' the Wizard was saying, chattering on with more of his incomprehensible explanations, 'at the Poles gravity loops round in a circle with a radius of a few kilometres, or less – you *feel* the arc of gravity here, where in the middle of the world it feels like a straight line. It's a curious sensation, I think you'll agree.'

Pulling himself on to the ladder felt like hanging upside down, and climbing up was extremely hard. He wasn't helped by the fact that, every now and again, the craft would lurch a little, as if unsettled.

He made his way up into the upper room. From somewhere (Tighe couldn't work out exactly where) the Wizard had brought out a body suit. 'You'll need to put this on,' he said. 'It's fierce cold out there. Cold enough to freeze you solid.'

Tighe inspected the suit. It was made of a black material and the inside was as soft as finest goat's fur. He clambered into it, relishing the softness against his skin. It was too large for him, but when he was inside it the Wizard pulled some ruckling threads, which dangled from the belly of the costume, and its legs, arms and torso closed around him.

'Comfortable?'

'Very,' said Tighe, as the Wizard fitted a hood about his head.

'You'll need these as well,' the Wizard said, handing him two gloves. 'The gloves and the boots have special threads in them, do you see? They'll enable you to cling to the side of the wall when it's sheer. Do you see? Do you see?'

Tighe nodded. The hook was shrinking around his head to press tight against his scalp. He felt the ring around his face where the fabric framed his eyes and mouth. 'What about you, Master Wizard?' he asked, in Imperial. The Wizard took his arm and stood them both in the middle of the room.

'Me?'

'Will you not wear warm clothes, Master?' The Wizard was dressed in the loosest black shift and leggings. His brown leather skin was bare from half-way down his forearms; his neck and head and his feet were equally naked. Tighe watched and noticed the Wizard touch the floor with one toe; a delicate, ballet-like gesture.

'No no,' said the Wizard, as they started to rise. 'No need, no need. I told you, there's a microfilament mesh that runs underneath this leather skin of mine. It can heat up to keep me warm, or chill to keep me cool. Necessary,' he confided, leaning closer to Tighe. 'There are no sweat glands in this particular skin, you see.'

As they rose, Tighe felt himself overbalancing, and tried to lean forwards, but the Wizard grabbed him. 'Illusory,' he said. 'You'll fall if you lean too far.'

The roof-hole opened, and a great hissing sound poured in. Tighe looked up, nervous. The sky was full of torn-up fragments of white, buzzing and whirling back and forth.

Then they were on the roof of the Wizard's craft.

6

All around was a blurring of blue and white. It was bitterly cold, just as the Wizard had foretold; colder than Tighe had ever encountered before. Tighe's face juddered with the chill; he felt his sinuses hum. In front of him was what seemed to be an impossibly brief, curving section of wall, with nothing above or below. It was pure white.

A flurry of the white fragments thickened until the whole air was full of them. Then, as abruptly, it cleared and the air was clear. Tighe could see the strange white rock up ahead, marked with thin runnels up and down. But the wall went nowhere; putting his head back he could see clear blue sky above it. The top of the wall!

'Snow,' said the Wizard. He was shouting, to be heard over the rush of air. 'Ice. You've surely not seen them before.'

'Galioshe had a refrigerator, in the village,' Tighe replied, calling loudly to be heard. 'I've seen ice. Never so much though. Wizard – is that truly the top of the wall?'

'What?'

'Is that truly the top of the wall?'

The Wizard shook his head. 'Can't hear you. Hearing not what it should be.'

'I said – can that truly be the *top* of the *wall*?'

'Go and find out,' he said, 'then I'll show you what I've come for. Come to the very end of the earth for; quite apart from wishing to escape from my Lover.'

He stepped forward and Tighe gasped. There was no ledge on which to step, not even a slender crag. But instead of falling, Tighe saw glinting filaments of silver snake out of the Wizard's palms and feet and anchor into the sheer curving wall of ice. He started moving up and west, like a bug on the wall. 'Come along,' he called.

With his throat contracted and his chest pulsing with excitement, Tighe stepped forward off the Wizard's craft. Threads flew out from his gloves and from the boots of his outfit. The next thing he knew, he was fixed to the side of the wall, the ice close enough to chill his nose and eyes. He shouted out with joy. When he twitched his arm muscles to move, the filaments adjusted, and he shifted to the side.

'Easy, isn't it,' called the Wizard, pulling himself past Tighe a little below with easy motions of arm and leg.

'I'll go to the top of the wall,' shouted Tighe, joyfully. He thought of adding *I'll escape from you, for at the top of the wall I will see God*. But there was no point in prolonging his dealings with the Wizard. If there were unanswered questions, God would answer them for him. If there was no God on the top of the wall, then at least he would know.

He began hauling himself up and sang out in pure delight at the speed with which he started up the wall. Craning his neck back, he couldn't judge just how far he had to climb. There was a sense of the wall curving back away from him. He had always expected the top to be a clear, flat edge; a right angle away from the rest of the wall. But it made a kind of sense that the wall did not have such a sawn-off look, but rather curved over.

He hurried upwards, expecting at any time for the sheer face to start to curve over to the flat. After a few minutes something came into view; a shining beacon of some kind. Snow flurried around him briefly and the ice made the end of his nose go numb. But surely the beacon was a marker that the top of the world was near-by.

As he approached, he saw that it was another silver craft, just like the one possessed by the Wizard. He shimmied up past the spindly legs and the bulging hourglass shape of the body. Then he saw another human being. With a sense of dislocation, mixed in with a sort of disappointment, he saw that this was the Wizard.

'How did you get here?' he shouted, breathless with the effort of the climb. 'How did you get here so quickly?'

'But I've not moved,' said the Wizard. 'You have – you've climbed right round the world. I thought you said you understood my explanation.'

'The top of the wall,' insisted Tighe. 'It's just up there – it's almost within our reach. I'll go again!'

'No, no,' said the Wizard, 'we have not got all of the day. My Lover is near-by and I don't like being away from my craft when he's prowling through the air. Come: I'll show you why I came here.'

It was so cold that he looked absurd in his skimpy clothes. But he didn't seem to mind the chill. He pushed with one hand and a crag emerged from the ice wall like a board of wood. It was white, but seemed to be made of metal rather than ice. The Wizard stepped on to it.

'Be careful,' he said. 'It's slippy. Frosty.'

Uncertain, Tighe stepped on to the platform. The Wizard was fiddling with a panel that had emerged, and suddenly a man-sized hole irised into existence.

'Well,' said the Wizard, looking briefly at Tighe. 'Come through, then.'

He stepped through. Tighe looked around him. The silver bulge of the Wizard's craft stood out briefly against the bright blue sky and then a grainy mist of fluttering snow obscured it. He reached up and rubbed the chilled end of his nose with the palm of his gloves. The cloth felt warm to the touch; that must be how he was being kept warm in the chill of the ice world.

Then he stepped through.

He emerged into a hollow space, groined with metal and – apart from the flat metal floor – arched and circular. It was perhaps fifty yards from side to side and twice that in length. Along the sides near the entrance were parcels; many almost as large as Tighe himself. Further along the metal floor was bare. The Wizard himself was fishing in an open metal box on the right, bringing out an assortment of things.

'What place is this?' gasped Tighe.

'My little storeroom,' said the Wizard. 'Impressive, isn't it? I wish I could claim I had dug it all out myself, but the truth is I deposited some machines and they dug it for me whilst I travelled elsewhere. Still, you can enter it from either side – it goes right through the world! Imagine that!'

Tighe stepped forward and felt the odd sensations he had felt before, inside the Wizard's craft, in strengthened form. He felt as if he were leaning backwards, bent in the middle. It was freakish: as if he were folded about his waist, with both his torso and his legs leaning sharply backwards. He kept looking down at himself to reassure himself that he wasn't, but the sense of positioning was too strong. He hunched himself as far forward as he could, but it was difficult to walk.

'How comical you look,' exclaimed the Wizard. But his voice did not express much amusement.

'What are you looking for?' asked Tighe. He reached forward with each leg in turn, but the closer he got to the middle of the strange ice cave, the sharper the sense of being bent in the middle became.

'Oh, supplies. Some electrical things. A bit of food. Need more food now, now that you're here. This side of the cavern is food, don't you see. That side is something else. I do believe my Lover has not yet discovered my little cache, which rather surprises me. But if he had I suppose he would have taken it all away.'

He looked up. 'Go to the exact centre of the room. There are some delicious experiences there.'

Tighe couldn't walk any further. He sat down, and began inching along on his behind. He felt wrong, queer inside. It flashed upon his brain that he was upside down, crawling along the ceiling. As he moved he got lighter and lighter. The floor, which seemed perfectly flat when he first came into the space, now sloped down away from him. With a cry of fear, he turned to scrabble back to where he came from, but there was ice on the metal floor and suddenly he slipped.

Before he knew what was happening he was in the air. He fell. The room swung about his head. He saw the silver metal of the floor sweep past, missing his head. The white roof swept past. The floor again.

'Wizard,' he called out, scared, 'what's happening?'

'You're falling, young warrior,' called the Wizard.

Tighe twisted in midair and got a better view of his position. He was circling through the air, following an arc that echoed the larger curve of the roof. The Wizard, upright against the silver floor, swept past and past his vision.

'Try to control it,' suggested the Wizard. Tighe couldn't see if he was looking at him or not. It seemed that he was rummaging in another box. 'Spread yourself and fly like a kite.'

'But there's no wind!' Tighe complained. He followed the advice, though: putting his arms by his side and his legs together. His kite training was still there, inside himself. He tried to angle himself inwards. With a lurch, the angle of his spin tightened; he was now going round much faster, in a smaller circle. He felt sick. He abandoned himself and kicked furiously with his legs. There was another lurch and he felt the logic of the world – or gravity – redefine itself around his midriff. His legs felt dissociated from him.

He was still spinning, but now he was rotating about an axis that was his own belly-button, as if strapped to a circling wheel. The floor was several yards away from him, but it seemed an arbitrary point, not down. His head was up but so were his legs. 'Help me, Wizard!' he called.

'You're at the centre of the world,' called the Wizard. 'To all intents and purposes.'

'Help me. I feel dizzy. I feel sick.'

Something thread-slender gripped his leg, and with a jerk Tighe was pulled away: it felt as if he were being pulled sharply up, but when he came to rest he was sitting on the strangely curved-but-flat metal floor at the Wizard's feet. One of the filaments that came out of the Wizard's palm was wrapped around his ankle.

The Wizard loosened his filament and drew it back inside his palm. 'A nice adventure?' he said flatly. 'Do you understand my explanation now, young scholar that you are?'

Tighe shuffled along the floor away from the Wizard, towards the other side of the room. He felt profoundly disorientated. His stomach was still spinning. 'What happened to me?' he demanded.

The Wizard turned his attention back to the box through which he was rummaging. 'You can never find the one thing you want, can you?' he said. 'You think you know where it is, but you never know.'

For several minutes he searched through in silence. Tighe sat, trying to calm himself, to breathe slowly. He didn't like the way his breath spored out of his mouth in puffy white clouds.

On the other side of the room were square and hexagonal boxes. On Tighe's side the parcels were lumpy, bulgy, like sacks filled with vegetables and frozen solid. Tighe turned and examined the one nearest him. With a start, he realised that it was a human being. He reached up and with the warmth of his palm he cleared the layer of frost from a face. A blue-white set of features revealed itself: clenched lips, shut eyes. There was a black dribble from one nostril.

'Wizard!' he squealed. 'Wizard!'

'What?'

'These are people! Dead people, all frozen, over here.'

'Yes,' said the Wizard, and chuckled his raspy high-pitched chuckle. 'That was what I wanted to show you. A fair number of people have visited the East Pole, but few have visited it and lived.'

Tighe, alarmed, tried to stand up, but the weirdness of this odd room was too much for him and he staggered, overbalanced and fell again. He managed to get himself up to a sitting position, and in that posture he shuffled over to another individual. It didn't take long to clear the frost from this one's dead face. It turned out to be a pale-skinned woman. Or at least Tighe thought she was a woman.

'Who are these people?' he asked.

'They? Some are family, so to speak. Others are just people. Only people. Nothing to worry about.'

'Family?' hissed Tighe, horrified. 'People?'

'Well, yes. Harvest, so to speak. They grew what was required and it didn't work out, or there was some problem. But I was able to salvage something worthwhile from many of them. The others – well, assorted individuals. One or two are explorers; people who made their way further east than anybody else.'

'You killed them?'

'Well,' said the Wizard, scratching his leather face, 'I can't take the credit for all of them. Many just died of the cold. Without that suit I've given you, my precious, you'd die too. But, yes, some of them. They're only people, my ice-prince. Only family. None of them are actually *us*; none of them are Lovers.'

'Lovers,' echoed Tighe, looking around in horror.

'Talking of which,' said the Wizard, turning his attention to his box, 'we can't spend all day here.' He continued speaking over his shoulder. 'I hoped you'd be impressed. One of the advantages of the material I put in your head is that you won't be as disabled by conscience as many would be. Think of the freedom I have given you! I impress myself, actually. It usually only results in a more or less severe series of mood swings and disorders. But you seem perfectly level, perfectly placid. I've perfected things sooner than even I thought I would.'

Tighe, listening to the Wizard without really understanding what he was saying, moved amongst the frozen bodies. He found one with a skin as dark as his own. His eyes were open, but the eyeballs were pure blank whiteness, like eyes of ice. Tighe saw that he was clutching something in his lap.

'One or two were more problematic,' said the Wizard, still rattling on as he searched through his box. 'Others were perfectly acquiescent. Funny that. Still, they didn't die in vain, that's the important thing. Each step brings us closer to undoing the disaster that has afflicted humanity.'

Rubbing with his glove, Tighe saw that the dead man was clutching a small rifle; one of the compact, short-barrelled rifles that could be held in one hand, the sort that Tighe had seen the Otre carry about. He glanced over his shoulder, but the Wizard's attention was elsewhere.

'How do we do that, Master?' he asked, hoping to keep the Wizard distracted. His mind felt clear.

'Well, it's a complicated business, more complicated than your uneducated mind could comprehend, I fear. But we must lay the wall flat! We must lay the wall flat for humanity to be able to grow. That is my plan. My Lover wants the same thing. If we could work together, we could achieve marvels. But he doesn't trust me, that is the thing. He doesn't trust me.'

'What did you put in my head, Wizard?' Tighe asked. The handheld rifle had almost come free from the ice that held it. Tighe rubbed with the warmth of his gloves.

'Eh? What? What did I put in your head? Well, I hope you can see how impressive my achievement has been. I hope you can understand it.'

The gun came free and Tighe pulled it out. It was black, with a short barrel and a handle like a horn. There was a trigger like a nipple tucked in at the junction of handle and shaft. Tighe had seen soldiers shoot such devices. He knew what to do.

'When you were born, a year old or so, I came by your village and inserted my equipment. I put in several things, in a complex of pollenmachine polymers. Think of it this way: I planted my seed, my metal seed, at the base of your head, a little above your neck. That is where your strength comes from, your mental strength. But, like any seed, it takes time to grow, and with something as complex as the integration into a whole living cortex – well, it's impossible to predict success.'

Tighe sucked in a breath. 'Is my pahe here?' he asked.

'What?'

'In this ice room? Is my pahe here?'

The Wizard turned to look at Tighe. 'But we're talking about your implants!' he said. 'Why would you be interested in your pahe?' Then he registered what Tighe was holding in his hands. 'What's that?' he asked.

Tighe swallowed quickly. 'I found it,' he said, holding it between both gloved hands. It was a moment of intense focus in his head. To avenge his pahe. To make things right for pashe. He pressed his hands together, feeling the trigger resist, resist, and then click in.

The gun exploded, bounding out of Tighe's hands, and a bullet sped through the icy air towards the Wizard.

7

For a moment time seemed as frozen as the location. The Wizard was standing there. The gun had thrown itself out of Tighe's hands and landed amongst the frozen corpses.

The Wizard reached down with one hand and his long leather fingers fumbled at his stomach. He pulled out a black pellet and held it up to his face. His skin had not been broken.

'Sorry,' said Tighe.

'You ought to be careful with that,' said the Wizard. He sounded mildly irritated. 'You could harm yourself. That *would* be a waste of your potential.'

'It must be the cold,' said Tighe. 'It just, sort of, went off.'

'I can see it went off. Still!' He beamed. 'It shows off how excellent my new skin is. The microfilament mesh I told you about is very strong and very clever. It distributes the force of the bullet's impact over its whole structure almost at once, so I barely even feel the blow. Isn't that clever?'

'Very clever,' said Tighe. His head was swimming in and out of focus. Even in the bitter cold of the ice chamber he was sweating. 'How clever you are, Wizard.'

'Yes. Anyway, where was I?'

He turned back to the box, and started rummaging through again.

'My implants,' said Tighe breathily. He looked about frantically and located the gun. 'You were telling me.'

'Yes. Well, yours are basically the same model as I tried out on several other people. Some of them now sitting frozen around you; some still living on the worldwall.'

Tighe grabbed the gun and stuffed it into the pocket in front of his clothing. 'Really?' he said.

'Your pashe's implants were very similar.'

'You put things in her head too,' said Tighe, looking around for some other weapon. There was the dandelion-puff device, but that was in one of his own pockets, underneath the clothing the Wizard had made him put on. He couldn't think how to undo this outer clothing and reach the little device without drawing attention to himself. He wasn't even sure how to operate the little thing. And he wasn't sure – he realised with a sensation of doom in his heart – wasn't even sure it would penetrate the tough skin of the Wizard.

'Yes,' the Wizard was saying, 'I inserted her implants when she was a child. It may have been too late, actually, because she suffered from all manner of emotional instabilities. Still, you haven't inherited them. Either I reached you in time or else your metabolism was simply more suited to the implants. Ah!' He lifted something from the box, and turned to face Tighe.

Tighe looked up. He smiled weakly.

'Back to the craft, I think,' he said. 'Enough time in here.' He hoisted up a sack that rattled with the things that he had gathered, and made his way back to the door.

Tighe, slowly and cautiously, got to his feet. He felt the strange tugs and weird angles, as if he were fevered and the world were warping around him.

He staggered over to the Wizard's side and held on to his arm as he made the door appear again. They stepped out on to the little platform and then the Wizard was away over the sheer face of the ice. Tighe, braced by the mess of icy snowflakes that fluttered against his exposed face, reached out. A filament snaked out and he pulled himself along.

In minutes he had joined the Wizard on top of his craft.

Inside the upper, green room, the Wizard poured the contents of his sack on his bed-couch with the excitement of a child with its presents. 'Let's go down below,' he said. 'First, go downstairs and check to see what my Lover is up to. He's a wily one, my Lover. We'd better keep him in view, that's all.'

He ushered Tighe down the ladder, still wearing his oversuit. He expected to feel too hot, wrapped up as he was. But in fact he felt pleasantly cool. He stepped off the bottom of the stairs and made his awkward way through the twist in space to settle beside his pashe.

'Pashe,' he whispered, as the Wizard made his way down the ladder. 'I tried killing him, but his skin is magic. Strong.' He pulled off one glove and pressed the ends of his fingers against his mother's lips. The Wizard was standing now, making his way gingerly over towards his cradle.

Tighe watched him. His pashe, staring straight ahead, started sucking, absently, on Tighe's fingers' ends.

'So,' said the Wizard, examining his screens. 'He is close. Close! We may need to leave at a moment's notice. Still, the flurries and blizzards do a good job in masking where we are.'

He stood up. Tighe pulled his fingers from his pashe's mouth.

'So!' he said. 'I think we can spare an hour or two before we have to go.

342

What can I say? My jaunt on the ice has tired me out. If you'll excuse me I'll have a little lie down.'

He wandered back to the ladder and climbed up to the top room, pulling the hatch closed behind him.

8

For a while Tighe did nothing but sit still, with his arm around his pashe. His mind circled round and round, just as he had spun round and round in the Wizard's strange ice cavern. Most of what the Wizard had told him made no sense at all. The world was not the way he had thought the world was; no. But he had no clear idea of the version that the Wizard seemed so wedded to. This strange part of the wall was unlike any place he had been to before, that was true; but as Ati had once said, the wall is cluttered with wonders. Perhaps the Wizard possessed powers beyond his machines; or machines that Tighe had not yet seen. The more he thought about it, the more likely it became that it had been some magic of the Wizard's that had spun him through the air in the ice cave. Some tantalising magical trick of the Wizard's that had shown him the top of the wall and then baffled his attempts to climb up to it.

'He is a powerful creature, pashe,' Tighe whispered into the ear of his unresponsive mother. 'But perhaps he can nevertheless be defeated.'

For some unfathomable reason, this leather-skinned man had been present in his family life, a hidden thing, a secret. Tighe stroked his pashe's hair. She seemed to be shivering.

'Don't fret, pashe,' hushed Tighe, trying to calm her down. 'I have a thing in my pocket – it is a device of the Wizard's own. He won't expect it. I believe it will harm him. I believe that!'

Pashe was trembling hard now. From sitting placidly, she was suddenly in the grip of something; it was as if she was having a fit of some kind. Her lips were working. 'Pashe!' said Tighe, feeling a lump of fearful anticipation in his throat. 'What is it?'

She started rocking backwards and forwards, and a thin sound forced itself between her lips.

Tighe clutched her more closely. 'He did something to you, I think,' he said, his voice hoarse. 'He killed pahe and put him in that cave of ice, I think. He did something to your head. To mine.'

For a while pashe struggled against his embrace, moaning faintly, a most pathetic sound. Then suddenly she stopped. She turned her head and looked directly into Tighe's eyes. It was the first time she had looked at Tighe since his arrival on the Wizard's craft. Her eyes locked with his. He saw the little sparks of lighter brown freckling the darker brown of her pupils, like flaws in a jewel. Her brows were pressed together in pain, or puzzlement.

Tighe felt tears clog the corners of his eyes. 'Pashe,' he said.

'I remember you,' said his pashe. She lifted a wobbly hand and touched the side of Tighe's face. 'When you were a baby. You were a smooth baby. Sweet-smelling. A nice baby.'

'Pashe,' said Tighe, the tears tickling down his cheeks. He felt his adam's apple as a tightness in his throat, a knot of emotion.

'He came,' she said and Tighe knew at once that she was talking about the Wizard. 'He came and he fiddled with your head. He made me sit and watch it; he made me happy to see it. He can do that, he can twist the inside of your head from a distance, make you happy or sad, give you pleasure or pain. He can manipulate his machines from a distance. He made a doorway in the back of your head and put in his machinery. But after he went I had a temper and I pulled as many wires as I could out of the back of your head before the wound healed over.'

She dropped her hand, and turned her face away, looking again at the wall across the floor from her.

'Pashe,' said Tighe, softly, meaning to ask a question. But she cut back in.

'Your pahe didn't like it. He said best leave alone, that you'd die. But I was in a state, I wouldn't be told. I pulled the wires out of the back of your head where he had bandaged it. You bled and bled. You didn't even cry. I don't think I got them all, but I got much.' She was starting to tremble again, to shiver from side to side. 'It was all like stalks of grass, very fine, very fine. A thin wire. I threw it off the world, never told *him*. You didn't even cry. Bled and bled. Bled and bled and bled.'

'Pashe,' said Tighe, wiping his tears with his gloveless hands. 'Pashe, stop now.'

'Your pahe tried to stop me and I hit him, hit him hard. Then I pulled it all out, all that badness, out of your head.'

'Pashe – stop. You're hurting yourself.'

And it was obvious that she was. Every word was an effort. There was something wrong. Her eyes were thrumming up and down, and a tendril of blood dribbled down from one nostril. Her words became indistinct. 'Pashe!' cried Tighe, coming round and trying to embrace her fully. 'Pashe!'

She jerked back hard and cracked her head against the wall behind. Then she was fitting fully, her tongue out and her eyeballs white. The violence of her seizure knocked Tighe away and he scrambled over the nightmare landscape of the warped-but-flat floor back to her body. Blood was squeezing from the corners of her mouth where she had bitten her tongue, mixing with her saliva into a pink froth. She was grunting in rhythm, her arms straight at her side. Then she went quiet.

Tighe laid her out on the floor on her back, and pressed his face to her chest. He couldn't sense any breathing.

Panic was swelling inside his chest. He couldn't believe this was happening. 'Wizard!' he cried, lurching over the treacherously shaped floor to the ladder, and climbing it awkwardly. 'Wizard! Wake up! Wizard!' He hooked one arm round the top rung and hammered on the bottom of the hatch with the other. 'Wizard!'

There was a grumble through the floor from above. 'What?'

'Come down here, Wizard!'

'Leave me sleeping, boy.'

'Come down here Wizard! It's pashe. She's had a seizure.'

'Leave me be. I *need* my sleep.' The Wizard sounded impossibly querulous and distant.

'Please come down! Please come and help me!'

'Oh very *well*, tiresome and troublesome.' Tighe heard a rustle, and some footsteps from above. 'You can have five minutes, then I'm going back to sleep.' The hatch started opening.

Tighe dropped quickly down the seemingly curved ladder to give the Wizard space to come down. He made his way back to where his pashe was lying.

'What is it?' said the Wizard, coming up behind him. 'Fallen over, has she? Coma, is it? I can't say I'm surprised. You can't muck around with somebody's cortexes the way I was compelled to do and expect everything to work properly afterwards.' He leant over, putting his leathery hand on Tighe's shoulder for support. 'Yes,' he said. 'Yes, yes. I thought this might happen.'

'What will you do?' Tighe asked. 'To bring her round? What will you do?'

'Bring her round? Dear me. Dear me. You seem *much* more agitated by this than I should expect. I'll turn up the dials, if you see what I mean. I'll adjust my fine-tuning of your mind, so that you don't feel so upset by this.'

'It's my pashe!'

'Yes, I know it is. Obviously there *will* be a part of your mind that knows that. I couldn't eradicate the fact from your consciousness without losing important aspects of who you are. So, I suppose, in an *intellectual* sense you might feel a little disturbed by her death.'

'She's dead?'

'But I can *tweak* other sensitivities, so that it shouldn't *feel* too bad. I'm surprised,' said the Wizard, getting to his feet and making his way over to his cradle. 'I'm surprised that you feel as bad as you seem to do, to be honest. The adjustments I've already made should have dampened down a lot of that.'

He settled into his cradle and fiddled with one switch, prodding it with a single leathern finger whilst watching the corner of a screen. 'There,' he said. 'Better?'

'Dead,' said Tighe, looking down at the body of his pashe.

'Yes – yes. You sound more neutral about it already. I don't mind boasting that I've gotten myself *quite* skilled at the fine-tuning. There . . . there. How's that?'

Things went calm inside Tighe's head, like a snowstorm clearing to leave a patch of blue sky. It was clear to him what he had to do. He reached over to pick up his spare glove, holding it in his left hand. His right hand was empty. He stood up.

'You see, how much better that is?' the Wizard was saying. 'I like to think of it as a kind of emotional analgesic. A painkiller for the soul, if you see what I mean. It's one of the many things we can do, you and I.'

Tighe concentrated on the Wizard in his cradle, fixed his eye on that destination so as not to be distracted by the strange topography, and started walking towards him. The floor seemed curiously curved. He reached into his front pocket with his ungloved hand and drew out the gun. It felt chilly against his skin.

'Eh, my boy?' said the Wizard, looking round. He saw the gun. 'I see you still have that,' he said. 'A souvenir? You can pick up more if you like, since we'd better shift your mother's body to the cavern. Back inside the cavern. Lots of goodies there.'

Tighe stopped, standing beside the Wizard's cradle. The Wizard's leather face was in full profile as he examined one of his screens.

'It's a good job you woke me, actually, my boy,' he was saying. 'I think my Lover is closer than is entirely comfortable. It may be this is the time to leave.'

Tighe lifted the gun and levelled its stocky barrel at the side of the Wizard's head. The old man was staring at his screens, his face in profile; his eyes, from Tighe's perspective, lined up one behind the other; his eye-holes the only weak space in his strengthened skin.

The Wizard glanced round, before turning his head back, focusing on the screens before him. 'Yes, yes,' he said indulgently. 'I saw it already. It's very nice.'

Tighe fired the gun.

The bullet passed through the Wizard's left eyeball, snapped the bones in the bridge of his nose and passed directly out through his right eyeball. It sheared away and ricocheted off the curved metal wall behind the Wizard's cradle, bounced once, and then twice, screeching with each change of trajectory. It smashed into one of the Wizard's four screens a heartbeat after having been fired, whistling so close to Tighe's own head that he felt the puff of air as it passed. The screen cracked and splintered. But the Wizard did not see this because both of his eyeballs had been mashed by the shot.

The Wizard howled. For a moment that was all he did. He didn't move a muscle, except to let out a high-pitched howl of agony and surprise. Then both of his hands came up, clutching at his wounds as the blood started coming out of the holes in his leather face.

Tighe stepped back, his heart pumping hard. There was a deep terror lurking somewhere inside him. He didn't want to think about that. He didn't want to look at the body of his pashe on the floor behind him. He didn't want to stay in this space at all.

The uncanny screechy howl of pain from the Wizard's face did not seem human. It did not seem to Tighe that he had injured a human being.

He stepped awkwardly over to the ladder and hauled himself up it. Just before he passed up into the green room above, he saw the Wizard's cradle spin round, so that the Wizard's sightless head turned to face him. 'Boy!' screamed the Wizard. 'Boy! What did you do?'

'For my pashe!' yelled Tighe, and pulled himself up into the upper chamber. As an afterthought he yelled down, 'For my pahe too.'

'I've turned the pain off now,' came the Wizard's voice from downstairs. 'You idiot boy! What did you think you were going to do?'

Tighe stumbled awkwardly, trying to position himself in the exact centre of the upper room without falling over. 'Your magic won't help you see in your blindness, I think,' he called. He felt a pervasive sense of exhilaration.

There was the sound of movement in the room below. 'Idiot,' shouted the Wizard. 'I thought you were stable! How obvious that you're not! Where do you think you're going? There's nowhere for you to go.'

'I'm going away from you,' yelled Tighe.

'Idiot – I'll turn off your muscles with a switch! I'll operate you by remote control. I'll force you to cut off your own fingers, to break off your own teeth and use them to scratch out your eyes! You'll know what my anger is like.' The Wizard's threats sounded bizarre in his high-pitched voice. 'There!' he called. 'There! I told you. Maybe I can't see for now, but I can *feel* my way over my controls. How do you like *that*, eh?'

Tighe did feel a twinge, a tingle of cramp that ran all the way down his spine, like the uncomfortable numbness of an arm caught underneath during sleep that flails helplessly when you wake up. But the sensation soon passed.

He reached with his foot, stamping on the patch of floor that he had seen the Wizard press when they had left the craft earlier. Nothing happened.

'You can't control me!' he called gleefully to the room below. 'My pashe pulled your machinery out of my head just after you installed it! I'm free.'

He pushed down on one of the nubbins on the floor. Still nothing happened. He was too excited to think clearly. How had the Wizard operated the elevator device? Where had he put his foot?

There was a bark of what might have been laughter from below. 'Did she, now? That doesn't surprise me. She was never stable.' Another laugh. 'Ironic! I thought this one was doing so well! Still, she can't have got *everything* out, or I wouldn't have been able to track you. There was something left behind, and it will have grown into *something* in your head.' There was a stamping noise, and then a crash, and the Wizard cursed. 'Damn you boy, this is *most* inconvenient. Have you any idea how long it will take me to fit new eyes?'

Tighe stamped furiously, as if performing a ritual dance, dabbing at dozens of points round about the centre-point of the room with his toe. There was another series of crashing noises, this time close under the hatchway.

'I can hear your feet, boy,' growled the Wizard from below.

Suddenly Tighe was rising. He must have hit the right spot. He was lifted up, and the hole in the roof irised open. The cold air rushed and swirled, and tiny pieces of snow flurried in. And then he was on the roof and the cold was bitter. He knew it was, because his ungloved hand, still clutching the gun, felt the chill immediately. Tighe stuffed the gun into his pocket and fumbled the glove over his numb fingers. Then he stepped forward, hoping that the Wizard did not have a way of turning off the filament devices in his gloves and shoes. A thread leapt out to meet the ice and Tighe started away from the Wizard's craft.

9

He made his way through a prolonged snowstorm, climbing away east-ward. He had no idea where he was going, or what fate awaited him, as long as he could put as much distance as possible between himself and the Wizard. He passed rapidly over the ice.

After a while the air around him cleared and Tighe looked over his shoulder. The sky was a blue so intense it seemed unreal. It seemed bright and clean as newly washed plastic, close enough to kiss. Tighe paused, panting. His sinuses hurt with breathing in the freezing air.

He looked up and saw a blurry-edged cloud of snow descend the wall until it was all round him and he couldn't see anything more than his own gloved hands before his face. He clambered further along.

The air cleared again, and a shadow passed over the wall in front of him. He looked over his shoulder to see the silver shape of the Wizard's craft swing through the sky. He whimpered in terror.

'Tighe!' boomed a voice from the craft. 'Tighe!'

Tighe stopped and clung to the ice, pressing up against it, hoping that motionlessness would protect him. *He cannot see*, he told himself. *His eyes are gone. He cannot see me, he is hoping I will call out or move and give myself away to his devices. But I will not.*

The silver shape passed away to the east and then with a whine of motors it rose and passed up.

Tighe breathed heavily. He looked away to his right; looking east. This was the end of the wall, he could see that. Instead of a continuing vista, there was a stretch of ice perhaps fifty arm's lengths, perhaps further (it was difficult to gauge it), and then blue sky. The sky was not only behind him; it was above and below and away to the right. Soon there would be nothing but sky. And then what would he do?

And then what?

Looking up, Tighe could see the silver shape descending again. 'Tighe!' boomed the amplified voice of the Wizard. 'Tighe! Make yourself known, boy! Make yourself known.'

Tighe clung as still as possible. He even tried to still his breathing.

'Don't be a fool, boy! My sensors tell me you're around here somewhere. Shout out – move around and my sensors will pick you up more precisely. Then you can climb back aboard.' The words distorted and echoed strangely against the ice.

The Wizard's craft disappeared downwall, his words still booming and echoing. They dissolved into the general hiss and hurry of the snowflake-filled air. When he could no long hear it, Tighe started climbing eastwards, palm over palm.

Then, growing in volume again, the Wizard's voice swelled into hearing once more. Tighe cursed silently and stopped where he was. The craft was coming down from above, the words wailing and grumbling incomprehensibly until Tighe was able to tune into what they were saying, '. . . rather than let that happen.' *Aphen–aphen-phen·phen* wobbled the words. 'I can do it! I control all my machines from where I am. I'll turn off the heating in your suit and you'll freeze to death!' The echo bounced about in diminuendo, *death! death! death!* 'I'd rather kill you than let you go – I spent such effort trying to *find* you.' The words smeared and Tighe lost track of them. *Find* you. *Find* you.

The Wizard's craft disappeared below. Tighe resumed his eastwards climb, uncertain of his destination. But it made him feel better to be moving.

There was another blinding flurry of torn-up snow fragments and the cold pushed itself deeper into Tighe's face. It seemed to catch because although the flurry cleared the cold continued worming its way inside. Tighe's fingers started hurting; then his feet. Soon the chill had spread all over his body. It seemed the Wizard had made good his threat: whatever magic it was that provided heat in Tighe's suit had been cancelled.

From above came the warbling and humming of the Wizard's magnified voice once again. It called down to Tighe from above and slowly angled to the horizontal as the silver craft descended once again.

Tighe could feel the chill in his bones now. He was shivering, which made it hard to place his hand-holds. He could no longer feel his fingers. The Wizard's voice came into focus.

'. . . you. Don't fight it! Believe me this cold will kill. I know you're suffering. I can do more!' More! More! More! echoed the ice. The wind scuffed and hissed around the words. 'I can disable the filaments that work from your gloves and feet; you won't be able to grip! You'll fall off the world.'

Tighe tried barking his defiance, but his throat seemed to have frozen. Breath hissed painfully out. No!

'Idiot boy!' came the Wizard's booming voice.

The silver craft was passing much closer to the ice on this occasion. It was a little above and an arm's length to the side, and was drifting down. Fearful that it would knock him off the wall, or squash him like an insect, Tighe struggled to make his pain-chilled limbs move, to clamber a little to the side.

There was a crack that buckled the air and a wash of a sharp, metallic smell. Tighe looked up to see a second silver craft sweeping down from above. The cracking noise percussed a second time, so loud it actively hurt. A beam of white light flickered into existence between the two craft; and the Wizard's machine dazzled, light shining in all directions. There was a huge whining noise and then another crack. This time a strand of blackness appeared, reaching from one craft to the other; as purely defined against the blue sky as if it had been black thread. This did not produce a glittering light-effect off the silver of the Wizard's craft. Instead there was a rapid series of croaky *whomph* noises and a bole of smoke coughed out of the side.

Tighe glimpsed, briefly, a hole in the side of the Wizard's calabash and black smoke sputtering out, as the whole machine veered sharply into the wall. It crunched enormously against the ice and Tighe felt the wall itself shudder.

With a sinking sensation in his belly, Tighe felt the world slip, slide downwards.

The Wizard's craft, rebounding from the ice, part fell and part flew down and away. Tighe had a fleeting sense of a crushed-in side of silver, of smoke dribbling from the machine, and then it sped with a rush of following air and dwindled rapidly into nothing.

Tighe clung more desperately to the ice; but it lurched and slid again and then it was falling.

He knew he was falling because his gut told him; but he pressed himself against the chilly bosom of the ice, turned his face towards the wall. He couldn't see movement.

The frozen air pushed at him from below.

The world heaved and danced. His frozen joints burned with sudden pain as everything stumbled sharply left. The world was shadowed and then lit, and Tighe had the vague apprehension that he was tumbling strapped to an enormous flake of ice. Then the ice began to break into pieces.

A portion of ice tore away to Tighe's right, and then another, peeling itself away from Tighe's filament grip. He looked over at it, too chilled and icy to feel fear. He could see the wall of ice sweeping up past him, the ripples and folds in the wall scrolling past.

A crack appeared in the ice directly in front of his face, and with a twitch of muscle Tighe disengaged his filament grip. He started to separate from the ice just as it fragmented. A gust from below caught him and turned him upside down, and then he was tumbling. He put his frozen legs together and his kite-pilot's instinct operated his body beyond his stunned semi-consciousness. He flattened his angle, brought his head back up.

The second silver calabash, the one that had attacked the Wizard's craft with its beam of black light, swept past him again and again. It was as if there was an endless supply of these machines, each hanging in the air a thousand yards above the other: as if Tighe were stationary in air, and this parade of upward-rising silver machines were streaming past him.

There was an explosive, sore percussion, and Tighe's head creaked with pain. He had, he distantly realised, been hit by one of the pieces of falling ice. The collision pushed him away. The repeating image of the rising silver machine dwindled, shrank.

Tighe may have passed out; he wasn't certain. He didn't feel so cold any more. In fact, he could feel a delicious warmth seeping through his bones. His fingers flared into achy life again and then warmed to a more comfortable temperature.

But he was passing in and out of consciousness.

10

It seemed to Tighe that he was falling in pure space; there no longer was any wall. All around him was blue sky, with an iterated pattern of white patches that might have been clouds, sweeping up and past and away over and over again. Tighe was warm, except at his face where the chill wind through which he moved made his lips and nose numb and spread blunt fronds of pain into the bridge of his nose, into his forehead. But otherwise he felt almost babyish.

He stretched out, then curled himself up again. Hanging in pure nothingness. Only the intensity of the wind, only the level of its roar, increased or decreased. He was freed of all constraints: this was pure existence.

He wasn't certain how long he fell. He couldn't think where the wall had gone. He started to feel thirsty.

5
The Godman

1

Tighe was conscious of the silver craft's approach in a dreamlike fashion because he was fearful it was the Wizard come to claim him again. He cried out, but – as in a dream – his voice didn't sound. There was a great rushing, as of a waterfall, all about him.

A metal tendril snaked out and grabbed him, and this was a clumsy, painful sensation. It jolted him; this sensation no longer felt like a dream. The tendril dug painfully into the flesh of Tighe's waist, catching a fold of skin in sharp agony. He screamed, started thrashing.

It drew him in; or – as it seemed – it was as if Tighe reeled the craft in towards *him*, such that it grew and grew until it towered over him. Up close he saw that it was not the same as the Wizard's machine: it was larger, taller, and there were many more devices and artefacts fixed to its outer skin.

A mouth opened in the silver fabric and swallowed Tighe whole. Inside, away from the enormous push and howl of the constant wind, it was suddenly so quiet that Tighe passed out with the exquisiteness of it.

He woke again in the dark, and with a miserable aching from the chafed skin of his waist. He was still dressed in the suit the Wizard had given him, but he took off a glove and fumbled with the toggles and the ties in order to be able to wriggle a hand inside at his torso. The fingers touched wetness.

He may have swooned again because the next thing he knew he was sitting upright on a kind of bench, with a bright blanched light all about him. He sat still. For a while there was nothing but a quiet hum. Directly in front of him a tiled white wall dissolved out of the wash of light. The more his eyes got used to the gleam, the more he saw: the outline of a doorway, a constellation of silver-cream and white bricks, or tiles, in a diagonal pattern.

The back of his head felt peculiar.

He tried to stand up, to step forward off the bench so that he could examine the wall more closely. It was then that he realised his head was tethered. As he moved his body forwards his head yanked backwards, cricking his neck. He almost fell. Carefully he sat back down and reached behind him. A plastic cord, finger-thick, came out of a fitting in the wall and buried itself into the back of Tighe's head. Tighe's fingers explored the point where the cord entered the head: the hairs back there had been shaved clean, and the cord buried directly into the skin. There was a tiny ridge of scalp that circled the point of entry.

It bothered Tighe. He didn't like the thought of it. But, with a puzzling sense of strangeness, he realised that he was in a way more bothered by the fact that it didn't bother him all that much. It was another bizarre eventuality in the bizarre sequence of events his life had become.

Everything went black.

There was a whistling noise in the darkness. Tighe focused on it. A series of cyan-blue flickers pulsed in geometric patterns. A pink blur, like the neon torch a tinker had once tried to sell around the village, hazed through the black-purple darkness, settling around Tighe's eyes. He reached out to flap his hand in front of his face, but he couldn't see anything.

There was a strong smell of burnt sweat.

White light. A series of scratches and scribbles, so intimate as to appear imprinted on Tighe's corneas, wriggled past the lower part of his vision. He barely had time to register that they were letters and numbers – not enough time even to read what they said – when everything went black again.

There was a voice. 'Open your eyes,' it said in Imperial.

Tighe opened his eyes cautiously. He was back in the white padded room. Three versions of his Grandhe stood before him.

'Grandhe,' he said. His mouth was sticky; his lips crackled and adhered against one another. Then, bizarrely, his mouth was full of saliva, so much and so suddenly that Tighe couldn't stop it dribbling down his chin. 'Grandhe!' he said again.

'No,' said the middle individual. He looked like Tighe's Grandhe except that his skin was glossier, blacker, and he was much younger. The one on the left had much paler skin, a reddish copper tone. The one on the right had a knobbled, rough-looking texture to his skin; like the bark of a tree trunk, only on a finer scale.

Tighe swallowed, and gasped. 'Where am I? Grandhe?'

'No,' said the middle Grandhe. 'That's not who we are. We have nothing to do with that.'

Tighe tried looking from Grandhe to Grandhe, but he couldn't turn his head too far because the cord fixed into the back of it was too short to allow much movement. 'You look like my Grandhe,' he said. 'You three do.'

'Your hardware is incomplete,' said the Grandhe on the right. 'We can barely connect with the interfaces we have established.'

'It is at a primitive level,' said the central Grandhe.

'The Wizard put the metalwork into my head,' said Tighe.

'Wizard?'

'I was in another craft, like this one I think. There was a man with leather skin.'

The central Grandhe smiled very slowly. 'You called him the Wizard?' he said, softly. 'He called *himself* the Wizard? How droll.'

'You know him, I think,' said Tighe. 'You are his Lover. He talked about his Lover often.'

'We are all three his Lover,' confirmed the one on the right, 'and he is ours.'

'How is it you are all the same?' Tighe asked.

'One hundred and eighteen eggs were taken from one woman,' said the Grandhe on the right, 'many hundreds of years ago. They were all fertilised out of the same stock.'

'My stock,' said the central Grandhe. 'I am the original.'

'I do not believe that you are,' said Tighe, a little surprised at his own boldness.

The two outer Grandhes looked at the central one and then back at Tighe.

'As far as anybody is concerned,' said the central Grandhe, 'I am. It is not cloning and therefore we are all slightly different; but there are strong resemblances, it is true. We may not be clones, but we share many qualities.'

Tighe didn't follow this. He reached up to fiddle with the cord that passed into his head. Taking it between his finger and thumb he tugged to see if it could click out. It was firm. Each tug sent flickers of light sparkling at the edges of his vision.

'Leave that,' advised the central Grandhe. 'We have not finished checking the work done by our Lover.'

'Which one of you was the Lover he spoke of?' Tighe asked.

'We all are. We don't distinguish in a way that you are likely to understand.'

'You tried to destroy him in the air,' Tighe recalled, picturing the swooping silver craft and its black beam of fire; 'but I think he escaped.'

'He escaped,' confirmed the right-hand Grandhe.

'You are pursuing him. Why do you look like my Grandhe?'

'Grandhe?'

'When I was growing up,' Tighe started to explain, 'in my village . . .'

'Ah,' said the central Grandhe. 'This was one of the areas used by the man you call the Wizard. He planted versions of us, of him – stolen versions – in several places and performed various experiments. You are not one of us, though: you are the *offspring* of one of us.'

'Perhaps you are the offspring of the offspring,' suggested the right-hand Grandhe.

'It is a more remote genetic connection, certainly.'

'You say your mother removed some of the hardware that was inserted into your head? When did this happen? When you were a baby?'

'What experiments was the Wizard undertaking?' asked Tighe. He felt an itching sensation right in the centre of his head. It was not pleasant. He put both hands to his head and tried massaging and scratching the skin of his face and scalp. But the itch was directly in the middle of his head.

'He wants what we want,' said the central Grandhe. 'We must return the world to a flat condition. Humanity cannot go on living this precarious existence.'

'Precariousness', said Tighe, distractedly, 'is the point of existence.'

'Metaphysics,' said the right-hand Grandhe, in a cross voice. 'Don't scratch at the back of your head like that!'

'How does putting machines in peoples' heads', said Tighe, grumpily, 'and letting them grow and then cutting them out – how does that help anything?'

'Our Lover', said the central Grandhe, with a hint of awe in his voice, 'has the most ambitious plans. He would like to turn a person into a machine for manipulating gravity; in something after the manner with which a craft such as this one converts power into gravitational resistance, a person might warp gravity in a local context. It is an astonishing dream.'

'An impossible dream,' said the right-hand Grandhe.

'He wants other things as well. He wants power, particularly; and he is testing out machinery that has grown in the minds of genetically appropriate subjects until he has developed one that functions neatly in harmony with consciousness. This is not a small task.'

'You admire him,' said Tighe.

'Of course.'

'And yet you want to destroy him.'

'Of course. Naturally, he wants to destroy us. He was one of us, we were Lovers together, before he fled away.'

'He was trying to kill *you*,' observed the right-handed Grandhe. 'He had remote-turned-off the heating in your suit. You would have frozen to death if we had not overridden the command.'

'Are you going to kill me?' asked Tighe. It was funny how placid he felt in this environment. All his sensations were concentrated in his head.

'Well,' said the right-hand Grandhe, vaguely, 'we usually destroy the offshoots of his experimental dabblings. If may not be safe to leave them climbing around on the wall.'

'Don't kill me,' said Tighe, without emotion. He felt ambivalent either way. 'I have information about him. I'll trade it for my life if you like.'

There was a pause. 'It seems', said the central Grandhe, 'that we cannot access your rapid memory. The hardware is not complete.'

Tighe looked again: the central Grandhe was the red-skinned Grandhe who had been standing a moment before – he was sure – on the right. The Grandhe with the skin like liquid oil was now on the right. When had they changed places? He didn't remember.

There was a stabbing odour, a potent chemical smell, but it passed directly. Transparent blobular creatures floated over Tighe's field of vision. 'What is happening?' he said.

'What information do you have?'

'The Wizard has a cave in the ice,' he said. 'In it are his supplies and many bodies. He showed me. I took a gun from there and shot him.'

'Stories,' said the central, red-skinned Grandhe. 'Metaphysics. He has a new skin now with a microfilament underlay. Shooting him would do no good.'

'I shot him through his eye-holes,' said Tighe, shutting his eyes. But even though he shut his eyes, he could still see the scene in front of him in perfect detail. It was as if his eyelids were transparent. He wasn't even sure he *had* shut his eyes. He fluttered them up and down, feeling them slide over his eyeballs, but the scene in front of him did not go away.

The black-skinned Grandhe smiled his slow smile again. 'He won't like that.'

'He said that he'd fit himself some new eyes,' said Tighe.

'But of course he'll do *that*,' said the right-hand Grandhe.

The three of them flickered out of view and a drifting pattern of blue triangles floated aimlessly through the white spaces in front of Tighe.

Then they were back: three versions of the same man, black, red and textured. The order in which they were standing had changed.

'I don't follow . . .' said Tighe.

'We should apologise, really,' said the black-skinned Grandhe. 'It is not your fault that you are caught up in this. We are playing for larger goals. Individuals – well, they take second place. Which can be a shame for the individuals concerned.' The space he occupied abruptly emptied, impossibly, to be filled with a patch of grey light scratched and criss-crossed with shimmering lines. The black-skinned Grandhe flickered back into space.

'The future of everything,' said the red-skinned Grandhe. 'We need to lay the wall flat on its side. Then life can begin again.'

'People will still fall,' said Tighe. 'That is the nature of being alive, living on the wall or living elsewhere makes no odds. People will still fall.'

'Our Lover has been foolish,' said the black-skinned Grandhe. 'We will soon destroy him.'

'He had high hopes for me,' drawled Tighe. 'He thought I was important to his plans.'

'He hoped to use you to destroy us, we think,' said the Grandhes in unison.

Then one added, with what sounded almost like a chuckle, 'Your hardware is incomplete. Some has grown, which is how we are able to interface you now. But it is at a primitive level.'

'When you snatched me with your metal tendril,' said Tighe, a distant sensation of crossness registering itself in his mind, 'you nicked the skin around my waist! It still hurts. You weren't very careful.'

'Once upon a time,' said the black-skinned Grandhe. He was the only Grandhe present. Tighe felt that the others had not vanished, but were somehow still present. Or perhaps they had never been there in the first place. Certainly, he could only see the black-skinned Grandhe now, outlined against an environment of dull blue sparkles, each glint of which caused a pricking sensation inside his head. 'Once upon a time,' the black-skinned Grandhe said again. His voice was suddenly huge, drowning out every other sound, drowning out every other sensation, as huge as the wind, as huge as the wall itself. There was nothing now but the voice, no vision, no feeling or taste, no smell. Only the voice.

'Once upon a time! There lived a man! He hollowed out himself, renewed his organs with new organs, made machine enhancements of cerebral material, recreated ancient technology! He was the godman! He was the godman! This is where people find themselves, *beneath* the godman! Once upon a time the world was different. Now it is as we know it. It will be different again. Who survives the difference? Who survives the change? Who *creates* change? The godman! Who controls change? The godman! Who *creates* change? The godman!'

Then there was nothing; everything black except for a tinny, semi-musical humming. Far, far away Tighe thought he could make out a distant echo, like the echo he had heard when he was clinging to the ice, a minute tinkling sound that repeated *death! death! death!* as a metallic whisper.

Then nothing at all.

2

When Tighe woke again he was lying on a crag, with grass tickling his face. He sat up, disoriented. The sun was bright below him, throwing shadows off the lip of the crag. Everything was crisp, bright.

He touched the back of his head. There was a scab of blood there, a large one that covered a patch of shaved scalp. He scratched at it with his fingers, bringing away rusty flakes of dried blood under his fingernails.

He was still dressed in the Wizard's suit. Untying it he pulled it down over his shoulders. His old clothes, stained and a little tattered, were underneath. He pulled up the fabric of his shirt and examined his belly. There was a band of bruising, and two parallel lines of crusty scabbing. That had been where the metal tendril had gripped him.

How clumsy they had been!

Tighe settled himself with his back against the wall, pulled up a handful of stalkgrass and chewed it. He thought back over his experience. Much of it made no sense to him, but beyond that he had the intimation that the meeting with the three versions of his Grandhe had not taken place in a real sense. Together they were greater magicians than the Wizard. They had created some magic realm, partly in his own head, perhaps, and had talked to him there. Some of the things they had said had not really taken the form of words; maybe nothing he had said had taken that form. But the understanding had shaped itself in his head.

He dozed for a while and woke refreshed. His belly was empty, with an echoey ache of hunger fading in and out in his torso. He stuffed some more stalkgrass into his mouth and combed through the turf for a bit looking for insects. All he could find were tiny spiders, grey-bodied, that moved with extreme slowness despite their tiny proportions. He tried eating a few, but they tasted too sharply bitter to be palatable.

He made his way down from this crag with some difficulty, stepping from mini-crag to singleton, sometimes using nothing more than clumps of grass as foot- or hand-holds. Eventually, however, he reached a more substantial ledge and started walking westward along this. All the time he found himself meditating on what had happened to him. The things his Grandhes had said, speaking directly into his brain via the plastic tube. The things the Wizard had said.

The ledge shrivelled until it was barely two feet's width across; Tighe had to proceed carefully. After a while it started broadening out and Tighe marched briskly along, lolloping over his bad foot and striding purposefully with his good.

He passed an overhung alcove on the ledge, inside which a feather-worker was pulling flights off a dead bird and tying them into a chain to hang round her neck. At the back of the alcove a narrow doorway could just be seen. Tighe had seen few birds in the sky. He tried engaging this woman in conversation, but she did not speak Imperial and regarded him with some suspicion. She was muffled up in many layers and Tighe realised that the air all around was cold. His suit kept him so warm he had assumed the climate was mild.

He walked on. By the time of dusk, he was still on open ledge; but the dusk gale was light, the winds tugging gently at him almost horizontal. He slept on an empty stomach.

The next day he walked further west and passed through a number of farms, eventually coming to a village. He had decided on the way that it was foolish to speak Imperial. For all he knew he would be taken again and sold as a slave if he was identified as being from the Empire. At the outskirts of the village he encountered a man and a woman attempting to use spars of twisted platán wood to construct a shelter for their chickens. Tighe squatted on the ground watching them. When they called him over, their breath pouring like steam from their mouths, he grinned and acted as a simple-minded boy. Each of their phrases brought forth a grin and mannered gestures with his hands. He stood and helped the couple with the work, holding the spars and weaving the narrower twigs into a fretwork. By late afternoon the work was finished and the woman of the couple went off to begin fetching up the chickens.

The man sat and gabbled at Tighe and Tighe grinned and nodded, understanding not a single word. But when the woman returned, with two handfuls of shrieking wriggling chickens tied together at the feet, hung upside down, she also brought a loaf of grass-bread. The couple shared the food with Tighe, and he grinned and nodded and made child-like noises.

After eating, he helped the woman bring along the remainder of the chickens from inside their house. She chattered happily to him and he grinned and nodded.

That night he slept outside the couple's house and in the morning he shadowed the man as he went about his business in the village. At every job

Tighe contributed something and was rewarded with pieces of bread, or a few morsels of dried and peppered earthworm.

Tighe stayed with this couple a week or so, sleeping outside their door. It was enough time to learn only the rudiments of their language; a task made harder by the fact that at no stage did Tighe let on that he was starting to comprehend them. It seemed that they were recently married; that the woman's mother was the village matriarch, and had given them two dozen chickens as a wedding gift. Most of what the couple said passed Tighe by; but he gathered that they were puzzled by his dark skin and wondered why an idiot boy possessed so fine an antique coat. They intuited that it gave him protection against the cold – for how else could he sleep so comfortably outside the door through the cold nights?

Tighe helped the woman harvest grass seed to feed the chickens; cleaned the pens for them; sat and watched as the woman wove chicken feathers into a tightly worked shirt. He met several people in the village, who humoured him as if he had been a baby. After a week, the woman's mother came to visit: the village matriarch. Straight away the two women, mother and daughter, were arguing loudly. Tighe could only pick out occasional words, but he had the sense that the focus of the disagreement was the newlyweds' indulgence towards the strange voiceless boy who had wandered in from east. Don't trust him! He'll slit your throat in the night! The daughter complained in a pure tone, the old woman bickered away in a broken, deep-throated one.

Tighe decided it was time to move on. It pained him to do it because he realised it would vindicate the old woman's suspicion and hurt the younger woman who had been so kind to him, but he stole two of the chickens in the middle of the night. He broke their necks to stop them squawking and betraying him, and then he fled through the cold along dark ledges. By the dawn he was far west.

He stuffed one of the chickens into the capacious pocket at the front of his suit, along with the gun – which he was pleased to see had not been taken away from him by the Wizard's Lover. It made him look like a pot-belly, a pregnant woman. The other chicken he plucked, after the fashion he had observed in the couple's house, tying the feathers together with the beak and some of the smaller bones into a grass-weave parcel. This he carried under his arm. The meat he cooked all at once, building a fire with dried grass and lighting it with struck flints, as the couple had taught him to do. He ate the cooked chicken meat over the next few days.

It was impossibly delicious.

He travelled for a further week, passing through villages at night in case word of his theft had somehow travelled before him, until he judged that he was far enough away from his crime. Then he traded the feathers at a long, narrow village spread out along a heavily overhung ledge that barely saw sunlight, for some bread and a length of plastic twine. He plucked the second chicken and offered the feathers at the next village along. By now the meat of this bird was so game it was beginning to smell, and although he cooked and ate it, the flavour was too dense to please him.

He walked on. His bad foot was healing slowly, after a fashion, into a twisted sort of shape that hurt less and less to walk on.

Further west he found work at a farm which raised huge butterflies from maggots. It was situated on a broad, semi-circular meadow positioned at the end of a village shelf; the woman who ran it employed five young men to do the work. To begin with Tighe pretended to be from downwall and to the east, and grunted the few words he understood. After a week or so, though, he had picked up enough of this language – it was a variant of Otre – to get by.

The farm fed the maggots with old and rotting meat; gathering this meat was a lengthy business. At least two of the men were away from the farm at all times, ranging in a circle of six or seven villages upwall, west and downwall from the farm. They traded bits and pieces for meat no longer fit to be eaten; and sometimes came across carcasses of birds and other vermin on out-of-the-way crags.

The maggots, puppy-sized bags of pulsing flesh, fed avidly. The more they ate, the bigger they got; and when they metamorphosed into butterflies, the larger the wingspan. This was the crucial thing; because the verdant green and happiness-blue colourings of the wings were what the farm traded. Some wings were traded whole, others were scraped to harvest the jewel-bright scales that made up the patterns, each the size of a little-finger nail. The best butterflies had wingspans as broad as a man's height; most were smaller than this and correspondingly less splendid. Some of these were made into clothes and ornaments, others were plastered into church walls as decoration. The farm did good business. Tighe worked collecting the offal or did jobs about the farm itself. The woman owner, a short, froggish pale-skinned easterner, took a liking to him. She questioned him in detail about his origins and Tighe made up some things and inserted others that were based on the truth. He told her a story that included some truth about the Wizard's craft, explaining that this was the origin of his marvellous suit that kept him warm or cool depending on what he needed. She didn't seem surprised; the wall, after all, was cluttered with wonders, as everybody knew.

The woman, called Basch, decided to take Tighe to her bed. This was, the other farm-workers assured him, a great sign of favour. Basch's favouritism shifted amongst her employees from month to month, and they advised Tighe to make the most of it whilst he could. Tighe decided to go along with this development and took to sleeping in Basch's bed with her every night.

His first night with Basch was a nerve-racking affair, since Tighe had never been with a woman before. But he didn't confess this fact and allowed himself to be guided by her impatient hands – this was, as it happened, her preferred technique in bed. He was almost too nervous to enjoy it and when he came inside her she was cross. 'I don't want children,' she would say, slapping him on his back as he lay over her. 'You pull yourself out of me before you do that.' They started again within minutes and this time Tighe did just that. She was much more pleased.

Tighe's days oriented themselves around this new night-time routine. Basch did not become pregnant.

After a couple of months of this, Basch's eye shifted to another worker, an arch-nosed, lanky easterner called Pnex. Tighe returned to the general shed where the workers slept and endured a certain amount of mockery.

During his time at the farm he thought often of the Wizard and of the Wizard's Lover. If the Wizard had been able to track him because of the machinery inside his head, could he not find him again? After all, he had tracked him once, using only the remnants of the machinery that his pashe had not removed. But as week folded into week and the months began to pass, he began to wonder whether the Wizard's Lover had not removed the last traces of the machinery from his brain. His scab had healed and the hair had grown back over the scar. He could still feel the rubble of healed skin through the hair at the back of his head. When he was Basch's lover she had run her hand through his hair and asked after this circular scar. He had told her that he had been poked in the head with a military pike, but he felt that she didn't believe him.

The year swung slowly around; the frost of winter gave way to a chilly spring. Tighe debated with himself. He thought about waiting the full twenty months until the year had passed right round its cycle; but eventually he became eager to move on.

He said goodbye to Basch and his fellow farm-workers, and took a parting gift of cake-bread and a small bag full of scraped-off butterfly scales to trade. Then he stepped out one morning and, limping less than he had used to, made his way westwards again.

3

For most of the rest of that year, through the spring and into the summer, Tighe made his way westward. He went from village to village, finding work where he could, going hungry where he couldn't. He traded everything except his hand-sized gun, with its five remaining bullets, which he kept hidden, and his suit – although he had many offers for this latter.

One time he was ambushed by a gang of women, all dressed in many layers of wool. They jumped from a higher crag to the ledge along which he was passing and started striking him with poles, whooping and yelling. Tighe was knocked down and his face was bloodied before he was able to fish out his gun. Firing the pistol frightened them away, but it hurt him to breathe for a fortnight or more after this.

He stayed in one village for a month, pretending to be a doctor. He had no medical knowledge, but his command of the language was now good enough to enable him to spin out plausible stories. A child died of fever he had promised he could cure and the villagers chased him westways out of the village with shouts and threats.

He found a farm that kept goats; here he possessed real knowledge and did not need to pretend. He worked there for a fortnight before moving on.

Soon he began hearing stories about the City of the East, also called Bact, and, by some, Devildom. Tighe finally arrived there as the grasses on the wall started assuming the singed colours of autumn. He passed through a brief tunnel, and entered the city.

The City of the East was built over a dozen layers of ledge and shelf, and its myriad rooms dug into the wall were mostly connected by tunnels and in-ground staircases. A broad central shelf was home to a continual pageant and dramatic performance; as soon as one troop of actors dropped, exhausted, another would take up the play exactly where it had been left. There was shame in relinquishing the play and some of the actors played so hard and for so long that they were virtual corpses by the end, dropping down from sheer fatigue. New actors would not, by tradition, step into the arena until the previous actor had stopped speaking; but as soon as a gap opened up, actors would rush to the middle and gabble at the lines, or sing snatches of song, whilst they cleared the space of the bodies of their forerunners.

Crowds watching the play were not large, but they were continuous; as some of the audience left, new people would drift up to watch. The play was a lengthy, complex version of the history of the world, full of diversionary narratives and highly stylised, repetitive speeches. For some observers, watching the play was a religious ritual. For others it was a more conventional sort of entertainment.

At the back of this shelf were several ranks of prophets and doomsayers, whose hectoring tales of apocalypse filled the air and conflicted with the musical declamations of the actors. Occasionally quarrels would break out between actors and prophets, and the audiences would enjoy these fist fights as much, or more, than the ritual drama or religious speechifying.

The city was rich in springs; water flowed so copiously from a number of slant-lying pipes and holes in the wall that it wasn't possible to dam it up and charge money for it. This was one reason for the city's enormous population: water was free. It dribbled out of standing pipes by public ledges.

Tighe tried to find work amongst the maze of shops and hostels that occupied the lower ledges and shelves, but the city was crowded and work was difficult to find. He traded his suit, finally, for a bag of precious jewels, some electronic components and a sack of biscuits. He kept the gun, uneasy and thrilled by the ceaseless activity of the City and uncertain when he might need it.

His plan was to make his way back west, past the Meshwood. Partly this was an end in itself: he wanted to find out what had happened with the war, whether the Empire still stood or whether the Otre had conquered it all. But apart from that, it was an attempt to make his way homeward, back to the village. It ought to be possible, he thought, to find a way upwards; to buy passage in a calabash, for instance; or to work his way around. If he put his mind to it, it ought to be possible to find his home again.

He was nearly eleven: the age at which a child becomes an adult. One evening he pushed his way through a crowd in a narrow defile in the wall and bought some fortified water in a clay jar. The defile was crammed with people drinking this liquor, and singing and playing palm-on-palm games for money. Tighe laughed and joked with the people he met, but the crush of the crowd meant little to him.

He took his fortified water away and found a residential ledge where he could sit in peace. Slowly he drained the rest of the jar, feeling the petrol taste of the liquor on his tongue and the roof of his mouth, letting it fuzz his mind. He was greatly changed by his experiences. He thought often of the Wizard and of his Lover, who so resembled his Grandhe. Sometimes he tried to piece together the narrative, the ways in which the Wizard had manipulated his village, his family. It was complicated, and there were a number of different narratives that could explain it.

He dozed off, the jug in his lap. He was woken by two ruffians, both much taller and bulkier than he, who had jumped on his sleeping body. One was sitting on his legs and the other held back his arms; the one on his legs was running his moist hands through Tighe's clothes, looking for valuables.

'You foul drunk,' he snarled. Tighe, terrified, found himself laughing because there was a stench of liquor on the mugger's breath. The irony seemed comical. The ruffian behind pulled his arms back and he gasped in pain.

'I have a jewel!' Tighe blurted. 'It is valuable! It you take it, you might leave me in peace!'

'Foul drunk,' said the first ruffian, slurring the words a little, 'where is this jewel?'

'Free my hand and I'll reach it out.'

The ruffian seemed to be having difficulty following Tighe's words he was so inebriated. His head wobbled, perhaps in agreement or perhaps because he was so drunk. His fellow took it for confirmation and loosened his grip on Tighe's left arm. Tighe snaked his hand down to his boot and pulled out the gun, firing it almost straight away. The noise was enormous and sudden in the quiet evening. The ruffian on his legs fell backwards, shot or startled Tighe couldn't tell. The other released his grasp and started away, running awkwardly. Tighe stood up, aiming his gun, laughing hysterically; but he had enough self-control not to fire. Instead he hurried away in the opposite direction, leaving the mugger lying on the ledge.

After this incident Tighe decided he needed to act more like a man, less like a child. With some of his jewels he bought a slave, a short, skinny girl. She could, he decided, act as lookout when he was too tired, or drunk, to pay attention to the world around him. She herself was as fluttery as a bird; she slept little, waking at the slightest disturbance. Her eyes were surrounded by sunken, dark skin. Her hair was thin and portions of pink, inflamed-looking scalp showed through. There were yellow dots of infection in the pores of her face. Tighe started buying twice as much food, to make sure that she was fed; but she ate very little. 'This is why you are so thin,' he scolded her. But all she would say was 'Yes, Master.' She said very little else.

She was, however, a good cook, whenever Tighe felt more extravagant and hired a public oven as well as some ingredients for food. He thought sometimes of using her, since he had not experienced that physical release in many months and she was, after all, his: but the truth was he found her offputting and unattractive. She was so small, so scrawny, she looked as if she might break in use.

Week followed week, with Tighe simply staying in the city and living off the wealth earned by the sale of his antique suit. One day he saw somebody wearing it: a plump, rich man, striding up and down one of the ledges as proud as the sun. Tighe wondered how much he had paid for the thing.

There were hundreds living in the city; perhaps even a thousand. It was an enormous number, but eventually Tighe came to recognise most of the people on the shelves and ledges. It was possible to become familiar even with so large a number of people. As his supply of jewels began to diminish, he began to think that the City of the East was boring to him: the drinking, the endless theatre and preaching. He debated with himself what to do: secreting three of his most exquisite jewels in a twist of leather tucked into his boot, he decided he would make his way through the lands of Otre towards the Meshwood.

He explained his plan to his slave girl, and to his surprise she began to cry. 'What are you crying about?' he asked, alarmed.

'The city is my home,' she said. 'I have only known the city.'

'Are you not curious to see the wonders of the worldwall west of here?' he said. 'Come! You must be curious.'

'No, Master.'

'Well, perhaps I will sell you to a new master before I go,' he said, feeling compassionate. 'I'll tell you,' he said, feeling in a confiding mood, 'I was a slave myself once. Yes! I know the difficulties of being a commodity. I have been a Prince and a slave, and I have been to the end of the world. I have had such adventures! It is surprising to me that you would not wish to have adventures of your own.'

'I'm sorry, Master,' said the slave girl, weeping bitterly and hiding her face in the crook of her elbow. 'I do not have an adventurer's soul.'

'Well,' said Tighe, embarrassed and trying to comfort her by stroking her hair. 'Well, don't worry.'

4

Tighe spent an evening drinking, working through two jugs of fortified water, and then losing a whole jewel to a fellow drinker playing palm-to-palm. He didn't have the natural dexterity for the game and was hazy about some of the rules; but it was exciting playing, and even the bitterness of losing so much had its thrill.

In the morning Tighe woke with a drinker's head; his eyes were sore and his head throbbed. He was intensely thirsty and he stumbled unsteadily along ledges and up a stairway to a standing pipe, his slave girl following on behind.

There was an injured man at the pipe, wearing the yellow bandana of slavery. It was a common sight: a slave filling jars with water to carry back to his master's house – except that this slave had only one leg. Tighe didn't think he had ever seen a one-legged slave before.

The man balanced on a crutch that fitted under his armpit and was tied round that shoulder with a tether. Tighe barged him out of the way, forcing him to drop his jar and he cried out in terror, fearful that it would break and he would have to explain its loss to his master. But Tighe had a dry mouth and needed the drink.

After he had finished, he turned on the slave. 'How clumsy you are with your single wobbly leg! You can't keep your balance, you fool.'

The slave was sitting on the ground, his one good leg and his crutch stretched out before him. The pot was unbroken. Something twitched in Tighe's memory. He dropped to his haunches and looked carefully at the slave's face.

'I'm sorry, Master,' mumbled the slave, his eyes on the floor.

'You have a name,' said Tighe, slowly.

'No slave has a name, Master,' said the slave humbly. 'A slave is only a slave.'

'You're Mulvaine, I think,' said Tighe.

The slave twitched, but kept his eyes on the floor. 'No slave has a name, Master,' he said again.

'Mulvaine!' said Tighe, his heart tumbling in his chest with joy.

'Mulvaine – it's me! Tighe – you remember . . . the platon? The army? We carried you into the Meshwood – Mulvaine – ' He reached out and touched his severed leg, cut off high up near the hip. 'I thought you were dead, I truly did. Your leg!'

The slave, tentatively, looked up at Tighe. 'This is another lifetime, Master,' he said, in a wobbly voice.

'A year ago, no more,' said Tighe. 'Tighe! You remember.'

Mulvaine, a distant focus coming over his eyes, started trembling. Tears were coming out of his eyes. He opened his mouth to say something, but only sobs emerged.

'Why do slaves cry all the time?' Tighe demanded.

'Tighe,' said the slave in a low voice. 'I can't bear to think of my life before. It's too painful.'

'Come,' said Tighe, with sudden determination. 'Come, take me to your master and I'll buy you. I'll buy you!'

Mulvaine's master was a wrinkled man. He had fought in the war in a senior position as an Otre officer, Mulvaine explained to Tighe as he hobbled along, and had been wounded in the foot. Surgeons had removed the foot, and he had taken Mulvaine on as a slave because he did not want a slave who was more whole than he was himself. 'It flatters his sense of himself, I think,' said Mulvaine, 'to order me about. I have less leg than he, for all his missing foot.'

'My foot is broken too,' said Tighe, 'although not missing, for which I am very glad. But I think this man would rather have my two valuable jewels, and perhaps my slave, in exchange for you with your crutch and your ugly face!'

But Mulvaine's master was a stubborn old man. He lived with two other veterans of the war in a narrow corridor-like room high in the city. The other two old men shared a female slave between them; but Mulvaine's master was attached to him. 'But see these jewels!' said Tighe. 'See how valuable they are! They're worth far more than this cripple.'

'I'm *used* to him,' said the old man, scratching his stubbly chin. 'What good would those jewels do me?'

'You could buy five slaves with this!'

'What use would I have for five slaves?'

'Well, you could buy anything you like. And I'll give you my own slave in part exchange.'

'Don't like the look of her. Diseased look. She'll not last the winter.'

Tighe became more and more exasperated. 'Now, don't be stubborn,' he warned.

'You young barbarian,' said the old man, becoming heated, 'I commanded a dozen men! I gave my foot to the war! I'll not have you coming in here, calling me names.'

Tighe himself had taken on a more arrogant manner since coming to the city. He quailed before the anger of the man, before telling himself that he was a man now. 'But these are unusual, precious jewels,' he insisted. 'You'd be a fool to pass this by.'

'Are you calling me a fool now?'

'I say what I see,' said Tighe.

'Fool! I commanded a dozen men!' The old man reached up his staff, which he used to lean on when he walked, and made a pass at Tighe's head. Tighe leant back and the end of the stick swished past. 'How dare you!' the old man blustered.

At the far end of the long, narrow room the two other old men cackled at their compatriot's impotent rage.

'Only a fool would turn down so excellent an offer,' said Tighe coolly, encouraged by the mockery from the others.

The old man's face darkened in pure rage and he struggled to get to his feet, the better to be able to beat Tighe with his stick. Tighe leaned forward and pressed him back into his seat with a firm hand on his shoulder. The old boy struggled like a tantrum-struck baby, gasping and spluttering. There was a loud exhalation and his eyes glazed. He fell back into his chair, his face in a rictus of astonished pain.

Tighe stepped back uncertain what had happened. The other two old men were stumping up from the far end of the room.

'He's dead!' said one.

'Died of apoplexy!' said the other.

'Apoplexy!' said the first, with a tone almost of glee.

The second old man prodded the corpse with his own walking stick, and then turned to Tighe. 'You taunted him to death.'

'Taunted him to *death*!' gloated the other.

'Accidentally,' said Tighe, hurriedly.

'Them jewels is ours now,' said the old man, leering. 'You can take the cripple in exchange, he's no use to us.'

'But leave the girl,' said the other old man, leeringly. 'We can use the girl.'

Tighe sucked in his breath. 'I don't think so,' he said. 'The master's death frees the slave.'

'Nonsense!' snarled one old man.

'Nonsense!' said the other.

'What's his is ours now. We're his heirs.'

'He made us his heirs!'

'Then fetch a magistrate, I'd advise,' said Tighe, feeling himself gather inside. 'I dispute it. I think he died without heirs and I'm claiming his slave. You can have his other stuff. Come now, slave,' he said to Mulvaine.

'You can't do that!' screeched the first old man.

'Who are you? What's your name?'

'You speak Otre with a *western* accent,' said the first. 'You're a westerner – a dirty westerner. You have no rights here!'

But Tighe walked calmly out through the door, leading Mulvaine and his own slave as he went.

He took Mulvaine down to the lower ledges of the city and bought him some food. Mulvaine ate with gusto.

'You're a wealthy man now, Tighe,' he said, his eyes hesitating upwards and then tumbling back down in his habit of meekness.

'I thought you were dead, with the others,' said Tighe, slapping him on the shoulder.

'The others?'

Tighe coughed. 'Ati,' he said. 'Pelis. Ravielre. You remember them?'

Mulvaine was staring at the ledge in front of him. 'I assumed', he said, 'that the whole platon had been destroyed. I don't remember very much. I remember running along the ledge with you, Master.'

'Don't call me master,' said Tighe, with a strange twinge inside him. 'It doesn't feel right, somehow.'

Mulvaine blushed. 'No,' he said, meekly.

'It's all right,' Tighe said.

'I remember running,' Mulvaine said shortly. 'Then the pain in my leg – I was shot. But I don't remember anything else until I was awake in an Otre fort. My leg was bandaged, missing, and that's how I've been. They put me in a pen with other commodities, but nobody would buy me. I was lucky to find my master, I truly was. He was recovering himself and he fastened on me.' A tear crawled down the planes of Mulvaine's face. 'And now he's dead. Dead!'

'Don't start crying now,' said Tighe, with distaste. But it was too late; Mulvaine was sobbing, and rubbing his eyes.

'Why do slaves feel they must cry as much as they do?' fretted Tighe.

'Anyway,' said Mulvaine sniffing hard through his nose, 'you must have a story, I think, Master. Tighe, I mean. Master Tighe. Oh, the old days! They seem so far away!'

He was shaking his head, looking at the floor.

'Well,' said Tighe, settling himself down and staring out at the sky. It was shortly after ninety and the sun was bright, a white hole burnt through the perfect blue. 'I've had some adventures, Mulvaine,' he said. 'I can tell you that. I was a slave, too, just as you have been. But I escaped.' He rubbed his right eye. Since he had started drinking the fortified water for which the City of the East was so famous, he had started experiencing headaches that nibbled at the back of his eyeballs. He was getting streaks of white blankness over his vision, too: sometimes when he opened his eyes he couldn't see anything but a milky haze until his eyes settled and things came back into view.

'Escaped!' said Mulvaine, in a small voice. He was looking nervously around. 'Runaway slaves are thrown off the wall,' he whispered. 'Everybody in the city knows me. I've been here a year. I couldn't escape.'

'Well,' said Tighe. 'I was – shall we say – taken by somebody else. Just as you have been taken, freed, by me.' He smiled at Mulvaine, but the other's glance was still downwards. He rubbed his stump through his clothing.

'Ah, Mulvaine,' Tighe said, 'I have travelled further than you could imagine. I have travelled to the end of the world – to the East Pole. I have visited the ice caves there and battled with magicians and monsters. I have flown through the air, swum through the breath of God. When I return to the world of men and women, as I have done, it is hard to feel bound by the smallness of these customs.' He wrinkled up his eyes. His vision was not as sharp as it once had been.

'The East Pole?' said Mulvaine, looking up briefly. 'I have heard of it. It is not, then, a sort of myth?'

'No,' said Tighe, rubbing his eyes again. 'It is as real a part of the wall as the ledges on which this city is built. The wall is not as we thought it was. I remember, Mulvaine, when we were still in the platon. One day you said to me: you said, is it that the wall is big, or that we are small?'

'Did I say such a thing?' mused Mulvaine. 'It seems a very long time ago, Master.'

Tighe wrinkled his face. 'Don't call me so,' he snapped. Then he made himself regain his composure. 'Well, there was a kind of truth in that, but it was not as I thought it. I saw us as small and God as big. But now I have travelled and I know who built the wall. I have met with the mangod and he is, they are, as small as you, as small as me. It seems that God and man are exactly the same scale, exactly the same size. It seems that God is a part of our family, a part of our village, that he and she live as a single person among us. It seems that he is as overawed by the size of the universe as are we: that he is as likely to bicker with his Lover as we are. I had used to think that God was beyond change; but I have discovered on my travels that it is not so; that God is in love with change. Perhaps that is why he is in thrall to this world, to this worldwall. Change is a potent thing, like liquor perhaps, and has drawn us in.'

'What a lot you have learned, Master Tighe,' said Mulvaine, with an undertone of sarcasm. But he was still looking at the floor.

Tighe stood up and walked back and forth a little to stretch his legs. 'We come from a mighty people, Mulvaine,' he said. 'Our people achieved many things. And we will achieve great things again. This I have been promised. So I have pledged to return to my village. You will come with me.'

'It is hard for me to walk, Master,' said Mulvaine, in a miserable voice. 'I have only one leg and my crutch chafes under my armpit.'

Tighe didn't hear him; or if he heard him, he didn't really listen to his words. 'I shall return as Prince to my village,' he said. 'It is my right. If my Grandhe still governs, then I shall confront him with the truth. With what I now know about the worldwall itself.'

5

Tighe spent the rest of the day trying to dispose of his female slave. It was harder than he thought it would be; few people were interested in so sickly a creature. She cried every time Tighe took her to a new doorway, a new potential buyer, and she cried when the buyer abused her as diseased and a weakling. 'You are difficult,' chided Tighe, 'you cry at the thought I will sell you, and you cry at the thought that I won't be able to sell you. Are you sure that you do not wish to come with us?'

'I do not wish to leave the city, Master,' she whined.

'Well, Mulvaine and I will travel west. We will see wonders – do you not wish to see wonders?'

She shook her head miserably.

Eventually Tighe found a baker who was prepared to take her. 'She's small enough to climb inside my oven and clean out the corners,' he said. 'I'll pay you in bread.' Tighe cursed inwardly to think that he had wasted two valuable jewels on so hopeless a purchase, but it couldn't be helped.

He returned to collect Mulvaine and share some of this new bread. He had left him on the central shelf watching the never-ending play. 'Let's go now, Mulvaine,' he said.

'In a moment, Master,' said Mulvaine. Tighe had given up rebuking him for calling him 'Master'; there seemed little point. 'This actor is staggering and about to fall, I think.'

Tighe pushed through to get a better view. Mulvaine, as a slave, had not dared do so; but he was tall enough to see over the crowd. Tighe squeezed through and saw the actor enter into a lengthy monologue. He was dressed in bright red fabric, but he was plainly exhausted: his face was yellow with fatigue, and his hands trembled like vibrating machines of some kind. He croaked his lines rather than spoke them. Two young actors, eager and fidgety, waited on the outskirts of the stage space, to race one another and claim the role of the failing actor.

He pulled himself up, his voice dry and cracked. 'I am to take on the clothing of death himself,' he warbled. 'I am to take on the clothing of ending itself.' He span round in a slow, ritualised arc and ended with his arm outstretched. The tremor of his hand was painful to see. He was pointing at one of his fellow actors. 'I am to clothe myself as death,' he said again. 'I am to clothe myself as ending. I am to clothe myself as death. I am to clothe myself as ending.'

'The world is tall,' said the other actor. This had been her only line for the last half-hour. Tighe knew this because somebody in the crowd next to him said so, loudly and crossly. 'Over and over!' this audience member said.

'Hish!' said somebody else.

'The world is tall,' said the other actor. She was dressed in green cloth.

'As the sun rises,' said the first actor, breathlessly. He pointed at the shelf. 'As it rises and goes over the wall.' He pointed upwards. But this gesture was the final straw. His leg wobbled comically and then he simply fell straight down in a heap. The other two actors were hurrying on, fighting amongst themselves to take the position centre-stage and kicking the prone figure of the previous actor in their eagerness to clear him away.

'As the sun rises,' shouted the first actor.

'As it rises and goes over the wall,' yelled the other, and raised his arm, bringing it sharply down in a blow to the other's face.

Tighe turned away, and pushed his way out of the crowd again. 'Come along now, Mulvaine,' he said. 'You've seen the old actor pass out.'

'Master,' whined Mulvaine, bobbing his head to get the best view. 'Can't we stay half an hour more! It's the sunrise speech! It's a famous speech.'

'No,' snapped Tighe, his temper fraying. 'We must go now.'

Mulvaine hobbled along behind him in a sullen mood, but Tighe felt lighthearted to be leaving the city. Sharp needle pains came and went in his eyes and he had developed the suspicious feeling that these new headaches were somehow brought on by his being in the city itself. 'They'll go when I leave the city,' he told himself.

They climbed to a higher ledge that led west.

'Stop!' called somebody, from behind. Tighe and Mulvaine turned together. One of the old men from the same space as Mulvaine's old master was standing there, his walking stick horizontal, pointing straight at Tighe.

The old man had hired a young ruffian to reclaim Mulvaine. This thug was tall and his arms were fat with muscle. As he stepped along the ledge, the old man called after him. 'Take his jewels too!' he quavered. 'He's got jewels.'

The thug confronted Tighe. Tighe pulled out his gun. The thug looked at it.

'Is that real?' he asked, in a surprisingly mellow voice.

'Yes,' said Tighe and aimed a shot at the ledge. The gun struggled and fired, and a gout of dust flew up.

The thug took a step back and then turned and marched straight past the old man.

By evening Tighe and Mulvaine were out of the city and moving west. Most of the traffic on the ledge was going in the other direction, drawn into the city.

'Where are we going?' asked Mulvaine, as the two of them settled into a nook in the wall to sit out the dusk gale.

'We're going to my village, Mulvaine,' said Tighe. 'Going home.'

Mulvaine didn't say anything. After a while he said, 'My skin has been rubbed raw by walking so far, Master. My skin under my arm.' He said this in a pitiful, small voice.

'You'll get used to it,' said Tighe. 'The dusk gale is so mild this far east,' he added. 'Do you remember how harsh the dusk gale used to be, back in the Empire?'

But Mulvaine was not to be drawn by nostalgia.

The next morning Mulvaine shared out rations from his pack and the two of them started marching west. The air was clear and the strong rays of the sun from below illuminated the wall before them with streaks of beauty. The sunlight was hurting Tighe's eyes, but he tried not to think about that. Soon enough his eyes would get better; his eyesight would become less misty and the pain would stop. Soon enough they would pass through the Meshwood and find their way up to his village.

The path led out along a stubby spur of worldwall. At its furthest point Tighe looked back. The distant outline and haze of the city was still visible, just. Tighe breathed deeply and waved languidly. Mulvaine waited, poised on his crutch, looking at the floor and panting. For a moment Tighe pondered his time in the city; but the sense of freedom was so exquisite it made his hair prickle and stand on end. Freedom, and the path home.

After this short pause, he and Mulvaine walked on. Rounding the spur and starting down the far side.

The Wizard was there, waiting, as if he had been waiting all this time. His eyes were red lamps. He was wearing a black plastic cloak that flapped and curled around his leather skin.

'Tighe,' he said in his squeaky voice, but with an edge of malice. 'My Lover has been at you, tampered with my machines, and I've found it hard to track you. Hard! And I've had my own worries, my own battles to fight.'

'Wizard!' said Tighe. The manliness, the swagger and the self-belief – all of it fell away, like sheets and great flakes of ice falling off the end of the world. He was a boy again, a young boy in front of his Grandhe. 'Wizard!' Sweat started on his face.

'My sweet young Tighe,' said the Wizard, a tone of menace in his voice, 'I've been so looking forward to seeing you again.'

Appendix

Notes on the World of On:
The Physics of the Worldwall

1.1. The Worldwall. Gravity, which operates in the universe as a whole at 90° to a body of mass (such as a planet), has on this particular world been twisted by Hawking's over-efficient experiments. Instead of operating perpendicular to the flat of ground, gravity is operating parallel to it, in a spherical standing-wave vortex extending from the notional centre-point of the planet to a circular plane less than a kilometre beyond the surface of the globe. This vortex draws energy through superstring elasticity from surrounding space-time and has currently lasted some 430 standard years.

The dynamics of the change are difficult to theorise clearly. Of the underlying principles of gravity (that it be always additive, always infinite in range, and always attractive) the first two are unaltered by the shift; were gravity, notionally, to shift through more than 90° clearly the last would be violated. Any shift of less than 90° lacks quantum stability. The gyroscopic rotational realignment alters the equations trivially, but it otherwise satisfies physical necessity.

1.2. Equations. The standard equations for gravitational attraction have usually taken for granted the linear, lagrangian properties of the gravitational effect, such that each particle exerts line-of-sight pull on every other. In fact, equations contain a blind element that eliminates the torque effect of superenergetic quantum foam. Accordingly, for a spherical body of mass M and radius R, containing N molecules each of molecular weight A, the Newtonian gravitational binding effect of energy E_g will be as follows:

$$E_g \approx \frac{GM^2}{R} \approx \frac{GA^2m^2NN^2}{R} \; \bar{\omega}$$

where $\bar{\omega}$ is the necessary alignment of the vector of attraction.

Theorists from Podkletnov onwards had postulated localised gravitational instabilities, particularly with reference to certain condensate attributes; and these states were always directly related to the linear part of the gravitational lagrangian L. This in turn involves the very small negative intrinsic cosmological constant of space-time. The older definition of 'critical regions' as those where $\delta^2(\chi) > |\Lambda|/8hG$, applied prior to the uncovering of over-efficient power sources that drew their energy in a more direct way from quantum foam.

Gravitational theory had, similarly, long known of certain unstable modes of the classic Einstein space-time dynamic, named 'zero modes', which have the same probability to occur as the $h=0$ configuration (flat space) and a higher probability than all other field configurations. (The probability is proportional to $\exp(iS[g]/h_{\text{planck}})$, and for the zero-modes one has $S=0$). Thus a gravitational field would always embody a certain instability towards these configurations. What prevents this in the general bulk of space-time is a certain intrinsic cosmological term $\delta L_{\text{Cosm.}}^{(2)} = +|\Lambda|h^2$, favouring an $h=0$ configuration.

The coherent coupling $\delta L_{\text{Coherent}}^{(2)} = -\Lambda^2 h^2$ of the gravitational field to *any* atomic-molecular aggregation, for instance a central node of mass, always amounts to a local positive cosmological term (which is to say, gravity must be an attractive rather than a repulsive force). This cancels the intrinsic stabilising term $\delta L_{\text{Cosm.}}^{(2)}$ and leads to a local instability.

Therefore, while the regular coupling of gravity to incoherent matter produces a *response* – a gravitational field – approximately proportional to the strength T_{cont} of the source, the coherent coupling induces an *instability* of the field.

Things go as if a potential well for the field were suddenly opened. The field runs away towards those configurations which are now preferred (although whether this is compatible with the cosmic energetic balance remains moot). The runaway stops at some finite strength of the field, where higher order terms in the lagrangian, which usually can be disregarded, come into play. This duration of this condition is difficult to determine because it depends mainly on the non-perturbative dynamics of the field, and very little on the initial conditions.

1.3. Doomsday Possibilities. There are two opinions as to what will happen; one is that this gravitational disturbance will exhaust itself within (estimates vary) fifty to five hundred years and gravity will revert to normal. The other is that it will distort superstring alignment in a chain-reaction, interrupting and perverting the universal gravitational constant. This 'doomsday' scenario sees the situation of the worldwall as cosmically fatal, with the actual weave of space-time disintegrating over a period of some hundred thousand years, the unravelling beginning at this world but spreading logarithmically throughout the galaxy and possibly further. Should this happen, the basis not only of gravitational attraction, but of atomic coherence, could disintegrate, and the universe as a whole reduce to a sort of chaotic sub-particle soup extremely attenuated through the expanse of remaining space. The greatest danger posed by this eventuality is that it would disrupt the balance of forces maintaining the singularities beneath the event horizons of black holes. Arguably, a shift in the vector $\bar{\omega}$ would release enormous amounts of stored energy from black holes, with devastating effects.

It is unclear which of these two hypotheses is the more likely.

The effect of this shift in the coefficient and alignment of gravity has been to angle the vector of living through 90°. Instead of operating, as it were, from the sky to the ground, gravity on this world now operates from the 'west' to the 'east', turning the entire world on end and replacing what had been an endless flat plain (punctuated with mountains and valleys) into an endless *vertical wall* (punctuated with ledges and crevices). West is now 'up', and East is 'down'.

2. Attributes of the Podkletnovian configuration

2.1. The Pause.
At the surface of the world (or worldwall) gravity is running parallel with wall, rather than conventionally at right angles as is normal. As yet, however, gravity is operating 'normally' in the rest of the universe – such that, for instance, the world continues to orbit around the sun. There is accordingly a place where the 'horizontal' gravity stops, and the usual gravitational laws reassert themselves. This boundary is known to the inhabitants of the worldwall as the Pause. This barrier, although theoretically navigable simply by pushing through it, in effect creates a seal on the atmosphere of the world. This has significantly raised the air density and pressure between the world and the Pause (something of which the inhabitants of the world are, of course, unaware).[1]

2.2. Sunrise and Sunset Atmospheric Turbulence.
The worldwall as a dynamic system has now achieved a precarious equilibrium. The atmosphere is under a constant gravitational pull and will tend to fall. There is, of course, no 'ground' to prevent this fall, and in effect the atmosphere rests upon itself. During the day the air is heated by the sun and will tend to rise, or at least to stop falling; and at night it chills and falls more rapidly. This means that at the cross-over points of dawn and dusk cold falling air meets rising warm air – creating dawn and dusk gales. These gales are most pronounced at the central latitudes (or verticalitudes), and least pronounced out near the Poles.

---

[1] Tighe, falling from his village ledge, fell more slowly than a sky-diver would in the present world for this reason; although such falls will nevertheless, of course, usually be fatal.

2.3. Days and Seasons. From the point of view of an inhabitant of the worldwall, the sun now appears to rise from beneath, to ascend through the sky and to disappear 'over the top of the wall'. Over the years since the catastrophic realignment of gravity, the earth has – as would be expected – picked up rotational momentum. With the globe spinning faster the day now lasts a little under half the previous twenty-four-hour period. Seasons, on the other hand, are longer drawn out than before. Partly this is because the planet's solar orbit is counterset by the gyroscopic increased rotation, partly the increased air-pressure (see below) stabilises the shifts in temperature occasioned by the elliptical passage of the planet about the sun. The population of the worldwall continues to count time in 'months', for now forgotten reasons; but there are twenty months in a year (divided into ten *tithes*, two months to a tithe). More specific timekeeping varies from region to region. One popular system divides the day into one hundred and eighty 'degrees' from sunrise to sunset; another divides the day into ten 'hours', each of a hundred 'minutes'.

2.4. History. At the time of this catastrophic realignment of the gravitational field the large bulk of the world's population perished. The world's water, chiefly contained in oceanic form, was removed from its usual position and fell through the space between the world's surface and the Pause; evaporation was significantly reduced by the presence of the Pause, and this heavy rain lasted for a considerable time, although eventually the bulk of this body of water 'froze out' at the two poles, creating what would on a normal world have been two enormous mountains of ice. The amount of loose matter, chiefly earth and biomass, which was also dislocated by the change in gravity was small compared to the mass of water, but significant in terms of erosion, as well as constituting the main cause of fatalities. Eleven billion people died in this event, the small population of survivors mostly subsisting underground (or 'inside the body of the wall') until the outside environment had reached an equilibrium. A significant proportion of the loose matter lodged itself back on the wall, building up on ledges and overhangs, but the bulk of it was frozen in at the poles with the loose water.

After a hundred years or so, the remaining population of the planet – minuscule in comparison with what had been before – had settled into a habitual lifestyle. There are enough horizontal spaces (ledges, platforms, crevices and the like) to support small groups of people; springs and rain provide a degree of water, and a variety of plants and animals grow on the surfaces available to them. High amounts of oxygen, raised humidity in the central latitudes (or 'verticalitudes') and the presence of many springs and water-sources – chiefly subterranean aquifers fed from the pressure of polar water-ice – enable extensive forestation of certain areas.

3. Flora and Fauna

3.1. Claw-caterpils and Other Insect Life. The higher air pressure has changed the dynamic of the fauna and flora of the worldwall. In particular it has allowed many insects to grow to much greater size; the main limitation on insect dimensions being the efficiency of spiracles as a method of diffusing oxygen throughout the organism. At higher pressures, this efficiency is viable over greater distances, and insects can become much larger. With the majority of insect predators destroyed in the catastrophe, and with insects more able than many organisms to adapt to the new environment, a great variety of forms of insect life flourished; larger and larger bugs evolving rapidly in the rapidly changing circumstances.

Various breeds of insect, particularly the variety known to inhabitants as 'claw-caterpils', have developed habits of predation upon non-insect fauna, including human beings. These creatures are strongly attracted to the smell of blood and will eat all components of their prey. They have evolved a variety of coagulant saliva. This prevents the blood from draining out of victims and being lost off the face of the world, and enables the insects to maximise their feast. Claw-caterpils prefer densely forested areas and are rarely seen outside meshwood or tanglewood locations.

Acknowledgements

I would like to thank Simon Spanton, for excellent editorial and other advice; Malcolm Edwards, Oisín Murphy-Lawless, Steve Calcutt, Rachel Cummings, Abraham Kawa, Tony Atkins, Julie Roberts, David Harris, Bob Eaglestone, Roger Levy, Cathy Preece and Sarah Kennedy. For advice on gravitational matters, I'd like to thank the workers at the Gravitational Institute of Staines, particularly Robert Ayamanski and Francesca Frenacapan.

This is a book about precariousness, and it necessarily reflects the precariousness of my life during the last years of the last millennium; but none of the people listed here bears any responsibility for that.

This book is for R.

Barker